## ALSO BY CAMMIE McGOVERN

**Young Adult**

*Say What You Will*

*A Step Toward Falling*

*Just Breathe*

**Middle Grade**

*Just My Luck*

*Chester and Gus*

*Frankie and Amelia*

**Adult**

*Eye Contact*

*Neighborhood Watch*

*The Art of Seeing*

**Memoirs**

*Hard Landings*

## Praise for *The Last Letters of Sally and Walter*

"What a dearth of stories we have about love after a certain age, and what a welcome treat is Cammie McGovern's tender and absorbing novel come to fill the void. I loved Walter and Sally, and most surprising to me, I loved their passion for Scrabble. This is a beautiful, hopeful, and exhilarating gem about second chapters, second chances, and fresh beginnings."

—Lily King, acclaimed author of Read with Jenna pick *Writers & Lovers* and *Heart the Lover*

"*The Last Letters of Sally and Walter* is a funny, tender, deliciously nerdy, wildly romantic love story. Nobody celebrates oddballs and second chances like Cammie McGovern. Nobody better understands the body's inevitable failings and the heart's indomitable courage. It's so good it made me get out my Scrabble board and invite my husband to play, just so I could live in Sally and Walter's world a little longer. It's so good I cried when it was over."

—Catherine Newman, *New York Times* bestselling author of *Sandwich*

"With love, wit, grace, and the seasoned hand of a gifted storyteller, McGovern invites us to be unashamed of our beautifully ephemeral and ever-evolving humanness. This bighearted book will make you believe in people again. It just might make you believe in yourself again too."

—Matthew Quick, *New York Times* bestselling author of *The Silver Linings Playbook* and *We Are the Light*

# The Last Letters of Sally and Walter

# The Last Letters of Sally and Walter

A NOVEL

CAMMIE McGOVERN

Published by Sourcebooks Landmark, an imprint of Sourcebooks
1935 Brookdale RD, Naperville, IL 60563-2773
(630) 961-3900
sourcebooks.com

Library of Congress Cataloging-in-Publication Data

Names: McGovern, Cammie author
Title: The last letters of Sally and Walter : a novel / Cammie McGovern.
Description: Naperville, IL : Sourcebooks Landmark, 2026.
Identifiers: LCCN 2025040340 | trade paperback | epub
Subjects: LCGFT: Romance fiction | Novels | Fiction
Classification: LCC PS3613.C49 L37 2026
LC record available at https://lccn.loc.gov/2025040340

Printed and bound in Canada.
MBP 10 9 8 7 6 5 4 3 2 1

*For my mother, Katie, who has inspired all who know her by so graciously embracing this second chapter in life…*

# CHAPTER 1

# Sally

*OH DEAR*, SALLY THOUGHT WHEN SHE WALKED IN THE LIBRARY AND spotted one man sitting alone. She'd been living at Golden Grove for only a month when she saw lime-green flyers advertising a Scrabble club taped up in the elevator. Technically, Scotch-Taping papers in random places was against Golden Grove rules, though occasionally people did. Given how many flyers she'd seen, Sally could hardly believe only one person had shown up: Walter Kretzer, a man her neighbor Connie had recently described as "a bit too intense for my taste."

Connie hadn't meant it cruelly. She was trying to be helpful, welcoming Sally by offering tips on navigating the nightly dinner shuffle, which could get overwhelming. Some residents began congregating in the lobby around four thirty to suss out the options for dining companions. A hostess was supposed to seat everyone in groups of four or six, and usually that worked out. If one person was particularly quiet, someone else was usually garrulous enough to fill in the conversational gaps. Connie had decided early on that she didn't care for blowhards ("I was married to one for thirty-six years. That was enough"), so her advice tended to steer Sally toward the soft-spoken folks, the ones who (in truth) didn't mind if Connie dominated the conversation for a meal.

Golden Grove was an independent senior living facility, which meant that even though all residents were over sixty-five, most were reasonably healthy and independent. The facility only kept a skeletal nursing staff (during the daytime, to pass out Band-Aids and help people check their blood pressure). They had no "tiered system" of assisted care, no medical facility, no memory wing locked every evening for sundowning Alzheimer's patients. Admittedly the line blurred as the folks who'd lived at Golden Grove for a decade or more crossed their eightieth or ninetieth birthday and began to fail.

Just last week, Sally sat at a table with a woman who'd once been a state rep and could still hold forth about local politics but halfway through dinner couldn't remember what she was eating. She stopped her story with a surprised look at her plate. "What's this called again?" she asked. "Fish, dear," the woman sitting beside her said. To Sally's surprise, no one remarked afterward about the memory lapse. She was catching on now: They all had these moments, and soldiering through dinner conversations was the least they could do for one another.

Based on the tour Sally took before putting her name on the wait list, she knew the emphasis at Golden Grove was on an activity-heavy "robust retirement lifestyle." No one was meant to sit in their apartment alone for long, and in the month since she'd moved in, Sally had tried four different clubs—the Green Thumbs gardening group, the easy-pace Wednesday Walkers, the classics-only book club, and the Keeping Current news discussion. All had been assertively welcoming. "Our focus is having fun!" leaders chorused. "We don't pressure people with a lot of expectations." On a second visit, she discovered each meeting was usually a repeat of the week before: introductions made, the emphasis on fun repeated. It was all fine with Sally, but still an adjustment, as was everything about moving to Golden Grove.

Early on, Connie told her one activity a day was the optimal schedule to keep. "Then you build the rest of your day around that. For instance, on days with the garden club or the Wednesday Walkers, you can dress accordingly that morning."

At the time it struck Sally as a sad admission. Everyone planned their life (and their day's outfit) around readying for a *club*? After a few weeks, though, she saw the common sense in Connie's suggestion, and it didn't seem sad at all. Living at Golden Grove felt a little like being on the longest, slowest cruise ship in the world. Fellow passengers shared one meal a day. Most chose dinner, though lunch was also an option. Some paid extra and did both.

So far, Sally liked everyone she'd met, but that didn't mean any of them felt like *friends* exactly. Even after a month, she still had a hard time remembering names and telling people apart when they all looked (though she hated to admit it, of course) so generically *old*. Most women's hair color varied from silvery white to battleship gray; they all wore hearing aids and cardigans and slip-on shoes.

"Do I look as old as they do?" Sally asked her daughter, Rachel, one evening on the phone in an uncharacteristic moment of self-pity, forgetting that Rachel—honest to a fault—was the last person she should ask.

"Well, you've slowed down a lot, and yeah, you have a kind of hunch these days, but that's only because you wore yourself out taking care of Dad for so long," Rachel replied.

Sally had stayed thin when most women her age widened with menopause. She was always getting compliments on her lovely skin, but *there you have it,* she thought. Offering an excuse hadn't exactly softened the truth. She was seventy-three now, which didn't feel old until she realized she'd already outlived both her parents, who'd seemed (in her mind, at least) ancient when they died. Yes, the last five years of her life had been consumed by managing the medical care of her husband, John, and his chronic heart condition. It *had* been hard, and it was the reason she'd put their names on the Golden Grove wait list two years ago, knowing that when their time came, she might be moving in alone.

After so many years as a caregiver, she couldn't bear the idea of her own care falling to her children. Still, it had been an adjustment in countless ways she never expected. That people might look old but seem so energetic. That at the end of their lives, people might be judged not by their careers or their children but by the number of hobbies they had.

After that conversation with Rachel, she made a point of staying positive and telling her children that living at Golden Grove was energizing. "No one sits still for a minute here! I'm doing something every day!"

She tried to make it sound exciting, like Rachel's early updates from college when she breathlessly reported, "There's a party every weekend night and if you're a freshman girl, you get invited to all of them!"

But when Sally said, "It's like there's a club meeting every day, and if you're new, you get invited to *all* of them," Rachel had no idea what she was talking about. "That sounds potentially horrible, Mom. You need to be careful about not doing too much. You remember what the doctor said."

Count on Rachel to leave no unpleasant topic unmentioned.

Sally saw the Scrabble club flyer with its unusual start time—after dinner, when most people watched a movie in the meeting room or went back to their apartments—and decided, in defiance of Rachel's warning, to go. She wasn't sure what she expected, but surely not this: one man seated alone at the center table in the library beside a battered maroon game box. So far, she hadn't attended a single club meeting with fewer than ten members.

"Here for Scrabble?" he said without a trace of self-consciousness.

Given the effort put into posting flyers, she was shocked. "Where is everyone?" she said, realizing too late what a deflating question this might be. Most clubs were organized and run by residents. If turnout was a barometer for social success, this poor man must feel terrible.

Apparently not, though. "We used to get a pretty big crowd, but it's been petering away unfortunately. Too much competition, I suppose."

She remembered Connie's warning and wondered if he meant competition from other clubs. Or he was too competitive? He seemed affable enough.

"Would you like to play a game?" he asked. "You don't have to. Other people have walked in and left when they saw it was only me."

It was almost too heartbreaking to bear, except he didn't seem to realize this. He smiled and gently caressed the box top. How could she not sit down and play a game? He had lovely, clear blue eyes that looked—in spite of his smile—in danger of filling if she said no.

"Of course," she said, pulling out the chair across from him. "I'd love to. Though I should warn you it's been years since I've played. I might be a bit rusty."

"We'll just have to see," he said, pulling out the game board and a cloth bag that apparently held all the tiles.

About a third of the way into the game, Sally understood why this club had no members. Walter was a strong player and not inclined to hold back to spare a beginner's feelings. The first time he played all seven tiles on his rack and gave himself a 50-point "bingo bonus," Sally laughed in surprise. The second time he did it, boosting his score to 176–52, she wondered if anyone had ever spoken to him about the poor sportsmanship suggested by overly lopsided victories. She didn't say anything because, in truth, she liked watching his plays and learning from them.

He frequently laid one word parallel to another, making four or five two-letter words and effectively doubling his score. The next turn, he'd do it again, making a row of three-letter words. "I didn't realize you could *do* that," she gasped.

"Oh yes," he said. "Once you learn the acceptable two- and three-letter words, you'll see: This is where the fun of Scrabble lies. The delicate finesse of parallel plays." He smiled down at his construction the way an artist might look at the part of a painting they felt particularly proud of.

Connie was right: Walter *was* a little intense.

But he was also *interesting*.

Sally lost the first game by 200 points but surprised herself by suggesting another.

"*Really*?" Walter said.

"Why not? I can't do any worse, and I'd like to try some of the tricks I just learned watching you."

He smiled and shook the tile bag. "Splendid. I suspect you're going to be a fast learner."

She was. This time she played EYE under COMBER, making four words at once. "Very nice," Walter said. On his next turn, he played CHIDS.

Sally narrowed her eyes. "I think you need an E there, Walter. You mean CHIDES, don't you?" She'd spent the majority of her life teaching third graders, which meant correcting their spelling mistakes, most of them so glaring (like this one) she wondered if they'd ever read the word they were trying to spell.

"No. My word is CHIDS."

"But that's not a word, I'm afraid."

"Are you challenging it? If you're wrong, it'll cost you a turn."

She bent to catch his eye. Was he serious?

Apparently so. Well then. "Yes, I suppose I have to challenge 'CHIDS.' Or suggest adding an L? Maybe you could make it 'CHILDS'?"

"I wouldn't try that in a tournament. The plural of 'child' is 'children'; possessives aren't allowed."

She shook her head. He was right of course. Who better to know the plural of *child* than a former elementary school teacher? Silly to make such a meager peace offering. "All right. I'm challenging. Do we have a dictionary?"

"Right here," Walter said, pulling out a thick, red-covered paperback from under his chair. "Yes. Here it is. Unfortunately you're right. 'CHIDS' as a plural is not acceptable. I wasn't sure and took a risk. You were smart to challenge."

After this, she surprised herself. Instead of giving up when Walter pulled ahead—again by 200 points—she aggressively borrowed as many strategies as she could from him, making more parallel plays after realizing how many two-letter words were acceptable. Like the musical notes, for instance, which she learned when he played FA with an F on the triple-letter square twice for 34 points. Three turns later, she played TI as part of a 22-point turn.

"Very nice," Walter said, with apparent delight. "You're learning quickly."

She was, as a matter of fact. Later, she played QAT, a word he'd used in the first game.

Soon, she played AXIOM using his XI to hit a triple-word square and earn herself 82 points. He applauded her triumph. "My goodness. I might regret everything I've taught you soon."

Three turns later, when she bingoed, having had no idea what that meant an hour earlier, she looked up to see him staring at her, suddenly serious.

"Would you like to go to a tournament with me?" he said.

# CHAPTER 2

# Walter

THE NEXT MORNING, WALTER WONDERED IF 7:00 A.M. WAS TOO EARLY to email this woman. He rarely used email, though he knew it was the preferred method of communication at Golden Grove. "If you want to invite someone anywhere, use email," his neighbor Irene had told him when he first moved in. "That way the person has it written down. With a voicemail, you never know. Some people live here for years and never learn how to pick up their voicemail."

Indeed, after two years at Golden Grove, Walter hadn't learned how to pick up his own voice messages, but then again, there were many aspects to socializing here that he hadn't mastered. His own fault no doubt, because he hadn't (in all honesty) tried very hard. Or more accurately, whenever he did try, he felt so self-conscious afterward that he usually had to hustle back to his apartment and lie down on his bed to erase the memory of his own foolishness. All part of a pattern of socializing errors he made early on and never quite recovered from, he feared.

But last night felt different. Really different. He'd all but given up any hope of resurrecting his moribund Scrabble club after everything that happened, and then she walked in, a woman he was almost certain he'd never seen before. When she told him she'd been living at Golden Grove for over a month and they'd once eaten dinner at the same table, he nodded sheepishly. Walter tended to be oblivious to certain matters that others kept track of. "I'm not good at remembering people," he admitted. "I'm especially bad with names. I used to advocate for name tags at dinner, but then last year, we tried it and no one could read the tags without glasses, so we all stood too close and squinted at each other's chests and that was that. Idea abandoned."

She laughed. "I like that image, though. I'm having a little problem with names too," she said. She then made a fairly impressive play, added up her points—27—and leaned across the board to whisper, "If I'm being honest, my problem is that everyone looks the same to me. It turns out I can't tell old people apart."

Oh, this made him laugh because this had been his biggest problem when he first moved in, too. "For my first six months, I could only remember one woman's name: Isadora. She wore a bright-red wig and a shawl that looked like a fringed tablecloth and spoke in a loud Russian accent. Her, I could remember. Everyone else not so much."

Sally laughed. "She sounds delightful. What happened to her?"

He shrugged and shuffled his tiles around. What happened to any of them? If he really wanted to know, he could study the bulletin board next to their mailboxes where somebody posted announcements of extended hospital and rehab stays. They also put up death notices and funeral details, but at a certain point, who wanted to keep track? Easier to keep his friendships at Golden Grove superficial, he'd decided. For him, people came and went. Names hovered on the margins. Maybe this attitude partly explained the mysterious implosion of his once popular Scrabble club, but he pushed the thought out of his mind.

"Who knows," he said, playing JOE for a ridiculous 64 points.

"Is that JOE like coffee?"

"Yes," he said. "And I apologize for that. Sometimes you get more points than you deserve."

Now, he'd woken up at seven, and he wasn't sure if it was too early to email. Of course he could, he decided. Email didn't wake people up. But what was her name again? Sarah? Susan? He'd meant to write it down last night and cursed himself for not doing so. He could remember the lovely color of her eyes (a gold-flecked hazel) and the pretty scarf she wore (lilies on a dark background), but he couldn't remember her name. Then it occurred to him: the score sheet from last night! He ran to his game box and found it there on top: the record of two glorious games against Sally R.

He rifled through a stack of weekly newsletters in his recycling bin for the once-a-month column called "Please Welcome," which always ran a picture and an introduction to new residents. At last, he found her: Sally Reynolds. To his surprise, her bio sounded like all the others:

> Sally comes to us from Putnam, MA, where she lived for forty years and taught elementary school for thirty. She is the mother of two children, Andrew and Rachel. She enjoys gardening and reading and is excited to pursue both these pleasures in her time at Golden Grove.

Honestly, Walter thought. *This* was what they wrote for her? A woman as smart and funny as Sally was a rare jewel at Golden Grove, and they'd made her sound like everyone else. But Sally was *different.* She was competitive and curious and didn't seem particularly interested in talking about either her old life or her children (or, even worse, grandchildren), which was a rarity in Walter's experience. Admittedly he couldn't remember what else she was interested in besides Scrabble, but that was okay. He'd find out soon enough.

He took thirty minutes composing his email, looking to strike the right note. He wanted her to know what a pleasure it had been for him to play her last night, but he didn't want to overwhelm her with enthusiasm that might seem off-putting or slightly desperate:

> I hope you won't think I'm overstepping if I forward information on the tournament I mentioned last night. There are others you might consider, but I've been to quite a few and I like this one. I realize it's also possible you were only being polite when I asked if you were interested in entering a tournament. I've been told that I sometimes project my own passions onto other people.
>
> Please forgive me if I've done that here, but I'd be remiss if I didn't say that you showed a remarkable natural ability last night. You said that you hadn't played Scrabble in decades but I wonder if you've dabbled in other anagramming games? Perhaps you're a Boggle player or a newspaper word jumble enthusiast?
>
> At any rate, here is the information on the tournament I mentioned. If you're inclined to study a bit more ahead of time, might I suggest learning a list of acceptable two-letter words? Memorizing these 100 (or so) words will boost your score an average of 30 to 40 points. Possibly more. For some players, just learning XI, XU and QI does that.
>
> Respectfully yours,
>
> Walter Kretzer

There, he thought, reading the note over for the seventh or eighth time. He told himself that his anxiety about sending this had more to do with the collapse of his Scrabble club than with Sally, who was obviously an attractive, smart woman but not a reason for him to be clammy-handed as he typed this note. Goodness. He'd gotten so he didn't understand his own impulses. After he finally pressed Send, he stood up, went to the bathroom, and returned a moment later to see if she'd responded.

Soon, he feared he might suffer a repetitive wrist injury from refreshing his inbox.

# CHAPTER 3

# Sally

"HE THINKS I OUGHT TO ENTER A TOURNAMENT. HE SAYS I HAVE potential!" Sally trilled the next morning to Rachel.

"Oh my God, Mom. What did you say?"

"I said okay!"

"Mom, I'm sorry but I'm not only thinking about what the doctor said. You have to be so careful when you choose your activities at these places, especially in the beginning. You don't want to get pigeonholed, where suddenly you're the person always talking about tai chi."

"I don't like tai chi."

"Right, that's what I'm saying. You've already said you didn't love the tai chi crowd. What if people start thinking of you as the Scrabble Lady?"

She reminded herself that Rachel was a constant worrier with too little to focus her nervous energy on beyond her struggles to procreate. She and her husband, Barry, had been doing IVF for three years, and a few months ago she told Sally she couldn't bear to discuss it anymore, that she would let her know if anything happened but until then, she needed to talk about other things. Hence the focus on Sally's Golden Grove social life, apparently.

"I don't think anyone here will think of me as the Scrabble Lady," Sally said. "I only played for one night."

"Right, but that's another reason not to go to a tournament. Won't everyone there be really good?"

"Which will make it interesting! I'll learn a lot!"

"I don't know, Mom," Rachel said. "That worries me."

Was this the kind of mother Rachel would become? An anxious hoverer who planted doubts every time her child took a risk?

That afternoon she read Walter's note and laughed out loud even though she was alone in her apartment. She could have easily written back: *Don't worry about overstepping! I've already visited three different Scrabble-related websites!* Instead she wrote this:

I believe I've already got the two-letter list memorized, though admittedly this isn't hard when so many of them are notes from the musical scale or letters in the Greek alphabet. I have to ask though: Is AA really a word? What could it possibly mean? It doesn't seem right, does it?

Best, Sally

PS: In case you can't tell from the above, yes, I'm interested in entering this tournament.

A few minutes later, she received a reply.

AA means rough, cindery lava. I used to enjoy learning definitions along with spellings. AI is a three-toed sloth, QI (also spelled KI) is the vital force in Chinese thought. Sadly, I've come to realize knowing definitions doesn't improve one's Scrabble game a jot and I've stopped out of fear that my brain has a finite storage capacity. Let me know if you'd like me to send along another list. U-less Q words is the next one most people turn to. You'd be surprised. There are 50 of those. Shall we try for another game soon?

She waited until after her Keeping Current news discussion group that afternoon to write him back. Admittedly, though, her mind wandered a bit during the meeting, running through a list of two- and three-letter words containing at least one high-value tile. QAT was a good one. Also, COZ. Walter was right—definitions didn't matter; letter combinations did. Some letters combined beautifully for high payoff. For instance, Z paired with A, and K with an A or I. Find a triple-letter square to play it as two words, and your score for the turn was at least 60 points. She certainly hadn't known this two days ago. That afternoon, she wrote Walter back:

I've officially signed up for the tournament! When asked to assess my Scrabble experience, I wrote rank beginner. Is that a mistake? Will I be playing children I once taught as third graders?

Had she told him that she taught elementary school? Had he mentioned his own career? Oddly, she couldn't remember. One of the many surprises of living at Golden Grove was how little people talked about the work they'd done most of their life. Almost as if there was a tacit agreement that whatever one did for the five decades before moving in here didn't matter all that much. Again, Walter was quick to answer. He was either sitting in front of his computer awaiting her response or a very fast typist. Or both.

Wonderful news. No, it's not a mistake to call yourself a beginner, and believe it or not, yes, children over eight are allowed to enter and play against adults. In my experience, it's a bit like chess—the children interested enough to enter tournaments can be fearsome competitors. I've lost to players as young as eleven and recently had a nail-biting close call with a nine-year-old. How would a Thursday evening game work for you? We could meet in the library?

Because she was sitting there, she responded right away:

Yes, as luck would have it, I'm free Thursday evening for a rematch. I'll warn you ahead of time, though, I might be better than I was. I just spent a whole meeting of the current events news discussion club secretly memorizing the U-less Q words. I have no idea what's going on in the world, but I do know that QIBLA and FAQIR are acceptable Scrabble words. Does this make you nervous at all?

When she read this over, Sally had to laugh. She sounded like the bespectacled boys from the high school trivia team where she'd spent four years as the only girl member. It had been ages since she'd thought of them and the way they talked about being overprepared to psyche out the competition.

"Everyone's memorized the titles and leading characters' names of all of Shakespeare's plays, right?" one would say loudly after arriving at a tournament as they waited to check in. "Right. Plus sonnets," another would say and nod. She always blushed in those moments. Now here she was, sounding just like them.

I'm delighted to learn that someone else has attended the Keeping Current group and walked away feeling less informed than when they walked in. I usually spend the hour counting

> the number of attendees who've fallen asleep. You've found a much better use of the time. I applaud you. Shall we meet in the library at seven?

Now that they'd set a date, she thought of Connie's warning about Walter being "a little intense" for her. During their game the other night, he'd told her the Scrabble club had once been very popular and he wasn't sure what had happened. "In our halcyon days, it was all very jolly. Some nights we had twenty people. A few times we ran out of game boards. Lots of Scrabble talk in the dining room, with everyone discussing plays they'd made the night before. I loved it."

*So what happened?* She didn't ask, though the question had hovered in the air. She could see it was a tender subject. She remembered the way her old trivia teammates fought bitterly over narrow wins and losses, and how quickly it became agonizing for all of them. For a moment, she wondered if meeting him in the library—a public spot where others would see them—might unleash a spate of warnings similar to Connie's. Was it possible Rachel had a point and she might regret being associated with Walter so early in her time at Golden Grove? It had been more than fifty years since she'd graduated from high school, and suddenly this felt like she was back in a place where rumors spread quickly and public opinion weighed heavily on everyone's mind.

Apparently she'd taken too long with her response, because after a few minutes he wrote again.

> We could also meet in my apartment, though I'd have to warn you, it's small and I'm much better at Scrabble than I am at housekeeping.

She snapped out of her reverie. No, if she was worried at all about being seen with him in public, she definitely shouldn't go to his apartment and knock on the door.

Let's meet at seven in the library. See you then.

## CHAPTER 4

# *Walter*

"I HAVE TO TELL YOU, WHEN I FIRST GOT TO GOLDEN GROVE I MADE some mistakes," Walter said, a few plays into their game that evening. "I wasn't used to being around other people all the time. It took me a while to adjust."

He wasn't sure why he was admitting this. Sally hadn't raised the subject. If anything, she seemed as if she'd rather *not* discuss his unpopularity, but for some reason, he couldn't stop himself from detailing his disastrous introduction to Golden Grove, starting in the first week when he couldn't get anything to work: his television remote, his window blinds, his mailbox key. "I worried that I looked like I was losing my mind just as I was meeting new people I was meant to befriend. I'll admit I might have overreacted."

She nodded sympathetically, which prompted him to keep going. "I made a silly scene by the mailboxes one day when a few women tried to show me how to use my key. I accidentally screamed, 'I know how to insert a key into a lock!'" He stopped talking and played the word he'd been staring at without seeing it for almost two minutes: YURT. "I learned my lesson that night when everyone gave me a wide berth in the dining room, and I ate my dinner alone. Unfortunately, there were a few more incidents like that. I committed the cardinal sin of attending an exercise class wearing corduroy slacks and dress shoes, and afterward four women asked if I'd ever heard of sweatpants or sneakers and did I know about the internet where you could order almost anything these days?"

Sally laughed. He hadn't told this story before, and it hadn't occurred to him that really, it *was* kind of funny. "I had to tell them yes, I had heard of the internet, just to stop them from following me home and ordering a new wardrobe for me. Nice play, by the way."

She'd just laid MOOD parallel to CLUBBED, creating five words and scoring 34 points.

"For a while I made the mistake of bringing a book to the dining room and asking for a table by myself. I wanted to look smart, I suppose, and convey the idea that I hadn't lost my mind. Instead I'm afraid I looked like a misanthrope."

Sally nodded as if none of this seemed particularly surprising. "It's hard to get used to eating with different people every night."

In the three days since their first game, he'd watched her in the dining room. She always moved graciously, with no trouble finding a table and people to eat with, which was always a problem for him in spite of the fact that a hundred and forty people lived here. Could that be an act to cover up her own awkwardness? "My secret is, Sally, I've never really gotten used to it, but I've made a few deals with myself. I ask for takeout three nights a week. The rest of the time I force myself to socialize in the dining room, and I pretend to enjoy it."

What was it about Sally that was eliciting all these confessions? He couldn't say. Golden Grove was full of people who'd had remarkably accomplished lives; sometimes it seemed to Walter as if most residents had either worked in impressive-sounding jobs or had accomplished impressive-sounding things: taken trips to Antarctica or read all of

Shakespeare. One man had apparently invented a retractable ladder system that was still used by firefighters today. Early on, these revelations left Walter quiet. What could he say about his own work to people like this? *Insurance is more interesting than you might think*? Everyone knew that wasn't true.

"So where does the Scrabble club fit in?"

"That was my brilliant solution! Or at least I thought it was. About ten years ago, I joined a Scrabble club that met at a local VFW hall. I loved it and became a pretty regular tournament player. After I moved here, I still went to my old club since it wasn't that far away, and it hadn't occurred to me to start one here. But then I realized Golden Grove had plenty of game lovers who might be ready to take a break from bridge." He gave her an overview of the rest of the story—how exciting it had been in the beginning when eight people showed up to the first meeting and twelve the next. A few weeks later, the numbers peaked at twenty-four and hovered there for a while, until he began incorporating tournament rules.

More issues flared up the first time he brought a copy of the *Official Scrabble Players Dictionary* and stipulated that it should only be used for official challenges, not for word hunting with a tough rack of letters. "But what if we can't think of any words for the tiles we have?" one woman asked, genuinely surprised.

"That's the idea," Walter had said. "You have to think of the words yourself, but I promise it gets easier over time. The more we play together, the more words we'll learn."

"I don't think so, Walter," one man said, along with a sad admission. "I'm forgetting more words than I'm remembering."

From the beginning, he'd stuck by the *OSPD* for word adjudication, but some people thought he was "too extreme" on that front or, conversely, allowed too many words that were in the dictionary but no one had ever heard of. Like ZA, a word that bothered people once they learned the definition: slang for pizza.

"Oh for heaven's sake," Shirley had said. "That's ridiculous, Walter. Absolutely not."

He tried to explain the rules to the group as gently as possible. "It's not up to us to determine which words are allowable. Dictionaries have done that for us. If a word seems unfair to you, we shouldn't ban it; we should all remember it and put it in our arsenal!" For him, this was the fun part: imagining them all headed into battle, armed with word lists as ammunition.

"But what if we don't *like* all this slang and don't want to fill our life with words like ZA? Can't we just vote and agree no ZA allowed at Golden Grove?"

He wanted to point out that ZA gave them all an easy way to use a Z that could otherwise sit unusably on a rack for treacherous lengths of time.

He was also shocked at how quickly petty disagreements and poor sportsmanship became an issue. "I don't like this business of the other person scoring double for the tiles left over on my rack. What if I get a Z on my final draw? It's really not fair," Iris complained.

"But those are the *rules*," Walter said. Even as he insisted on protocols, he could see doubt take root in the expressions around him.

"Can't we change the rules if we all agree?"

To Walter, it was unimaginable. Apostasy. He looked around to see who was with him, but a half dozen pairs of eyes looked away. He made no pronouncements that night, but already he saw the writing on the wall. Judging by the nodding heads, Walter knew he was fighting a losing battle. More consternation erupted the following week when Leanne Walters laid down YID with only a dim recollection of what the word meant.

"Absolutely not!" Ellen Levine decreed. "Walter! We have another issue here!"

Years ago, the National Scrabble Players Association had addressed the thorny question of swear words and ethnic slurs by arguing that words were divested of all meaning when laid on a Scrabble board and therefore could not cause harm. They were simply letter combinations, no more, no less. But after the earlier dustup, Walter conceded quickly. He made an announcement that "offensive words will not be allowed," and at the next meeting, he brought along the NSPA official list of those identified words. By that point, though, the early enthusiasm was waning and attendance was down.

He also understood that he was part of the problem. He enjoyed playing competitively, but after a few complaints, he was careful not to press too hard, and he rarely challenged opponents' words. However, he didn't hold back from running up his scores, because what would be the sense in that? Others could learn from watching him. If they were interested, they could borrow one of the Scrabble strategy books that he donated to the Golden Grove lending library.

This was where the fun started! Anyone could improve with a little knowledge and practice. "Ten years ago, I was terrible! Then I started studying and my rating improved dramatically!" To him, this story was the embodiment of optimism. How many new skills could the over-sixty-five crowd learn well enough to master? Scrabble *was* learnable, with insider tricks that paid off. For most people it was a simple equation: The more words you learned, the more ammunition you had.

Hard to sell people on this idea, though. Some arrived at Scrabble night and asked to play anyone other than him. "Not you, Walter! I can't keep up with you!" Rita Weller once said in the booming voice of the newly deaf, smiling beneficently, which apparently gave everyone else permission to say the same thing. As the numbers continued to decline, some people wandered in, saw him sitting there alone, and spun around quickly as if in a hurry to check that they hadn't left the oven on.

"Don't take it too badly," said Harold, the closest person Walter had to a male friend at Golden Grove, on a night when only four people showed up. "Some clubs aren't meant to last very long. People enjoy novelty and then they get tired of it."

That was two months ago. Now he understood he'd been a fool to think it would last. He shifted to meeting once a month in response to Phyllis, Harold's wife, who suggested that weekly games might be too onerous on people's schedules. "An obligation rather than a welcome diversion." But even that hadn't been enough to lure back Harold and Phyllis, nor any of their pals who followed the popular couple from one activity to another like lemmings.

Last month, in spite of flyers posted on every wing, no one showed up. Soon, people weren't even feigning excuses anymore but instead were shouting across the crowded dining room, "No Scrabble for me tonight, Walter. I've decided it's not for me!" Honestly, why did people yell such things? He certainly wouldn't bellow, "I don't like that blouse you're wearing! It's not for me!"

As he relayed a shortened, hopefully not-too-pathetic version of this story to Sally, he also managed to find a seven-letter play with a terrible rack of one-point tiles, mostly vowels. His heart fluttered a little as it always did at the prospect of a bingo bonus and a whole new set of letters. "This is what we fondly refer to as a vowel dump," he said, playing his word, ABOULIA.

"My goodness, that is pretty, isn't it?" Sally marveled. "All the vowels except E. I'll have to remember that one."

This was all he wanted to find when he started the Scrabble club in the first place: another person who looked at ABOULIA and felt the same thrill he did.

# CHAPTER 5

# Sally

SALLY COULDN'T GET OVER THE WAY WALTER TALKED ABOUT HIS SOCIAL missteps. She'd never heard a man speak this way, and it made her curious to ask a question she'd wondered about since moving in: "Do you think people at Golden Grove make *real* friendships here, or are they more like cordial acquaintances and really they don't know each other all that well?"

For weeks, she'd been puzzling over the surprise of how upbeat everyone seemed—full of hearty welcomes and reassurances that she would soon love it here. "Everyone does!" they inevitably said. Was it possible these folks worked a little too hard to sell this place because they were trying to convince *themselves*? After she asked, she worried about sounding too critical, because she *did* like it here. She did.

Walter smiled. "It's a good question," he said. "I'm not sure I can answer for others. I'm sure *some* people here would say they've made good friends."

"What would you say?"

He considered his answer. "I would say I enjoy most of my conversations."

Sally laughed. "Tell the truth, Walter."

"Okay, I'm not sure I've made any deep friendships, but that's more of a comment on me than on people at Golden Grove. I've always been an outsider. At work, I spent the vast majority of my time trying not to be the butt of practical jokes."

"Oh dear. Did you have pranksters at work?"

"Some people spent hours setting jokes up. The only thing they wasted more time on was retelling the story afterward."

"I'm guessing you didn't have many soulmates there then?"

"Well. I met my wife at work, so yes, there was one."

"Was she a fan of practical jokes?"

"I suppose you could say that she appreciated that group more than I did." He seemed to remember something. His expression changed and he shook his head. "Until they turned on her the way those sorts so often do. Then she agreed with me and quit her job."

"Workplace drama is never fun."

"After she left, she never looked back."

"But you stayed?"

"Oh sure. Had to. She went back to school, got her degree, and became a librarian, which she loved but never got paid much for. I was the primary breadwinner."

She asked what he'd done for a job, a question so rarely posed at Golden Grove that people sometimes had to think for a moment, as if their careers had happened so long ago they'd almost forgotten. "I was an insurance actuarial adjuster. Don't ask me to explain what that means. I've already bored you enough."

"Did you like it?"

"I liked it for the first few years and hated it for the last thirty-five. Still it never occurred to me to do anything except stick it out until retirement. I didn't think I had a choice."

In spite of this being a fairly sad sentiment, Walter seemed his usual cheerful self, clicking tiles as he rearranged them on his rack. Sally thought about her own work and how exhausting it had been to spend every day with eight- and nine-year-olds and every evening preparing lessons for the next day. In the hardest times, her best teacher friends, Wendy and Pamela, carried her through, going out after work, drinking wine, and making fun of people at school. She sometimes feared she looked forward to those evenings more than she did to date nights with her husband, John, which happened three or four times a year. Fine dinners, always, but nothing like the fun she had with her friends.

And then, within a two-year span, Wendy got breast cancer and Pamela had a brain aneurysm, which she survived, but she was never the same afterward. Pamela had once been the one who goaded them into funny confessions after two glasses of wine—which janitors they liked, which children they didn't. After her "mini-stroke," she still laughed at jokes but it wasn't clear if she understood them. Eventually she moved to Florida, and a year later Wendy died, leaving Sally to wonder if teaching took a greater toll on one's health than anyone wanted to admit. By that point, it was too late to make new friends. The younger teachers were fine, but no one ever suggested a drink after school.

She hadn't known what to expect moving to Golden Grove. Could friendships like the ones she'd once had be forged over bingo cards and craft projects? She didn't know.

After a few minutes of silence, Walter surprised her by saying, "If you're really asking, I've decided the secret to Golden Grove is that everyone here is superficially friendly and no one is really friends. At first I found that disturbing; now I think it's a big relief. If we knew each other better, we'd have to worry when other people got sick. This way, we don't have to listen too closely when someone talks about their health. We can smile and nod and immediately forget everything they've said because we're not here to keep track of these things. We're here to be pleasant distractions for one another."

Sally marveled at the thought, especially when he followed it up with a bingo he'd been shuffling his tiles around for three full minutes to find: KETONES, with an N hook on CRAVE, vaulting the score on this one turn into the three digits.

"Goodness," Sally said, shaking her head.

"Are you unsettled by this play or by what I just said?"

"I'm upset that I actually thought I had a chance of beating you this game." Sally smiled. In truth, she didn't mind the idea of living at a pleasant, superficial distance from other residents. In fact, she found it comforting. This last year had produced any number of topics she'd rather not discuss, including Rachel's struggle to get pregnant and Andrew's surprising return, at age thirty-nine, to live with his parents, after losing his job and his apartment in a two-month stretch.

Whenever the subject of children came up and someone asked what hers did, she grappled with euphemisms. "My son is in a transition period," she'd say with a hand wave that was meant to imply *don't ask*. To her surprise, most people assumed this meant he worked in technology. "Everyone moves around in that field," people said. She never corrected them because she appreciated the assumption that he would probably be fine.

Never mind that Andrew had almost as much trouble working his iPhone as she did, and his difficulty "adapting to a new software system" was the reason given for his work layoff eight months earlier. For seven years he'd worked for a small government agency that helped low-income families apply for food stamps and assistance paying their utility bills. On his last day, he was told he'd be replaced by a computer.

"That's an exciting development for us," said his boss, who was five years younger than him.

Some part of Sally understood that the current holding pattern of her children's lives might be one reason she'd started spending her mornings studying word lists and her afternoons playing Scrabble with Walter. It was a relief to worry about something other than her children. It was—as he put it—a nice distraction.

At their next practice session, Sally told Walter, "I believe I've spent more time studying Scrabble this week than I've spent learning anything since college."

"My goodness." He grinned. He'd brought his tournament timer with him but warned her that it was old so they shouldn't expect it to be terribly accurate. "It will give us the feeling of being timed better than it will actually time us. Each player has twenty-five minutes to use throughout the game. In tournaments, it's important to use your time wisely."

She nodded, intrigued by this added challenge. For some reason, she felt mystifyingly confident—as if the few recent tricks she'd learned might translate into unexpected brilliance.

They didn't. She lost both games again, but Walter reassured her, "You're even better than you were last week. You really have a natural talent for this, Sally Reynolds."

She might have some talent, but as she pointed out, Walter had the words. After the fifth time he'd played a word she'd never seen before, she admitted, "It's like you have twice the vocabulary I do."

"Three times actually. You have to remember I've been playing seriously for about nine years. Top players know about 140,000 words. The average person has a vocabulary of about 20,000. I'm somewhere in between."

About halfway through their next game, Sally played a word she hadn't heard of a week before, KEDGE, as a parallel play, making four different words. It was a lovely move and also scored her a surprising 42 points. Walter clapped. She smiled as she wrote her score.

"I believe I can beat you someday, Walter. I just have to memorize half the dictionary."

Though her children were stumped by their mother's new Scrabble passion, for Sally, it made sense. They didn't know the girl she'd once been, the one who loved words and used to keep notebooks full of new ones she learned for no reason other than the pleasure of revisiting them: *lament, subterfuge, acquiesce*. In elementary school, she always won her classroom spelling bees, and one year—fourth grade—she won the school-wide bee in a surprising upset over three fifth graders who expected to be each other's only competition. The following year a bout of mono kept her out of the bee, though a teacher told her afterward she would certainly have won. "'Transistor' was the winning word," her teacher said with an eye roll. "Enough said."

As she moved through school, Sally discovered that she liked academic competition even though it often put her onto teams where she was the only girl. In junior high, she competed on the Geo Bee team, memorizing details from the continents of Australia and Africa (longest river, deepest lake, former names of countries). Though geography wasn't a particular interest of hers, she had the surprising revelation that in the heat of competition, she could remember details from other people's continents in addition to her own.

Tidbits she hadn't intentionally memorized but must have overheard in practice sessions burbled up and offered themselves, often as her teammates stared at one another in a panic. Though they sat in a row of four, they never turned and looked at her, never included her in their discussions. Inevitably, she had to lean in and say quietly, "The answer is Lake Titicaca."

Astonishingly, she was never wrong.

Her teammates were nice enough to acknowledge her contributions but not make too much of them, as if they all understood: *Better for a girl not to be known for this kind of thing.* When she supplied the winning answers, they spoke of the triumph in whispers, the implication being, *We all know who cemented this victory, but let's keep it our secret.* It wasn't until her last year of high school that she fully understood the price she'd paid for being the only girl on the team.

At the end of junior year, Ben Gelfound, the teammate she'd had a crush on for three years, grabbed her hand under the table after the victorious moment when Sally remembered Winston Churchill's minister of defense during WWII was actually Churchill himself. She assumed this meant he liked her too and now they would start dating. The next fall, Ben told her nervously at the first practice, "After the final competition last year, when I—you know—" He didn't say *held your hand under the table behind the school banner.* "I thought maybe I'd ask you out and we could even date this year, but I've gotten the feeling from the other guys that it's not such a good idea."

"Okay," she said, dumbfounded.

"Because of the team, obviously. We still have this year's competition ahead of us, and we can't let ourselves get distracted."

It was sensible, of course, and at the time she felt relieved just to hear him acknowledge what had happened and know she hadn't imagined the feeling of his damp hand in hers, the way his thumb caressed the soft pad below her own thumb. She nodded in agreement and took away the main point: *We like each other, partly for the very reasons that prevent us from dating—we're both responsible, intelligent, and future-focused.* Dating each other (while tempting) was an unnecessary distraction from more important matters like clinching a senior-year victory for their team. For weeks she smiled supportively at him and complimented his wrong answers in practice sessions. She praised his efforts right up until she learned that he'd invited Beth Markham to the homecoming dance.

For the rest of that year, she watched, stunned, as each of her teammates managed to secure a girlfriend, in spite of their thick glasses and tendency to replace decent conversation with factoid recitation. Ben had at least acknowledged her femaleness; the others didn't seem to recognize it beyond the vague discomfort they felt in the face of her (often) superior ability. She remained dateless that year and determined that the high school Knowledge Bowl would be her last academic team.

She never regretted the decision. She loved college and the discovery that her exceptionally good memory had more pragmatic applications than retaining trivia; she also understood that her braininess had left her delayed in developing other skills. She was shy at parties, unable to determine the difference between flirtatious overture and polite conversation. She hovered in corners, nursing one glass of punch and keeping a careful eye on friends for drunkenness. One by one, she watched them pair up, leaving her alone most weekends, wondering where she'd gone wrong.

She met John three years after graduation, when she'd started teaching elementary school and one of her newly engaged college friends suggested a double date. She was twenty-four years old and spent most of the evening trying to hide her inexperience with men, talking about fun times and college parties she'd witnessed but hadn't (in all honesty) been part of. If doing this meant occasionally feigning uncertainty about a word she knew well or pretending she'd never heard of a writer she'd read, so be it, she thought. After eighteen years of schooling, she'd finally learned a formula that worked.

Three days later, John called for another date. Within six months, they were engaged and the relief she felt was enormous. As if she'd been holding her breath her whole adult life, and at last, she could exhale. Was this the same thing as love? John was always kind and dependable in their courtship. He held doors open and called when he said he would. If his shyness about discussing his work, his past—anything really—made her wonder how well she really knew him, she only admitted this the week before the wedding, to her mother, who waved the worry away, saying, "You'll know him soon enough. Believe me."

Did she continue the pretense of simplemindedness after they were married? She didn't mean to, of course, but those early years of marriage were so marked by the surprising discovery of John's moods and the way they fluctuated like weather. One day he'd return from work quiet and unresponsive and stay that way for days, forcing her to watch him carefully, looking for triggers to the sadness that would take hold of him and then vanish just as mysteriously. What did she talk about to fill the silence that so often defined their family dinners after the children came along? Did she tell him about the books she read to distract herself from the loneliness of solitary child-rearing? She honestly couldn't remember, just like she'd almost forgotten her old game-playing prowess lying dormant all these years.

But here it was again, waiting to be tapped.

# CHAPTER 6

# Walter

MUCH TO HIS DELIGHT, HE AND SALLY BEGAN PRACTICING SCRABBLE every evening after dinner. If the library was being used, they went to her apartment, a space that Walter loved. Though the apartments only varied slightly in layout and paint color, hers seemed brighter and more cheerful than others, with interesting artwork on the walls and not too many cloying family photos around the living room.

He didn't want to go overboard, complimenting her taste with every tchotchke he picked up, but she *did* have wonderful taste. He also tried not to comment on her clothing or her lovely scarves too much, but again, sometimes he couldn't help himself. "You're wearing my favorite scarf today," he said one evening and immediately wondered if he'd overstepped. So far, their conversation had been composed of about 80 percent Scrabble talk, 10 percent discussion of other Golden Grove residents, and 10 percent talk of other matters.

"Am I?" She looked down and touched it, surprised. "Why is this your favorite?"

He stammered. What could he say that wouldn't embarrass both of them? Other Golden Grove women regularly fished for compliments. Once, a woman had asked what Walter thought of her new shoes, forcing him to stand up and come around the table to look at them. "Lovely!" he'd stammered because he'd never been good at this sort of thing, never noticed his wife's haircuts or new clothes. But with Sally it was different. He couldn't stop noticing little things. "The green brings out your hazel eyes," he said and looked away. Yes, he decided. He'd overstepped.

Then she surprised him. "Nice try, Walter, but you're only hoping to distract me from the triple-word lane you just opened up, and it's not going to work."

Sally seemed to be a rare example of an older woman entirely at peace with her appearance. While some still went to great trouble to dye their hair and, in between touch-ups, walked around looking like they had a narrow white runway of powdered sugar on their head, Sally had a glorious mane of thick silver hair, cut shoulder length. Slim from all the walking she did and the fish she usually ordered at dinner, she also never denied herself pleasures. Never touched her stomach when dessert time came around and said, "Oh I shouldn't," obligating every dinner companion to contradict her.

Even his wife, Elyse, the most strong-minded woman he'd ever known, had had mystifying spells of self-doubt when it came to her looks. "Why didn't you tell me I'm getting fat," she once wept, unable to fit into an old party dress for a cousin's wedding. "I had no idea! You should have said something!" He never knew how to react in those moments because truly, he never noticed. To him, she was always Elyse, the woman who'd come into his life and changed it so completely. How could he see her as fat or thin when he'd spent his whole life so grateful for her presence? Occasionally he wondered if maybe his slavish gratitude had been part of the problem. He didn't see *her*; he saw the effect she had on him.

The week before the tournament, Walter found himself growing more anxious. Yes, Sally was a terrifically promising novice, but had he warned her how unrelenting and exhausting tournaments could be? Had he mentioned that playing with such intense concentration for eight hours in a single day could turn ordinary people into nit-picking super-nerds with hair-trigger tempers? Unfortunately, he was a prime example of this phenomenon, and the one whose behavior he worried most about. At the first tournament he played in, Walter shocked himself by finishing in third place behind two Scrabble veterans.

In his best game of the day, he'd beaten Ken Grant, half his age and rated 300 points above him. Ratings were determined by the National Scrabble Players Association, using a Byzantine formula after qualifying tournaments turned in their results. Beating a well-known player meant your rating jumped up. After the game, Ken shook Walter's hand and said, "Welcome to the big leagues. I suspect we'll be seeing a lot more of each other." Ken was known for his bushy beard, his long, thin braid, and the way he liberally used words that looked misspelled to fool his opponents into turn-wasting challenges: APATITE, CIGARET. Walter had read about this trick in the NSPA newsletter and studied the word list on the outside chance that he might get the opportunity to play Ken. Beating him was beyond Walter's wildest dreams.

Soon after that victory, though, Walter began his long, slow descent downward. At the very next tournament, he developed a headache halfway through the day and lost six games in a row, missing crucial plays and wasting far too many turns looking for places to play a Q or a J with a decent payoff. By his last game of the day, his shirt was soaked through with a flop sweat he hadn't experienced since adolescence, and he found himself pitted against a child who played SEQUINED for a triple-triple bingo and said, all innocence, "That's a word, right?" Walter lost that game, 495–235.

He never bounced back after that. Not really. He told people he'd let his rating fall intentionally, that he wanted to play at a lower level to build his skills before returning to the upper echelon of competition, but even playing weaker opponents didn't help the anxiety that plagued him at every tournament. It became a mystifying private war, waged with himself. Could he make it through without embarrassing himself? The answer was mostly no.

At the last tournament he'd entered over a year ago, he'd paced the hallway in between losing games, unable to get over his terrible luck and the garbage letters he kept getting stuck with. By the end, he'd become what he always abhorred in club players: a tile whiner. He started his final game of the day by announcing, "I suppose you'll draw both blanks and all four S's this game. All my other opponents have."

His opponent gave him a quizzical look, as if he wasn't sure he'd heard him correctly.

"There's just a lot about this game that's luck-based and unfair," Walter said to clarify, realizing—too late—that he sounded like a petulant child. He couldn't help it.

These last few weeks of playing with Sally had reminded Walter of what he loved so much about the game: the delight in new words, the beauty of placing them artfully onto a grid. Once, when she threaded REIKI through a cramped little spot forming four separate words, he broke into a spontaneous round of applause. She stood and took a little bow. "It won't be the highest-scoring play of the game, but it might just be the prettiest."

She was right. Later he outscored it by 30 points by stretching KNIGHTED across two double word squares. "I still think REIKI is the best play of the game," he said.

"It's not really about winning, is it?" she said graciously, and then laughed. "But then again, if it's not about that, what *is* it about?"

"It's about the lovely surprise of finding someone who enjoys this game as much as you do," Walter said, blushing the moment the words were out of his mouth. He hadn't meant to sound so sentimental.

She smiled and looked away as if she understood what he was trying to convey but couldn't say aloud: *I like you, Sally Reynolds.*

The night before the tournament, he lay awake fretting. What if this went the same way his last three tournaments had gone, and he became a bellicose fool, ranting about bad luck and unfair matchups? Last time, he lost seven out of eight games, which meant he'd start with a lower rating and probably get paired with beginners. Surely he could pull off one or two wins against lesser opponents and be able to keep his cool, he told himself. Still, he tried to warn her on the car ride to the tournament. "Nerves are a problem for me. I don't play as well at tournaments. Sometimes I overreact about bad luck in a way that might be unattractive."

Sally, who was driving, turned to smile at him. "Are you telling me that if I get paired with you today, I might finally win?"

"I can almost guarantee you would. My hope at this point is that I don't make a fool of myself, ranting about my bad tiles. Not doing that would be a victory for me. I also don't want you to get discouraged if you don't do well today. You're a *good* player. You might even be a *great* player." He wanted to add that she was also a great driver, but he feared going overboard with compliments. Only about half the Golden Grove residents still had cars. Judging by the stories told at dinner, many who still drove probably shouldn't. Walter had a mild fear of driving with a fellow resident and always took a Golden Grove shuttle van to market and doctors' appointments and Uber anywhere else. But Sally was a fine driver. Better than fine.

To his great surprise, she reached over and squeezed his hand. "Don't worry about me at the tournament, Walter. I don't have any high expectations. I just want to have fun."

Walter shook his head. "We all *say* that and none of us means it."

He looked down at the hand she had just squeezed, still resting on his thigh. Why hadn't he squeezed her hand back? Or better yet, taken it into both of his and said, *We don't have to go to this tournament! We can go back home and keep playing games, just the two of us! That's been the most fun I've had playing Scrabble in years!*

A few hours later, Walter could hardly mask his surprise. He won his first two games! Granted, the first was against a newcomer, but still he managed two nice bingos halfway through the game. More surprising was his second victory, against a woman he'd lost to at a tournament three months earlier. He wasn't sure if she remembered their previous game or his desperate strategy of playing phonies that got challenged off the board until the end of the game, when she said, "I see you're not taking the risks you used to. Or else you've read a dictionary."

This was what passed for a joke with the Scrabble crowd. He feigned a limp smile and prayed that no one was making the same "jokes" with Sally.

His biggest surprise of the morning was a close loss to a player rated 200 points higher. Walter played his best game in ages; his opponent got lucky and admitted it. "I drew both blanks and two S's," he said afterward. "Otherwise I would have lost. You played great defense and blocked every big move I wanted to make."

When was the last time anyone had said anything nice like this to him at a tournament? He floated back out to the lobby to meet Sally for the lunch hour. "I've had a terrific morning," he said, hoping he didn't sound like a braying fool. He'd never had anyone to talk to at these events and had never made anything but awkward stabs at rudimentary chat over bagged lunches. "This is very unusual for me. Lately, I've spent most tournaments losing all my morning games and falling into an afternoon of despair. Today feels different. Maybe you're my lucky charm."

Obviously this was a silly thing to say. He believed in luck, but courting it was a bargain one played in private and should never talk about. Around them, other brown baggers sat in empty chairs eating out of Tupperware and plastic baggies. In the past, Walter had always liked how Scrabble drew such socially awkward people. Most spent their lunch hour discussing controversial moves that hadn't worked out in their last game. Today was different, though. He'd not only broken his own losing streak but also had someone to eat lunch with! It occurred to him that these two factors might be related.

Before each game that morning he'd looked around the room to see if he knew who Sally was playing. Invariably, he didn't. As an unrated beginner, she was probably paired with others who were also at a tournament for the first or second time. Most were either very old or surprisingly young. On the car ride here, she admitted her greatest fear was getting paired with a former student and losing badly. "I was a stickler for spelling back when I taught third grade," she'd told him. "It'd be embarrassing to lose to someone who used to misspell 'such.'"

Walter considered this. "How do you misspell 'such'?"

"You add a T. It's a contagious problem. Once one child does it, they all do. Or you add an O and attach an A. 'I had "soucha" good summer' was an old favorite."

"Oh my," was all he could say.

"Any former students?" he said now, still grinning. They'd both packed tuna fish sandwiches, which seemed like a happy coincidence.

"No, thank goodness. Though I did play one ten-year-old who was frighteningly good. I'm proud of the victory I squeaked out at the end, but he had me nervous for a while."

"Children can be surprisingly competitive. Their advantage is practicing online."

In the Scrabble world, there were endless debates about playing online. Most people agreed—yes, it improved your game, but there were important facets to Scrabble that a computer couldn't teach you and, just as importantly, couldn't use itself. Walter often repeated this argument, but he was beginning to suspect it might not be true, as evidenced by a small but growing number of teenagers climbing up the Scrabble rankings.

"Never underestimate a young opponent," Walter said equitably. "I've lost to quite a few players who would technically qualify as children in any other context. Fearsome players all. I'm impressed that you won."

"It was my last game of the morning. I think I might be improving with each one. Maybe that's not saying much, but I'm definitely learning."

He smiled at her. She was astonishing, really—to seem so calm and upbeat halfway through her first tournament. At his first, he'd gotten so sweaty he had to change into his souvenir T-shirt at the lunch break to escape the cloud of nervous BO he was moving around in. He wondered if maybe her serenity was rubbing off. "I told you I've had an issue with anxiety at tournaments in the past. It's led to some humiliating displays of poor sportsmanship, but your presence has calmed my nerves and everything feels different today, I'm happy to report."

Sally smiled down at her sandwich. "That's nice of you to say, Walter, but I certainly wouldn't give me credit."

"Why not? You've reminded me of the pleasure of playing the game. In the past I've gotten far too fixated on using my rating as a measure of my brain's current status."

"You have a wonderful memory. What would you be afraid of?"

"Unfortunately my father prided himself on what a terrific memory he had straight into full-blown dementia when he occasionally forgot to put pants on before he walked outside."

Her expression froze, somewhere between sympathy and a smile. Oh, why was he offering her these frightening glimpses into his past? Suddenly he feared what else he might reveal in his buoyant spirits: *I wasn't a good father! Or a good husband for that matter! I didn't realize until it was too late!* He'd spent a lifetime unable to talk about his feelings and suddenly they were all right here, just below his paper-thin surface.

Thankfully, she let the subject go. She finished half her sandwich, wrapped up the other half, and tucked it back in her bag. "That should make a lovely dinner," she said, just like they all did in the dining room when they packed up half the dinner they hadn't eaten.

## CHAPTER 7

# Sally

OVER THE COURSE OF HER MORNING GAMES, SALLY SAW COUNTLESS words she'd never encountered before. GIPON, FOVEAL, GLAIVE. After each game, she made a list of words she wanted to look up at home. The most satisfying discovery of the day was playing words she wasn't sure how she knew. DRUPE, for one. And MOILERS for her first bingo. Both had been challenged; both had been good. Yes, she'd had a decent morning, but two games into the afternoon round, something shifted. She began seeing more plays on every rack. Suddenly she understood why Scrabble champions spent their downtime playing anagram games: Every rack of letters was a bonanza of them. If you saw one word in your tiles and stuck with it, you might miss a host of other possibilities.

Every new group of letters looked like nothing until you opened up your mind and suddenly there it was: a TION that made a dozen words right off the bat. Or INTER, which did the same. She could feel her brain stretching. On some turns, it took her by surprise and she had to catch her breath. *I'm good at this*, she marveled. When was the last time she'd made such a discovery? Four Thanksgivings ago when, after years of saying, "I can't make a pie crust," she actually did? The hardest part of aging, she once thought, wasn't the battle to retain your abilities; it was the absence of a chance to develop new ones. And here she was. Doing just that.

Much to her surprise, she won her last two games, though to be fair, this might have been more of a comment on her afternoon opponents. One was a woman older than herself who took out her hearing aids, set them beside the board, and explained, "It helps me concentrate if I can't hear anything." Apparently, it didn't help enough because she missed some obvious plays and Sally won 389–319. The other was a polite young man who started the game by saying he was having a migraine and might need to leave at some point to throw up. In the end, he played the whole game with such labored concentration that she wanted to squeeze his hand and say, "Why don't we just stop and tell them you won." She didn't because she feared that might be more insulting than actually beating him. Which she did, handily.

After it was over, he pushed his chair back and let his head hang between his knees. She quickly came around and put a hand on his back. "Let's get you some help. There's a first aid station in the hallway. You need some Tylenol at the very least." He couldn't speak by then, only nod. She took his elbow and steered him out of the main convention room into a "first aid room" with a leather sofa and a young woman reading a magazine. "Is there some place where Daniel might lie down? He's having a migraine. He could probably use some water," Sally said. Daniel stretched out on the sofa with a groan. The moment he was horizontal, he rolled over on his side. His eyes closed, his teeth clenched, he rasped, "Thank you."

The "nurse" in attendance (who didn't look old enough to have graduated from college) said she couldn't administer any medication, so Sally went to the hotel gift shop and bought an envelope of two

Advil and a bottle of water. After she gave him these, he took her hand and squeezed it. "Good game," he rasped.

She smiled. "You should have won. You're a very good player."

"Not necessarily. FAMULI was nice. So was COOEE to go out."

She remembered Walter saying that true Scrabble aficionados were capable of analyzing a game longer than it took to play it. "We can be terrible bores," he'd said. Here was poor Daniel, trying to do this in the face of blinding pain. "You should close your eyes," she whispered. "Don't try to talk."

Even as she said this, she couldn't explain the stirring that she felt in her heart. When was the last time she'd been able to help a young person who wasn't one of her children? She couldn't remember. For that matter, when was the last time she'd helped one of her children?

# CHAPTER 8

# Walter

WALTER ARRIVED AT HIS FINAL GAME OF THE DAY EXHAUSTED BUT CALMED by his respectable 4–3 record. He hadn't experienced anything close to his collapse in recent tournaments and, in fact, had made some of his best plays in years. Over the afternoon, his confidence soared so high he began writing down his letter racks so he could go over each play later on. It would be lovely to relive this day.

His final opponent was a 12-year-old boy named Toby, who seemed unusually polite for someone so young. Before the game began, he shook Walter's hand and said it was an honor to play him. *My goodness*, Walter thought, wondering how this boy might have heard of him. "Likewise," he said. In the few minutes they had before the game started, the boy said something about learning to play Scrabble from his grandmother, and Walter realized he'd heard his name before. Dorothy, from his VFW Scrabble club, had played him a few months ago at a Framingham tournament and called him a "prodigy."

"Remember this name," she'd said. "Toby Weir. He lives with his grandmother and he's going to be a top player someday, mark my words. He beat me by a hundred points but he was very polite about it, and afterward he praised a few of my moves."

Dorothy's friend, Lena, chimed in with her own story about Toby: how he came in second at a Framingham tournament when he was only eleven years old. "Later he told people that he had a photographic memory but he'd only read the first half of the dictionary, up to the letter M. 'I think I'll do better once I get to the end of the alphabet,' he said. Apparently the judges went back and it was true: Every bingo he'd played started with a letter from the first half of the alphabet.'"

"Are you the boy who finished second in Framingham?" Walter asked.

Toby closed his eyes as if he needed a moment to remember something like this, then popped them back open. "That's right. I did."

Walter narrowed his eyes. "Didn't you go 6–1 that day?"

"Oh, I don't remember things like that."

A Scrabble champion who could remember the first half of the dictionary but couldn't recall his own win-loss record? Walter could only dream of having such a selective memory. "Do you *really* not remember or are you just trying to seem modest?" He was genuinely curious.

"I really don't remember those things. My grandmother says it affects your game if you get caught up in tracking your wins. Then you're remembering numbers, not words."

"What's your current rating?"

Toby shrugged. "I don't know. My grandmother might."

Walter shook his head. Lately, even if he tried, he couldn't forget his current rating, which was 200 points lower than it used to be.

The bell sounded. Toby held the tile bag above eye level and dug around for a tile to decide who would go first. He smiled and showed his pick to Walter: an A. Usually luck like this would send Walter into a spiral of negative thoughts. *Here we go again. I bet my first rack will be all vowels. He'll probably open with a bingo.* But this time it didn't happen. Instead, Walter stared at the boy and tried to decide: Did he *really* not know his own Scrabble rating? "Doesn't she show you your rating when it comes?"

"Sometimes. Usually not, though. She says it's better for me to concentrate on learning my word lists, so I work on those instead."

Walter smiled. Here was a crack in the story of the boy genius with the photographic memory: Maybe he hadn't read the dictionary once and closed it halfway through. Maybe he'd been memorizing word lists like all the rest of them, sweating it out, toiling in private. Yes, he was still impressive of course—he was *twelve* years old, for heaven's sake—but he wasn't a freak. Instead of the disproportionate resentment Walter usually felt toward a new opponent lucky enough to start the game by drawing an A, he felt something else entirely: He *liked* Toby. He was curious what he might learn from him.

"How much time do you spend studying?" Walter asked. Most prodigies tried to make the work of being a champion look easy. *I study when I can. A little bit on weekends.* Making it look easy was a prerequisite to being a prodigy. *I don't try hard. Trophies fall in my lap.* Apparently Toby hadn't gotten that memo. "A *lot*," he said, rearranging his tiles. "Like all the time. My grandmother thinks I'm an oral learner so she makes tapes of herself spelling out word lists and I listen to those."

Toby laid down UMIAK, an old Scrabble favorite meaning Alaskan canoe. Walter studied his own rack and made a quick play. Suddenly he didn't care about the outcome of this game as much as he cared about this grandmother and her study tips. This first one sounded crazy. Wouldn't most Scrabble players agree that learning words was a *visual* exercise? Walter learned his lists by writing them onto index cards, but could there be a more effective way to do it?

He let a few turns go by without speaking. In tournaments, it was considered impolite to talk during a game. It was called coffeehousing, and some players were famous for using it as a weapon. Distraction, trash talk, even praise, could throw off another person's concentration. Once someone complained that Walter clicked his tiles too loudly while rearranging his rack. The game was three-quarters over when Walter dared to return to their conversation. "I think you and your grandmother might make an interesting story for the NSPA newsletter."

"What's that?" Toby said, making his play, unfazed by the interruption.

"The newsletter? From the NSPA?" He reminded himself, sadly, that young people probably never read newsletters. Walter got the old-fashioned paper version, sent by mail, but he knew it was also possible to read it online.

"I've never heard of that."

"The newsletter or NSPA?"

"Either one."

Was this even *possible*? Could a budding champion not recognize the organization that oversaw these tournaments? "The National Scrabble Players Association? The people who do the Scrabble ratings?" In his darker moments, Walter had thought of them as the power-mongers who issued the new rules and triggered the nervous, self-destructive play that had put his rating on a downward spiral a few years ago. In one of those moods, he would have told Toby they were the enemy and should not be as powerful as they were.

In reality, he knew they were probably a handful of overworked, underpaid staff who toiled in a grim office somewhere in New Jersey, collecting results from tournaments and configuring new ratings. He told Toby this. "Plus they put out a newsletter once a month that includes human interest stories. You and your grandmother would make a great one."

"Oh no, she wouldn't like that."

"How do you know? She must be a member."

"I don't think so. What does it take to be a member?"

"Not much. You pay dues and get a card." Suddenly he shifted his attitude toward the group entirely. "They're a worthy organization and should be supported. You should definitely be a member if you aren't already. Your grandmother can help you. There's a small fee, but I'm sure they'd waive it for you if you needed that."

Toby thought about this for a moment. "Is that 'waive' like W-A-I-V-E?"

"Yes."

"I always wondered what that spelling meant."

How extraordinary to have so many words at his disposal with so few of their meanings, Walter thought. "Here, I'll show you what you get when you join." He pulled his wallet out of his backpack to show Toby his membership card: the color of a Scrabble box with NSPA written out in letter tiles. When Walter first got his in the mail, he kept it out on the kitchen counter because it was fun to look at. "It'll look like this." He held it out. "Only with your name on it."

They weren't supposed to open any bags during a game, but they were two turns away from the end of this one, and for the first time in his tournament career, Walter didn't care about the outcome. Once he figured out who Toby was, he gave up on winning and was happy to keep the point spread near 40. He was seventy-four years old and might someday be able to say he lost a reasonably close game to a national champion. It had been a great day.

"Here it is," Walter said, flipping through his wallet. "My NSPA card. Does it look familiar? Have you seen your grandmother's?"

Toby had managed to use all his tiles and slap his clock timer down with seventeen seconds to spare. "Can I see it?" He held out his hand.

Walter smiled and put it back in his wallet. "You'll have to get your own, kid."

Oh, if only his own son had been a fraction more like this boy at his age! Forgiving of Walter's awkwardness, impressed by a few shining baubles like this silly card.

Afterward, they carried their score sheet up to the official's desk. Walter didn't want to get sentimental, but in his exhaustion, he couldn't help himself. "It's been a real honor playing you, Toby," he said, shaking the boy's hand for the second time. "I suspect you've got an exciting future in Scrabble. I'll be rooting for you."

To his surprise, the boy looked sheepish. "I don't know about that," he said.

"Oh I do. Trust me, I've been playing in tournaments long enough to say you most definitely have a big future ahead."

"Yeah, maybe," Toby said, waving as he walked away.

Walter looked forward to telling Sally this story on the car ride home, but first he needed to find a private bathroom before they started the fifty-minute drive. He'd already experienced the stomach-knotting embarrassment of her lifting his backpack at lunchtime and looking down in surprise. It was weightless as a pillow, so she must have wondered what was inside—a lucky blanket? A stuffed animal? No, just a handful of Depends that he was in dire need of changing. It wasn't until he got to the bathroom, dug around for a while, and finally emptied his backpack completely that all the joy of the day drained away with a single realization.

"We need to file a report with the tournament organizers, Walter," Sally said after they'd spent twenty minutes looking around the table where he played his last two games, and then the lost and found.

"No. Absolutely not. The wallet is gone and it's my own fault. If we tell the authorities, they'll blame the boy, and I can't be absolutely sure he's the one who took it."

"But you just said the last time you saw it, it was lying on the table because you'd taken it out to show him your card."

"I was a fool not to make sure I had it back, that's all."

The more Sally pressed him, the more he insisted. No report. No notification. On the car ride home, he was quiet, though Sally had a hard time letting the topic go. "Protecting children when they make a mistake doesn't help them," she said. She was probably right, but what did he know? He'd made so many mistakes with his own son over the years that he didn't trust his instincts anymore.

He and Elyse had always had their worst arguments about Gavin and the way he flitted from one expensive passion to the next. First hockey, then electric guitar, then photography. "It's robbery," he once said and Elyse glared at him.

"It is *not* robbery to support your son," she'd snapped.

He'd spent the last twenty years realizing he'd been too hard on Gavin, and now it was too late to do anything about it. He thought of other moments—when Elyse lay in bed beside him, staring at the ceiling, and said, "Maybe it's more important to be *kind* than it is to be *right*. Maybe that's especially true when it comes to your own child."

Without mentioning Gavin, he tried to explain his reasoning to Sally. "I think this boy has had a difficult life. I don't know what happened to his parents, but he lives with his grandmother and he's a real talent. He has a chance for a future in Scrabble, but if I made a police report and word got out to the judges, they would disqualify him from future tournaments. I don't want to be responsible for that."

"But stealing a wallet is a *big deal*."

"I had seven dollars in it. I only have one credit card, and I can cancel that."

He hoped she'd let it go. Elyse had been right. Sometimes it *was* more important to be kind than to be right. To his surprise, Sally didn't say any more. They drove in silence for a while until finally she asked, "Other than the wallet business, did you have a good day?"

He smiled and thought of an old joke. "Other than that, Mrs. Lincoln, did you enjoy the play?" Sally laughed, which momentarily replaced the unsettled feeling in his stomach with satisfaction. "Very good actually."

"Why don't you tell me about your games and then I'll tell you about mine."

He was happy to oblige and soon found himself describing each of his matches in the painstaking detail he'd warned her about. "My strongest opponent of the day played ILIA, hoping to block passage to a triple word, but apparently he forgot that if I played a C on the front, I could add an E at the end for a plural and grab the triple-word square."

"CILIAE is the plural of CILIA?"

"To be honest, I wasn't sure, but he didn't challenge, which he should have because it turns out it's not acceptable."

He told her about a few bingos he was proud of and some more phonies he'd gotten away with because they sounded so much like real words. "That's the trick of course. I got away with DINNERER because LUNCHER is a real word, which doesn't make sense. Someone who eats lunch?"

Amazing how easy it was to fill conversation with someone as interested in Scrabble as he was. In the dining room, he struggled every night to hold up his end of the conversation. With Sally, before he knew it, they were pulling into the Golden Grove parking lot.

# CHAPTER 9

# Walter

WALTER WASN'T SURE WHY HE FELT SO NERVOUS ABOUT APPROACHING Sally during the Tuesday coffee/tea hour, held in the library. He rarely came to this event, though he knew some women dressed up for it in flowered skirts and pearl necklaces. He was grateful to see Sally wearing her usual sensible brown slacks with a pastel turtleneck. She didn't see the word *tea* and reach for her jewelry box, thank heavens.

She smiled when she saw him and still, he hesitated. In the three days since the tournament, he'd intentionally given her a break from any emails about Scrabble or invitations to play. Impossible for him to know if he was coming on too strong with his Scrabble enthusiasm, and it was best to err on the side of caution, he reasoned.

"Hello, Walter!" She smiled, to his relief. "Any news about your wallet?"

"No, I'm afraid not."

"So you've canceled your credit card and all of that?"

Ginny Hendricks, a well-known Golden Grove busybody, perked up. "Have you misplaced your wallet, Walter? Did you ask at the front desk if they've seen it?"

This was why he avoided sharing personal problems in public: Tell one person in the lobby that your shoelace was broken, and within minutes, a crowd of ladies would swoop in with solutions so obvious he might as well be a child. *You need a new shoelace, then, Walter! You should go to the store and buy one!*

It took Ginny all of twenty seconds to enlist others. "Rhoda, did you hear? Walter's lost his wallet!"

Rhoda took a large bite of cookie before offering a spray of crumbs with her advice. "Did you try looking in the last place you had it?"

Walter looked at Sally, whose smile was unreadable. He didn't want to be mean, but some of these women wouldn't leave you alone until you were. "It wasn't misplaced, ladies. It was stolen and I have the matter well in hand. Cards all canceled. Crisis averted."

"*Stolen?*" Rhoda gasped and clutched at her necklace, a string of green plastic beads. "Oh, Walter, how did it happen? Were you *robbed*?"

"It didn't happen here, rest assured. Your valuables are safe."

Ginny leaned in for a hug that Walter had no choice but to accept. "Still. Poor Walter. You should come to our tai chi class. Learn a few self-defense moves."

"That's a wonderful idea, Ginny!" Rhoda trilled. "Lillian, what do you think of Walter joining us for tai chi?"

As far as Walter could tell, the twice-weekly tai chi group consisted of a dozen women standing behind chairs and holding out one arm as if they were collectively stopping an invisible train hurtling toward them. "Would you really call tai chi *self-defense*?"

"Oh absolutely," the trio chorused. "That's the main focus."

"It doesn't seem as if there's too much *moving* in the class."

"That's the whole point." Ginny nodded. "Self-defense can be about standing very still."

It did no good to argue a point like this, Walter had learned.

He'd also learned that trying for a joke often had the opposite of its intended effect and so didn't say the first one that came to mind: *I've always thought walking away quickly from a mugger is probably the best self-defense*. Two years at Golden Grove had taught him there was really only one response possible: "Yes, I'll consider that. Thank you, ladies." He bowed his head in the hope of ending the conversation, but instead the three women leaned closer, as if readying to demonstrate some tai chi with teacups.

Sally excused herself with a warm smile. "I'm afraid I can't stay. I'm expecting a call from my daughter this afternoon."

Did she think these women were as silly as he did? Impossible to tell. "I did have a question for you, Sally. If you have a minute."

Three sets of eyebrows lifted, as if they were all in junior high school and he'd just asked Sally if he might carry her books. He moved away from the trio, who he feared were now adjusting their hearing aids for easier eavesdropping.

"I don't know if I told you about this local Scrabble club I sometimes go to. It's more casual than a tournament, just friendly games, a wide mix of players, at our local VFW. Might you have any interest?"

"I'm sorry, Walter. I can't hear what you're saying."

He was so self-conscious that he'd lowered his voice to a whisper. He shot a look at the other women. If he pulled her out of the room altogether, he feared they'd be a topic of conversation for the rest of the day.

"Would you have any interest in going to a local Scrabble club with me?"

"I thought you *were* the Scrabble club."

"No this is a real club, in town, at the VFW on Thursdays."

She seemed to need an inordinate amount of time to consider his invitation. Did she really have such a busy schedule that she might have to move things around to go out on a Thursday night?

"Let me look at my calendar and think about it," she finally said. "I'll let you know. Thank you for thinking of me, Walter."

She squeezed his shoulder in reassurance as he imagined her reassuring her students when it was time for math. He was surprised by how disappointed he felt after she walked away. He'd spent an entire day debating whether or not to invite her at all because the VFW Scrabble club could be an unpredictable combination of overly serious players on the one hand and, on the other, lonely people looking for an excuse to get out of the house. Too often, Peter, who oversaw the group, didn't do a good job of pairing opponents, so Walter had some matches where he had to explain the rules of the game and others where a better player resented having to play *him*. Once he heard one of them complain about "getting matched with the aging farts."

He'd invited Sally with a plan to pretend not to know too much about the group, in case they arrived and found an unfriendly mix of people. It honestly hadn't occurred to him that she might demur from the whole idea. It made him return to his apartment and rethink everything about the tournament and wonder where he might have gone wrong. He remembered their happy lunch and nice drive home after they got past the unpleasant business about the wallet. Had she decided she didn't like Scrabble anymore, the way everyone else at Golden Grove had? To him, she'd seemed so different from the others. More talented to begin with, and more interested in putting in the work to improve her game. He'd thought they were becoming friends, but of course, he'd never really understood the ins and outs of friend-making.

This was the reason he started playing games back in school, starting with the chess and war games club, a group of misfit boys who carried baggies of chess pieces around like an advertisement of their social-skill deficits. In college, Walter attended one weekend of fraternity rush parties and felt so overwhelmed that afterward he gratefully returned home every weekend to play gin rummy with his mother, who was battling cancer by then. Because she was too weak to move much, they spread the cards over her bed and talked almost entirely about their games: which strategies had panned out, which ones hadn't.

His father, who'd always been an unpredictable and angry man, grew more eccentric as Walter's mother worsened until finally, after her death, something snapped. He began dressing inappropriately for the weather and eventually walking outside in his underwear or, worse, nothing at all. Halfway through Walter's sophomore year, a neighbor called him at school to tell him that his father had been wandering the street at night naked, ranting about topics no one understood. There seemed to be no other choice except for Walter to move back home and finish school as a commuter.

Curtailing his father's erratic behavior wasn't easy, but to Walter's surprise, here again, games were a help. While his mother's mind had stayed razor-sharp to the end, his father's had not. Cloudy with confusion, he did best with simple games: checkers or Authors, a card game they'd played when Walter was a child. Six months before Walter's college graduation, his father died, leaving him free at last to attend parties, though by that point he never got invited to any.

Walter's first year working for Farmland Insurance had served as a reminder of how inexperienced he was at socializing. Going out for drinks with coworkers became an excruciating exercise in fiddling with drink coasters and coming home some nights unable to recall if he'd said a single word. Eventually he understood that the other actuarial adjusters were coarse jokesters who liked to rank the secretaries' looks on a scale of one to ten. How relieved he was one lunch hour to stumble upon a group of those secretaries playing hearts in a small, rarely used conference room.

Elyse had seen him watching from the doorway. "Want to join us?" She smiled as if his sitting down—the only man in a group of six women—would be perfectly normal.

"Maybe I'll just watch, if you don't mind," he said softly.

From the start, Elyse's card skills had mesmerized him: how she shuffled and dealt without looking down, how swiftly she arranged her hands into suits. After a few days, he joined their game, and after a month, she invited him to a Friday night bridge party she hosted.

"Oh, I don't play bridge," he demurred. He'd only ever heard of married couples having bridge nights. "I've never learned how."

Elyse touched his hand with her fingertips. "Then you let someone teach you," she whispered with a warm, slightly maternal smile. "I'd be happy to."

He assumed it would be the same group of women he'd come to know from the lunch-hour games, but no. The group of eight was split evenly: four men and four women. He'd contemplated wearing a work suit and was relieved he hadn't when he arrived to find the other men in casual slacks with their sleeves rolled up.

Relieved, that is, until Elyse touched a button on his sweater and said, "Nice sweater. Did it belong to your dad?"

She was teasing him, he suspected, but unfortunately the sweater *had* belonged to his father. He smiled sheepishly. He was beginning to think that maybe Elyse *liked* his awkwardness and his terrifying lack of real-world experience. By that point, he was a year out of college and had only been on three dates in his life, all set up by his mother's friends, with girls as shy as himself, where conversation necessitated preparing questions ahead of time. "What's your favorite season?" was a standby until one woman looked confused and answered, "Garlic powder, I guess."

With Elyse's crowd, no conversation starters were needed because no awkward silences ever developed. The men poured drinks in highball glasses and the women smoked cigarettes. People fought for airtime to finish a story as they called for more nuts or held up their glasses for a refill. After a few bridge nights, it was easy for Walter to see that the men cared less about the games than the women did, so he had an opening. Bridge *was* complicated but hardly impossible. He could buy books and teach himself. He could study the bridge column every Thursday in the paper. Those evenings introduced him to the wonder of game playing as a remedy for the socially awkward.

After a few months, Elyse declared him the best male player they had. Considering the alcoholic way some of the other men downed their scotches, this was, in truth, damning him with faint praise, but Walter was thrilled and the next week asked Elyse out on a real date. "Maybe we could get dinner," he said, his throat suddenly dry.

"With cards or without?" Elyse said and his heart fell.

"Maybe…without. Just this once?"

"I'm teasing, Walter. Yes, of course I'd like to go out with you. I wasn't sure if you were ever going to pick up on my hints."

After that, things moved quickly and every outing brought new revelations of how much Walter didn't understand about the opposite sex. "Lots of girls at the office have tried flirting with you," Elyse said. "You're a little slow on the uptake, but that just means you don't think you're God's gift the way some men do. You're definitely not like them, thank heavens."

Games filled their courtship, and after their wedding they brought a card deck and a cribbage board along on their honeymoon. Later, they conceded they'd probably spent more time playing cards than having sex. "But that's only because a game lasts about thirty minutes," Elyse pointed out. They both continued working at Farmland Insurance after the wedding, though Elyse admitted that the typing pool was an awkward place for married girls to linger for too long. "Everyone's just waiting for you to announce your pregnancy and leave."

When she failed to get pregnant that first year—or the next—she stayed on to irk the higher-ups. Walter knew their managers weren't tracking their fecundity the way he and Elyse were or noticing how, every month, Elyse's moods rose and fell alongside her cycle. One night, lying in bed with the lights off, she told him, "I'm afraid God knows some of the thoughts I've had and he doesn't think I'd be a fit mother."

Walter, who thought they mostly went to church for the social aspect—it was a congregation full of young marrieds like themselves—turned to her. She'd never mentioned God before, and it scared him. "Does anyone think God can hear our thoughts?" he whispered.

"I do. I just told you."

"Wouldn't we all be in trouble though?" He thought of his poor father and his wild rantings, which were, no doubt, only the tip of the iceberg of his disturbing thoughts.

"Mine are worse."

This was unsettling. "How?"

"I can't tell you. I just think about things that aren't right sometimes, and I'm pretty sure that's why I haven't gotten pregnant."

The next morning Walter tried to forget this conversation but couldn't. It haunted him six months later when Elyse finally got pregnant and again, two months after that, when she lost the baby. After two more miscarriages (one almost seven months along), he thought about it even more: What secrets was she keeping that God might disapprove of? He knew she was a friendly, outgoing girl before he married her. After all, she was the one who first invited him to join their games. "I've seen you watching us. I know you want to play," she'd said. He'd blushed at that (the way he blushed at everything back then). He *was* interested in the game, but if she knew that much, what else could she discern about the contents of his brain?

Her confession cast a shadow over his memory of their courtship. She never went to college, which meant she worked for almost five years before he arrived. Had those been five long years of inviting others to play games? Why hadn't he even considered this possibility before they married? He couldn't say, except that his relief at meeting her was so huge there wasn't room for other emotions—like skepticism, perhaps. Or doubt.

After four years without successfully producing a baby, they learned that Elyse had a heart-shaped uterus, which wouldn't rule out carrying a pregnancy to term but would make it harder. "A fertilized egg needs to implant in just the right spot for a healthy placenta to grow," the doctor said. "Keep trying. Hopefully it'll happen sooner rather than later."

Reassuring words, certainly. A medical explanation to replace the spiritually indicting one. As they continued trying, though, he wondered—but never asked—if she thought about her confession, whispered in the dark. He remembered her parties, filled with men and women so comfortable in her apartment that they fetched their own ice and poured their own drinks.

They still played bridge occasionally, though not as often because most of the old crowd was busy with families and babies of their own. It was the early seventies by then and the generation coming up behind them looked like long-haired strangers, even if they were only a few years younger. He didn't understand all their stormy protesting, though apparently Elyse didn't share this feeling, a fact he only learned when he overheard her announce at bridge that she was joining a civil rights protest.

"They're right about everything," Elyse declared. "One hundred percent."

"But Elyse, sweetheart, you're not black," Linda said, taking a long drag on her cigarette. Linda was seven months pregnant, which had almost stopped them from coming. For Elyse, some pregnant women were harder to be around than others. Linda was six years younger than Elyse and had been married less than a year.

"Does that mean I shouldn't care about the injustice I read about in the newspaper?" Elyse said. "Did Jesus tell us to only care about the people who look like us?"

Conversation stopped at the other tables. Elyse, once the glue that held these evenings together, had become a loose wire, Walter suspected. A nervous source of worry. No one ever knew what might set her off. The mention of Jesus was strange. As far as he knew, everyone in this crowd went to church but no one ever talked about it afterward. They certainly didn't reference Bible teachings like a Baptist.

"Just forget it, Linda. You go ahead and have your baby and hope it doesn't bring home a black boyfriend or girlfriend someday. That's fine."

Oh, it was too much. Fearing Elyse had had one too many drinks and might say anything at all—*God is punishing me for having sex with other men before marriage! I did it because I wanted to!*—Walter hustled her out of there with phony excuses about needing to be up early in the morning. Afterward, he assumed that evening had killed the bridge club, but a few months later, Walter heard two coworkers make a bridge joke and realized the group was still playing. They just weren't *being invited.*

That afternoon, he stopped at JCPenney on his way home and bought their first Scrabble set. He knew it was a game easily enjoyed by two and also knew Elyse would probably be better at it than him. She did the word jumbles and crosswords every morning in the paper. His heart soared, thinking how much she'd like the gift. Then he got home and found Elyse sitting in the dark, weeping. "Guess what? I'm pregnant," she whispered. She was smiling, even as tears spilled down her cheeks. "Here we go again."

They steeled themselves. They told no one and made no plans. When the pregnancy held on into the eighth month, they painted the nursery yellow but waited to buy a crib. A crib unfilled would be too painful down the line, they reasoned, right up until she went into labor two weeks early and her heart-shaped womb produced its miracle—five-pound three-ounce Gavin—and it swiftly became clear how ill-prepared they were. They had no bed for him, no tiny clothes, no ribbon-tied booties or little hats.

With Elyse still in the hospital, Walter shopped frantically, working from a list she'd made, adding a couple items of his own: a copy of *The Lion, the Witch and the Wardrobe*, a junior edition of Scrabble. "I know this might be a little premature," he said, showing her his purchases in her hospital room. "But this way, we'll have them. Whenever he's ready."

The first time Walter pulled out the Scrabble Junior set was eight years later, on a rain-soaked Saturday when Gavin's baseball game was canceled. "You'll love this," he told his son, though he wasn't sure. Gavin was far more focused on sports than Walter had ever been. "Your mother and I used to play this game a lot." (In truth, they'd only played a few times. Elyse liked it but was too preoccupied with her pregnancy to concentrate in her usual competitive way. He won all of their games.)

"Why don't you play anymore?" Gavin asked, stopping Walter short for a moment. Why *had t*hey stopped playing games? Before having a child, days seemed so much longer, time something that had to be filled. After his arrival, there was never enough, certainly not a few hours to play a game.

"I'm not sure," he said.

A year earlier, Elyse had started a new job at their local library. Because she was new, she had to take the weekend shifts that no one else wanted, which meant Walter spent most Saturdays alone with his son, and this wasn't always easy. Walter wasn't much of an athlete, and the only activities that held Gavin's interest involved throwing and hitting balls. That day, Walter was happy for the rain and the excuse it provided to stay inside, but Gavin was bored. He started by going first and playing "THE."

"Really?" Walter said. "That's your play?"

"Yes," Gavin said.

On his next turn, Gavin spelled "TOOF," down from his first T.

"Sorry, Gav, you're not allowed to spell going up," Walter said.

"I didn't," Gavin insisted. "It's 'toof.'" He tapped one of his teeth.

Walter tried to be magnanimous. "Good try," he said, privately thinking, *He's eight years old, for God's sake. Do they not teach any spelling in school?* "Unfortunately, that F should be a TH, though."

"I spell it this way," Gavin said, unfazed.

Walter drew the line and removed the offending word, explaining the simple but fundamental rule: "If it's not a real word, you have to take it back." To counter Gavin's sulky pout, he added, "But you can try again with another word. Like FOOT going down!"

"I don't like FOOT," Gavin said, pushing his rack away. "I don't like this game."

Walter never played Scrabble with Gavin again. Just as he and Elyse stopped playing games, as well. He never understood what happened exactly or why he seemed to drive people away when he came near them with a board game or a deck of cards. He just did. That was that. Lesson learned.

# CHAPTER 10

# Sally

SALLY KNEW SHE'D BEEN OVERLY BRUSQUE WITH POOR WALTER, AND she felt bad. Maybe it was because he occasionally reminded her of her son, Andrew—the way he hugged his backpack to his chest as he ran through the rain to her car; the way he talked to himself at the tournament, pacing between games; the intensity with which he studied the tournament matchup lists. Back in high school, Andrew had a hard time making friends, mostly because he was so academically competitive. He couldn't stop himself from asking what everyone else got on a test, couldn't see how off-putting it was to highlight his own spot on the far end of the bell curve. Sally despaired of him ever making a real friend, and then, his junior year in high school, he shocked them all by announcing he had a girlfriend. At her first dinner with the family, he told everyone, "Karen has a higher grade in physics than I do." When she demurred and said that wasn't true, he insisted, "Yes, it is. She's got a 97.8 and I have a 97.2."

Sally liked Karen immediately and shared her general embarrassment—that Andrew would memorize not only his own grade but someone else's too seemed like proof that he wasn't ready for a real relationship and might even be in this one to get a look at Karen's study notes. But apparently not. They stayed together all of senior year, and when it came time for the prom, Andrew surprised everyone by using birthday money to rent a tuxedo with a lilac cummerbund and bow tie to match her dress. He was earnest about every aspect of preparation: "Everyone thinks orchids are the only flower for a corsage but that's not true. They didn't have any in the color I wanted so I ordered a lilac dahlia."

A *dahlia* corsage? Sally had wanted to gasp. To her, that sounded a heartbeat away from a squirting clown flower.

"Karen will love it, I know."

Sally held her tongue. Just as she held her tongue when he emerged wearing a tuxedo with pants so short his lilac socks showed.

"I asked for this hemming," he announced. "I want Karen to see the lilac socks I found."

*You could always show her in private*, Sally didn't say. *Or when you're sitting on the sidelines watching other people dance*, she also didn't say.

Sometimes Sally wondered if that period of awkward first love marked the pinnacle of Andrew's happiest days, when he was willing to dress like a lilac-spotted clown to court his ladylove. They lasted through one year of college, then Karen broke up with him, and for years afterward, he plotted ways to win her back. Three summers after their breakup, he saw his opening in a social media post that implied she'd broken up with her most recent boyfriend. The next day Andrew showed up at the pool where she worked as a lifeguard with a five-page handwritten letter detailing the reasons they should get back together, which he asked her to read and respond to on the spot.

Rachel told Sally this story after she'd heard it from friends—how he'd stood in khakis and a button-down shirt at the bottom of her lifeguard chair and waited. "I'll watch the swimmers while you read," he'd said. As if this weren't unsettling enough, he pointed to some children in the shallow end and screamed at them for spitting water at each other. "People pee in this pool. You know that, right?"

"He looked like he was dressed for a job interview, Mom," Rachel had told her. "Surrounded by people in bathing suits and swim diapers."

"Poor Karen," Sally had said, shaking her head. "What did she say?"

"She tried to tell him they should talk later, somewhere else, but he was weirdly insistent. He said he needed an answer right then. So she said her answer was no, and he should leave."

After that episode, he vowed he would never date again, a threat he'd kept as far as Sally knew for two decades.

For reasons that Sally never fully understood, Andrew's academic career peaked in high school and never recovered from the meltdown he suffered when Karen broke up with him after freshman year of college. For a few weeks afterward, he stopped going to classes. At Christmas he came home and announced he was taking the rest of the year off. Thankfully, he returned, but he never found his old competitive edge, graduating with a meager 3.1 GPA and talk of teachers who gave everyone else a break except him.

After graduation, he moved back home and worked a variety of jobs that had all been disappointments: as a market researcher, a paralegal, and—in a particularly ill-advised move—a door-to-door salesman of solar energy plans with a script that included the opening line, "Do you care about the environment? Because I do." It all lacked a sense of purpose until eight years ago, when he got a temp job working for the local state assistance office, which helped families get access to low-income housing and help with winter heating bills. To everyone's surprise, this turned out to be a good match for someone who had difficulty navigating social expectations. The office was defined by the rules to be followed and forms to be filled out. Because he didn't like being judged himself, he judged none of his clients, even the ones who talked to themselves or resisted his help.

"The system isn't always fair to people who don't speak English or haven't been to college. I like trying to make it fairer," he said.

To Sally, this sounded generous and surprisingly empathetic. It was easy to see that Andrew felt good there, secure enough to move into his own apartment where he'd lived for ten years, until about nine months ago when his boss announced that the department was facing cutbacks and replacing his position with a software program that could do all the organizing and filing Andrew had previously been in charge of. The manager was sympathetic and arranged for Andrew to interview for positions in related departments, but nothing came through. Andrew admitted that he might have gotten too emotional in one interview and cried a little. "I never realized how much I liked that old job until they asked me to describe it. Then I couldn't help it. I got sad."

Eight months ago, he'd moved back home just as his father was recovering from his first stent surgery. "He's here to help with his dad's recuperation," Sally would call out to neighbors until finally, one afternoon Andrew asked her to stop. "We all know that's not true. I'm here because I have nowhere else to go."

It was the saddest, truest thing any of them had said in a while, and she had no idea how to respond.

Walter didn't remind her of Andrew because he was intelligent but bad at practical matters (like keeping track of his wallet—something that could have easily happened to Andrew). It was this awkward sweetness. Where she could see his good intentions along with a version of Andrew's old teenage intensity—about games and strategy, rules and fairness. Any time Walter talked about the rise and fall of his Scrabble rating, she thought about Andrew's tallies of his own GPA and overall class ranking. Dwelling on these measures of validation scared her a little. It had all been so sad with Andrew, watching the bright fire of his potential burn out to nothing.

Then she thought of something she'd been puzzling over ever since the tournament. Why had Walter been so surprisingly protective of the boy who'd taken his wallet? On the trip home, she'd prodded him but he wouldn't say. Though she hadn't seen the boy, she imagined him looking like Andrew at age thirteen: greasy-haired with a goatee of acne. For years, she was grateful to any teacher who looked past Andrew's carapace of rudeness and saw the sad, lonely boy quivering beneath it. Surely Walter had done this, even if he hadn't said as much. He was a kind man. Nicer than he allowed people to see. Now that Andrew was starting over—still living at home and still looking for a job—there was little she could do to help except hope that he'd find people as forgiving as Walter had been.

After hanging up with Rachel, watering her plants, and reading three pages of her book club pick, she picked up the telephone. "Walter?" she said. "It's Sally. I've decided I'd like to try your Scrabble club."

# CHAPTER 11

# Walter

WALTER TOLD HIMSELF NOT TO GET NERVOUS. WHAT WAS THE WORST that might happen? Sally had seen the oddballs that Scrabble attracted, so why was he nervous about bringing her to this meeting? Still, on the drive over, he warned her. "The Scrabble club meets in the back of the VFW. To get there you have to walk through the bar full of sad sots. You'll wonder if you've stepped back in time because they allow smoking and that's pretty much all anyone does. Plus drink."

"Do some of them wander back and play a little Scrabble?"

"Only if they've gotten lost looking for the bathroom."

The real problem, Walter realized as they pulled into the parking lot full of pickup trucks, was that he actually *liked* this group and thought of them, for better or worse, as the closest thing he'd had to family in the last three years. Like with family, he knew them well enough to know that some people were fairly off-putting. For instance, Gene, who came to meetings even when his gout was flaring up badly enough to necessitate propping his odorous foot on a chair beside him, invariably closer to the nose of his opponent than his own. Or Peter, president of the club, who started every meeting with announcements that went twenty minutes longer than necessary because he loved hearing the sound of his own voice on the unnecessary microphone he'd purchased for the purpose.

The list of people Walter might have to apologize for afterward went on and on, and still he was fond of all of them. They *knew* each other. True, he couldn't say what most of them did for a living, but he could tell you who had poor rack management skills and who held on to their Q's and Z's for too long. He could also tell Sally what he admired about some of the members he'd gotten to know over the years.

For instance, the way Iona had nursed her daughter through leukemia, distracting herself by memorizing three- and four-letter words in the *OSPD* while she sat through chemotherapy appointments. "What else could I do?" she told them afterward. Eight people from the club, including Walter, had gone to the funeral, which was packed with people her daughter's age—only thirty-eight. By the speeches he heard, Walter guessed that her daughter was gay with no life partner but many friends. He liked hearing their stories and the flexibility with which they called each other "our chosen family." Maybe such a swipe hurt Iona's feelings, but it didn't seem to. For Walter, it was surprisingly comforting. Maybe you *could* choose your family if you'd come from one that disappointed you. Maybe Gavin had done just that. Maybe Walter had, too.

When Elyse died, Walter shared the news with the club, without ever mentioning the fact that she'd moved out of their house nine months before. With them, he was able to say the truest thing he felt. "My wife died last Monday. I came to play this week because I feel so unmoored." He played Reggie Cox in the first round that evening.

"It's a shame," Reggie said. "But from what I hear, all the ladies will be after you now." Reggie was in his late fifties and never mentioned having a wife or a girlfriend, so this was an especially surprising—if strange—thing to say.

Was he looking forward to his own old age when the field of competition for women might winnow a bit? Walter didn't ask. "There's that," was all he said.

Everyone in the club meant well, just as Walter did. Still, he was nervous. "It can be a funny crowd," Walter said to Sally as they got out of the car. "And by that I don't mean ha-ha. You might wonder if there's something about Scrabble that attracts misfits."

Sally smiled at this. "Oh, I don't mind that."

"Nice of you to say, but you might change your mind. We'll see."

As a preventive measure against a calamitous pairing, Walter whispered to Peter, "Sally's new to the game but very promising. She's only played in one tournament, and her rating doesn't reflect her potential. Please don't pair her with any beginners or nutjobs."

Peter had been running this club for as long as Walter had been coming. He was younger than Walter, but not by much, judging by his thin fringe of silver hair, as neatly cut as a Benedictine monk's. As was his wont, Peter followed up his overlong introduction by dragging out the pairing announcements for drama. "Today Nora Adams… Where is she? Hello, Nora! Nora will play—" He smiled and waited. Someone must have told him this was an effective suspense-building technique. "Harriet Moore-Westhaven. A rematch of last year's memorable April face-off when Harriet scored a personal best for a single play! Does anyone remember what word she made?"

*ESTRANGED*, Walter thought but didn't say anything for fear of encouraging Peter too much. Someone from the back of the room called out, "ESTRANGED!"

"That is correct! Next up we have—"

Walter waited anxiously for Sally's name to be called. He'd be playing Byron Zorick, an older man who'd once had a rating in the 1500s but was now approaching his nineties. He'd stopped playing tournaments when macular degeneration took most of his sight, though he still showed up for club meetings and got through his games by holding his rack inches from his eyes and asking his opponents to place his tiles. He was a nice man but, in truth, he embodied Walter's worst fear for his own future. Stooped and slow-moving, Byron sometimes showed up with a helper at his side, making him seem even more fragile than his sunken cheeks and walker already did. Tonight, Byron looked okay.

## CHAPTER 12

# Sally

SALLY DIDN'T GET HER ASSIGNMENT UNTIL AFTER EVERYONE ELSE WAS paired, and then it looked as if she'd play Peter, who told her this was the usual solution when an odd number of folks showed up to a meeting. (If the number was even, Peter sat out to adjudicate any word challenges or disagreements.) At the last minute, however, a late arrival came in. Peter seemed nervous as he handed Sally the scorecard. "I'm sorry to do this to you, but I had no choice. You'll be fine, though. Don't worry."

Sally smiled and thanked him. Maybe this was one of the club members whom Walter had warned her about when he said a few people could be terrible bores? At the table, her opponent introduced himself so softly Sally couldn't hear his name. Joel maybe? Or Jack? He played PURSE for an opener. She managed a quick response with STRETCH with the S as a hook. He raised his eyebrows in surprise. She'd had a rack full of consonants that hadn't looked promising a moment earlier, but then she remembered her list of one-vowel bingos.

"Lucky tiles," she said softly as she recorded her score—88, including her bingo bonus. It went like this for the next four turns.

A strong play from him matched by an even stronger play from her. Each time she finished and hit her clock, his eyebrows went up. It reminded her of John, who, twenty years into their marriage, still raised his eyebrows whenever she was better than him at something unexpected, like math or taxes. *You're good at this*, his eyebrows would say. *I'm surprised.* Why hadn't she ever realized how irritating such a small gesture could be? Her annoyance fueled her. She *was* getting lucky with letters, but even when she didn't have much on her rack, she stared hard and dug deep until the tiles offered up something.

Eventually her opponent's eyebrows stopped going up because his eyes never left his own rack. At one point he bingoed with UNSTUCK, pulled ahead, and leaned back in his chair with a sigh as if the world had righted itself again. Whoever this man was, he clearly believed he was meant to win. Three turns later, she played the word she'd been building for a while, QUARTZ, for 115 points and returned to the lead. She heard Walter's voice somewhere behind her. He must have finished his game early and come over to watch. She spun around, surprised to see not only Walter but four others—including Peter—watching. Walter was grinning from ear to ear but his face was bright red, as if perhaps his delight at this triumph was making it hard for him to breathe. "Are you okay?" she whispered.

"I'm fine," he rasped. "Turn around! Concentrate!"

"No coffeehousing please," Peter said loudly, and Sally turned back to her game, now all too aware of the growing crowd behind her.

Strangely, the pressure didn't make her more nervous. Quite the opposite, in fact. She imagined the crowd lifting a sea of eyebrows as she followed QUARTZ with the deceptively simple TAKE played parallel to HALO so that the K on a double-letter square got counted four times. "Fifty-four points," she said loud enough for the crowd to hear.

Someone whistled softly.

Her opponent—Jack or Joel—made several valiant tries at a comeback and then, just before the end, said, "It's hard to win when your opponent draws every power tile in the bag."

He sounded childish, like a middle-aged man who hadn't learned basic sportsmanship. At the game's end, he held out his hand but didn't look at her as they shook.

"Thank you," she said and only as she stood did she realize the crowd behind them had swelled to include the whole club. Peter started a polite golf clap that grew into a round of applause that was confusing. Did every newcomer who won a game get this response?

A few minutes later, Walter pulled her aside and explained. "You just beat Jack Trotter, the New England divisional champion for two out of the last five years. He's never played at this club before. He lives an hour away in Connecticut. I have no idea why he came."

"Oh my," Sally said. So this explained the raised eyebrows. "That *is* surprising. But I also have to tell you, he was right. I got very lucky with my tiles. That's the only reason I won."

"You might have gotten lucky, but I watched the second half of that game. You made three moves I hadn't found. I was looking for something longer with your K and you were three steps ahead of everyone, dropping TAKE so decisively. It wasn't just lucky tiles. You're an extraordinary player, Sally Reynolds! I saw Peter take a picture of your board afterward. He's probably sending it to the NSPA officials right now. This might be the most exciting thing that's ever happened at this club. No, I take that back. It *is* the most exciting thing that's ever happened at this club. Once, on the way to the bathroom, Dorothy's drawstring broke and her pants fell down. Up until tonight, that was the high point. Now this is it."

He was obviously enjoying inflating this victory as much as possible. She rolled her eyes. For her next game, Sally played against Dorothy, whom she liked, though she couldn't stop imagining her with her pants down. Toward the end of the game, Peter came over and passed her a folded-up piece of paper with a note: *Jack Trotter is requesting a rematch with you. Are you willing to play him again?* She looked around the room until she saw Walter standing next to Peter. *It's up to you*, he mouthed.

Did he *want* her to say no? Would it ruin his story if she accepted and lost as she undoubtedly would? She tried to read his expression and couldn't. Then it occurred to her: She *wanted* to play Jack Trotter again. She'd like to learn more Scrabble strategies, and what better way to do so than playing the best? "Sure," she said, handing the note to Peter. "I'd be delighted."

Peter's eyes widened, as if she were Daniel announcing her intention to stroll back into the lion's den. "It's nice of him to ask." She smiled. "I look forward to it."

Dorothy grabbed her arm. "Bless your heart, honey, we're all rooting for you."

Sally smiled and thanked her. Walter grabbed her other arm. "Please, Dorothy, I just need a few minutes to speak privately with Sally."

When they were alone, Sally whispered, "Why is everyone making such a big deal? I just played him a half hour ago."

"Exactly. And you won. The stakes are a little higher now. For him, at least."

"Hardly, Walter. I'm not going to win again."

"But you might. I watched you play. You made moves I've only seen professional Scrabble players do."

Sally took a deep breath. Were there really *professional* Scrabble players? Suddenly she felt nervous. Not just for herself, but for everyone in the club who now seemed overly invested. "I don't know, Walter. Maybe this is a mistake."

He held up a hand. "It's not a mistake. You beat this man once.

You can do it again. Look at me. Look into my eyes." She did, and she had to admit…he had lovely eyes. Pale blue and kind. "You can beat him again."

The room went quiet as they walked back in. People stepped aside to clear a path to where Jack Trotter sat with his chin in both hands staring down at a game board as if he was already imagining the battlefield he would eviscerate her on. As she pulled out the chair across from him and sat down, she closed her eyes and saw Walter's face—his kind eyes, his furrowed brow, his whispered invocation: *you can beat him.*

Trotter opened with a gamble: GRIDE, which obviously looked like a phony. Why use this word when he could have played RIDGE unless he was hoping for a challenge that would win him an extra turn right off the bat? She also had to wonder why he was playing so many letters that were useful in making bingos—ED, ER, DGE. It was a risk unless he had something bigger in mind and needed these letters on the board to make a grander play out of. She made the best defensive play she had: TARRY down the middle to cut off any use of G or R.

It went like this for the next seven turns. She foiled his bigger plays but in the process made none of her own. The board grew cramped with no tentacles to score off. For two turns in a row, they both played three-letter words. She didn't mind losing, which she was doing now by more than 40 points, but she hated playing this way. It felt claustrophobic, like they were trapped with each other in a small house with no escape. Then she saw a possibility. With a rack of one-point tiles, she found a bingo on a risky line that would open up two triple-word squares. It would also give her a bonus and the promise of seven new tiles. And this: It would give their audience a better game to watch. So she did it.

A few people clapped, but the applause died away when they

realized the risk she'd taken for a relatively small payoff in points. The play hadn't even put her point total ahead of his. Trotter's eyebrows went up in a different kind of surprise. He reshuffled the tiles on his rack now that an invitation had been issued to triple the points on his next play. Which he did. But Sally couldn't help thinking, her move had thrown him off. He didn't bingo in response, which most competitive players tried to do. He used one triple-word square and she used the other. This time around, she had better tiles and managed to get 65 points with JOKIER. A few turns later, she pulled ahead with another bingo using both a blank and an S, eliciting a decidedly unsportsmanlike sigh from Trotter. She wanted to lean over and whisper, *I haven't gotten that lucky with my tiles; I'm just using them well.* Which she was.

Somehow, this second bingo left Trotter even shakier than the first. He took a full minute before finally playing PELT for 12 points. He'd attached it with the T to form TO so he couldn't score the P twice. A quick glance around the board and she could see better options: PLEAT through an A that would double his P. Was this part of a larger strategy she couldn't see? Was he having a stroke?

For the next three turns, she watched his endgame collapse completely. He lost his lead and then, with four tiles left in his hand including a Q, he lost the game by 13 points.

# CHAPTER 13

# Walter

WALTER WOULD GRANT SALLY A FEW CONCESSIONS. YES, SHE'D BEEN lucky with her letters in the first game, and yes, in the second Trotter had disintegrated in an epic endgame collapse, the likes of which Walter had experienced himself but never actually witnessed. Certainly not in a nationally rated player. But he also wanted to make it clear: Something extraordinary had happened last night. "Time will tell, of course, but I believe it will one day go down as one of the greatest upsets in Scrabble history."

"Oh stop, Walter," Sally said, waving a hand over the coffee she'd just poured him. He'd called her at nine this morning and asked if he might come over "as soon as possible to discuss your triumph."

"I had some good luck and he had a few—I don't know—issues, I guess."

"Sally, the man fell *apart*. He collapsed under the weight of your tactical genius. Twice! It was extraordinary to witness. In fact, that might have been the most thrilling two hours of my life. I understand that I'm supposed to say the birth of my child was the best, but if

I'm being totally honest, watching those two games, Sally—that was better." He got up and paced around the room.

"You're a unique phenomenon. I suspect they'll soon be writing about you in the NSPA newsletter. In fact, I wouldn't be surprised if you got a call today requesting an interview. I'd be happy to field your media requests if it becomes too much." He couldn't stop grinning. "There might be some photo shoots involved. I think you should wear your green scarf with the lilies to bring out your eyes." He chuckled to himself and then stopped. "Seriously, though. How *do* you feel about giving interviews?"

"Oh no, Walter. No one likes a gloating winner. I enjoyed those games, and yes, it was nice to win, but I'm not going to walk around trumpeting my success in public."

"You mustn't say that, Sally. Women always downplay their achievements and I've never understood it. To my mind, it's the most infuriating thing women do, right after suggesting that I should put a sweater on when I'm not cold."

She laughed. "You might be right. Most women don't have the same competitive edge as men. Or maybe we really mean it when we say we like to play for fun. Men *say* things like that, but I'm not sure they mean it."

"Of course we don't mean it. There's nothing fun about losing. Eating ice cream is fun. Losing isn't fun." Walter sat back down. This wasn't the debate he wanted to have. He'd come with a proposition, but he knew he'd need to broach it carefully. Sally obviously hadn't spent last night googling all the tournaments Jack Trotter had played within a three-hundred-mile radius in the last few years, as he had. Out of the twenty-two tournaments Trotter had entered, he'd finished in the top five fourteen times and had been the overall winner twice, bringing home total estimated winnings of close to $3,000.

Walter wanted Sally to recognize that she could start playing at this level, too. Yes, she hadn't been playing long, hadn't memorized the word lists the others had, but this only made her potential greater. What would her game look like after a few months of serious word study? The possibilities were astonishing. She might even make it to the top division at Nationals this year (a rarity but not unprecedented for a player in their first year of competition).

After that, she might qualify for the Scrabble Word Cup. In his excitement last night, he'd imagined the two of them taking the twenty-hour flight together to Sydney, Australia, where it would be held this year. He pictured them both confessing to a fear of flying and holding hands for takeoff and landing. He wasn't sure why this particular fantasy took hold, except that he *was* afraid of flying and always avoided it if he possibly could.

"You mustn't be afraid of competition, Sally. You need to think about this in a different way: You could be a role model for every person over the age of seventy-five who's ever been underestimated. You, my dear Sally Reynolds, are not in cognitive decline. This should not only be acknowledged but celebrated. Openly. Loudly."

"Walter."

"What?"

"I'm seventy-three."

"You are?"

"Did you really think I was over seventy-five?"

"I apologize. To me, you don't look a day over sixty. I got carried away by my point. Your victory last night was a triumph for all retirees. You stand as proof positive that we all have the potential for new discoveries and second chapters. Let *that* be the story that resonates from your victory." He stopped talking and waited.

Sally took in one deep breath in, and then another. "I see what you're saying, but I didn't win because I'm a Scrabble genius. He underestimated me and made some significant mistakes. I also got lucky with my tiles."

"Luck doesn't explain *two* wins."

She smiled. "Fine. You want me to gloat, I'll gloat for five minutes but no more."

"Actually—" He reached into his pocket and pulled out a piece of paper. "I want you to do a little more than gloat. I want you to consider entering a few more tournaments. I've made a list of the ones I'd recommend."

Sally took his list and looked it over. "I don't know, Walter. If I want to get serious, I'd have to practice a lot more. I still can't beat you, in case you've forgotten."

"With your nerves of steel in pressured situations, you'd most certainly beat me in a tournament. Also I know more words! That's memorizing a word bank. You'll need to do that, too, but your gift is different. It is extraordinarily rare and it needs to be nurtured." He stared at her now, unwavering. It was hard to look away. "I've watched these top competitors. They spend four to six hours a day studying word lists. They carry key rings of laminated flash cards and stand in public bathrooms, flipping through them. They never let up."

"Walter, I can't possibly—"

"Listen to me, Sally. You just beat one of the top fifty players *in the country*, having about one-third the word inventory he does. Think what might happen if you doubled that. The next big tournament is in Hartford and offers more prize money than most, so it draws the best players and establishes the playing field before the Nationals. It also takes place in a casino and is open to all players, regardless of experience, which means there's an element of unpredictability at all levels. This is the tournament where big upsets happen, and the Scrabble gods reveal their feet of clay. A few years ago, a two-time world champion was bested by an MIT student who'd only started playing three months earlier."

He couldn't tell what she was thinking. Sally was still new to Golden Grove. Did she realize that he was proposing an extensive time commitment to a single activity over the next two months—an idea that ran counter to the core philosophy of Golden Grove, where every resident was meant to dabble superficially in half a dozen activities and no one was meant to take any of them too seriously? They were all "learning tai chi" and "writing their memoirs" and "studying noir films from the 1940s," and no one spent more than an hour a week at any one thing. Saying yes to this would mean saying no to most other activities. Would she agree?

She opened her mouth and he held his breath. *Her saying no doesn't mean she dislikes me*, he reminded himself. He felt like a teenager: hands damp, blood rushing to his face. Good Lord, he thought. Given this level of overreaction, maybe it would be best if she *did* say no.

"All right," she whispered softly. "Let's give it a try."

# CHAPTER 14

# Sally

SALLY'S TRIUMPH AGAINST JACK TROTTER MADE THE *GOLDEN GROVE News and Notes* "Weekly News Roundup" distributed every Monday, which must have been Walter's doing. Because the Roundup also ran menus and a calendar of scheduled activities, most people read it from cover to cover. By Wednesday, they all knew about her triumph but missed some crucial details. "I didn't realize you were the North American Scrabble Champion," Connie said in the elevator the day the notice appeared. "You ought to meet Walter Kretzer. He's our local Scrabble whiz." She repeated her warning that he was a little intense for her but this time added, "He's a nice man. Especially if you like Scrabble."

At dinner that night, there was a polite round of applause from her tablemates when she sat down. "Beating a champion at our age!" Valerie said. "That really is something."

Sally felt a little silly and then thought of Walter's words: *You'll inspire others. How many of us learn something new at our age and get really good at it?* "I have to admit it was a surprise. A few weeks ago I hardly remembered how to play." Did that sound too braggy? She couldn't tell.

Regardless, it meant Scrabble was a topic of conversation in the dining room again, which was exciting until she overheard Rhonda, two tables away, ask Walter if he really thought it was a good idea to spend time playing a board game when there were so many bigger problems in the world. "In the face of climate change, don't board games seem a little frivolous?"

Sally felt awful. Golden Grove folks could get terribly sanctimonious about their political views, but Walter surprised her: "Not at all. I believe board games give us a way to connect with people we otherwise wouldn't meet. You should see the variety of people who come to tournaments. Janitors, business CEOs, retirees, children. At my last tournament, I played a young man who'd just moved here from the Philippines. His English was terrible but he was a stellar Scrabble player based on word memorization alone. I think we need *more* opportunities to meet people with different life experiences, not fewer."

*Good for him*, Sally thought.

That night on the phone with Rachel, she tried to make a similar point. "I know it might sound silly to put energy into studying a board game, but it's also an interesting, diverse community. I'm learning a lot about people I'd never meet otherwise."

"Right, Mom, but didn't the doctor tell you to avoid stressful, physically taxing activities?"

*Here she goes again*, Sally thought. "Scrabble isn't taxing. You sit the whole time."

"But, Mom, a day-long tournament where you're playing six or seven games in a row? I'm sorry, but that sounds exhausting. I'm just thinking about what the doctor said."

Of course Sally hadn't forgotten what the doctor said. Just that morning, it had taken her an hour to get dressed and make a pot of coffee before Walter came over. By the time he arrived, her medications had kicked in and she was moving better, thank heavens, but no, she hadn't forgotten. "He also emphasized staying as active as I could for as long as possible." She wondered if Rachel liked to worry about other people's problems to avoid looking too closely at her own. "I won't know if it's too much unless I try, right?"

Thankfully, Rachel was happy to change the subject. "Actually, this wasn't the reason I called. Have you spoken with Andrew this week?"

Sally felt bad admitting that she hadn't. When she moved to Golden Grove, she'd left Andrew living at home with a promise that he could stay for six months before she'd have to sell the house. At the time, he'd seemed appreciative and promised to fix a few things up before the house went on the market. When he first moved back home, he started a few home renovation projects to make the house more accessible when John returned from rehab. He put a railing on their front porch, grab bars in all the bathrooms, and no-slip strips in the showers. Unfortunately, though, Andrew wasn't much of a handyman. The bars wiggled when you grabbed them, and the shower strips buckled the first time water hit them. She almost said, "Oh no, sweetheart. You just work on finding another job," but she held her tongue, afraid there was no need to remind him again of the sad reason he'd moved home in the first place.

As a family, they'd never spoken openly about difficult subjects. Easier to tiptoe around them—and kinder, she hoped, though she could never be sure. Was it kind to have gone so long avoiding the subject of Andrew's empty days and his emptier life?

"I haven't talked to him, no. Why? Is something going on?"

"Karen's back in town. He ran into her in the grocery store."

"Oh my," Sally said. Hard to imagine how nerve-racking this might be for poor Andrew. "Isn't she married now? With a child?" No need to remind Rachel when she was the one who'd told Sally these updates in the first place.

"Exactly. I guess the husband is still in New York, and she mentioned the words 'trial separation.'"

For a long time, Sally said nothing. A worst-case scenario played out in her mind: Andrew getting his hopes up as he did the summer Karen worked as a lifeguard. Would he write her another five-page letter hoping it might go better this time? "Did they talk? Is she moving back here?" Sally tried to make her voice sound light as if this was a casual encounter for Andrew, not the equivalent of strapping his heart onto a roller coaster.

"That's just it, Mom. She *is* moving back. And apparently she's a real estate agent now."

CHAPTER 15

# *Walter*

WALTER DIDN'T WANT TO OVERWHELM SALLY, SO HE BROUGHT ONLY three books to their first practice session. *Scrabble Strategies for Winners, 1,000 Scrabble Words You've Never Heard of Before,* and, of course, the Bible: *The Official Scrabble Players Dictionary.*

"Goodness," Sally said, looking down at the stack.

"I have a few more in my apartment." He wasn't sure if he should admit that he owned more than twenty Scrabble-related books. "When you're done with these, you can return them for others. Except for the dictionary. That's my gift to you."

"Thank you, Walter. That's very sweet."

"Never mind sweet. We've got a lot of work to do." He'd already drawn up an outline of topics to cover, starting with rack management and tile tracking. "I don't want to overwhelm you, so I'd like to start with these two." He tried to keep his excitement at bay. In the past he'd been told that his enthusiasm wasn't always infectious. "You load people up with one tip after another, Walter," Phyllis once told him. "It drains all the fun."

He watched Sally's face as he went over the primary points of rack management—that in choosing between two or more plays, one should consider the combination of letters being left behind as much as one considered the points earned on a play. "Good rack management is the secret to bingos down the line. High-scoring words must be built over several plays." He studied her face. Was he overdoing it? He couldn't tell. "Maybe we should just start with a casual game. No coaching. I'll give you a few notes afterward on what I see."

"I don't mind coaching, Walter. That's what we're here for, right?"

He grinned and clapped his hands together. "Fine then! I won't hold back!"

And he didn't. At their second practice session, he told her he'd like to work on vowel dumps. "You probably know TAENIAE of course. The opportunity to use it won't come often, but others will: AECIA, AWEE."

"I don't like AWEE. I don't like throwing away E's. They're better than that."

"I suppose you're going to say you don't like EPEE either."

"I hate EPEE." She smiled.

"If you have four E's on your rack, could you part with a few of them?"

"I suppose, but this idea of *dumping* implies that there are good letters and bad letters."

"But there *are* good letters and bad letters. The point values help you tell the difference."

"Some people might have different feelings about letters than you do."

"I don't have feelings about letters, Sally. You shouldn't either."

"Well, I beg to differ. Just calling this exercise vowel 'dumps' tells me you have *feelings* about letters."

"Fine, you're right. Would you like to hear my least favorite letter in Scrabble?"

"I already know. It's V."

His jaw dropped. "How did you know?"

"We've been playing almost every day for a month, Walter. You're not exactly a stone-faced mystery. You cheer every time you get rid of a V."

It was a strange feeling, he had to admit. He knew these quirks about other players but had never had anyone observe his own play closely. "Well, you're right. I do hate V's. With good reason. I would argue you should, too."

Walter was pleasantly surprised. As their practice sessions continued, they hardly ever spoke of personal matters. The few times she asked any questions about his past or his family, he usually deflected. "Oh, you don't want to know about my family stuff," he said once, waving his hand to change the subject. He found it easier to discuss his lack of friendships at Golden Grove. "A lot depends on being the club-joining type, I've learned, and I haven't done too well with that. I go to meetings and then I fall asleep, which is embarrassing. Once, I attended a poetry discussion and only woke up when they were vacuuming the carpet afterward." Sally always laughed at these stories in a way that made him consider telling her the truer, less funny story of his life—everything that happened with Elyse and Gavin.

Then, about three weeks into their daily practice sessions, he did. Or the start of it, anyway. She asked if he'd ever considered joining the Green Thumbs gardening group. "They have gardeners, of course, so we just do the fun things—deadheading, replanting, a little pruning. It combines a bit of exercise with being productive," she'd said. "You might like that one, actually. No one will care what you wear either." (He'd told her the story of showing up to exercise class in dress shoes and the tidal wave of offers he got to help him shop online.)

"My wife, Elyse, was more of the gardener than me," he said quietly.

Sally let that sit for a turn and then casually asked, "What other hobbies did she have?"

He felt his heart begin to race. He shifted in his seat.

"Did you play games together? You must have, I assume."

"In the beginning, yes. Games brought us together, actually." He stared down at his rack as he spoke, but the letters blurred. "She was a demon at cards. She organized a hearts-playing group at work and a bridge club after hours."

Much to his surprise, he found himself telling her the broad story of his marriage—the happy, game-playing start, the struggle to get pregnant, the Scrabble set he bought that they hardly ever played. Then he really surprised himself and told her something he hadn't told anyone else at Golden Grove. "Nine months before she died, Elyse moved into her own apartment."

A silence followed that was hard for Walter to read.

Finally, she said, "I'm so sorry, Walter."

"We already knew she had cancer. When we got home from the doctor's office, she said this felt like a wake-up call. That if she had to fight to save her life, she wanted to have a happier life. Which apparently meant living apart from me. The hardest part, I suppose, was that I didn't realize she was unhappy until then."

# CHAPTER 16

# Sally

THAT NIGHT SALLY STAYED UP LATE THINKING ABOUT WALTER'S STORY. She wanted to be honest with him as well, but how would she even start? How could she explain what was happening with Andrew when she didn't understand it herself? He'd been so good at school, the salutatorian of his class, right behind Karen, who'd delivered the valedictorian's speech with him seated behind her, beaming up in pride. Andrew assumed they'd get married. As silly as it seemed now, they *all* assumed this.

At seventeen, they seemed so much older than their peers. Older, even, than their parents in some ways. Sally remembered watching them at dinner after graduation—the way Andrew touched the back of Karen's hand and leaned in to her shoulder to whisper something that made her smile and pinken. Sally told herself it was normal to feel envious in the presence of young love. Wouldn't we all like to go back and feel that way, she told Wendy and Pam, her teacher friends, who sighed and nodded in agreement. She never told anyone the truth: She wasn't sure she'd ever felt that way.

What she felt when she met John was relief; at last she could move on and join her friends who'd gotten married right after graduation. She was twenty-five when she met him, and compared to her previous boyfriends, John seemed like a paragon of predictability. He called when he promised, took her to nice restaurants, was always polite. True, he was never overly romantic and never said "I love you" until he proposed, and then it almost got lost in a longer sentence ("I think if I love you, we should just go ahead and take the next step"), but she didn't mind. *This is how it's supposed to go*, she told herself. *This is what a mature relationship looks like.* If they sometimes ran out of conversation before dinner was over, she looked around restaurants at other married couples and saw the comfortable silence many of them sat in. *This is how it's meant to be*, she thought.

Yes, she admired and maybe even envied Andrew and Karen, who'd given each other nicknames no one else understood (Flea and Glub), who touched anytime they were in arm's reach of each other, but where had it left Andrew twenty years later? Alone, unemployed, and living in his parents' house, sleeping in most mornings like the teenager he'd never been. She didn't talk about Andrew because she didn't know how to explain it. How sad it seemed sometimes, and also how she admired the way he'd stayed true to Karen even when she married a doctor and moved to Westchester, where they had their first child.

"I'll always love her," Andrew had said when he heard she was married. "I won't talk about it, I promise, but I'll always feel the way I did in high school. I can't help it." She understood that this was essentially a sad story and still she wondered sometimes: Had she ever known such love?

In the early days of their marriage, Sally told herself she was lucky to have a husband so disinterested in the details of their domestic life that she was free to make most of the choices. She picked out their wedding china, chose their first apartment, decorated and painted the baby's nursery. As a new associate in his bank, John spent ten-hour days at work, often culminating in dinners with clients that he never enjoyed. "I'd be happy if they'd just let me get my work done," he'd grumble, arriving home at nine at night and carefully putting his suit on a hanger, only to put it back on eight hours later.

After Andrew was born, she noticed a change in John that she couldn't explain. He grew quieter in the evenings, even more withdrawn. Sometimes he seemed almost absent from his body. At dinner, she tried not to focus on the challenges of her day—the endless work of second-guessing why a baby was crying—and focus instead on John. But even when she asked about work, he often didn't respond. The house grew quieter, conversations even more labored.

When Andrew was about six months old, John's mood darkened until finally Sally broke down and mentioned it to her sister. "Sometimes it almost seems like he's depressed," she said, so afraid of the word that she instantly backtracked. "I mean not *depressed*, but hard to reach sometimes."

"Yes, I can see that," was all her sister said.

That year they hosted John's extended family for Thanksgiving. Sally spent all day cooking, and when their guests arrived, John never offered to make anyone a drink. When his mother came into the kitchen and whispered, "Will John join us at the table do you think?" Sally understood this behavior wasn't a surprise to any of them. Eventually that first episode passed.

Over the years, his dark spells came and went, and Sally weathered them by reminding herself that he rarely lashed out at the kids or her. He kept going to work where it didn't seem to be an issue. He just...disappeared. Sometimes for days at a stretch. Sometimes weeks. Later, when Andrew was in college and having his own struggle after Karen broke up with him, a psychiatrist asked Sally if there was any history of depression in the family. She hesitated. Did it count if John had never been diagnosed? Because she'd never had the courage to broach the subject with him. She told the doctor, "There might be some depression on his father's side."

"How severe?" he asked.

She hesitated. How did one quantify what had never been spoken of? "His father had an uncle. John never knew the whole story, but people said the uncle might have committed suicide." The word sounded foreign on her tongue.

The doctor nodded and made a note. "Usually that means something."

To Sally, it never seemed fair to dwell on this. When John was in a good state of mind, he was *fine*. True, he didn't help around the house much, but lots of men didn't. He allowed her to go back to work after the children went to kindergarten. She thought of that as a gift; many husbands didn't want their wives to work.

"No closer family members?" the psychologist asked.

She'd wanted to say it then. *His father has these moods where he seems to disappear. I don't know what to call them because we've never discussed it.* In the end, she didn't because Andrew's struggles seemed so different from his father's. He wasn't overly withdrawn or quiet. If anything he was the opposite—angry with Karen, of course, but also with his professors, with the school policy that didn't allow cafeteria food to be taken out of the cafeteria. Everything, really.

He talked endlessly at dinners, monologuing his litany of complaints, starting every sentence with, "Here's another completely ridiculous thing about school." He stayed home for the rest of that semester, awakening a fear that he might waste his scholarship out of misplaced spite, but no. Over the summer, he came to his senses and decided to go back, "even if I don't agree with most of my teachers." Her relief confirmed that maybe she'd been right not to ask—even once—what he talked about with the doctor.

After Andrew returned home as an adult, the silence deepened, in part because John's heart condition had worsened. When was there time during those trips to the hospital and those bedside vigils to ask Andrew, *Are you happy? Could we have done something different?* Not talking about hard subjects was what they'd always done. After John's memorial service, she asked Rachel why she thought none of them had cried at the ceremony. Rachel rolled her eyes. "God, Mom, when was the last time any of us cried?"

The next day before their afternoon practice session, Sally poured Walter a cup of coffee and sat down across from him. "Before we get started, there's something I'd like to say. You were very honest yesterday about your marriage. More honest than I'm used to, frankly, and I wasn't sure how to respond. Now I've had a night to think about it, and I want you to know that a lot of people have stories like yours. I know I did. My husband struggled sometimes. Though we didn't talk about it, he had dark spells where he became very withdrawn. I never understood them, but they scared me, and I wish now that I'd had the courage to discuss it with him."

"Was he depressed?"

"We never used that word, but if I had to describe it, I'd say yes, he had some kind of depression. When the kids were younger, we did things together as a family, but after they got older, we didn't as much. I tried to get him interested in the things the rest of us were doing, but usually it didn't work. After a while, I stopped asking or trying, really. I did things with friends and he stayed home, which should have been okay, except I felt guilty most of the time." She looked down at her hands.

"I've never told this to anyone before. I'm saying it now because I know it wasn't entirely John's fault. We fell into a pattern where I assumed his criticisms of our children—or our friends, or anything, really—were a criticism of me. I'm afraid women of our generation thought it was our responsibility to keep our husbands happy. Except you can't really do that, even for a spouse. So we resent the person who made us feel like a failure. I don't know if that was your situation or if it helps at all, but I wanted to say that."

He drew his tiles and put them on his rack. "I had periods of my life where I wasn't very happy. With work, or anything else, I suppose. I never blamed Elyse, though."

"She might have blamed herself." She drew her tiles and arranged them as she always did—consonants on the right, vowels on the left. "And she might have gotten tired of feeling that way. It wouldn't have been your fault is what I'm trying to say."

# CHAPTER 17

# Walter

WALTER WORKED TO KEEP HIS EYES ON HIS TILES. WAS THIS THE KINDEST thing a woman had ever said to him? He couldn't be sure, but it felt that way. "Looking back, I wish I'd figured out how to be happier earlier. With my work and all that." His voice sounded shaky. He couldn't help it.

"Have you been happier since you retired?"

"Oh yes. Much."

"Can you say why?"

"Well, Scrabble for starters." He wasn't sure how silly that sounded. Until the day Elyse told him she was moving out, Walter had never thought his marriage had any serious problems. He had other problems that seemed far more pressing: his frustration at work, his relationship with Gavin. After she made her announcement about leaving, he hoped this was a delayed part of the consciousness-raising she'd dabbled with in the seventies, when she joined a group of women who sat in a circle and talked about the lifetime they'd spent being "silenced by men." Elyse had grown up with a difficult, alcoholic father, and for some reason, Walter assumed her departure had more to do with her dead father than with him.

He told himself that his best strategy was to let her do what she needed to do without protest from him, and eventually she'd change her mind. Maybe she'd even admit that he'd never done anything wrong. He'd been a good husband, she'd say, but even so, she felt as if something was missing. After she moved out, he waited for a knock on the door or a late-night phone call. *I miss you. I'm sorry.* He told himself he wouldn't be angry. He'd simply say, *I missed you, too. More than I thought possible.* Then a few months passed without a word.

As Thanksgiving approached, he assumed Gavin would come home and they'd make dinner the way they always had, but a week before the holiday, he ran into Mary Sue, Elyse's friend, in the grocery store produce section, her cart full of sweet potatoes and bags of cranberries. She teared up to see him, which he initially took as a good sign. *Elyse is so sad without you that I'm crying!* But no. "Haven't you heard, Walter? She's back in the hospital. The cancer is everywhere. They've put her on hospice."

He managed to see her twice before she died, but by then it was too late to tell her that he'd always loved her, more than she knew, more than he could ever express. That her strength frightened him sometimes. Her clarity of purpose. That his issues with Gavin were complicated, perhaps, but could also be boiled down to the simple jealousy he felt when he saw her bottomless love for her son. Why didn't she love *him* like that when she'd captivated him for more than thirty years? He told Elyse none of this when he visited her in her new apartment, three small, sunny rooms with a hospital bed in the living room and a rolling table covered in pill bottles. Everything he wanted to say got bottled up in his chest and refused to come out. "I'm sorry," he managed after five minutes. "I'm just so, so sorry."

She drew a breath through her cannula. It sounded like the opposite of a sigh. Like she had no regrets because she'd freed herself from the baggage of *him*. "I know you're sorry, Walter," she finally whispered. "I don't know if it helps to wish things were any different."

But he *did* wish things were different. For years after her death, he wished he could go back in time and be a different person—more open, more expressive. Would it have helped? Were they fundamentally incompatible, as she once suggested, or could he have tried harder and changed the outcome? He didn't know. It certainly didn't help his relationship with Gavin, who blamed him for Elyse's move out of the house and, ultimately, for the failure of her cancer treatments. "I just wish you'd supported her more," Gavin said once toward the end.

"*How?*" Walter asked. "What could I have done differently?" It was a genuine question, though Gavin didn't hear it that way.

"Oh God, Dad," he muttered. "If you have to ask..."

This was the problem. He *did* have to ask. He *didn't* understand.

Nothing had ever been easy with Gavin. As a child, and later as a teenager, he seemed to lurch from one passion to another, all with expensive price tags attached to lessons and equipment. One minute he asked for an electric guitar, and the next he wanted a membership and lessons at a local tennis club. To Walter, these seemed like the affectations of someone endlessly reinventing himself because even though he was very good at some things, he wasn't, at his core, a very confident or happy person. He cared too much about how he was seen and what other people thought of him. They had bitter fights while Gavin was still in high school, with Walter returning often to what he believed to be an unassailable point: "I'd just like you to stick with one thing!"

Was he guilty of showing disdain for the parade of Gavin's short-lived, overpriced passions, as Elyse accused him of? Possibly. "He's fourteen years old," Elyse would say. "He's not meant to choose his career yet."

"But isn't it dangerous to dabble in everything and stick with nothing?" Walter would say, and Elyse would call Gavin a "renaissance boy," alleging, "He's interested in learning a little bit of everything." Even she worried when he got to college and drifted through majors until finally, at the start of junior year, he declared himself (seemingly out of nowhere) a studio art major. Gavin had never taken a single art class until he got to college, so yes, Walter might have reacted badly. "So now you're into *painting*?" he'd said.

"I've always liked art. I've never given myself permission to pursue it. Now I am."

That was the way Gavin spoke. *Given myself permission.* What about asking his parents' permission to waste the four years of college tuition they were apparently throwing away on an education that had no chance of landing him a job?

In his early twenties, Gavin must have decided that the best way to get out of his stormy adolescence was to stop fighting altogether. His rare phone calls home were short and newsless; his visits the same, usually two or three meals punctuated by some inevitable moment of casually dropped character assassination. "Well, Dad, it's not like you and I have ever had an easy time talking," he once said in the middle of what Walter had thought was a pleasant dinner.

Another time, seemingly out of nowhere, Gavin announced, "You've always had a lot of issues with anger, Dad."

Walter was shocked. *What issues with anger?* he wanted to scream.

To his surprise, Gavin *had* stuck with his painting and Walter *had* been impressed, by Gavin's diligence and eventually by his art, too. What did Walter know about painting, of course, but when Gavin was part of a show in New Jersey featuring a dozen young artists, Walter thought his work was *very* good, but he didn't know how to say this. *Your colors are so bright! I can really see this one going in someone's living room!*

By that point, they knew Gavin cared a great deal about his art, but he seemed to affect the casual demeanor of someone who didn't. He shrugged at compliments and barely smiled at people, including his parents, who'd come. From their point of view, Gavin got as much attention as any of the other artists, but something was obviously off. He seemed defeated, as if there was a competition he already knew he'd lost. At the end of the evening, when they went to hug him goodbye, he gave Walter a quick, stiff squeeze and held on to Elyse for far longer. When he finally broke away, Gavin was crying.

For six months after that, they hardly heard from him. At Christmas, he came home for forty-eight hours and said very little. He thanked them for their presents but brought none of his own, which wasn't typical. In the past, he'd given them elaborate paintings, some so large they had to be wrapped in a bedsheet. That year, he offered no explanation until just before he left, when he announced over morning coffee, "I've decided to give up painting. Dad'll be happy."

Walter certainly *wasn't* happy to hear this. "I never said I don't like your art. All I asked was that you stick with something. It seems like you have with your painting."

Gavin didn't want to talk about it. Cryptically he said, "Some bad things have happened that you guys don't know about." Elyse went closer and hugged him, but he stiffened at her touch. "I should get going," he said, though his bus back to New York didn't leave for an hour and the station was only fifteen minutes away.

He meant it, though. His bags were packed and waiting by the front door. Walter thought of something Elyse had said the night before, alone in the bedroom they no longer shared unless Gavin was home. (They'd long ago migrated to separate rooms when sleep became so mystifyingly elusive.) She'd wondered if Gavin might be on drugs. "He seems so muted. Like he's not really here."

"Aren't drugs supposed to make people *more* chatty?" Walter had said, because what did he know? He'd certainly noticed the monosyllabic responses and noticed, also, the whole dinner they ate without Gavin saying a word about his mother's food. "Do drugs make people forget common courtesies?" After Gavin announced his abrupt departure, Walter felt bad. Obviously, he played some role, in his son's mind, though he wasn't sure exactly what it was. Voice of doubt. Chorus of criticism. They drove in a heavy silence to the bus station with Walter weighing the different points he wanted to make. *I never said you should give up your art. I like your work. I don't know how to talk about it, but I like it.* In the end, he waited too long. As they neared the station, he slowed the car down. "Your mother and I just want you to find something you can really commit yourself to. Happiness comes from that."

He'd parked the car by the time Gavin responded. "Does it really, Dad? Would you say you loved insurance?"

"Well, no. But I loved the things that working hard in a job afforded me."

Gavin turned to his father. "Like what? I'm curious. What do you love passionately? So much that working at Farmland for all those years was worth it?"

Of course Walter knew what he was supposed to say: *You. Your mother. Having a family.* But at that moment Gavin was looking at him with a half smile of derision, like he might laugh at whatever Walter said. His eyes were alight with more animation than Walter had seen in the whole two-day visit. It was a trap. Gavin could be brutal when his jokes turned sarcastic, and his sharpest barbs were always reserved for Walter. This felt like one of those. Walter could walk into the firing line with a bull's-eye on his chest or he could slink away quietly. Let Gavin go back to New York with his gym bag full of resentment and sort out his problems alone. He said nothing. He turned away from Gavin and prayed for the bus to arrive thirty minutes ahead of schedule. The silence stretched out, endless and full of castigation.

"You can't think of anything, can you, Dad? There's nothing you really love that's made the drudgery of staring at actuarial tables for the last thirty-eight years worth it, is there?"

Once, Walter had made the mistake of explaining actuarial tables to Gavin, who was scraping through the lowest level of algebra his high school offered, barely clinging to the C his father's help had earned him. He was obviously mistaken to think the real-world applications of math might spark an interest. Ever since, Gavin had relished any chance to insert the phrase *actuarial tables* whenever Walter's work had come up.

"Nothing, Dad?" Gavin finally said.

Walter had no idea how much time had passed. When he turned to look again, Gavin's smile was wider and the glint in his eyes sharper. He felt as if he could hear Gavin's thoughts. *I might be pathetic, but not as pathetic as you.* Gavin was more than capable of saying such cruelties aloud. He had in the past. "I have passions you know nothing about," Walter said, so passionately a bit of spittle flew from his mouth.

"Take it easy, Dad," Gavin said, reaching behind his back to open the door. "I'm sure you do. Hiding away somewhere so no one knows about them."

A minute later, he was gone.

After that, Gavin came home to visit, of course, but only intermittently at Elyse's prideless urging. "*Please*, Gavin. We *want* to see you." He shared snippets of news but never really told them what he was up to. He moved into the house of a friend in upstate New York. "It's temporary," he said. "He asked me, and I said okay." Walter never understood the fuller picture until Elyse finally told him. "James is more than a friend, Walter. He's an...important part of Gavin's life."

Walter shook his head, not because he couldn't believe Gavin was gay but because he couldn't believe Gavin and *James* were lovers. James was old. Possibly as old as Walter. Everything about him seemed middle-aged. His taste in clothes, his sense of humor, his inability to work his own phone. Walter told himself he wasn't uncomfortable with James being a man; he was uncomfortable with James looking and acting old enough to be Gavin's father. "I wouldn't understand it if he was with a woman that age either," he told Elyse. He couldn't admit the other part out loud, at least not to her: What did it say about your parenting to have your child fall in love with someone who could so easily replace you?

"I see it as a relief," Elyse told him. "He's being taken care of, but he's also learning—I hope—to take care of someone else."

A few months later, they visited Gavin at his new house in upstate New York and saw no sign of any paintings in progress. Instead he showed them around their two-acre "compound," which included a chicken house, two goats, and an elaborate composting area, complete with a worm farm that Gavin had designed himself. He was most animated—by far—about the compost. Nothing was more miraculous than the speed at which a bin full of food scraps, cardboard, and grass clippings could become dirt if you added a few Dixie cups of worms.

"Sometimes I'll throw a whole banana in and come out the next day just to check and I'm telling you—it's completely gone," he told them.

Elyse lapped it all up, bending close to smell the fetid loam, digging her hands through the dirt pile beside it, pulling out a fat worm and laughing as she threw it into the bin. Elyse didn't see the country house as a mystifying new affectation; she believed that restless Gavin had at last settled down. "He seems to have found real peace with James, hasn't he?" she said in the car ride home.

Did she really think this, or was she trying to convince him so she could believe it herself? Impossible to say. Those drives home from visiting Gavin were often filled with a heavy silence that contained an entire unspoken argument. *"We have to support him. He needs our approval."*

*"Don't you find it hard though?"*

They never said these words aloud, but he feared they were there, even so. His judgment. Her defensiveness.

Everything worsened after Elyse moved out. Whether she planted the idea or he hatched it himself, Gavin blamed Walter's inability to express himself on latent homophobia. "I know you don't *think* you're homophobic, but you are. That's why I waited so long to tell you. I knew you'd be weird about it." The only thing Walter felt weird about was the ten years Gavin spent dating women before announcing he was gay. Was he so wrong to think maybe a few of those women deserved an apology? He'd barely made the point when Gavin jumped down his throat. "You want me to call up every woman I dated and tell them I'm sorry for being gay? Yeah, no, Dad, I'm not going to do that. I'm proud of who I am. I'm *not* sorry."

*Oh honestly*, Walter thought. He wasn't homophobic and he wasn't sorry that Gavin was gay. He was sorry that Gavin wouldn't give his father any benefit of the doubt. They barely spoke during the final stage of Elyse's illness and took no comfort in each other's presence after she died. Walter tried. He called; he went through old photo albums and filled a manila envelope with snapshots of Gavin and his mother. He suggested visiting and going out to dinner. "I'll bring the photos and we can talk," he said, afraid his voice sounded small, like a child's.

"I don't know, Dad," Gavin said, his own voice cracking. "Sometimes talking to you just makes it worse."

In the end, Walter decided that his real transgression against his son was outliving the mother who'd loved him so unconditionally. Looking back, he understood the larger problem he'd never recognized at the time. His own college years had been so dominated by caring first for his cancer-stricken mother, then for his senile father. He never talked about the two frightening years he'd lived alone with his father, trying to curtail the old man's irrational impulses with Post-it notes and door locks and eventually (because the doctor agreed, he had no choice) sedatives. He certainly never told Gavin that a fear of aging in the way his father had was the reason he'd put his name on the Golden Grove list. In the end, his greatest gift to Gavin would never be appreciated or acknowledged: He made arrangements to ensure that he would never need Gavin's help the way his own father had.

"You're moving into a *nursing home*?" Gavin had said when he told him. By that point, they only talked about once a month, possibly less.

"It's not a nursing home. It's an independent living facility. Quite a different thing. This provides activities and community, and later on, if I need it, some support as well."

"So like bingo and tea parties? Don't you hate all that stuff?"

"Well, for starters, they offer much more than bingo." He tried not to sound defensive. With Gavin, it was always a challenge to make it through ten minutes on the phone without one of them taking umbrage. "They have book clubs and news discussion groups. They also have a lecture series." He rattled on for a while, thinking of every impressive-sounding perk he could. By the time he got to "They have a lovely garden and are committed to sustainability," he felt a little silly. The truth was they did offer bingo. Twice a week.

"Great, Dad. Sounds like fun."

Now that he'd started revisiting all this with Sally, he understood: The truth was, Scrabble *had* saved him. Or at least it had given him a "chosen family" after his own had abandoned him. When he finished telling a shortened version of his struggles with Gavin, Sally surprised him by talking about her own son, Andrew.

"He's had a hard time finding a path for himself." She hesitated as if she, too, wasn't sure how much to say. "I wish he'd found love, but he hasn't yet. Or he was in love once and I don't think he ever recovered from it."

Walter felt his chest loosen. Usually when the topic of children came up at Golden Grove, people either bragged about their offspring's accomplishments or complained about their hovering worry—the daily calls, the constant visits. Walter never knew how to respond: *My son rarely calls and appreciates it when I don't call him either. Since his mother's death, we've established a competition for which one of us can ask the very least of the other.* He never said this, of course.

If anyone asked directly, he might have said, "My son was very close with his mother. We're still figuring out our role in each other's lives," but so far no one had. Of course Sally was different, though. She wasn't afraid of the topics other people avoided.

"Do you think Gavin's life is happy?" she asked now.

Her question surprised him. He hadn't thought too much about this. "I suppose so. He has a nice partner and they live a fairly simple life. He hasn't had much of a career, but I don't know how much that troubles him." He didn't mention the composting/worm farm.

"For a parent, I think that's the main thing. You can rest easy if your children have found some happiness. So many of them don't. I'm not sure how much responsibility a parent should feel about that."

With this simple observation, she'd managed to shift something in Walter's mind: Maybe he wasn't entirely a failure as a father.

# CHAPTER 18

# Sally

SALLY LIKED LISTENING TO WALTER. SHE APPRECIATED HOW HONEST HE was about both his marriage and his relationship with his son. She sympathized and told him a little about Andrew without going into too many specifics. Since her phone call with Rachel, she'd called Andrew twice. When he didn't call back, she wrote him an email, saying it must have been lovely to see Karen again but they probably shouldn't ask for her help selling the house. *It's never a great idea to mix friendship with pleasure, right?* she wrote. Was he getting these messages and intentionally ignoring her? Hard to say.

She couldn't ask Rachel, who was going in for her fourth IVF treatment and had already announced this would be her last. "I don't think my body or my marriage could survive any more," she said. Rachel used to spend a good part of their conversations complaining about her husband, Barry, but recently she hardly mentioned him. Sally hadn't pressed the matter because she couldn't bear to think about the possibility that Rachel had married a man like her father—dutiful but emotionally distant.

The more Walter talked as they played, the more Sally appreciated his honesty, but she also understood she could never be so honest herself. How could she when they were this far along, readying for a tournament she might not be able to finish? What would he even say if she told him the whole truth about herself? Instead, she made smaller confessions. She admitted that she didn't really listen during the current events club. She said she sometimes feared that she was responsible for pressing her daughter into an unhappy marriage. "She came to me with doubts before her wedding, and I said, 'Oh everyone feels this way. I'm sure it'll be fine.'"

"Has it been?"

"I don't know. Maybe 'unhappy' is the wrong word, but they don't seem to have much in common except for trying to get pregnant so they can have a baby who will give them—presumably—more to talk about." She sat up straighter, as if surprised. "Goodness. I can't believe I just said that."

Walter still topped her in making surprising revelations. The day after he talked about his difficulties with his son, he announced: "Gavin's also gay. I should have said that yesterday, but I didn't want that to sound lumped in with other criticism. I don't mind the gay thing. I really don't. I don't know why I didn't mention it before."

She wanted to reassure him: *Because it's hard to tell our real stories. I don't know how to talk about mine either.* Sooner or later, she knew, the truth would come out. About herself. And Andrew as well for that matter. If they were becoming real friends, as she suspected they were, she'd have to tell him. *Just not today*, she thought. *Not before the tournament.*

Instead, she told him something Rachel had once said: "Some people say homosexuality is a spectrum and everyone is a little bit."

Walter pursed his lips at this. "Gavin dated women until he was twenty-five. I thought that was interesting, but when I asked him about it, he called me a homophobe."

Sally whispered, "I'm sorry. These conversations can get so thorny, can't they?" and turned back to study her tiles, where she found a bingo: REPARSE. After playing it, she watched his face move through a series of grimaces. "*Re* parse?" he said. "Is that like parse *again*?"

She had to bluff because she wasn't sure if this was a word or not. "What you like to do with every game you play."

"Very funny." He looked at her and back down at the board. "I know you're not sure. I can tell by your face. The question is am I sure it's *not* a word?"

He must have decided not, because he laid down his own word: CWM. "Before you challenge, I'm going to tell you this is an acceptable word."

"But it can't be, Walter. It has no vowels."

"Which leads us to today's lesson." He flipped through the file folder he always brought along and handed her a new laminated study sheet titled REAL WORDS WITH NO VOWELS. "You'll be shocked when you see what's on there. Shocked and grateful."

She realized then: This was one way they normalized telling the truths about their lives. They listened, nodded, and returned to Scrabble. She knew that eventually the secret she'd been guarding more closely than her marriage or her children would emerge, and Walter would be angry that she hadn't told him sooner. Which was why she prayed they could make it through to the tournament without incident.

Was that too much to hope for?

Walter promised her he'd never knowingly play a phony during their practice sessions so she could assume every word he played was acceptable in future games. Still, she questioned him occasionally. "BOZO?" Sally said a week later "Isn't that the name of a clown?"

"It comes from a Spanish word, 'bozal,' meaning stupid, unable to speak Spanish well."

"That's how Bozo got his name?"

"Watch your time, Sally. Best not to get sidetracked."

They had recently started using a more accurate game timer that Walter ordered online. "I'll stop the timer when I'm offering tips, but you need practice playing under time pressure."

Though that was the intention, Walter didn't stick by it. He stopped the clock often to analyze a choice one of them had made. "If I'd played VENAL instead of LEVY, I'd have gotten more points, yes, but I would have opened up a lane to the triple word."

She considered this. "Still. Opening up the board isn't always a mistake. Yes, it gives your opponent opportunities, but it also gives *you* more to work with." Recently, Sally had discovered that she played better and scored higher when she made bolder moves, sending out tentacles that reached perilously close to triple-word squares. She did this once, playing CELLAR so that the R landed beside a triple-word bonus.

Walter stared at her. "You're not worried that I'll play an S hook and triple word twice?"

"Not particularly," she said. "Because you don't have an S."

"I might have a blank."

"You might, but I'm guessing you don't. You usually do a funny shifting in your chair when you get a blank."

He stared at her. "No, I don't."

She smiled. "Well, I'm sorry, Walter, but yes you do. Your body tells the world: *Well, look here. This changes things.*"

"And you made this bold play because you think you haven't seen me do this and therefore I must not have a blank?"

"That's correct."

He huffed and shifted the tiles on his rack. "Well, you're right, I don't. But you shouldn't start making risky plays because you think you can predict opponents you don't know."

As it turned out, the risk was rewarded the next play when Sally drew the blank and used it for her own triple-word hook. "Sometimes it works that way, too."

One afternoon, Walter opened a game with CUTUP. "That's two words," Sally said.

"You've never heard a funny guy called a cutup?"

"Oh maybe so," she conceded.

When he played ZINCY on his next turn, she put her foot down. "Now you're pushing it. Don't tell me something full of zinc is zincy."

"That's right. Or resembling zinc. You've heard of tinny."

She smiled. "I've also heard of irony."

He hooted with laughter. "Oh, that's good. See how much fun words can be?"

"When you're winning."

He grinned. "Which you will be soon."

A week before the tournament, Walter brought a notebook to their practice session. "You don't have to write down every tip I offer, but maybe this will help you remember the important ones." She took notes that session because she wanted him to know that she appreciated his efforts, but in the last year or so her handwriting had changed from the beautiful penmanship of her teaching days to the cramped scrawl of someone trying to save paper.

Even when she willed herself to write legibly, she couldn't. Walter didn't notice because he didn't know her old writing, but her heart sank when she realized her writing had become illegible, even to herself. For her "homework" that night, Walter gave her a new assignment—take six-letter stems using the most commonly drawn letters and add one letter to the mix. She started with TESAIN and added D to find seven other words including DETAINS, SAINTED, and STAINED. The next day, he looked over the lists she'd made. "What's this word?" he said, pointing to one.

Sally leaned over and squinted. "I don't know. I can't read it either."

"But you wrote it."

"I told you, my handwriting has always been terrible. Let's move on."

She was already nervous, but she tried to cover it up when they started to play. Three turns later, she spotted a rack-clearing bingo and picked up all seven of her tiles with both hands, too late to realize her left hand was in a full-blown tremor. The farther she extended it, the worse it got. Three tiles spilled from her shaking hand.

"Oops," she said, cleaning things up and laying out her word with her right hand.

"What's going on with your hand?" Walter asked after she'd added up her points.

The tremor wasn't always there, thankfully. Usually it stayed under control thanks to medication, though she often kept her left hand in her cardigan pocket and made an effort to sit to the left of others in the dining room in case it showed up. Silly, perhaps, when she often ate with Mary, whose eyes were terrible, and Nancy, who spent so much time personalizing her orders that she probably wouldn't notice if Sally came to dinner missing a hand entirely.

But Walter… Walter was different. Walter noticed.

"Nothing. Why?"

"Seems shaky."

"Hands shake sometimes, Walter. It happens when you're old."

"Yours don't. Not usually."

She took a deep breath to settle her racing heart. "You're right. I do have a tremor in my left hand. Not all the time, but occasionally it crops up like that." Would he let it go with this?

"You have to see a doctor, then. As soon as possible. You can't ignore these things."

"You're right. I have."

He stopped flipping his tiles and looked up at her. "And what did the doctor say?"

"You don't want to hear all this. It's not a terribly cheerful conversation."

"Yes, I do. What did he say?"

"She. Some doctors are women, remember? She said that I have Parkinson's."

"Oh my God."

"Lots of people have Parkinson's, Walter. It's not the end of the world. I could give you a whole list of famous people if you're interested."

He shook his head. He didn't care about famous people.

"There are probably four or five people at Golden Grove with it. I take medication that keeps symptoms in pretty good control. Most days, I don't think about it too much. Every once in a while, the tremor comes out and I take more medication."

She hadn't come to Golden Grove with any intention of keeping her diagnosis a secret. Nine months earlier, she'd gone to the doctor with a host of symptoms she believed were related to the stress of caring for John—exhaustion, slowness, a tremor in her left hand. The doctor referred her to a neurologist, who watched her walk up the hallway and asked to look at her shoes. "Yes," she said, studying her soles. "I'm pretty sure this is Parkinson's." She pointed to the uneven wear on the outside of the left shoe. "It changes your gait." The next test, she told Sally, was to try medication. "If it works, we'll know I'm right."

Two days after starting medication, Sally's tremor went away. Within a week, she felt like her old self. At her second appointment, the doctor confirmed the diagnosis. "The good news is that Parkinson's can be controlled with medication for a long time. People won't know you have it unless you tell them."

As it turned out, she was right. Four months later, when Golden Grove called with an opening, she asked the doctor what she thought of moving into a facility that didn't offer extensive medical support. "You should be okay for at least five years. Those places are all about 'active lifestyles,' which is probably the best medicine for you. Plus you'll have your medicine."

After moving in, Sally remembered the doctor's earlier words—*People won't know you have it unless you tell them.* She certainly hadn't planned on keeping it a secret; she'd just been so surprised by all the talk of activities and club-joining. She'd also been surprised by how few people talked about the bigger health issues they were all facing. Sure, they all complained about their eyesight and their hearing, but those were manageable, shared indignities.

Most people didn't talk about chronic, progressive conditions or the larger cloud hovering on the horizon ahead for all of them. Even Nora, who wore scarves over her bald head, never said the word *cancer*, at least not that Sally heard. Maybe this shouldn't have been a surprise, because what could anyone say? They didn't know each other well enough to mourn a diagnosis or grieve a setback.

Would Walter let this acknowledgment, without any details, be enough? Hard to tell. He considered it for a while and then nodded his head: "Well, your mind is still sharp and you're playing well. You have no worries there."

She smiled. "I'm playing very well, Walter. I believe I'm beating you by 30 points."

"You've gotten lucky with the tiles this game, no question."

*Good*, she thought. *That's over.*

But it wasn't, of course. Walter could google a disorder as easily as anyone and a day later, he had questions. "Before we start..." he said. His voice sounded different—tentative in a way she hadn't heard before. "Would you mind if I asked about this"—he waved one hand nervously—"Parkinson's business?"

Did she have a choice? "Of course. Go ahead."

"It's progressive, is that right?" She nodded. "Meaning it will probably worsen over time." He spoke slowly. Chose each word with care.

"That's what 'progressive' means, yes."

"Your brain and your abilities won't be affected but your body will be."

"Some people with Parkinson's do have cognitive issues, especially later on, though that doesn't seem to be a problem for me yet."

"Good." He exhaled with relief. "So how do you control the symptoms?"

"The main thing you're told is to exercise as much as possible and be consistent with your meds. So far, that's worked for me."

"Until yesterday."

"Yes, until yesterday I suppose. Parkinson's means your body stops making dopamine, so you take synthetic dopamine. The problem is that it doesn't last all day. You have to time your doses carefully. If the dopamine wears off, the symptoms come out. It's hard to predict when it will happen. It depends on what I've eaten, stress levels, things like that."

"So maybe entering a high-stakes tournament isn't a good idea for you?"

"Now you sound like my daughter."

"From what I've read, people with Parkinson's should avoid stressful situations."

She wondered if he was going to suggest they shouldn't go to the tournament. Just that morning, she'd spent an hour on the phone with Rachel, who continued to argue that it wasn't a good idea. "It's going to be harder than you think, a whole day of game playing."

"Trust me, Walter, I've given this some thought. It isn't a death sentence. In fact, it isn't even fatal. People die *with* Parkinson's, not *from* Parkinson's. I'm not deluded. Yes, it will limit what I can do in the future, but it's also motivating to me. I want to do this while I still can. Everyone is telling me I need to be careful, so there's no need for you to add to the chorus. I've weighed the risks, and I've made my decision. Period. End of debate."

"That's not what I want to say."

"It isn't?"

"No." He took a deep breath. "I'd like to help you. Or at least I'd like to learn more so that if you need help I'll know what to do. At the tournament naturally, but around here as well."

For a long time, Sally said nothing. This wasn't what she expected him to say. "That's very kind of you."

"I'm not saying this to be kind. I didn't do a good job helping my wife or my son when they needed it. I don't seem to have good instincts on that front. I have to be told explicitly what to do. Even then, I often fall short. Still I'd like to try, if you'll let me."

Sally feared that if she tried to respond, she might get emotional, which she certainly didn't want to do in front of him. This was her strange, Scrabble-playing friend Walter, not someone she could break down and cry in front of. She let the moment pass with a whispered, "Thank you. Right now, I don't need help. Hopefully, I won't anytime soon." She picked up the tile bag and shook it. "Ready to play?"

As the game proceeded, she thought about his offer and tried to put it in perspective. Of course he wouldn't abandon her right away. He was too polite for that and also (she understood instinctively) too lonely himself. They'd continue to play Scrabble as long as she was physically able, and when she wasn't, he'd gradually begin to avoid her so as not to have the person she'd one day become diminish his memory of who she'd been. Once she thought of this, she decided: It wouldn't be his fault, and she wouldn't blame him. When the time came, she might even appreciate it. She'd done enough reading about Parkinson's and what it would be like. She wouldn't want to see it either. If she was lucky, that would be far down the road, in five or ten years. If she wasn't lucky, sooner.

She was glad the game ended on an upbeat note for Walter. He found an open I to play his Q on, with a double-letter score, no less. She'd been tracking the tiles and knew he'd be stuck with the Q if she didn't offer up an opportunity for him. "Yes!" he hissed with a grin, slapping his Q down. "That's 21 points for me!"

She still won by a comfortable margin, but the fact that he made this valiant last move said that for now, in spite of her news, things were still the same between them.

# CHAPTER 19

# Walter

WALTER SUSPECTED HE'D DONE A TERRIBLE JOB RESPONDING TO SALLY'S news. He remembered that Stanley, one of the few work colleagues he'd genuinely liked, was diagnosed with Parkinson's at fifty-seven but waited four years to tell anyone. Only after people had noticed his slurred speech and halting gait did he say anything to reassure people that no, he wasn't drinking during the day. After the announcement, his symptoms increased dramatically. Suddenly he walked with an old man's shuffle, hunched over like someone using a walker, which soon enough he was. In quiet discussions, his workload was redistributed, and the understanding was clear: He wouldn't be asked to retire, but everyone agreed the sooner it happened, the better. Six months later he was gone, after a goodbye party made excruciating when he burst into tears before the cake was even cut.

Stan had been one of the few friends who stood by him after Elyse left her job in such a blaze of anger. Thirty years later, he still recalled how Stan had invited him to lunch and talked of other topics before finally asking, "Everything okay at home?" ("Oh sure," Walter had said, with the cheerful update that Elyse was returning to school for a degree in library science.) After Stan's retirement, Walter had certainly meant to visit him or, at the very least, call to check up on him, but he never had, afraid of Stan's tears and the awkwardness of such emotional displays. He told himself people experiencing health declines probably preferred their privacy.

He should have known better. He'd seen how his parents' friends abandoned them with his mother's illness. By the time his father's dementia set in, there were no friends left, and even his sisters avoided coming home. Fragility was hard to look at; weakness, terrifying.

He'd never known how to handle news like this. He did a terrible job when Gavin came out, and again when Elyse got sick. He wanted to be different this time. The night after Sally told him her diagnosis, he practiced speeches he might deliver: *I'm a different person with you than I was with my wife and son, two people I disappointed terribly. I'd like to do better. Let me be your friend and help you with this. Please.* The problem was he had composed similar speeches in the past, and they'd always gone badly when he tried to deliver them. Even when Elyse lay dying in her new apartment, he couldn't offer comfort, so what could he possibly say to Sally, a woman he'd only known for a few months? *You've become a dear friend to me, more important than you might realize.*

For now, he decided this was good enough, and maybe the best strategy would be to change the subject. Besides, he wanted to hear more about her life. Why had she married John in the first place if she admitted, "That first year of marriage I realized how little we knew each other." Everyone had mysteries in their past, it seemed. Why did both his sisters—eleven and nine years older than him—move so far away after they married, leaving him alone to care for their parents? Was it their father's temper, which didn't come out often but was terrifying when it did? Was it silly to think about questions like this when one sister was dead and the other in a nursing home with no memory of who he was the last time he'd called her, about a year ago?

Of course he and Sally still needed to work on Scrabble and move through the curriculum he'd outlined. But he found himself distracted at times, wishing he could find the words to invite her to eat dinner with him or spend an evening with no Scrabble talk at all. In the dining room, Sally usually ate with the same four or five women who'd lived at Golden Grove for years, the women who made it a point to snap up any new arrivals with some wit, poise, and decent conversational skills.

Walter found that group confusing to be around with their dominating ways. ("Oh don't order that," Linda had said to him once. "They never do salmon right. It's always dry.") A few had come to his Scrabble club and liked to joke about it afterward as if it had been a disaster on the scale of the *Titanic*. Once, in the discussion of starting a new club, he overheard one of them say, "Let's not get too serious and kill all the fun the way Walter's Scrabble club did."

How often had Sally been privy to throwaway insults like this? Once, he worked up the courage to ask what her dinner group thought of her tournament plans. "Oh I don't talk about it," she said. "If I told them I spend every afternoon playing Scrabble with you, I think they'd force me to join more clubs." She laughed as if she didn't care what these women thought, but of course she must. She was human after all. He couldn't invite her to eat alone with him at one of the tables for two in the dining room—that would elicit too many questions. But what were his other options? Invite her to his apartment, which was decidedly more depressing? Show up one afternoon with a bottle of wine and a box of crackers? Every idea seemed fraught with peril.

Instead, he continued reading about Parkinson's in the hope that what he learned might prove useful in the future. He found websites; apparently an actor named Michael J. Fox was one of the famous people she alluded to, but there were others: Muhammad Ali, Janet

Reno, Pope John Paul II, for heaven's sake. They'd all lived for years with Parkinson's, productively and happily. It was generally agreed that early on, the greatest danger with Parkinson's was a risk of falls due to "freezing of gait," a terrifying symptom where one or both legs stopped moving completely. "As if your shoe was glued to the floor," was how one woman described it. "It happens out of the blue, usually when you're under some pressure, like leaving an elevator or crossing a street. Suddenly you're frozen." *Dear God*, Walter thought. Golden Grove had three floors. They rode in elevators three or four times a day.

He hoped his offer to help didn't come off as ham-handed. After her first two rounds of chemotherapy, Elyse had asked him not to stay with her during treatments because he talked too much and bothered other patients. "You don't realize how your voice carries. People can hear you even through their headphones." That year, Elyse's most reliable emotion was annoyance, her most consistent topic of conversation the grating habits Walter didn't realize he had. Eventually, he understood: Better to keep a distance.

He discovered the VFW Scrabble club during her second round of chemotherapy, when she specifically told him, "The most helpful thing you can do for me is find something for yourself to do." He'd thought he was helping, going out to play Scrabble two nights a week and traveling to tournaments that lasted all weekend. Only when Gavin called, furious that he hadn't been with her for a doctor's visit with unexpectedly bad news, did it occur to him that maybe he should have given her a ride even when she insisted she didn't want one. Impossible to second-guess what the best strategy with Sally would be. He had decades of experience getting this wrong and very little (if any) of doing it right.

He had made one effort to help Sally that he'd told her nothing about. A week earlier, he'd written an email to Esther Newsom, a longtime pillar of the Scrabble community, who was now director of the Hartford tournament. Esther had been the best female player for almost a decade, back in the 1990s. Since then, only a handful of women had cracked the top ten rating, with much speculation on why when women made up 70 percent of club players. Surely her past as a woman in the top echelon of Scrabble players would make her interested in Sally's story.

> Dear Esther—I'm writing to let you know about Sally Reynolds, a new player with exceptional promise. She'll be competing in the beginner division of the regionals in Hartford this year, but I don't expect her to stay there long. This will only be her second tournament, but whatever she lacks in experience, she makes up for with board vision, anagramming ability, and a nerves-of-steel endgame. You've probably already heard that she beat Jack Trotter (twice!) when he stopped by our club a few weeks ago. She's 73 years old and has only been playing for a few months. Just wanted to let you know about this exciting player. Best, Walter Kretzer

Though he knew there was a danger in raising expectations for Sally, this was one of the few important tournaments that didn't extend over a weekend and instead compressed all play into a single day. Every game had higher stakes. For Sally to have any chance of placing in the finals, she needed to be paired early with opponents strong enough to raise her rating when she beat them. She couldn't waste her morning playing the elderly crowd who pulled out knitting between rounds. Early matches were meant to be assigned randomly, but Walter had long suspected that initial pairings were orchestrated by tournament directors to produce the surprising upsets that garnered the most excitement. If this was true, he wanted Sally to be the beneficiary.

"You are going to do well. I feel it in my bones," he told her the night before the tournament. "This time tomorrow you might be the talk of the Scrabble world." He knew he shouldn't inflate expectations but he couldn't help it. He'd just gotten a message back from Esther saying, Yes, I've already heard about Sally Reynolds. We've got her on our radar.

Peter, no doubt, had written them as well.

"I'm worried I'll disappoint you if I collapse completely."

"Impossible," he said. "No matter what happens tomorrow, you could never disappoint me." Did she understand what he was really trying to tell her?

That night he lay awake, surprised by a new fear: If Sally did well and became a Scrabble news story, she'd get endless invitations to join clubs and play other Scrabble obsessives online. He'd pushed her because he wanted everyone else to know how special she was—a late-blooming prodigy, a phenomenon as rare as Halley's Comet. But why hadn't it occurred to him that once they did, he'd lose the lovely privacy of their afternoons together? The more he thought about it, the more he regretted suggesting she enter the earliest major tournament on the calendar. Why hadn't he targeted the East Coast Championship in Baltimore, six months away? Then they would have had more time to practice and a trip in the bargain—a train ride side by side, two nights in a hotel.

The next morning on the bus to Harford, he tried to tell her all this. "Whatever happens today, I want you to know how much I've enjoyed our time together, and I hope we can continue to play again in the future."

Sally stared at him. Did he sound ridiculous?

He must have because she laughed. "Honestly, Walter, do you think I'm going to lose so badly that I'll go from playing every afternoon to never reaching into a tile bag again? That seems extreme."

"No. The opposite. I'm worried you'll do so well you won't have time for our games anymore. Everyone will want a turn playing you."

"Well, stop worrying. I probably won't make it out of the beginners' division, and if I do, I certainly won't last long." She turned and gave him a piercing look. "Okay? Now you can stop staring at me."

But he couldn't stop staring at her. He didn't want to. He wanted to tell her the most important revelation he'd had, lying awake last night: *I did all this as an excuse to spend time with you. I find your company calming, though I'm not sure why because you also make me nervous. It's a combination that takes me out of my head and erases the last three years I've spent ruminating on my failures. Being with you feels like a glorious relief.* Even as he thought this, he understood how ridiculous it sounded. Maybe he should say: *I'm sorry I've put so much pressure on you. I don't care how you do. I love playing Scrabble with you and I want to keep doing it. That's all.* He almost said this, but suddenly, his heart was beating too quickly. He feared a film of sweat might break out on his face.

What, exactly, did he want to say but couldn't?

It was simple, really: *Being with you makes me feel like less of a failure.*

Saying this, though, would mean pulling back a curtain on his heart and letting her see what a mess it was. Even a suggestion of the truth—a whispered *Just do your best. I don't really care how this tournament turns out*—might make him sound like a lunatic. She'd probably laugh with relief initially and then turn blunt. "Then why did we work so hard? What was the point if you don't care how I do?"

*I wanted the time*, he'd have to say. *That was the point.*

He wondered if this made him no better than a thief, stealing her hours, afternoons, whole days that she could have used to make friends at Golden Grove or explore other activities. Now that he had this thought, it seemed horribly possible. He'd poisoned her with his own unpopularity! She arrived a tabula rasa with a sense of humor and her memory intact—a rare enough combination that surely they all wanted her time as a dining companion, a walking partner, a member of their group. Had he intentionally cloaked her in a shroud of Scrabble eccentricity for the sole purpose of keeping the others at bay? Suddenly he feared he had. Not only had his "help" not really been helpful, but it had been a deterrent to her adjustment to "healthy Golden Grove living." Even when he tried not to be selfish, it seemed he couldn't help it.

# CHAPTER 20

# Sally

NO QUESTION ABOUT IT, PLAYING IN A CASINO WOULD BE A distracting challenge, Sally realized within minutes of arriving. Though the tournament took place one floor above the slot machine room, they could hear the tinny plinking of the machines along with the muffled cries and shouts of people winning and losing. Sally had never been to a casino before—had never seen the spectacle of so many people gathered in a fluorescent-lit room to stare silently into machines. "Oh my," she said as they made their way past to the escalator.

"Oh my, indeed," Walter said.

Arriving at their floor, surrounded by familiar faces wearing Scrabble T-shirts and homemade hats with wooden tile messages glued to the brim, was a relief. It felt like the earlier tournament, just with four times as many people. As they sat in the lobby awaiting their first game, Walter explained, "You offer a $5,000 purse, and people flock from everywhere, including Canada. Scrabble is very big in Canada, probably because of their long winters with nothing to do." Poor Walter had seemed so nervous all morning, and now he was rambling in a voice too loud, probably offending people nearby. "Shhh," she said, touching his arm, surprised by the spark it produced. "Sorry," she whispered.

Her first opponent of the day was a middle-aged man who shook her hand without making eye contact and spoke so softly she couldn't hear a word he said. Once the clock started, it didn't matter, of course. The game was close. They swapped leads until the end when she eked ahead by knowing that he had a Z and blocking all his chances to use it. He not only lost 20 points for the Z left on his rack, but he'd gone three minutes overtime, trying to find a place for it.

"Ack," he finally said. "I'm surprised. You win."

For Sally, it had been clear a few turns earlier just who would win.

Because their game had gone over, she didn't have time to find Walter and give him a thumbs-up across the room. On her next game, she got lucky, winning not only the initial draw but also pulling an S and a blank on her first rack, letting her open with a bingo. Even as her heart raced at these breaks, she could hear Walter's warnings in the back of her mind: "Don't dwell on good luck for too long. Champions are the people who play well with bad tiles."

She feared this test had arrived during her third game, where she started with a rack of three O's, two U's, an I, and a V. Her opponent took all of three seconds to make his opening play for a tidy 24 points, leaving Sally with almost nothing to play off. And then she saw it: OVOLI. It wasn't a bingo but it emptied her terrible rack of vowels, her primary goal. The game continued like this. Every high-scoring play by her opponent was answered by one that felt like a desperate attempt to rid herself of bad letters. She almost bingoed twice but fell short both times. The only thing going for her was the sheer volume of tiles she was taking and using.

After wading through the morass of a dozen vowels early on, she pulled both blanks and used them for two bingos in succession.

Her opponent responded with a play that felt surprisingly timid: WIRE for a modest twelve-point score. As their game stretched on, his posture sank lower. He rested his chin on his hands as he studied the board. She looked around the room and wished she could catch Walter's eye to tell him: *You were right when you said that if you have a bad hand, you should play as much of it as you can. Get rid of the terrible letters and get new ones.*

He never made a comeback. In the end, she played GLOM for 30 points, so the score wasn't even all that close.

# CHAPTER 21

# Walter

SITTING ACROSS FROM HIS FIRST OPPONENT OF THE DAY, WALTER understood that he'd made a mistake entering the tournament himself. He'd signed up at the last minute, afraid that hovering over Sally might become annoying or, worse, detrimental to her concentration. Now he looked around nervously. He'd forgotten how crowded this tournament could get and how impossible it would be to keep track of how she was doing if he couldn't stay close by. He tried to concentrate, but he couldn't stop replaying his speech on the bus this morning and wondering why he hadn't simply said what he meant: *I'd like to do more than play Scrabble with you.*

What would she do if he asked her to dinner or a movie? Dates had never gone well with Elyse, who had trouble with rich restaurant food and who didn't like seeing movies in theaters with other people crinkling their candy wrappers. If he proposed a date with Sally, what would the end of the evening look like? Would they stand in the hallway outside her apartment door, unsure whether to hug or to shake hands? Would he begin to sweat profusely the way he had on the bus?

For the time being, he needed to stop thinking about Sally and twisting around in his seat every two minutes to look for her. She certainly hadn't given him any indication that she returned his feelings. If anything, she seemed mystified. *Of course we'll still be friends after this,* she'd said, patting his hand. *Honestly, Walter, why wouldn't we be?*

*Because I want to be more than friends*, he couldn't bring himself to say. Nor could he say, *Because I might be in love with you.*

Because his rating still put him in the intermediate division, Walter's first two games were across a crowded conference room from Sally. In the twenty-minute break after the third game, he pressed through the crowd but still couldn't find her. He tried calling her phone but got no answer. It was terrible not to know how she was doing. At the start of his fourth game, Walter arrived at his assigned table and realized he was two tables away from a player he hadn't thought about for weeks: Toby Weir, the wallet-stealing child prodigy.

Dear God, Walter thought, looking around. He should have considered this possibility sooner and told Esther to make a general announcement warning people to keep a close eye on personal belongings. Another problem with this Scrabble-obsessed crowd: They all left their backpacks and purses around the edges of the room because none of them cared about anything as much as going over their games they'd just played with the hairsplitting attention of Talmudic scholars. He'd certainly have a word with the authorities during the lunch break, he thought, and then watched as Toby's opponent arrived and Toby stood up exactly as he had with Walter, shook the man's hand, and told him it was an honor to play him.

The opponent looked as stupidly flattered as Walter undoubtedly had. Oh, this kid was a phony. A wallet-stealing charlatan who, unfortunately, could also play Scrabble like a demon. What a shame when he had a bright future ahead of him, if only he could keep his hands to himself. Maybe this opponent had the same pitiful thought Walter had: *If only my son were more like this kid.*

He watched as Toby and the other player checked the tiles laid out on the board in a five-by-five block. The other player opened the drawstring bag as Toby swept up the tiles to deposit inside. This ritual began every tournament game Walter had ever played to ensure no tiles were missing, except this time something different happened. Instead of dropping all the tiles into the bag, Toby pinched two with his pinkie finger and held them in his palm. The other player didn't see the move, but Walter, sitting behind him, most certainly did.

He watched, dumbstruck, as the hand holding two tiles disappeared into his pocket.

Walter's heart went into overdrive. He looked around the room. He needed to alert an authority quickly, before Toby played whatever tiles—blanks, no doubt—he'd just slipped into his pocket. With no proctor at the judge's table yet and no referees in sight, Walter went out to the lobby check-in desk where a young man and woman stared glassy-eyed into their laptop computer screens. "Excuse me, but I need to report an incident I've just witnessed."

Both pairs of eyes reluctantly left their screens. "Is it about a word challenge or unsportsmanlike conduct? Conduct issues have to be reviewed, and I can tell you from experience, the best you're likely to get is a warning to the other player."

"This isn't about my own game. I've just witnessed another player pocketing two tiles before play began. He's in there right now with two blanks in his pocket."

The woman looked at her desk partner. "What should we do?" The other guy shrugged.

"Someone needs to go into that room, stop the game, and have the player empty his pockets."

"Yeah, we can't really do that. We're not in charge."

Walter felt his face redden. "Could you contact someone who is in charge? If we wait too long, he'll play the tiles and there won't be any proof."

They both picked up their phones and started texting.

Walter stared in disbelief. "Could you try *calling* someone?" He looked around the lobby, now empty as the game bell rang at least two minutes ago. He'd have to sacrifice his own game if someone didn't show up in the next minute or so. "I know Esther Newsom," he said, hoping he didn't sound ridiculous. "Could someone please contact her?"

Usually, Walter wouldn't have claimed to know Esther, but earlier at check-in, she'd not only recognized him but also thrown her arms around him in a surprising hug. "Walter is an old favorite at this tournament," she'd said to Sally, leaving Walter dumbfounded. He'd played Esther twice and both times lost due to self-sabotage. The last time he played in this tournament was three years ago when he performed so atrociously, he left before his final game and vowed never to come back. Apparently his stock had risen by virtue of his connection with Sally.

When Esther finally appeared a full five minutes later, he told her what he'd seen, afraid it might already be too late. She squinted, as if she needed time to consider her options.

"When I left, the tiles were in his pocket. We've got to hurry before he plays them."

"I understand your concern," Esther said, making no moves. "But I'm trying to decide. This player is currently doing very well. If we stop the game and find nothing, we'll tarnish the results. Potentially, it might throw off the ratings for the whole day."

"He's only doing well because he's *cheating*!"

"But we don't have proof, do we?"

"I do! I saw him! With my own eyes!"

Infuriatingly, she still wouldn't move. Instead she turned away and made a phone call, speaking too softly for Walter to hear. A minute later, she turned back to him. "All right, Walter, I'll tell you the truth. This boy is the youngest player in his bracket and we're having a hard enough time getting younger players. I'm hesitant to focus negative attention on one of the few we have."

Walter could hardly believe what he was hearing. *You're so desperate for young people, you'll let them cheat?* "You can't be serious, Esther."

She held up a hand. "Please, Walter. You haven't seen the registration numbers. If we're not careful, our tournaments are going to start looking like happy hour at a retirement home."

Just then her phone rang again. "Yes," she said. "Okay, fine; we'll proceed. Thank you." She tapped her phone and turned to Walter. "Well, you'll be happy. They just gave me approval to go ahead with the search."

By this point, nearly twenty minutes had elapsed, more than enough time for Toby to play his stashed tiles. Walter's heart hammered as he watched Esther and a security guard interrupt Toby's game and ask him to follow them into the lobby. When he emptied his pockets, Walter tiptoed close enough to see: two Starburst candies and a handful of quarters his grandmother had probably given him for the soda machine. No tiles. As Esther walked Toby back to his game, Walter heard her say, "I'm sorry about this. Some people can't believe a young person is doing so well, that's all."

Walter was dumbstruck and furious with himself. Why hadn't he alerted officials to this wallet thief months ago? He staggered back out to the lobby, where Esther approached him a few minutes later with her arms outstretched for another unwelcome hug. "Poor Walter. I'm sorry about that. We'll keep our eye on this boy, I promise."

All the emotions he'd been trying to tamp down—his feelings for Sally, his fears about this tournament, his general anxiety—were here now. Much to his horror, he felt tears prick his eyes.

# CHAPTER 22

# Sally

SALLY'S MOST SURPRISING DISCOVERY IN THE COURSE OF HER MORNING games was that the pressure of tournament conditions seemed to make her *better*. With a clock ticking at her elbow, she found obscure words she didn't remember learning. Instinctively she knew they'd survive a challenge, and each time they did. It was unlike anything she'd ever experienced. Instead of closing down, her brain was opening up. She couldn't wait to tell Walter about the instances in which his teaching informed a choice she made, and every time, he was right! She wasn't sure how to describe the feeling of his voice inside of her head, talking her through moves he hadn't even seen.

In the middle of her fourth game, however, something shifted. Her mind was still sharp but she felt a heaviness settle into her torso and move up her arms. There was no tremor in her hand, thankfully—just an ominous feeling like her arms were moving through water, against resistance. She tried a few breathing exercises. She coughed and readjusted her legs. At some point in the last twenty minutes, her feet had gone numb, which was new. She panicked: What if she couldn't walk after this game? She'd considered bringing a cane to this tournament but at the last minute hadn't, afraid that carrying it around all day might be cumbersome. Now she realized a cane would at least alert people to her balance issues. Soon there'd be an hour-long lunch break, but how would she find Walter if she couldn't move?

As it turned out, she *could* walk, but just barely. Each step necessitated consciously picking up her leg and placing the foot she couldn't feel on the ground in front of her. She moved so slowly, the river of people heading to lunch parted around her. When she finally made it to the lobby, she stopped and looked around. No sense taking her slow time getting anywhere if she couldn't see Walter. Someone bumped her from behind, nearly knocking her over. She swayed precariously and a woman with white hair caught her elbow. "Are you all right, dear? Do you need help?"

She did need help, but she felt self-conscious accepting it from someone who looked ten years older. "No, I'm fine," she whispered, and the woman disappeared.

She wasn't fine. Her left leg was frozen in place. She'd had episodes like this before, but never in public. Her pulse quickened as she looked around again for Walter. Could that be him, sitting in a chair against the wall, bent over, his face obscured by a large white handkerchief? It must be, she realized. She remembered him carrying the handkerchief—such a throwback to the past, a memory of her own father. But why was his face buried in it now? "Walter!" she called, her voice too soft for him to hear.

She needed to take about six steps closer to get his attention. She tried again but couldn't move her left leg. In the past, she'd used tricks, like throwing something on the floor to step over or shouting "WAKE UP!" at the stubborn, immobilized leg. She couldn't do those things here.

"Walter!" she called again in a raspy whisper, like a stagehand trying to cue an actor without being heard by the audience. Again, people moved in a wide berth around her. "I NEED YOUR HELP!"

He looked up. His face was damp, and for a moment, her heart caught in her chest. Slowly he looked down and took in what was happening. So did she.

## CHAPTER 23

# Walter

WALTER HAD SPENT ALL MORNING SEARCHING FOR SALLY, AND HERE SHE was at last. It felt like he hadn't seen her in *days*. But why was she standing halfway across the room? Had she seen him getting emotional and was too embarrassed to come any closer? He tried to say with his expression: *Don't worry! I'm a foolish old man who cares too much about a board game!* Then he saw: She wasn't worried about him; she was having an episode.

He was up in a flash and at her side. He put one arm around her waist, stamped one of his own feet, and shouted, "MOVE!" He'd read about this trick on a Parkinson's chat site, and miraculously it worked. Her left leg loosened and moved forward. She wobbled a bit and leaned against him. He tightened his hold. He got her seated, found two pill bottles in her purse, and held them both up. She pointed to one and held up two fingers. Wordlessly, he shook out two pills and found a bottle of water in her bag, remembering something he'd read in his research. "This is the medication that won't work if you eat protein too close to it, is that right?"

She nodded, still too breathless to speak.

"Let's find something in our lunches that will work for now. Fruit? I've got a tangerine and a bag of potato chips. They're no salt, I'm afraid, so they taste like cardboard. I'm also happy to look around for a vending machine."

She squeezed his forearm and shook her head. *No. Please stay.*

They sat quietly for a moment, though neither of them ate. Instead Walter let his breathing fall into a rhythm with hers—in through the nose, out through the mouth. He'd never made it to a mindfulness class at Golden Grove, but he had to admit that breathing like this, sitting quietly, he felt a little better. After about ten minutes, Sally finally spoke—very softly. The first thing she said was, "Thank you, Walter. That's never happened in public before."

"Has it happened when you're alone?"

She nodded. He hated to imagine it—one foot glued to the floor, leaving her unable to reach the phone. "What do you *do*?"

"Play tricks with my legs. Yell at them like you did. Brilliant move, by the way. My voice was too soft for my legs to hear." He looked over and saw her eyes were closed but there was a smile on her lips. She was a miracle, really. Just sitting here with her, breathing side by side, had restored his equanimity. He almost couldn't remember why he'd been so upset.

As the lunch hour wrapped up, he asked if she wanted to keep playing in the afternoon games. She looked surprised. "Of course!"

"But are you feeling better? Can you move?"

She lifted her good leg and flexed her foot. She tried to do the same with the other and couldn't. "I might need a few minutes, but I'll get there."

"Shall I request a short delay of game? Will you be okay sitting here?"

"Yes! Go! Thank you!"

Walter made this suggestion, assuming the judges would deny

the request. They might turn a blind eye to blatant cheating, but he'd never heard of a game delay approved after a tournament had started. In a one-day tournament, timing was everything. They had to make it through four games this afternoon. No one could be indulged with staggered start times. Which would be *fine*, he told himself. Better, perhaps, after the emotional roller coaster he'd been riding all morning. They'd quietly withdraw from the afternoon games, catch an early bus home, and return to Golden Grove with their lives exactly the same as they were yesterday.

But no. The same young man at the front desk typed Walter's request into his laptop. "Did you say Sally Reynolds?" he repeated. Walter nodded. "Yes, I'll inform her opponent. That should be okay."

He was surprised. He hadn't even asked what the "medical emergency" was. "Who is she playing?"

"Winston Pryor."

*Winston Pryor?* Surely not. Pryor had won this tournament two years ago and was on the American team that traveled to the World Scrabble tournament in Sydney two years ago. He had a higher rating than Jack Trotter. "That must be a mistake," Walter said.

More scrolling and squinting. "She's in ninth place right now. He's eighth."

"Sally Reynolds is in seventeenth place? In the whole tournament? That's impossible."

"She's 3 and 0 this morning with a 317-point spread. She's having a great tournament."

Walter stepped away from the desk and looked back across the room to where Sally was seated, her head thrown back, her eyes closed. He could hardly believe what he'd just heard. Sally had won every game this morning?

## CHAPTER 24

# Sally

SHE OPENED HER EYES TO A SIGHT THAT MADE HER SMILE: WALTER pushing a wheelchair across the lobby, waving one hand and pumping his fist. "You've made it to the big leagues, Sally! Your next game is against Winston Pryor!"

"Who?" she asked when he got closer.

"I can't give you a rundown of his whole career but suffice to say he's won this tournament twice. We've got our game delay but we've got to hurry." He held out his hand to help her into the chair. "I've watched his games on YouTube. He's very aggressive, unafraid to play phonies, famous for making bingos through two separate words. If you give him that option, he'll figure out how to use it. He knows his nine-letter words like no one else."

Sally tested her left leg, which seemed better, but she accepted the wheelchair ride so she could concentrate on Walter's words. As he pushed, he whispered in her ear. "Don't be afraid to challenge. He's going to make assumptions about you. You're an older woman, he's never heard of you before, he's going to amuse himself by making risky plays early on. That won't mean they're phonies, only that they're risky. He'll underestimate you. Capitalize on that."

"How certain should I be before I challenge a word?"

"Good question. Watch his face for giveaways. Some people can be surprisingly obvious playing phonies. They immediately reach for the tile bag so you don't have time to consider your challenge. Other people do the opposite and wait forever. They smile like they want you to challenge, which makes you question yourself. Trust your gut."

He wheeled her over to table three, where Pryor was already seated, reading from a newspaper. Walter had explained that a player's table assignment went along with their rating in the tournament. She was now sitting two tables away from the top two players, apparently.

"Are you Winston Pryor?" Sally asked softly.

He smiled at the idea that she hadn't recognized him or, at least, was pretending not to. "Guilty," he said, revealing a piano keyboard of perfect teeth. "And you are—" He squinted down at the game assignment sheet. "Sarah? I'm sorry, no… Sally?"

"That's right. I apologize for the delay. I twisted my ankle during lunch."

"Ah." A wider smile, with more teeth, as he took it all in: the wheelchair with the hotel name on the back. "Lucky your husband found that chair."

"He's not my husband, just a friend. Thank you, Walter." Using her good leg, she managed to transfer herself to the chair. "There. Ready to start when you are, Mr. Pryor. Though you'll need to put away your newspaper, of course."

Three plays in, and Sally was already grateful for Walter's advice whispered en route. Pryor's first bingo, SCRIEVE, seemed like a test. He could have played SERVICE, but he was hoping for a challenge. She wouldn't fall for it. She nodded and answered with a bingo of her own, hooked on to his: STIFLER.

She was getting good tiles, not great ones, but she used what she had well. Instead of getting more anxious when she got stuck with too many vowels on her rack, she found IONIZED and bingoed while landing her Z on a double-letter square. She wondered if it was possible the extra medication was helping her. She couldn't test her leg right now, but her brain felt even sharper than it had been that morning.

Of course playing well didn't mean she was winning. Six turns in and Pryor had upped his game. Gone was any affectation of casual disinterest. He shuffled his tiles, face bunched in concentration. Twenty minutes later, he stopped flashing his high-wattage smile entirely. They traded the lead back and forth, neither one gaining more than fifteen points on the other.

Soon enough, it was clear: This would come down to their endgame and a question of who got lucky with the tiles still in the bag. Sally knew there was still an X, a K, and one S. She made a low-scoring play for the chance to draw four tiles from the bag of ten, a risk she knew Walter would advise against. *Don't get too attached to any dream play. Your opponent will see it too and block it.* But miraculously it worked. She pulled what she needed and readied her play: HEXES as a parallel, which doubled her points for the X. As she tallied her score, Winston played his own word in the space she was eyeing: FEIN.

Here it was, she thought, her heart skipping a beat. Exactly what Walter had warned her about. He was already reaching into the tile bag.

"Hold please," she said tersely. According to tournament rules, her timer kept running as she decided whether to challenge or not. She knew FANE was acceptable (an Indian temple) and FEIGN, of course, but was this an acceptable alternative spelling? She was currently 6 points behind him. If he got stuck with the K, it was possible she could win without challenging this word. Possible, but not likely. If she challenged and lost, she wouldn't recover the points from this lost turn. It was a big risk. Instead of looking to Walter for any clues, she remembered his words: *Trust your gut.*

"I challenge," she said.

Ordinarily a challenge would necessitate both players walking up to the judge's table. "Given the situation with my ankle, I wonder if we might ask the judge to come to us," she said.

It took the judge five minutes to make his way over. Because of their delay, they were one of the last pairs playing, and a small crowd had gathered along the sidelines to watch. Sally didn't take her eyes off the board. She could hear the shuffling around her, the collective anticipation of the group holding their breath. The judge stood beside them, his open laptop cradled in his arms.

"The contested word is..." He looked up at Winston over a pair of reading glasses. "Unacceptable."

An audible gasp escaped from the crowd.

Sally had won the game.

## CHAPTER 25

# Walter

IT WAS EXTRAORDINARY, REALLY. INSTEAD OF BEING COMPROMISED BY a physical setback and heightened pressure, Sally was playing better than she ever had before, finding words Walter only dimly recognized from the lists he'd made for her. He smiled when she made KAF, for instance, a word from the KA trick—all the letters in BETSY'S FEET could be added to create acceptable three-letter words. But the longer he watched her, the more struck he was by plays she made with words he'd never seen before. He feared each one was a phony—how could it not be when he'd been studying for six *years* and she'd been at this for *four months*? When she played SCIUROID for a bingo, Walter held his breath. A brilliant move that he assumed would get challenged off the board. But no. Pryor raised his eyebrows, considered for a moment, and then nodded. Three turns later, she did it again with YONI. Behind him, someone looking down at a phone, whispered, "My God, it's an Indian term for vulva."

Though the players couldn't hear this kibitzing, it was dangerous even so. He spun around to quiet the onlookers and realized more than a dozen people were watching. This never happened. In the final rounds, yes, but they usually cordoned off spectators to rooms with closed-circuit TVs. Regular tournament games rarely drew an audience because most weren't like this one: a complete unknown giving a national champion a run for his money. It happened of course. National champions took home their trophies and prize money with three-day records of 17–6 or 21–9, meaning they won a lot of games but also lost, sometimes to lucky unknowns who undoubtedly spent years afterward reliving their onetime victory over a legendary figure. But this game felt different. This wasn't a fluke, where lucky tiles on one side and unlucky breaks on the other determined the outcome. This happened before a dozen witnesses who all felt like they were watching the birth of a full-fledged seventy-three-year-old phenomenon.

# CHAPTER 26

# Sally

SHE WAS PLAYING WELL; SHE KNEW THAT MUCH. BUT SOMETHING NEW started on the sixth turn of her next game: The tremor that had once been limited to her left side reappeared in her right hand. It had never happened before, but she'd never been in a pressured situation that necessitated taking an extra dose of Sinemet so soon after her last one either. Had the extra L-Dopa to get her left leg moving set off a new tremor in her right hand?

She froze. She could risk making a shaky play with two or three tiles, but not one that required placing five tiles in between two other words. She had a choice: There was a four-point difference, not really worth the risk. She went ahead with the smaller play so she could assess which hand was worse when it was outstretched and aiming for a target. The right was worse. Almost as if new to tremoring, it was delighted to dance freely however it wanted. She used her left hand to steady it well enough to place the tiles.

This time her opponent—a young man with curly black hair—looked up at her and back at the board. She'd started the game with the same apology about her ankle that she'd offered to Pryor. Now she wondered if he could see through it all: the wheelchair, the silly excuse of the twisted ankle, the earthquake in her hands.

"I have Parkinson's," she said softly. "And my hands are shaky at the moment. I'm sorry." She exhaled with relief of saying this aloud rather than continuing any charade. Her opponent didn't respond, which was understandable. They weren't supposed to talk at all. With one to two minutes allotted for each turn, there wasn't time for any extraneous conversation. She'd said what she needed to. She knew Walter was probably watching this struggle play out. A victory at this point might not be winning the game but making it to the end of it without needing his help. For her next turn, she used the same strategy—one hand helping the other, which worked but took an extra thirty seconds off the clock.

Miraculously, her body held it together until the last play of the game. With five tiles left, she found a move that would empty her rack, leaving him with a C and a Y, giving her the 14 points she'd need to win. She felt a shudder of excitement move through her body as she lifted her five tiles. Then, as she neared her target, her right hand spasmed. Two tiles flew out of it and onto the floor.

# CHAPTER 27

# Walter

WALTER COULD SEE THAT HER TREMOR WAS GETTING WORSE. Miraculously, she was able to retrieve her tiles, and even though she lost precious seconds on the clock, she squeaked out a victory. Still, she was flustered. She couldn't let it happen again. He rolled her away from the game to a spot in the lobby where he could sit across from her. Because it was hard to watch her tremoring right hand, he picked it up and held it. "You've just had an extraordinary morning and two amazing wins, Sally, but it would be fine to bow out now. There's no reason for you to push yourself more than your body can handle."

He hoped Sally could hear what he was trying to say—*Your health matters more than this tournament*. Resting in his, her hand stilled and softened. She squeezed his fingers. A lovely, unfamiliar feeling. After the early days of their courtship and marriage, he and Elyse never held hands. "It just seems silly to me," Elyse once said. "Sweaty hands. All those germs."

"There'll be other tournaments," Walter continued, putting his other hand on top of hers. "You're only just getting started." Even as he said this, he knew this probably wasn't true. The same day they'd learned just how sharp her mind was under pressure, they'd also learned how badly her body responded to it.

"I don't want to leave yet," she said. "Today might be my only chance. I want to see how far I get."

To everyone's astonishment—even her own—Sally kept winning. Though her leg was better, she stayed in the wheelchair, which gave her a sense of security and a place to tuck her arms before they flailed. It also gave her an armrest so she could put her chin on her hand and stop her head from twitching, another Parkinson's tic she'd never experienced before today. During her games, Walter checked the updated results as they were posted. With a 5–0 record, she had moved up to sixth place. One more victory, and she would make it into the semifinals, which would start after the dinner break.

Forty-five minutes later, she'd done it. She'd made it to the finals.

Over dinner in the casino coffee shop, they were surprisingly quiet. Walter had lots of notes on her play the last three games, but it seemed more important to let her mind rest. Toward the end of the meal, she asked what he knew about the other finalists, and he realized he hadn't even seen the list. He got it on his phone and scrolled down, only recognizing about half the names, until he got to the bottom of the list and saw: Toby Weir.

Ten minutes later, he cornered Esther in the lobby. "Esther, this is unforgivable. How could this boy have made the finals after what I witnessed?"

Esther looked surprisingly flustered. "You're right, Walter. It shouldn't have happened. The judges looked over his record, and in the first three games, he drew every blank. We're watching him now, and we plan to issue him a warning after this."

"A *warning*? Good God, what if this boy wins the whole tournament?"

"He won't. Trust me."

Walter had only himself to blame. He should have reported his wallet theft at the last tournament, should have spoken up more insistently earlier today.

A few minutes later, game assignments were posted, and his worst fear was confirmed: Sally's next opponent would be Toby.

"Watch this kid carefully," he whispered as he pushed Sally. "He might be twelve years old, but he gets opponents to lower their guard with a big show of flattery and innocence."

"Have you played him before?" Sally asked.

"I might have. It's hard for me to remember. I've definitely heard stories about him."

She grabbed his shirtsleeve, which forced him to stop pushing her. "Am I about to play the boy who stole your wallet?"

Hard to say whether his face reddened from anger or embarrassment. "He might be," he sighed. "Though of course I can't prove it."

"Oh, Walter, this is terrible. I'm going to say something."

"Don't you dare. The main thing for you to do right now is beat the pants off him. That's it. That's all I'm asking."

# CHAPTER 28

# Sally

FIVE MOVES INTO HER GAME WITH TOBY, SALLY KNEW SHE WOULDN'T win. He was an unsettling opponent, mostly because his face looked older than twelve, but he was small and moved his body like a child. One leg folded beneath him, he sat on his foot and leaned over the board, moving his head around slowly to take it in. He obviously had an extraordinary memory and played two words she'd only seen champions on YouTube use—PLUTEI and GLUON.

About halfway through their game and 70 points ahead, he relaxed and pulled out a Pez dispenser. "Want one?" he said, flipping open the lion's-head top.

She studied him with narrow eyes. "No thank you." Then it occurred to her: If she wasn't going to win this game, maybe she could achieve a different sort of victory. "You're very good. How long have you been playing?"

"Eight months in tournaments. Longer than that with my grandmother."

"I've only been playing for four months." Ordinarily she wouldn't say such a braggy thing. *And look at me, I made the finals.*

"*Really?*" he said, obviously surprised. "How'd you get so good?"

"I have a very good teacher named Walter Kretzer." She watched his face. Surely if he had Walter's wallet, he would recognize the name, but his expression didn't change. "You might have played him once?"

Instead of answering, Toby made his play and slapped the clock.

"He's a wonderful teacher," Sally continued. "Very smart. Very good on strategy."

As if to prove her point, she made her best play of the game. HADJ for 52 points, but still not enough to pull ahead, unfortunately.

"Nice," Toby said.

"Walter taught me that." Did she sound silly? So be it. Walter *had* taught her everything she knew about Scrabble. Even if she was about to lose, the fact that she'd made the finals at all was entirely his doing and she wanted this boy to know. *The people you are beating (and stealing wallets from) deserve your respect.* Was the message landing? Impossible to tell. She'd only mentioned Walter because at some point, she realized he was no longer watching their game. It felt strange to have him disappear and also freeing.

She thought about simply confronting the boy: *You might win this game but you've also done something terribly wrong. I think you know what I'm talking about.* As a teacher, she'd been particularly good at getting children to admit their infractions. More than once, she'd elicited teary confessions from students by simply saying, "You know what you've done. You'll feel better if you tell me."

This time, sadly, she didn't get the chance. Toby finished her off with two decisive plays of five tiles each, effectively ending the game three minutes early. Walter reappeared as she was shaking the boy's hand and seemed shockingly unfazed by her loss.

"Okay good, that's over. Now we can go home." Walter pushed her away quickly without a word—or even eye contact—exchanged with Toby.

"I'm so sorry, Walter," she said when they got to the main lobby where they'd have to return the wheelchair. He'd become a pro with the footrests over the course of the day. "Use my shoulder if you need to," he said as she stood up and readied herself to walk again. "I've got a car waiting out front that will take us to the bus station."

"I'm sorry I lost to *that* boy," she said after they were in the car. "His word knowledge is incredible. He took control of the board three turns in, and I couldn't recover."

Walter turned to her, his expression unreadable. "He's very good. He's also a cheater."

"*What?*"

"I saw him pocket two tiles before the start of the second game this morning. I alerted the authorities, and they took so long responding that the tiles had already been played by the time they searched him."

"Oh, Walter, that's awful."

What else could either one of them say? They were quiet for the rest of the cab ride and quieter still in the station as they waited for their bus.

## CHAPTER 29

# Walter

WALTER FELT DEAD THE NEXT DAY. OR AS CLOSE TO DEAD AS SOMEONE who hadn't technically died could feel. For the bus ride home, they hadn't sat together—Sally wanted to stretch out over to two seats to see if it might help the ache in her lower back—which meant that he hadn't told her what he'd decided: He was done with Scrabble. Maybe he'd occasionally drop in to the VFW club to say hello, but even that seemed unlikely when every memory of the game now overwhelmed him with emotions—sadness being the first, fury a close second. Why had Esther hesitated so long before checking Toby's pockets?

Unable to stomach the idea of watching Sally's game with Toby, he'd wandered around the other finalists' games, and he saw possibilities for cheating everywhere. Phones on tables beside the boards, newspapers open on the floor. Rolf Hindergen requested a pause of game to go to the bathroom, which wasn't unheard of, but the standard protocol was to do so before you drew tiles so no one would know what letters they had when they stepped away from the board. Rolf managed to do this with six tiles on his rack and three left in the bag. Meaning he could reasonably plug a few letter combinations on his phone and get his best options. Recently the chess world had been rocked by a young champion confessing to exactly this—bathroom phone cheating in the course of a crucial game.

Enough. That was all. He'd seen enough.

The whole quiet bus ride home, he thought about something Gavin had said at his last art show when prizes were handed out and he hadn't gotten any. "It's not about the art really. It's about your social media following and who your friends are." No wonder Gavin turned to the comfort and company of mindless worms, who apparently reproduced by having sex with themselves, thereby ending any need to show off or manipulate anyone else.

The next time Walter saw Sally, he would offer a general apology for wasting so much of her precious time. Until then—what? He already knew he wouldn't venture out of his apartment today. For dinner or anything else. He didn't even feel like walking up to the front desk to fetch his newspaper because he didn't want to run in to anyone who might ask how the tournament had gone. With everyone's memory being what it was, thankfully a week from now, they'd forget to ask. In the meantime, he'd wait it out. Eat crackers and peanut butter. Watch TV.

He didn't call Sally or check up on her because he couldn't stop thinking about the embarrassing spectacle he'd made of himself on the bus ride to the tournament. Braying like a fool about "the importance of our friendship," and then weeping like a child when he realized that in an effort not to stir controversy, cheating was more or less condoned by the very people who made the rules. Maybe not condoned, exactly, but tolerated in the name of not confronting a promising young player. Thinking about this all made him so sad that he couldn't be sure that he could see Sally without getting emotional again. He allowed himself a quick check of the tournament results and saw that, thankfully, Toby had lost in the next round and didn't secure a place in the top finishers who were—unsurprisingly—all men between the ages of eighteen and thirty-five.

For years, Walter had made the same assumptions everyone else did about the gender imbalance in the elite top tier of Scrabble players: Women were less competitive, less willing to study obsessively, more apt to mean it when they said they played "for fun." He remembered once getting into an unpleasant fight with Gavin about "systemic misogyny and homophobia." How was this such a problem when so many women and gay people were successful, Walter had argued. Now he saw a clear example and wished he could go back and apologize to Gavin. He wondered if he'd instigated these fights because Gavin made him feel so small and narrow-minded sometimes.

Now he found himself composing arguments Gavin might have delivered himself: *Tournaments have built-in bias, favoring young men by allowing no accommodations for people with health issues or women with families.* How many mothers had to leave the tournament early because of family obligations? How many—like Sally—had physical limitations that prevented putting in a ludicrous twelve-hour day playing Scrabble?

In his mind, the letter to Esther began writing itself: *If we're ever to achieve a level playing field, accommodations must be offered along with shorter playing days. Otherwise, we'll spend the coming decades celebrating champions who all resemble the same mathematically inclined young men who came before.* (Another Scrabble anomaly—top-tier champions all tended to be math whizzes, not English majors as one might assume.)

As he composed the note he already knew he'd never send—especially if he was done with Scrabble as he'd vowed this morning—Walter remembered more pieces of the day. Why had he *cried* in the lobby when he hadn't even cried at Elyse's funeral? There, it would have made sense, if not for his beloved wife, then for how few pictures he appeared in during Gavin's slide show. But he didn't. Afterward he told Gavin he'd done a great job with the arrangements. "I wish I could have helped more," he'd said, hoping this didn't sound too needling.

"That's okay, Dad," Gavin said. "I just wish you'd helped Mom more these last six months."

Looking back, he'd probably spent that day too angry to grieve, and perhaps his breakdown at the tournament was overdue sadness at losing Elyse and, with her, seemingly any neutral tie to his son. He wept because even with Sally, he hadn't been completely honest. He told her he spoke with Gavin about once a month, but here was the truth: It had been almost three months since the last call he'd made, the one Gavin had yet to return.

## CHAPTER 30

# Sally

THE DAY AFTER THE TOURNAMENT, SALLY'S BODY COULD MANAGE nothing more demanding than a slow shuffle to the bathroom, the kitchen, and back to bed. She must have sounded so exhausted on the phone that Rachel came right over, and apparently the sight of her was alarming enough to elicit a gasp with one hand clamped over her daughter's mouth.

"Thanks, sweetheart; that's very reassuring."

"You just look so tired, Mom. And kind of gray. Your skin is a weird, ashy color."

"Well, you were right. Playing in the tournament was too much for me. My body fell apart at the end of the day."

"Oh, Mom," Rachel said, sinking down in a chair opposite the bed. "I didn't *want* to be right. I *like* that you're freakishly good at something weird like Scrabble. I mean, at first I wasn't sure, and then I started telling people at work and everyone texted me yesterday wanting to know how you'd done."

Sally smiled. "I did very well until the end when I fell apart against a twelve-year-old boy." Sally laughed and then, in an unexpected wave of emotion, felt tears fill her eyes. "It was *hard*, Rach. I don't know if I'll ever play again."

The tremor was gone this morning, thankfully, but in its place was a new, unfamiliar heaviness, as if her bones had been emptied and replaced by cement.

"Of course you'll play again, Mom. Just not in long, stressful competitions in weird public places like casinos. You'll play online, like everyone else."

"Serious Scrabble players hate playing online."

"Why?"

"Because people cheat and use their phones to look up words."

"Oh. But you can still play with your friend here, right? What's his name again?"

"Walter. I don't know. Something happened yesterday. He got very upset in the middle of it, but he wouldn't say why."

"That sounds a little dramatic."

"It was a lot of excitement for one day. Too much, I'm sure. I'm giving myself a day to recover, but I plan to be fine tomorrow. Why are you even here? I told you I'd be all right."

"Actually, Mom, it's not you I'm worried about."

Sally let her head fall back on her pillow. "I'm sorry. I never got a hold of your brother," she said. "Tell me what's happening with him."

"Okay, so Karen called me last night. I haven't talked to her in fifteen years, but she said some weird things were happening and she wanted to let me know. Starting with Andrew inviting her over to the house and asking her if she'd help us sell it."

"I told him not to do that—"

Rachel held up her hand. "Apparently, it wasn't really about the house, because she got there and he'd put their old prom picture on the mantel along with all these other old pictures of them from high school." She tried to ignore them and went around making an inventory of the things he should work on before they listed it, and then he told her, "I don't really care about the house. I care about you."

Sally thought about Andrew standing at the bottom of Karen's lifeguard stand, delivering his lengthy, handwritten love letter. How could a mother explain to her son: Better not to make these romantic gestures while a woman is *trying to work*?

"It gets worse, unfortunately," Rachel continued. "Karen left, and I guess he kept calling and texting her about having dinner sometime, and finally she told him she didn't think they should work together. So last night he showed up at her house at nine. She said he couldn't come in—that it was too late and she had a child to think about—but instead of going home, he stood on her lawn in the rain and drank a whole bottle of wine.

"She called the police. By the time they got there, he'd started to drive home, but he ran into her mailbox and the car got stuck in mud on her lawn. They issued a citation and took away his license. I guess the police drove him home, but Karen felt terrible and called me this morning. She thinks it all got blown out of proportion and she's happy to tell a judge that, but in the meantime, she wants to make sure Andrew gets some help."

Sally felt awful. How could all this have happened while she was busy studying word lists and worrying about Scrabble strategies? She had to get home and check on Andrew as quickly as possible. Enough with Scrabble and all the distractions she'd filled her life with in order—apparently—to miss an obvious crisis happening with her son.

Rachel was grateful. "Someone needs to talk to him, and he won't pick up my calls or answer the door when I knock."

"It's good that you've been trying, Rach. I'm sorry this all fell to you."

As Sally rallied her slow-moving body and packed an overnight bag, Rachel asked how long she could stay.

"What do you think he needs?" Sally asked.

"I don't know. Two weeks? Maybe three? It won't take much physically. He just needs someone with him."

Her heart fell. "Oh God, really?"

"He needs help. From a doctor, but also from us."

She packed a bag for her stay, and when she got home, she understood that Rachel was right. Hard to say which was in worse shape: Andrew or the house. Dirty dishes filled the sink. Open food containers covered the counter. He watched her fill the dishwasher and shook his head. "You shouldn't clean up. It makes me feel bad."

"If I'm going to stay here for a while, I need to have some dishes to eat off, right?"

After finishing in the kitchen, she sat down in the living room, where a box filled with his high school memorabilia had exploded across the floor: yearbooks, lab reports, old essays. Andrew sat down across from her, and for a long time, neither one of them spoke. His story was right here: Once a great student with infinite promise, he was now a forty-year-old man who'd never grown up, never moved on, never realized a fraction of his potential. In the silence, she turned and looked at the mantelpiece. Her throat constricted. Rachel was right—here was his prom picture with Karen.

"Did Karen really come here and see all this?"

"It was cleaner when she came. That was five days ago."

"What were you hoping would happen with her?"

"Well I was hoping she'd help us sell the house."

"Right, but were you also hoping you might get back together?"

"Was that so crazy? When I saw her in the store, she told me she'd separated from her husband. She said they were so different she wasn't sure why she married him at all."

"And you thought that meant she should have married *you*?"

"She's had four different relationships since we dated, and none of them worked out. To me, that means yes, she should have stayed with me."

"But it doesn't mean that, Andrew. She broke up with you, too."

"That was before."

"Before what?"

"Before I realized how much I loved her. When she broke up with me in college, it was because I'd never said, 'I love you.' She kept asking why I couldn't express my feelings more and I said I don't know, I just can't. Now I realize I was wrong and I'm trying to make it up to her and tell her how I feel."

Sally had never heard this. Surely Karen knew, though. Anyone with eyes could see how he felt by the way he readied for prom, the lilac socks, the silly corsage. Had he done all that and really never told her he loved her? Had this been the lesson they'd gleaned from their absent father—*Better not to care too much? Or if you do, say nothing?*

"Did you *ever* tell Karen how you felt?"

"I tried to. When she came over to look at the house."

*No*, she thought. *I meant when you were dating.*

"She said for now she was still married and she didn't think it was a good idea to talk about the past or our relationship. We could be friends, but that was all."

"So why did you go over to her house with the wine?"

"I wanted to change her mind. She used to say I was too passive about everything except grades, so I tried to show her I wasn't anymore."

"One way to show a woman that you care about her is to listen to what she says."

He stared at the empty fireplace, as if he wanted to look up at the prom picture but wouldn't let himself. "I get that now."

Sally hadn't let herself dwell on the image of Andrew standing in the dark of Karen's lawn. How scary that must have been for her. How sad for him. "Why did you bring wine with you?" She'd never seen Andrew overindulge in alcohol. In fact, she'd hardly ever seen him drink *at all*.

"I was hoping it would make me less nervous. Obviously that wasn't a good idea."

They sat for a while in silence, and she thought of something Walter had said about his dead wife. "There was a lot I didn't understand about her, and I was always afraid to ask. I was inexperienced when we met, and I was afraid she wasn't. But that was partly why I loved her, so what was I afraid of hearing?" Sally had avoided so many topics with her own children. She'd never talked about their father's depression, hoping (she supposed) that if she never named it, they might escape unharmed by it. But she'd learned something from Walter's surprising honesty. Talking might be hard, but silence was worse.

"Why do you think you've stayed so attached to Karen all these years?"

"She was the most exciting thing that ever happened to me. I couldn't tell her how I felt because I thought if I did, I might get really emotional." He took a deep breath as if just saying this was a relief. "I never found anything that felt as right as being with her. I was seventeen when we met, and I thought maybe being with her could be my job or something. Like she would have the career and I would take care of her."

"Even after she married someone else?"

"It wasn't rational, I know, but I just assumed it would work out. That's why I went overboard when I ran into her. In retrospect, I probably should have said, 'Let's have coffee some time,' like everyone else." Andrew hated coffee. "The problem is that I hate coffee." For a long time he said nothing. Then he added softly: "I didn't mean to get drunk."

"But you did."

"Yes. I did."

In the past, whenever Andrew stumbled badly, she always reassured him. *This wasn't your fault; this was a misunderstanding.* Along the way, she assumed he'd understand: *This was a little bit your fault.* Obviously he hadn't.

The next day, she drove with Andrew to the psychiatrist Rachel had made an emergency appointment with. On the drive over, Sally tried to keep up normal conversation, as if this were an ordinary doctor visit, which it obviously wasn't, especially when Andrew reemerged after forty minutes and said, "The doctor wants to talk to you."

The doctor asked about the specifics of the police incident, which Sally described as best she could. He told her he could confirm a diagnosis of clinical depression and wanted to start Andrew on medication but warned her that it would take at least four weeks to reach a therapeutic level. "In the meantime, he probably shouldn't be left alone for any extended period of time. An hour or two fine, but no more. Are you able to stay with him?"

"Yes," she said softly. She'd left her clinically depressed son alone to study for a Scrabble tournament. What else could she say?

As she collected her purse from the floor at her feet, she gathered her courage to ask something she'd never mentioned to a doctor or anyone else because she'd spent her whole life afraid of labels. "I've wondered sometimes if Andrew might have some kind of autism. Asperger's maybe, though I read somewhere that we don't call it that anymore."

She wondered if the doctor could hear her heart starting to race.

"It's certainly possible. I couldn't make a diagnosis, but you shouldn't be afraid to talk about it. Most adults who get the diagnosis around Andrew's age are relieved to have an explanation for struggles they've experienced most of their lives. There are support groups now—online and in person."

# CHAPTER 31

# Walter

FOR DAYS WALTER STAYED IN HIS APARTMENT, WATCHING TV AND, IN between, rewriting versions of a letter to Esther. By Thursday, he'd completed his third unsent missive:

> *Since the Hartford tournament, I've been trying to decide what the future is for competitive Scrabble. My problem wasn't just your hesitation to follow up on Toby Weir's cheating. The larger issue is what lay behind your hesitation and this general fear that we'll all be irrelevant if young people don't participate in our tournaments. In doing a little research, I've discovered the number of Scrabble players hasn't gone down by that much over the last ten years, and in many areas (including our own) it's not down at all.*
>
> *We're still here, enjoying our Scrabble communities; we're just a little older. Is this so bad? Must we fight this trend by simplifying the game, diluting the rules, or—worst of all—turning a blind eye to blatant*

violations? For many of us, the NSPA rule book has been a reassuring reminder that standards still exist. Isn't it more important for young people to learn to adhere to a code of honor than to soften that code so as not to scare them? Is it possible they have something to learn from us?

He'd written these two paragraphs, and already, he was crying again. What *was* all this weeping? He thought about the last time he should have cried and hadn't—a month after Elyse's funeral, when Gavin stopped by the house to ask if he could take back the paintings he'd given them. Walter had said nothing, too stunned to speak. Why would Gavin ask for them back, except that he thought of them as gifts for his mother alone? It seemed particularly cruel, even for Gavin.

"Fine," Walter had said. "Take whatever you want."

Gavin looked confused. "God, Dad, do you even care? About *anything*?"

"Of course I care. But I assume you're saying you never considered those paintings a gift to me, so yes, I suppose you should have them back."

"I mean about everything, Dad. If you care, it never *shows*. Mom never *saw* it."

Why hadn't he cried then?

There was a knock on the door that necessitated a stop in the bathroom to blow his nose and dry his face. He hoped it was Sally, of course, but knew it was probably Winona from housekeeping to ask if she could clean a day early. She often asked this because she was a single mother with three children with complicated schedules she had to work around. Every time he said fine, she said, "You're one of the nice ones, Mr. Kretzer. Thank you," which always made him feel good. Maybe a conversation with Winona would lift his spirits now.

But it wasn't Winona.

It also wasn't Sally.

It was Gavin.

"Hi, Dad," he said. He looked terrible—pale, unshaven, and heavier than the last time Walter saw him, which had been about six months ago. "Sorry I didn't call first."

Walter looked up the hall behind him. "Where's James?"

In the two years that Walter had lived at Golden Grove, Gavin had only visited once, at James's insistence. "We wanted to see your new home for ourselves!" James had said cheerfully and then whispered, "My mother ended up in a place that wasn't very nice. This seems much better." That whole visit, James showed more interest and asked more questions than Gavin did, making Walter realize the sad truth: James was easier for him to talk to.

"We broke up."

"Oh." Walter stepped back. This was a surprise. Should he offer Gavin a hug? Better not risk it. "Would you like to come in?" What else could he say? Gavin and James lived in upstate New York, a three-hour drive away. Surely he didn't intend to stay here, but he must have come with some purpose in mind. Maybe he wanted to pick another fight. Or blame Walter for this breakup.

"Thanks," Gavin said. He stepped in and looked around. "Is this a different apartment?"

"No."

"Did you always have a kitchen?"

"Yes." All the apartments at Golden Grove had kitchens.

Gavin nodded. "Huh."

Should he ask about the breakup? Say he was sorry? With anyone else, he wouldn't be so nervous. Gavin sat down in the leather La-Z-Boy chair that Walter reserved for watching sports on TV. After what felt like a long time had passed, Walter ventured a question. "Would you like to watch some tennis?" He pulled over a ladder-back chair from his kitchen table.

Gavin stared at him. "Are you serious?"

"I thought you loved tennis."

"In high school, Dad."

"Right, I'm not suggesting we *play* it. But it's on right now. Sometimes I watch it."

"You hated watching tennis when I played."

"That's not true. I hated the heat stroke that came with standing on the sidelines. It made it harder for me to follow the game. Watching it on TV makes me appreciate the sport more."

Gavin turned back and shrugged. "Okay."

For an hour they watched in silence. Had Gavin noticed that Walter was crying when he opened the door? Should he admit it was something he'd been doing off and on for three days? Gavin knew very little about Walter's Scrabble life and certainly nothing about Sally. It had been months since they'd last talked, and try as he might, Walter couldn't remember that conversation. Had there been a hint of trouble with James that he'd missed entirely? Was that why Gavin hadn't called him back?

For the next three hours, it was as if someone had privately dared them to spend an entire afternoon together without saying a single thing that mattered. Occasionally they mentioned the game. Once Gavin asked if it was always so warm in his apartment. "I can adjust the temperature," Walter said and did.

Dinner hour drew closer. Walter couldn't imagine bringing Gavin to the dining room where they might get seated with others who would undoubtedly wonder why they weren't speaking to each other. He had a fear that he might—in his awkwardness—admit the truth: *This is how we are with each other. We don't talk well. Or at all, really.* Instead, he said, "I'm not really hungry, but I can have my dinner delivered and we can share it if you're interested. I think it's pot roast tonight. That's one of their better meals."

"Dad." Gavin stared at him. "I'm vegetarian. Remember?"

Now that he'd been reminded, yes, he did remember. "That's right. Sorry."

Another long silence. Finally Walter tried, "Would you like pistachios? I've got some."

In the end, they ate crackers, cheese, and pistachios for dinner. At about eight, Gavin asked if he could spend the night. "I don't really have a plan right now. Or anywhere else to go."

"Of course," Walter said. He'd actually bought a pull-out sofa bed when he first moved to Golden Grove thinking guests might spend the night and then realized, sadly, he had no potential "guests" other than Gavin, who would, in all likelihood, never use it.

Now, as they put sheets on the bed, Gavin offered this out of the blue: "James thinks I need to grow up and decide what I want to do with my life."

Walter was surprised. Not only had Gavin ended up with a man old enough to be his father, but he'd also found a man who *sounded* like his father. "What did you say?"

"It's my life. I should be able to decide what I do with it."

Walter wondered if he'd ever been a role model Gavin could emulate. He'd made no secret of disliking the job he stayed at for thirty-five years. Outside of work, he had no hobbies or friends to speak of. He told Gavin, "In my day, we didn't have all these choices. You worked to earn money and you didn't think about it too much."

Gavin looked at him. "Was that better?"

"Oh, I don't know. It was easier in some ways, but I don't know if it was better."

"James wants to have a family but he thinks I'm not mature enough to handle it."

This was a surprise. Maybe he meant a family of pets. Walter waited for Gavin to clarify and finally asked, "Like a *family* family?"

"Yeah. He's been saving money for a long time to do surrogacy. We'd started the process, working with an agency."

"Is that what you want?"

"I thought so, but maybe deep down, I wasn't sure. James thinks I revealed my ambivalence in the interview with the agency."

"What did you say?"

"That it was hard for me to picture being a father sometimes."

Walter felt terrible at what this implied. *I didn't have much of a father so it's hard to imagine being one.* "I think you'd do a fine job. Better than I did, at any rate."

Gavin looked surprised. "What do you mean?"

"I could never say the right thing. I couldn't offer you reassurance. I suspect that didn't help your self-confidence."

Gavin considered this for a moment. "You weren't *that* bad," he said after a while.

It was the kindest thing Gavin had said to him in years. Walter took a deep breath. "It's hard to see things clearly when you're a parent because you're so scared all the time."

Gavin looked surprised. "What were you scared of?"

"That your child will make mistakes or miss an opportunity and then they'll be unhappy for the rest of their life, and it'll be your fault."

"Wow. That's giving yourself a lot of power. I don't think my whole life is your fault."

"You don't?"

"Some of it, sure." Gavin smiled. "But I screwed up a lot of things, too."

Walter thought about all their pointless battles, hard lines drawn in sand that had long since ceased to matter. About changing sports and musical instruments in high school. About "wasting" college with an art major. What had once felt so important was obviously beside the point now. Still, Walter couldn't shake the feeling that by waiting so long and saying so little, addressing those decades-old missteps would be hopeless.

It was simply too late.

## CHAPTER 32

# Sally

IN THE WEEK FOLLOWING THEIR VISIT TO THE DOCTOR, SALLY TRIED NOT to watch Andrew too closely. The point in staying here was to help him establish stable habits, not take the temperature on his mental health every day as they waited to see if this new medication would work. She managed to broach the Asperger's question the day after his doctor visit. "Yeah, Karen used to say that sometimes," he said.

Sally stared at him. *She did?*

"She has a brother with autism, but I never had the same problems he did."

"It's a pretty broad spectrum. It takes a lot of forms."

"Actually, what Karen used to say was she thought *she* had it, but no one understood what autism in women looked like. Then she'd say, 'You probably have it, too.'"

She reminded him of the words he'd said earlier—that Karen was the only person who really understood him. "Is it possible she was right?" What a sad irony this presented: two mildly autistic adolescent lovebirds kept apart by the very qualities that had also drawn them together.

"Yeah probably," Andrew sighed. "But what's the use in realizing this now?"

She sat up straighter, galvanized by the ease of Andrew's concession. "There's a lot we can do! We can read books about it and join support groups. You can find a community of other people dealing with the same issues."

"Like support groups have been so helpful for you?"

She sat back. She remembered the one Parkinson's support group she'd gone to after her diagnosis. "That was different, Andrew."

"How? It's depressing to be around people with the same problems you have. Isn't that what you thought?"

In truth, he was right. The group *had* been hard for Sally to sit through. They were all nice people, but all were more impacted by their Parkinson's. Most used wheelchairs or walkers. They were almost all hard to understand with their airy, soft voices and their uncooperative tongues. The focus of the one meeting she'd gone to was on swallowing therapy—the dangers of aspiration, preventing chin rash from drool. A terrible topic for a newly diagnosed person. The only one more depressing might have been medication-induced hallucinations, which was on the agenda for the following week. She never went back, though she told herself she would when it felt more "necessary."

Now she wanted to show him that she wasn't afraid of facing her problems head on. "I'm going back to that support group," she told him that night over dinner. "Will you come with me?"

As it turned out, the group was more or less the same twelve people she remembered from her first visit, all a year further down the Parkinson's road. Two more were in wheelchairs. One had an elaborate system of straps keeping him upright in his chair. "Oh God, Mom," Andrew whispered as they sat down. "I'm trying not to get *more* depressed, aren't I?"

"Let's just listen. We might be surprised."

Sadly, though, it was hard to understand most of the speakers. In some cases, their spouses (or caretakers) spoke for them. "We're wondering if anyone has any tips for some new dressing issues we're having," said one woman whose husband looked more like her father. Another woman asked if anyone had found shoe horns that actually work. "We've bought two, and so far, we think they're both more trouble than they're worth."

Toward the end, Sally worked up her courage and asked the question that had been on her mind all week: "I recently pushed myself too hard at an all-day event. I still haven't fully recovered, and I wonder if other people think taking a risk to do an activity you love is worth the toll it might take on your body."

The response was mixed. Most of the people with Parkinson's nodded and said, yes it was. Their caretakers were less sure. "I still wish we hadn't pushed Henry so hard for our daughter's wedding four years ago. Yes, he managed to walk her down the aisle and that was wonderful, but he hasn't walked independently since then."

Hard to tell if Henry would agree, because he seemed to be asleep in the chair beside her.

"God, Mom, can we please not do that again," Andrew said in the parking lot afterward. "I really don't think you have much in common with those people."

"I do though, unfortunately. My Parkinson's isn't going to magically go away."

They got in the car and sat for a moment without speaking. Finally she said, "Thank you for coming with me, Andrew. It's important for me to think about the future. I know it's unsettling, but not talking about it isn't the answer. I did too much of that with you and Rachel when you were younger."

"What do you mean? You didn't have Parkinson's when we were kids."

"I'm talking about Dad's depression." Though she'd been thinking about it a lot, this was the first time she'd brought it up. "I think it would have been better if I'd talked about it more. Then you would have known that your father's reticence wasn't your fault."

Andrew stared ahead. "I don't know. Maybe."

She started the car and for a while they drove in silence. Then Andrew surprised her. "Did you *really* like playing in that tournament?"

Andrew hadn't asked many questions about her life at Golden Grove and certainly hadn't asked about Scrabble. "I did! I won every game up until the last one. It was exciting."

"Do you think you'll play in another tournament?"

"I'd like to but I don't know if my body can handle it, which makes me sad."

That evening she gathered her courage and asked Andrew for the first time if he thought his medication was working. After the day they'd just spent—where he not only came to the meeting but also asked her questions afterward—she allowed herself to think, *Maybe he's better*. Of course he didn't agree. "If you're asking do I have dry mouth and a weird metallic taste in the back of my throat, the answer is yes. I can tell the meds are doing that much. I don't know if they're doing anything else."

*Be patient*, she reminded herself. *Don't say things that will only annoy him like, You seem better to me.*

That evening, Andrew surprised her again. Usually after dinner, he disappeared into his bedroom. This time, as she stood at the sink, he came up behind her holding a battered maroon box. "Want to play?" he said, holding up the old family Scrabble set.

She gasped in surprise and then felt a tightening in her throat. He was his father's child, yes, but he was also hers.

"Are you sure?" She smiled. "I'm pretty good now." When he

was younger, Andrew couldn't bear losing board games. As often as possible, Sally ensured his victories in subtle and not-so-subtle ways. She miscounted squares to land in jail. She sacrificed pawns and then rooks. By the time he was eight, it was such a habit, she was no longer aware of it, no doubt another mistake she'd made: He'd never learned how to lose.

"You think you can beat me?"

"Yes, I'm pretty sure of it, but only because I've been playing every day for the last four months. You'll get better, too, if you put your mind to it. The surprising thing about Scrabble is that it's more about your math ability than your vocabulary." Andrew's math SAT scores far exceeded his verbal ones.

"Huh," he said.

She turned back to her dishes. She didn't want him to see how pleased she was by the first activity he'd initiated. Maybe he'd change his mind now that he knew she wouldn't give him the game. And then, he surprised her again. After finishing the dishes, she walked into the dining room and found him seated at the table with the game board open and the tiles all turned upside down on the lid. "I didn't pick my letters yet. I didn't want you to think I cheated."

She smiled and sat down. "Why would I think that? Did you ever cheat as a kid?"

"All the time. Almost every game we played. You were never very suspicious."

She smiled. "There's a form of allowable cheating in Scrabble that you might like. Where you can play phony words and if your opponent doesn't challenge, you get away with it." She explained the rest—that if you challenge and it's an acceptable word, you lose a turn.

"Wow," he said, lifting his eyebrows. "That's interesting."

Was that a smile in the corner of his mouth? She couldn't tell.

They played without a timer and Andrew took endless minutes deciding each play. In the end, she won, of course, but to her surprise, he asked right away if she'd like to play again. "I've got a better idea of it now."

"Of course," she said, smiling.

# CHAPTER 33

# Walter

THREE DAYS AFTER GAVIN'S ARRIVAL, WALTER WOKE UP TO THE STARTLING realization that he hadn't talked to Sally in over a week. Unfortunately, he couldn't call her right away because Gavin was still here, and he was too self-conscious. He wanted to talk to her about the tournament, yes, but also the surprise of Gavin's visit. *What a relief to see that you were right*, he wanted to tell her. *Our estrangement came less from deep-seated resentment than a bad habit we'd both fallen into.* Walter still woke up each morning assuming Gavin would announce his departure, and then they'd get through another day and Gavin would say, "You sure it's okay if I stay?"

Gavin went shopping at a 7-Eleven, and they made a running joke out of eating junk food. "These are kettle-cooked," he'd say, pulling out a bag of potato chips. "And these are jalapeño-flavored." They also—admittedly—drank more than his usual. For Walter, having a beer with lunch had a pleasantly narcotic effect and he slept away most of the afternoon. Drifting in and out as they watched TV, he opened his eyes to see that Gavin was still there, and then he shut them again.

They let themselves get caught up in a tennis tournament. Walter picked the player he was rooting for and a second choice in case the first didn't work out. He cared, but not too much. He found comfort in the fact that tennis tournaments had referees watching every move and ensuring justice. He could close his eyes, abandon vigilance, and be assured that no one would cheat while he slept. Usually toward evening, he got a burst of energy and thought, *Maybe we should talk about what he wants to do from here*, and he'd venture a question. "Are most of your things still at James's house?" he tried. Did he dread going back and seeing James again? Did he secretly want to?

Gavin shrugged. "I guess, yeah."

After a week, Walter finally came out and said, "Maybe we should talk about what your plans are. I don't think you want to live here at Golden Grove forever."

Gavin considered this for a moment and then shook his head. "Yeah, no. I don't want to talk about this." But the next day Gavin surprised him, asking his own question out of the blue. "I know why I'm depressed, Dad, but why are you?"

Neither of them had said the word before. Walter almost protested and then looked around at the beer cans and the food wrappers and thought better. "Do I need to have a reason?"

"I guess not. But usually you're not like this."

Walter thought about Gavin's accusations in the past—that he was overly controlling. The hurt lingered because they contained a thread of truth, but was this true as well? Walter considered his answer. It was the tournament, of course, and the revelation that one cheating twelve-year-old boy could cast a shadow of doubt over years of work toward a goal that now felt empty and meaningless. But there was more to it than that. His depression also had to do with Sally. He'd wanted to tell her his feelings—had tried different times over the course of the day—and had come away with the distinct impression that she didn't want to hear it. Naturally, he couldn't tell Gavin this, so he tried to think of something else. "Maybe I'm depressed because at my age, my father lost his memory and his mind, and I assume I will, too."

"I remember you saying that. But didn't he walk around the neighborhood naked?"

"Just once," Walter said, as if it was important to defend his poor father. "But of course once was enough as far as the neighbors were concerned."

Neither said anything for a long time. Finally Gavin asked, "Why do you assume the same thing will happen to you?"

"The laws of genetics are pretty cruel."

"Right, but you weren't like your dad in most ways."

"Do you mean that in addition to his terrible temper, my father also slept with women he wasn't married to?"

Gavin shrugged. He wasn't sure what he meant by it.

Walter shook his head. "Impossible to watch that happen to a parent and not worry for yourself. Or impossible for me, at any rate."

"Is that why you moved into this place?" Gavin said. Walter didn't answer. "I never understood. I didn't think you liked superficial socializing, and that's all these places are, right?"

"That's not all they offer, but you're right. I'm still not particularly good at chitchat."

"Were you hoping to get remarried? James has a friend who says women go to those places to make friends, men go to meet women."

"That might be true for some."

"But not you?"

Why did Gavin seem so surprised? "No, of course not." Should he tell Gavin the real reason? "My father's care fell to me at the end of his life, and going through that scarred me. I didn't want the same thing to happen to you. I didn't want to be a burden."

If they'd had a different relationship—if they were both different people, really—this might have been a bonding moment. As it was though, a long, unreadable silence stretched out. Finally Gavin stood up. "God, Dad, I don't know what to say. That freaks me out a little," he said before heading into the bathroom.

The next morning Gavin announced that he was trying to find somewhere to stay. Walter felt hurt. "What did I say?"

"No, it's not you, Dad. Obviously I can't stay here indefinitely. I just wish I'd kept in better touch with some of my old friends."

In Walter's memory, Gavin's friendships were as mercurial as his interests. Walter had wanted to ask about this for a few days now. "Friendships are important, Gavin. They can sustain you as much as romantic relationships. Mine do."

"But you don't have any friends, Dad. Mom always talked about that—how you didn't see the point because they required so much effort."

Sadly, Gavin was right; he used to say such things because friendships came so easily to Elyse. After that first break with their bridge-playing friends, she quickly made new ones when she returned to school and later when she worked as a librarian. Even when Gavin was still young, she had "Ladies' Nights" and weekend outings with other women where she went to museums and shows and sometimes spent the night in New York City. She always came home flush with what he perceived as new secrets, stories she'd start to tell and then wave her hand and say, "Oh, never mind. You don't really know Penny." Yes, he used to resent those friendships, because where was he meant to find his own?

The men at work had all started out as her friends and all had decided, collectively it seemed, that marrying Walter had turned their former games organizer moody and unfun. Elyse didn't want to see any of those people outside of work, so he never did. He steered clear of their golf games and their halfhearted invitations to drinks.

If anyone asked after Elyse, he convinced himself they were looking for gossip—some proof that he'd snuffed the life spark out of the fun girl they remembered.

"You're right," he conceded to Gavin. "I used to find friendships complicated. Your mother was better at them than I was. She could judge who was worth investing the time into better than I could. It's gotten a little easier for me now."

Gavin looked surprised. "Are you saying you've made *friends* here? *You*, Dad?"

"Yes. Don't look so surprised. I have."

He narrowed his eyes. "Like who? I've been here five days, and I haven't seen you talk to anyone."

"For your information I started a Scrabble club that was very popular for a while. It had over twenty members."

"Scrabble, huh? I remember playing that once with you."

*Oh God*, Walter thought, wondering if they could go back to watching tennis in silence.

"What happened to the club? Did people play a little and realize it's a boring game?"

Here was the cruel streak Walter remembered all too well. The "jokes" he never laughed at because they hit too close to home. "None of the clubs here last forever but I've continued to play with one friend. She's an extraordinarily accomplished player and we've attended a few tournaments together. I consider her a very good friend."

"*She*?"

"Yes. Her name is Sally."

Gavin shook his head. "I have to say, this is weird to hear about right now."

"Why is it wrong for me to make a friend here?"

"Because for years Mom tried to get you to do things with her and you always refused."

This was only true with caveats. "She asked me to go to art museums and operas, things she knew I hated. She asked because she knew I'd say no. I assumed she preferred going with her friends."

"Did you ever ask her to do anything?"

He never had because he didn't know what to suggest. What interests did they share after Gavin left home? Now it occurred to him: They could have played games. They'd always loved games. He sat back in his chair. "I loved your mother, but I made some mistakes, Gavin. I don't want to live with the repercussions of those forever so yes, I've made a new friend who is important to me."

"Oh my God, Dad. Are you a couple or something?"

He looked at his son. "No, but I would like us to be."

"Jesus." Gavin shook his head. "I know I shouldn't be upset, but this freaks me out. Have you been hiding her this whole time?"

"No. I haven't heard from her in over a week. I've been eager to get in touch with her, but I didn't want to take time away from you, so I haven't called her."

Gavin held up both his hands. "Don't let me stop you, Dad. Seriously. Call her."

"I'm not going to call her now. I shouldn't have said it that way. You're not the only reason I haven't been in touch. It's complicated. As friendships can be." Gavin stared at him, as if waiting for him to say something more. "She has her own challenges, and I'm not sure how much help I can be to her."

Gavin shook his head. "Wow, Dad. That sounds like what you used to say to Mom."

Walter didn't understand. Was Gavin taking her side? Was he suggesting he should have done something different with Sally after the tournament?

The next morning, Walter sensed a change. When he walked out of his bedroom, Gavin was already awake and showered. The TV was off and coffee brewed. "I did a little grocery shopping," Gavin said. "You didn't have any milk. While I was there, I picked up some fruit and cereal. Plus oatmeal."

"I don't like oatmeal."

"No one does, Dad, because it looks like throw-up, but you still have to eat it."

Walter wasn't sure what to say. He'd been awake most of the night, stewing over what Gavin had said last night about mistakes he might have made with Sally. Later, he heard Gavin on the phone in the living room, speaking in a hushed whisper, and when he got off, he told Walter he was leaving. His bag was already packed and at his feet. "I talked to James." He held up his hands. "I'm not going back yet. He doesn't think it's a good idea and neither do I. But there's a house-sitting opportunity a few miles away. It means I can get back there and take care of the worms. And we'll talk about what's next."

Walter didn't want him to go. He wanted Gavin to stay so he could tell him every single thing that had happened with Sally and have Gavin tell him what he'd done wrong. No doubt Gavin would enjoy pointing out Walter's many errors in judgment, but Gavin was already packed and hustling himself out the door, leaving Walter alone to fear that he'd made the same mistakes with Sally that he had with younger Gavin—pushing too hard, focusing too much on his own agenda.

Why had he pressed Sally to work so hard learning his word lists? To her, there was no difference between coming in sixteenth in the tournament or sixty-seventh, so why had he insisted there was? Had he failed at so many tournaments that he wanted her success to carry him across some illusory finish line in his mind? If he couldn't wear the crown of laurels himself, he could at least stand near it?

That evening, Walter returned to the dining room for the first time in over a week. He hoped to see Sally of course, but she wasn't in the early-dining crowd that began gathering at four thirty for the five o'clock seating. If anyone asked him about the tournament, he planned to say that he was taking a break from Scrabble. Then he was surprised: No one asked.

A few people said it was nice to see him again and asked how he was feeling. "It must have been a nasty cold, Walter," Iris said. "We haven't seen you in a while!"

"Oh, it was," he said sheepishly.

They moved on to other topics and a few minutes later, Anita turned to him. "Have you heard about Sally? No one's seen her in a week, but they won't tell us where she is!"

Walter felt furious with himself. How had he let so much time go by without checking up on her? "Surely they've done a wellness check, though?" This was the euphemism for the knock on the door that came if you failed to show up for dinner without canceling ahead of time. It went without saying: They weren't looking for wellness; they were looking for bodies, fallen too far from an emergency alert button.

"Oh, they've checked," Wendy said. "She's not there. No one knows where she is."

*Dear God*, he thought, as his heart began to race. He waited another minute before stepping away from the group to call her but got no answer. Over dinner, he managed to ask a few more questions of Sally's friends without sounding too frantic. When was the last time they saw her? Had anyone talked to her on the phone? They all looked at one another, mystified.

After dinner, he marched to the front desk to ask for information about Sally's whereabouts. "She has more health issues than most people here are aware. I'm concerned that she might be in the hospital right now with no one visiting her."

"Oh no, Walter, she's fine," the older woman behind the desk said. "She's just away this week, visiting with one of her children."

"Which one?"

They couldn't tell him, of course. They could never give out information like this.

"I don't know what to do. She's not answering her phone, and I know she doesn't pick up her voice messages. Neither one of us does. We've both tried and it's impossible."

"Have you tried texting?" the girl behind the desk offered.

"Oh, for heaven's sake," Walter said in a huff, because of course the answer to one unmanageable technical obstacle was to suggest another one. Walter had never successfully texted in his life, but he occasionally suspected others might have texted him, judging by the mysteriously personal messages that occasionally appeared on his phone. Back at his apartment, he typed "How to Send a Text." He'd recently done searches on using his TV remote and replacing hearing aid batteries. He watched a video that made texting look easy, but how were grown people expected to type words on a keyboard with such small letters and no spaces between? After an hour, he went back to the front desk and asked if the girl would mind helping him. "I can type a message but it won't send."

"Have you been to one of our tech workshops?"

He didn't want to admit that he'd been to two actually, one about operating their TV and the other about getting on the internet.

"We offer some now on using your iPhone."

He showed her the issue. "I type the whole message and then—nothing."

She watched him. "Don't hold your finger down. Just give it a light tap." She brushed her finger over his phone and it worked.

"I'd like to try doing that for myself," he groused. Then, after he'd only typed two words—*Sally it's*—he miraculously managed to press Send successfully. He smiled for the first time. "I did it! I see what you mean... You just tap it really."

"That's right. Now maybe finish the message so she doesn't worry about *you*."

Walter spent the next day writing texts. Some took him over an hour to tap out.

I'm sorry I've been out of touch, Sally! We're all worried about you. The people at the front desk say you're fine but you didn't mention any visits upcoming with your children. Did something happen?

An hour later, he tried again.

I just want to know if you're okay. I know the tournament was hard on you physically. I'm worried that you had to go to your daughter's house to recover. I wish I'd never suggested going. I also wish I'd reached out to you sooner, but a surprising development in my life is that my son came for a visit and stayed for a week! Granted he had nowhere else to go after a lover's quarrel, but I relished the time regardless and got distracted. I wish I'd checked on you sooner.

The next day, he tried one more time:

I keep calling and getting the same message: voice mail not yet set up. Could whoever you're staying with help you set this up? I'm also wondering if you're reading these and haven't gotten a lesson in texting yet? You have to TAP LIGHTLY. Don't hold the send button or press too hard. Class on this topic being offered soon. I'm happy to sign us both up.

That afternoon, he sent what he decided would be his last text:

> In case you're wondering how well they protect your privacy at Golden Grove, I can tell you: Very. They say you're okay but they won't tell me any more. It occurs to me that it's been over a week now and if you wanted me to know what was going on with you, you would have been in touch. I will stop writing these notes which might be an annoyance during a family time and will wait patiently (I promise!) for you to be in touch.

After spending so much time composing and editing these notes to Sally, he found it hard to think of anything else to do with himself. He hadn't been back to the VFW club because he hadn't wanted to talk about the tournament, but they'd undoubtedly checked the results and would have seen how well Sally did. He could have spent an evening recounting her game against Winston Pryor and never mentioned Toby Weir at all, but he didn't want to do that. He didn't want to pretend everything was fine when it obviously wasn't, nor did he want to bury his head in the sand and continue to support a Scrabble association that didn't enforce the rules they endlessly bickered over.

What was the point of debating the merits of newly accepted word lists if a twelve-year-old could pocket and play with any tiles he wanted? His friends at the VFW club—Peter, Dorothy, Iona, and the rest—would understand the gravity of what he'd seen and be appalled, no doubt, but he feared they might shrug the same way Esther had. *We live in an age of internet and shortcuts. What can we do?* Better to turn a blind eye to cheaters than to be a group of overbearing dinosaurs, holding fast to rules as they watch their numbers dwindle to extinction.

Thankfully, he woke the next morning to a glorious surprise—a text from Sally:

Oh, Walter, I'm sorry I disappeared on you. My son isn't well so I've temporarily moved back home for a while. I'm all right and look forward to being back at Golden Grove soon. In the meantime, take care of yourself and send me all the updates from there!

Admittedly, it was less personal than he would have liked. Also fairly vague. What was wrong with her son? How long would she be gone? There was also the question of why she hadn't just called him when she got his texts. In the past, they'd spoken regularly to arrange games, so what was stopping her now? She must be busy. Maybe Andrew had pneumonia, something that necessitated cooking vats of soup. Over the course of the day, he reread the note half a dozen times and decided to follow her instructions and text her his updates. If nothing else, he was getting better with his thumbs.

Today, at afternoon tea, I asked Anita if she'd heard from you and get this, she said, "Which Sally?" There's two now, apparently! I told her I don't care about whoever this new Sally is and you shouldn't either. Apparently she's already made waves by complaining about too much sodium in our food and proposing the removal of salt shakers from the tables. As if she's *trying* to make herself unpopular.

He was going to the dining room every night again for dinner, still carrying a book with him in case he ended up eating alone, but much to his surprise, these days he usually got invitations to join others. One night he got two. The first from a woman who never remembered names but called everyone "dear" as she touched their arm. He was grateful when Sally's friend Connie rescued him with a wave. "Walter's sitting with us tonight, Louise! We want to tell him a new games night idea we have. It's brilliant." An overstatement perhaps, considering the idea was nothing more than "an evening where different games are offered at different tables—backgammon at one, cribbage at another. The possibilities are endless!"

Eating with the women he thought of as Sally's friends was a good distraction but by the end only made him miss Sally more. So much of their conversation tilted toward emphatic pronouncements of noncontroversial opinions. "The weather is getting warmer finally!" "I don't like watching television news anymore! It's all opinions!" He managed to smile and bob his head as if he was participating in this exchange of platitudes when really he was already composing his next text to Sally: Had a lively dinner tonight with the Green Thumbs group. Big pruning plans ahead! All top secret unless you ask me and then I'll tell you everything. He tried not to worry that she wasn't writing him back. Texting was hard work, doubly so for someone with shaky hands. The next day he wrote her again:

> The new Sally continues her campaign to alienate others by adding another class to our schedule. This one is called Learning to Live with Less. Taught by her! Her bio tells us she's been a "certified life coach" for thirty years. Did you know you could be certified in this? I didn't.

He was trying to strike a lighthearted, casual tone but didn't want to sound mean. Was this too mean? He couldn't tell. He tapped Send on his phone, though he must have let his finger linger a fraction too long because he was left with no choice but to add an "effect" to the text. He chose "gentle" with no idea what this meant. With the text successfully sent, Walter shut off his phone and closed his eyes, visited by the same fear he'd faced every evening after dinner: What would he do if Sally *never* came back? What if he was left alone in this commune of well-meaning oldsters without anyone he could have a real conversation with?

Over the next week, Walter dropped in on more of Sally's groups. He wasn't much help weeding with the Green Thumbs, but he made them all laugh, singing an old ditty from Gavin's childhood, "The Garden Song." "Inch by inch, row by row, gonna make this garden grow. With a rake and a hoe and a piece of fertile ground." He couldn't remember any other verses but it hardly mattered, judging by the way they laughed every time he moved a few inches and started up again. Why had he never noticed what an easy audience these ladies were? After four rounds, he realized if he didn't stop soon, either he'd look silly or they would.

It was midsummer but not too hot. It felt good to be outside and moving. No doubt he'd be sore tomorrow from holding his arms up clownishly as he sang, but never mind. When he walked back inside, he realized he was whistling.

"Excuse me. Mr. Kretzer?"

He spun around but saw no one. The lobby was usually busy this time in the afternoon—deliveries, visitors, staff coming and going—but there was no one. He turned back toward the elevator when he heard it again. "Mr. Kretzer?"

He squinted in the direction of the visitors' coat room and could hardly believe who he saw, standing in the shadowy doorway: Toby Weir.

"Could I talk to you for a moment?"

Walter's mind began to race. Had the boy's grandmother just moved into Golden Grove? Or worse—did he know who called for the pocket search at the tournament and now he was here to confront him? "Yes," Walter said, keeping his voice as neutral as possible. "Why don't we go up the hall?" If Toby was here to confront him, he didn't want others to hear it. After they were seated in one of the "conversational nooks" that no one ever used, Walter turned and faced him. "What are you doing here?"

"I wanted to talk to you."

*Here it comes,* Walter thought. *You accused me of cheating and turned the judges against me. I could've won that tournament. You owe me $2,000.* Even as he thought this, he had another realization: Toby looked older than he remembered, like he'd grown in the three months since he first met him. He steeled himself. "Go on."

Toby drew a deep breath. "I want to ask if you'd consider being my Scrabble coach."

Walter's jaw, quite literally, dropped. "What do you mean? I'm not a coach."

"When I played Sally Reynolds, she talked about you a lot. She said you had a philosophical approach to the game that opened up her mind. Your teaching helped her access words she'd never put on a list or intentionally memorized. I want to learn how to do that. I think I can. My memory is pretty good, but it's not photographic."

Toby didn't make the mistake most people did, calling it "photogenic." A niggling thought poked at the back of Walter's mind. "You're not twelve years old, are you?"

"No," Toby said. "I'm fifteen, but I'm short for my age. I don't lie on the official entry forms, just in conversation with other players. It disarms opponents. When they think I'm younger, they let down their guard and challenge fewer words."

"But that's cheating."

"Technically it's not. There are rules about not talking during games, but as you know, most people do, and there's no rules against lying in those conversations."

*Good heavens,* Walter thought, shaking his head. What other stories had this boy been telling? "Do you live with the grandmother who taught you to play?"

Toby looked down. Again, sheepish. "No. I live with my parents."

Remarkable how he seemed to age with every revelation. Would he turn out to be a short, beardless con man of twenty-three? "Why would you tell these stories and think you wouldn't get caught?"

"I used to watch a lot of WrestleMania. A big part of the competition is inventing a persona. I thought maybe the same thing was true in competitive Scrabble."

"But you know that isn't true. You've been to tournaments." Walter thought back to their first game and how charmed Walter had been by his innocence and questions about NSPA.

"I'd only been to one tournament before I met you. I was good—I *am* good—but I was a little insecure. You were nice to me in that game. Nicer than the other people I played. I remembered your name when Sally said it and then she kept talking about what an exceptional teacher you were, and I've been thinking about it ever since. I need someone to help me make it to the next level. I think I can get there, but not by myself."

"What about your grandmother?"

"I don't have a grandmother. Or not one who's alive. All that stuff I told you about recording word lists was stuff I did myself. I'm not sure if they were the smartest techniques, but they've gotten me where I am now. But if I want to go farther, I need a teacher."

Walter wanted to laugh. This kid certainly had some gumption. "You stole my wallet, Toby. And then I watched you openly pocket two tiles at the last tournament. *I saw you cheat.*"

"Okay, right." He took a deep breath. "Those are the two worst things I've ever done in my life. It's not like I have a long history of doing criminal things, but you're right about those. I came here because I suspected you were the one who saw me, and I want to explain myself. I also want to continue playing tournament Scrabble and make sure I never try anything like that again. Coming clean to you ensures that I won't. Let's start with the wallet—which I have, by the way—" He reached into the backpack at his feet and pulled it out. "I really hadn't seen an NSPA card before. That was all. I wanted to look at it and you wouldn't let me see it. You put it back in your wallet like you thought my hands were dirty, and you said, 'Get your own, kid.' Maybe you were joking, but it made me mad."

Walter *had* been joking of course, but he saw in this exchange a replay of a hundred unintended slights he'd visited upon Gavin. Holding something out and pulling it away at the very last second. How often had he done that? And more importantly—*why,* for heaven's sake? Because he liked the momentary power of holding something his elusive son was curious about and he didn't want to lose his attention too quickly?

"Stealing a wallet is a much bigger deal than stealing a club membership card."

"I know. I felt really bad. I didn't spend the money. You can look and see."

Walter did and indeed, it was there—a five and two ones—which surprised him. In all this time, Toby had never had the impulse to just go ahead and spend it?

"It didn't seem right to do that," he said.

"But palming two blanks at a tournament with a $2,000 prize seemed okay?"

"No, of course not. I only did it because I was so surprised that we were allowed to put the tiles in the bag ourselves when this was such a big tournament. I just thought, wait, won't everyone try doing this? It wasn't hard."

Walter stared at him. "No. No one's tried doing that. Most people don't think that way."

"I get that now. I really do. I feel like I've grown up a lot in the last four months."

Walter shook his head and looked up the hallway at two women, Pam and Patricia, walking toward them. One inched along with a walker; the other bent to hear what her friend was saying. Walter never knew their names until Sally introduced them with the surprising detail that although they'd both been married and had moved into Golden Grove separately, they'd now lived together happily for the last five years. "As a *couple*?" he'd asked her.

"Yes, as a couple." Sally had smiled. "Are you shocked?"

"No," he said and reminded her that his son, who'd seemed to like girls all his life, turned out to be gay. After Sally told him, he realized he hardly ever saw one of these women without the other. He liked seeing them together—always talking, laughing at the same jokes. He always felt like there was a lesson to learn from them, though he wasn't sure exactly what. Second chapters of life are possible? They passed with a smile and—surprisingly—even Toby seemed to realize there was something to envy about these two. After they were gone, Toby said, "I don't really have any friends. I used to be part of the games club at my middle school but not anymore. I thought they were my friends, but I was wrong."

Though Walter couldn't be sure, his instinct told him this boy was telling the truth—his transgressions haunted him and his remorse was real.

"Well," Walter said. "You can't exactly lie all the time and steal people's wallets and expect them to invite you out for lunch. If I agree to be your teacher my first rule will be: You have to knock it off with all that crap. Agreed?"

Toby nodded.

## CHAPTER 34

# Sally

THOUGH SALLY WAS THE FIRST TO BROACH THE TOPIC OF JOHN'S depression, suddenly Andrew wanted to discuss it. "Did you see the problem before you were married?" he asked her one evening over dinner.

"No, but we'd only known each other about six months before we were married." Would this shock someone in a generation who lived together for years before marrying? She assumed he was thinking this, but no. Instead, he asked: "Would you have married him if you'd known?"

The question took her by surprise. *Would* she have married John if she'd known how often she'd be left alone to make decisions and fend for herself? How lonely she'd feel for weeks and sometimes even months on end? She wanted to reassure Andrew—*Yes, of course. I loved your father unconditionally*—but she wanted to be as honest as possible from here on out. "I can't answer that for sure. I'll say this though: If someone had believed I was strong enough to hear the truth, I think I would have felt strong enough to handle it."

She bent down to look in his eyes. Did he understand what she was saying? *You don't have to give up on love; you just have to be honest.* Impossible to say when these conversations often ended as quickly as they started. She knew he wasn't contacting Karen, but was he thinking about her when he disappeared into his room every night after dinner? Was he still imagining a future together?

When she first discovered Walter's texts, Sally felt terrible. She hadn't looked at her phone in days and hadn't realized how worried he'd be. In spite of her shakier hands, she managed to text him back that night, but since then, with new texts coming in two or three times a day, she hadn't been able to keep up. She tried using her thumbs and the eraser end of a pencil but couldn't get her trembling fingers to produce anything beyond gibberish. She didn't want to call because she still wasn't sure what to say about Andrew. After three tries at texting, she took her phone to Andrew. "I need help texting my friend. My fingers won't cooperate."

Andrew took the phone and, instead of typing out what she wanted to say, read through all of Walter's texts. "I don't get it, Mom. Who *is* this guy?"

"My friend Walter. I told you about him, the one I play Scrabble with." Andrew nodded and kept reading. "You don't need to read them. You just need to help me text him back."

"It sounds like he's more than a friend, Mom."

She felt a blush rise up. "We're good friends, that's all. And he's worried because I disappeared without saying goodbye. I should have reached out to him sooner."

Andrew read aloud: "'Rest assured you're the only Sally who matters to me and the only Sally I care about.' Even I can tell he likes you, and I'm terrible at these things."

"He does like me. We like each other. We're friends."

"You know what I mean, Mom. As more than a friend."

Suddenly she felt self-conscious. "Never mind," she said. "Give me back my phone. I'll call him later."

"Do you like him too? Is that why you started playing so much Scrabble?"

"I don't want to talk about this anymore," she said, grabbing her phone and walking away. Suddenly she felt nervous about texting back. If Walter did have feelings, they were for the person he thought he knew—the Sally who learned Scrabble quickly and kept their games light, not the Sally who was coming to terms with her many failures as a mother and a wife. How could she explain to him she wasn't who he thought she was? Besides, her Scrabble career was over; that much was clear. She needed to concentrate on Andrew for now, not study a text thread from Walter and analyze what it all might mean.

After that, Sally made a point of leaving her phone in John's office and checking it as little as possible. She saw Walter's texts from time to time but she didn't respond. Texting was too unreliable, too painful a reminder of the permanent changes taking place in her body. A few months ago, she could text easily; now she couldn't.

Of course she could call him, and she almost did a few times, but that felt fraught with the possibility of awkwardness. She remembered his speech on the bus and wondered if she'd missed some bigger pronouncement he was trying to make. The whole business made her uneasy because he knew plenty about her anagramming ability and her surprising memory but very little about the rest of her life. True, she'd talked about her marriage with him, but she hadn't said much about her children and had told him virtually nothing about Andrew's struggles. How would she tell him about her failures as a parent now that she was brought face-to-face with them on a daily basis? Easier to wait, she decided.

The good news was that Andrew liked Scrabble and wanted to keep playing. They'd gone a week now playing two games a day, sometimes three, and while he still hadn't beaten her, he was definitely getting better, using her strategies, learning more words. Best of all, he was learning an important lesson he'd never mastered as a child—how to keep going in the face of disappointment. Only now did she realize what a mistake it had been, ensuring he won every game they played and enrolling him exclusively in activities he could succeed at. He never learned that it was possible to be good without being the best, or that he would improve if he cared about something and worked hard at it.

She thought about calling Walter just to share this lovely revelation: Scrabble is therapeutic! She didn't because she could guess Walter's most likely response. *Wonderful! Let's bring him to the club!* And even after deciding it was a mistake to shield Andrew from real-world competition, she couldn't bear the idea of exposing his fragile new interest to the tidal wave of Walter's enthusiastic support. It would be too much. He'd drown under a wave of Walter's word lists and strategy tips.

One morning as they played their first game of the day, Andrew surprised her: "How does someone get to be the East Coast Scrabble champion?"

She'd told him about beating Jack Trotter and had also explained that no, that didn't make her the East Coast Scrabble champion. "That gets decided at a tournament in the spring in Baltimore. But along the way there's a lot of smaller tournaments. If you play in those, your results are submitted to the National Scrabble Players Association. Then you get a rating that decides which division you're placed in for the regionals." The minute she said this, she remembered his old passion for GPA tracking. "In my experience, ratings don't necessarily reflect a player's true ability. My friend Walter is the best player I know, but he gets nervous and plays terribly at tournaments. Everyone agrees his rating doesn't reflect his true ability."

Surprisingly, Andrew didn't seem interested in this part. "Can you win money at these tournaments?"

"Sometimes, though not too much. The last tournament I played in had a $2,000 first prize, but that's rare. Usually it's more like $500. The Baltimore tournament has a prize of $10,000."

"The reason I ask is I'm considering entering a tournament myself."

Sally's eyebrows went up. "Really?"

"Is that a bad idea?"

This seemed to be a new, more self-aware Andrew. Admitting his uncertainty. "It might be a good idea, but you shouldn't be disappointed if you don't do well at first. That's important to remember. But newcomers are always welcomed." She was careful not to say the word *beginners*. He was forty now—late to be a beginner at anything.

Another week went by and they started playing more. She loved that they'd found a shared passion but sometimes wondered if this had become a version of therapeutic water-treading. Not harmful, of course, but was logging in days without incident the same thing as getting *better*? She honestly couldn't say until one evening when he, decisively and unquestionably, outplayed her in the last ten moves of the game.

The score had been close for most of the game, and in the end, he blocked all her plays to high-scoring squares and opened ones for himself that he must have known she didn't have the letters to use. She barked a triumphant cry of surprise as she added the totals. "You beat me! By 17 points!" She didn't want to overdo her praise, but this measured the surest sign of a return to his old self. If he had her genetic Scrabble skills—good memory, tracking ability—he was, for the first time in months, tapping into his strengths and using them effectively.

She squeezed his hand and bent down to meet his eyes. "You played a defensive game that left me with three bingos I couldn't use. Three! Amazing!"

The next morning, he woke up before Sally for the first time since she'd come home and was waiting for her downstairs with his computer open and coffee made.

"I want to enter the Baltimore tournament," he said.

# CHAPTER 35

# Walter

EVERYTHING ABOUT WALTER'S STUDY SESSIONS WITH TOBY WAS A surprise, starting with the biggest surprise, frankly—that he showed up at all. Walter had told him their practice sessions would have to take place at Golden Grove.

"No problem," Toby said. "I can take the bus."

Which he did. Two buses, in fact.

From the beginning, Walter told him, in no uncertain terms, that he must never lie to him again. "I'll know if you're not telling me the truth. Even about something small that you think doesn't matter. I'll stop all lessons if I catch you in a lie."

Toby nodded. "Okay."

At their first meeting, he asked Toby questions whose answers he could look up afterward: his parents' names, what they did for a living. According to Toby, his father worked for a pharmaceutical company. His mother worked in a lab that did research with mice. "What kind of research?"

"Diabetes."

Later Walter googled their names and found Toby was accurate on every detail, including the spelling of his father's company, Oronyx.

("Is that a Greek derivation?" Walter had asked. "No. I think it's the initials of the people who started the company. Plus an X." Walter was pleasantly surprised: Again, true.) At their second session, he asked Toby more questions about his life outside of Scrabble. Apparently he'd been in a chess and board games club in middle school but the teacher, Mr. Barghini, kicked him out because he thought he'd cheated. "He found extra tiles in his Scrabble sets and figured someone was bringing in tiles from home and using them to cheat. I was by far the best Scrabble player so he thought it had to be me, but it wasn't. I swear. He kicked me out of the club anyway."

This raised an interesting question. Had Toby cheated at the tournament with the twisted logic of a teenager—because he'd already been punished, he might as well commit the crime? "How many tiles did you palm at the Springfield tournament? Tell the truth."

"The ones you saw and the game right before."

"That was the fourth game of the tournament, and in your morning games, you'd drawn every blank possible."

"I got lucky the first two games."

"What did your parents say when you got kicked out of Mr. Barghini's club?"

Toby looked down. "I didn't tell them. They didn't want me to be in the club anyway. They don't like board games."

This surprised Walter. "Do they know how good you are?"

"Not really. They think games are a waste of time and I should have been in the science club, which came in second at the state science fair. I tried it, but that club was full of kids talking about going to medical school. I hate when smart kids do that."

Brag like adults? Suddenly Walter had a memory of pushing Gavin to join a math club in middle school instead of wasting his afternoons playing the guitar, though he refused to take lessons. ("I want to teach myself! Is that so wrong?" Gavin had said. "Yes!" Walter had bellowed. "It's one way to make sure you never get good at anything!" A terrible memory.)

"What do your parents say about your Scrabble playing now?"

"They say it's okay for me to do it if I can get myself to the tournaments, but they can't take a whole day off to drive me."

Walter had an unsettling thought. "Have they ever *seen* you play?"

Toby thought about this. "No. They think it's all kind of embarrassing."

Walter shook his head. What had been his default response to every new passion Gavin picked up? Some combination of doubt and chagrin. *Now you're playing tennis? Suddenly you're a rock-and-roll musician?* Why hadn't he let Gavin enjoy the novelty of exploration? Why had he never indulged him in that way? "Speaking as a parent, I can tell you that it's possible to care a lot and pretend not to because you don't want your child to be hurt."

They dropped the subject and didn't return to it for the rest of the session. At the start of the next one, Walter delivered the short speech. "I believe your parents will be very impressed when they see your unique talent at this game." Was he trying to atone for his own tongue-tied responses at Gavin's art shows? Probably. Did Toby recognize what he was really saying? *Parents make terrible mistakes sometimes. We all have regrets.*

Since his departure, Walter had spoken to Gavin only twice on the phone, and he couldn't say with any certainty how things were going for him. His answers about James were noncommittal. Though being with Toby made him think about Gavin, he hadn't told Gavin about it, nor had he mentioned his son to Toby. In both instances, the silence sprang primarily from a fear of awkwardness. What could he say that wouldn't sound ridiculous? *Remember my inexplicable obsession with Scrabble after your mother died? Well now I'm working with a fifteen-year-old compulsive liar who has asked for my help. I've enjoyed it so far; we're having fun.*

For their third session, Walter printed up some of the word lists he'd made for Sally. "Wow, thanks," Toby said. "These look great." By their fourth session, it was clear that Toby's greatest weakness was strategic planning—managing his rack, building bingos over time by leaving behind a good combination of letters to work with after each play. He also wasn't great at finding early plays that would pay off later in the game. "You need to open up the board."

Sally had taught him this with the octopus arms she created in the opening few turns. Yes, those gave her opponent opportunities, but if she stayed in control, it gave her more. "I used to be a more defensive player," Walter said. "Recently, I've learned the merits of a strong offense, even if it means taking some risks."

Toby didn't seem convinced of this until their fourth game, when Walter had managed the rare feat of playing two bingos in a row—one a triple-triple, scoring 139 points in a single play. "Wow," Toby said. "Maybe I should listen to you."

For Walter, the best discovery of working with Toby was learning that Sally was right—he *was* a good teacher. He could identify certain tendencies and point them out without seeming overly critical the way he'd been with Gavin. Equally important, he could highlight Toby's strengths to bolster a more strategic approach. Toby's tile counting was excellent. Halfway through a game, he'd ask Toby to guess what letters were in the bag and usually he was right. "That's a huge asset," Walter said. "If you need an I or an E, it's a big help to know your odds of getting one."

Once he pointed this out, he saw Toby using it—arranging his letters with spaces for the tiles he hoped to draw. His final lesson for Toby was perhaps the hardest one for a teenager to grasp. "I do think you'll need to step back and look at why you did all that lying before. I wonder if it was because you saw yourself as a prodigy. You want people to think you're an amazing player for a twelve-year-old, but if you're not twelve, are you still amazing? That's the question you've got to answer."

"I'm better than most fifteen-year-olds, right?"

"Yes, you are. But winning in Scrabble isn't about impressing others. It's about knowing yourself and your own abilities. Your greatest opponent will always be yourself. Victory will mean playing better this month than you played last month. That's the ultimate goal, and the only one that matters."

# CHAPTER 36

# Sally

"I'M STARTING TO WONDER IF THIS HAS BEEN THE WORST MONTH IN the history of this family," Andrew said one night, with surprising lightness. "Though I guess Dad dying was bad, too."

Indeed. John's death had been a difficult time, but this was a close second. It started early in the week when Rachel came over after her latest doctor visit with the news that her latest IVF hadn't taken. She sat on the sofa and cried in a way Sally hadn't seen in years. "All of these stupid women who work in my building can get pregnant and I can't," she wept. "They have no *idea*. They *complain* about being pregnant!"

There was very little Sally could do to help except sit beside her and hold her hand. In the three years Rachel and Barry had been trying, Sally had only seen Rachel cry like this after the first round hadn't worked. "What if we go through all this over and over, and it still doesn't work?" Rachel had said.

"That won't happen," Sally said, because she couldn't bear to consider the alternative. What did she know? It turned out Rachel was right: It had happened again and again.

"What does Barry say about trying again?" Sally ventured softly.

"He says we can't afford it."

One of the many cruelties about infertility was the gap between what was medically possible to try and what insurance would cover. "I could help you pay for it. Especially if we sell the house soon."

"Barry says no. He doesn't want to throw good money after bad." Barry had always been a little obsessive about money. He worked as a "financial adviser," but his office was in a strip mall next to a Stop & Shop, which made him a money manager for people who didn't have much money. "It's not a waste if the doctor says it's still worth trying."

A fresh wave of tears was answer enough.

Rachel had met Barry the same month she turned thirty and decided she was too old to keep "dating around," forgetting—apparently—the decade she'd just spent being ruthlessly discerning about every man she went out with. Usually she dated someone for three months before dropping him for reasons Sally could never keep track of. ("You didn't notice that he gets *manicures*?" she'd say. Or: "You probably never took any car trips where he played Moody Blues the *whole* time, I'm guessing.") Privately, Sally wondered if Rachel looked for excuses to dismiss men before they had a chance to break up with her, a defensive maneuver that left her playing musical chairs at her thirtieth birthday with Barry the only candidate left. After a lifetime of being overly critical, she suddenly insisted no one judge any of Barry's quirks—his braided leather bracelets, his gym obsession, his sideline pyramid scheme selling "health supplements" to cover his "fitness costs."

"How many fitness costs can one person have?" Sally had once asked Rachel, after a dinner where he'd spoken at length about new "benching goals."

"A lot," Rachel had said. At that point her eyes burned with an anxious fire and her lips looked chapped from biting back her words.

She seemed as if she wasn't irritated at Barry so much as at herself. After they got engaged, Sally only tried once to express the doubts she suspected Rachel was feeling. "Are you *sure* you and Barry have enough in common?" she had asked.

"Yes," Rachel told her firmly. "I'm marrying Barry because it's time to get married and I made a mistake being too picky in the past. Barry's fine. He's great. Even if he seems a little silly sometimes with his spray tans and his money-making schemes, he's nice to me. He *is*."

*Spray tans?* Sally had wanted to say but held back. And then, the week before the wedding, Rachel came into the kitchen and announced, with eerie calm, that she didn't think she could go through with it. Horrifyingly, Sally's first thought was of the florist with whom she'd just gotten off the phone. "It's too late. We've just taken delivery on the flowers," she said, regretting the words even as she heard herself say them. Why hadn't she stopped everything and *listened* to what her daughter was finally ready to say? Instead, Sally said, "Everyone feels like this the week before their wedding. I know I did and look! Everything turned out okay. You'll be fine." She had a to-do list in her hand that she waved around like it was a contract Rachel had signed. She should have torn it up and said, *Sit down and let's talk about this*.

In the days before the wedding, the only person who had the courage to address the topic again was Andrew, who, having known perfect love once at age seventeen, had no need to revisit the territory with anyone lesser. "The biggest problem with marrying Barry is then you have to be married to Barry," he said. "I don't think Rachel has thought about that enough."

Sally and John never said such cruel things aloud, though they must have both privately wondered what it would be like for Rachel to live with a man who watched a movie and needed any plot points not explicitly spelled out in dialogue explained afterward.

"She wants to get on with her life," Sally said to Andrew at the time. "She feels ready to start a family so she's doing it. There's nothing wrong with that." This was before Andrew's life had come to its mysterious standstill, when they could all still pretend he was fine, too; that they were all fine as long as no one looked too closely or questioned any of it.

In the end, Rachel went through with the wedding and for the last five years had been in a marriage she didn't talk about much except to say that Barry was fine and working (or working out) a lot. Though she still worked the first job she got after college at her old orthodontist's office—she started as the receptionist and now managed the office—she sometimes called herself a "professional volunteer." In the evenings, twice a week, she worked in a food pantry, Saturday mornings at an animal shelter.

In between, she checked on her mother and brother and a few other friends who she "worried about," which presumably meant they were lonelier than she was. Rachel had rightly insisted they deal with the crisis in Andrew's life, but here was the other problem they were collectively ignoring: Rachel came to them first, before she went home and told her husband about the baby they weren't having. Sally drew a deep breath.

"Barry doesn't want to talk about these things," Rachel explained. "He's sad, too, but he doesn't see how talking will help."

"Don't you have to decide this together? Is he open to adopting? Or using a surrogate?"

"He says those things are more expensive than what we're already doing."

Sally gathered her courage. "I hope he understands how much this means to you."

"He knows." Rachel blew her nose.

The worst of the crying jag seemed to have passed, which meant

Andrew felt free to come in and slump down in a chair across from them. For a full minute or so, no one said anything until finally he offered this: "Isn't it great to be home again, Mom, spending quality time with your children?"

Her sad children aside, there were other problems Sally could no longer ignore, mostly to do with the house. She went to clean the bathrooms and discovered mold growing out of the drain in one sink. Even more alarming were the cracked patches of plaster on the living room wall, suggesting water damage in an area where Sally hadn't thought there were any pipes. Last but not least, if she'd known how terrible the wallpaper in the downstairs bathroom would look twenty years on, she never would have spent a week wrestling with rolls and paste to put it up by herself. It now looked as if archaeologists had torn away strips to look for secrets revealed on the flaking plaster beneath. The more she looked around, the more she wondered if Andrew hadn't frightened Karen off so much as the state of their house.

"Do you think we might sell the house to a developer as a teardown and not do any of the work it needs?" she asked Rachel as she was getting ready to leave.

"If we want to get much less than it's worth."

Of course they didn't. With Andrew unemployed, Rachel's marriage in its current state, and what would only be rising medical costs for herself, Sally needed to get as much money as she could from the house. That night, she screwed up her courage, called Karen, and left a message. A few minutes later Karen called back and couldn't have been nicer. Sally started by apologizing for Andrew's behavior.

"It's okay, Mrs. Reynolds. I know he isn't a danger and wasn't threatening me. I was worried he might get hurt if he drove home. Is he…better now?"

"Yes. You did the right thing. It was a wake-up call for all of us. He's getting help and I think we can see the light at the end of the tunnel. The problem is we're still in the tunnel for the time being. We need to sell the house, and we need help figuring out how to prioritize the work that has to be done."

Karen said the first order of business might be addressing the roof.

"The *roof*?" Sally said. "I hadn't even thought of that when we have all these other problems inside—the bathroom mold, the water damage on the walls."

"Guess what's causing those?"

The more they talked, the clearer it was that Karen was not only good at what she did but had taken notes on her visit. The roof would need to be addressed but might not need to be totally replaced. The bathroom wallpaper could be easily removed and painted over. "Some agents might say you should paint the whole house, but I'm not sure that pays off. I'm a big believer in spot touch-ups." Sally exhaled in relief at the feeling of being in the hands of someone who was both capable and pragmatic. "Unfortunately, the biggest issue might be the septic system, I'm afraid. Some buyers can get squeamish about septic systems."

Sally remembered buying the house forty years ago and being surprised when she heard the sewer line didn't reach all the way down to the end of their street. Don't worry, she'd been told; a septic system will take care of the waste with a leach field in the back. Suddenly this felt like every other issue she'd chosen to ignore until it was too late. Once, she thought she'd had a nice life. Now she understood: Her Parkinson's was getting worse, her children were unhappy, and for most of her life, she'd been flushing her toilets into the backyard.

Sally felt a grateful tug in her chest the next morning when she opened the door to see Karen standing on the porch. "I just thought I'd take a quick look at that bathroom mold before you call any remediation companies. Some might say you need to spend thousands of dollars or you'll have mushrooms growing around your toilet. It's possible to treat some mold situations on your own. I have to admit I'm pretty fascinated by molds. I thought about going to grad school to study them."

Sally laughed for the first time in days as she showed Karen to the upstairs bathroom. Here was the smart valedictorian she remembered. Which raised the question: Why was a girl with a gift for science working as a real estate agent? And for that matter, why was a woman who'd gone to Cornell and lived in New York now living at home with her parents? Presumably it was temporary, as all these arrangements were. "Shall I take you up there? Andrew's here but I think he's still asleep."

Thankfully, Karen didn't seem fazed by the mention of his name. Nor was she put off by the state of the bathroom. In fact, she dug a bit of mold out of the drain with her fingernail and held it up to her nose before moving over to the tub and digging out some more. As she worked, Sally wondered how this bathroom managed to seem moldy, damp, and also mysteriously dusty. "I'm sorry I didn't clean before you came. That might be one solution."

Karen held the black scrapings so close to her face. "No, it's good you didn't. This gives me a fuller picture of what's going on. The more information I have, the better."

In the face of Karen's kindness, Sally had an impulse to share all their bad news: *I've got advancing Parkinson's; Rachel is struggling with infertility; Andrew needs a job that doesn't require technical know-how, computer programming, or interpersonal skills. It's been hard.* After spending a whole day together that started with her sobbing on the sofa, Rachel had said, with a sigh, "I better go home and tell Barry the news. Hopefully he'll be so tired from his CrossFit competition he won't care."

Sally had one overwhelming thought: *You hope he doesn't care?*

This morning, she readied herself for the speech she couldn't say before: *Your marriage shouldn't leave you feeling more alone. I should know. Mine did.* Was it terrible for children who assumed their parents' forty-year marriage was fine to hear otherwise? Would it only produce more confusion and uncertainty for them? Impossible to know the answer, but her friendship with Walter had convinced her: *When in doubt, be honest.*

As Karen poked around, a tremor started up in Sally's left hand.

"By the way, I was very sorry to hear about Mr. Reynolds," Karen said. "I didn't know him well, but he always seemed like a nice man."

*It's possible none of us did*, Sally almost said. "Thank you, Karen. He was sick for so long that it… Well, you know what they say."

"No. What do they say?"

"It might have been a blessing. For some people it's better not to live too long with diminished capacities."

"Oh sure." Karen nodded. "I can understand that."

Sally had heard others say this, but she'd never actually said it out loud before. It sounded reasonable enough but would it still, down the line when she was experiencing her own diminished capacity?

"Oh my God, Mom. What's Karen doing here?" Andrew stood in the doorway behind them wearing pajama bottoms and a T-shirt, with pillow-dented hair.

"She's generously volunteered to investigate our mold issue. Use the downstairs bathroom, please."

"Wow. Okay, I guess. Hi, Karen. Thank you."

"Hi, Andrew. You're welcome."

By the time Karen had made a list of economical home remedies they should try before calling the mold experts, Andrew had gotten dressed and combed his hair with enough water to tame it down. He stood in the kitchen with a mug of tea in his hand. "I'd like a minute to apologize to Karen, if that's okay."

Sally stopped and turned to her. "Is that all right with you?"

Karen hesitated for a moment, then nodded. “Yes, of course.”

She was right to hesitate. Andrew had always been terrible at apologies. As a child, any attempts usually became a long-winded rationale for blaming other people. For a minute, Andrew said nothing and stared at Sally.

“Fine then; I’ll leave,” she said, holding up Karen’s list. “I’ll start looking into these.”

Sally left but hovered near the doorway where she could still hear what they said.

“I was very wrong to come over and scare you that way. I suppose I was trying to seem less passive, but I could have picked about a hundred better ways to convey that message.”

Sally’s nervous stomach loosened. Not a bad start. She couldn’t hear what Karen said, but she heard Andrew again: “I honestly don’t know what I’m doing, Kar. I’m forty years old, and I’m trying to start over. I know you might feel the same way, but at least you have a kid and you’ve had a life. I had one job for a while that I liked, and then I got replaced with a new computer program that I couldn’t even operate.”

Sally took another deep breath. He was doing okay. Maybe even better than okay. He sounded surprisingly honest but also well intentioned. Only after she moved into her office and turned on her computer did it occur to her that she was blushing, along with the reason why: He sounded like Walter, and recently, anytime she thought of Walter, she blushed.

“I’m sorry, but should I be worried that you two are playing Scrabble every time I come over?” Rachel asked a few days later, unpacking groceries she’d brought to make dinner. It wasn’t clear what was happening with Barry, only that Rachel was stopping by more often.

The only explanation she'd offered: "You guys are more fun to cook for than Barry, who pulls out his carb counter every time I turn on the stove."

"No," Andrew said. "You should be worried that I've only beaten her twice."

It was true. He'd only repeated his earlier victory once.

"Wait—" Rachel said, pausing for effect. "Is Mom smarter than we've always thought?"

"Not by most standard measurements, but in Scrabble, yes."

"I'm sitting right here, guys. I can hear you."

"In Scrabble, I'd call her freakishly gifted. On simple math problems like determining a tip for someone delivering food, not so much."

Rachel nodded. "Yeah, that sounds about right."

Andrew was getting better, no doubt about it, and it was nice to see Rachel more, even if they hadn't talked about her marriage since the day she'd wept on the sofa. It reassured Sally to hear them banter with each other, but it also felt like a fragile and temporary reprieve.

At one of these dinners, Rachel mentioned an old friend of hers from high school, Charlie Fleishman, who'd come into the orthodontist's office with his nine-year-old son. She'd always liked him, she said, though he'd been too odd to consider dating back then. "He was into Dungeons and Dragons and other role-play games. Tory once saw him at a Renaissance fair wearing a velvet cape with lace-up leather boots and a sword. So no, I couldn't have dated him in high school, obviously."

"What's he like now?"

"He seemed the same but maybe I'm the one who's changed. You could tell he probably had kids so he could keep playing games, but it didn't seem so weird anymore. Mostly he seemed like a nice dad."

Was Andrew thinking the same thing Sally was—that she sounded a little smitten? "Did he remember you?"

"Oh sure—we were pretty good friends in senior year calc. He told me he'd wanted to ask me to prom but he never got the guts up."

Andrew made a face. "What did you *say*?"

"Well, I checked his kid's file to make sure he was divorced and then I said sometimes alumni volunteer at school dances."

"They do?" Andrew looked up, surprised. Was he remembering his old prom, the pinnacle of his high school years—possibly his life?

"Yeah, you'd be surprised how many people we went to school with work there now. Or just hang around and volunteer at special events."

Surely this wasn't a helpful suggestion for a forty-year-old man who'd had some trouble growing up, but Rachel didn't seem to register this.

"So yeah, maybe I was a little flirty with him, I don't know. When I got home, I had two texts from him."

Later, as they cleaned up from dinner and Andrew pulled out the Scrabble box for their fourth game of the day, Rachel asked Sally how she got so good so quickly. "My friend Walter helped. He made all these laminated word lists for me to memorize and loaned me a whole stack of Scrabble strategy books." Remembering all this made her think about Walter, whose texts had slowed down. The last one was a few days ago. *Top secret pruning plans ahead for the Green Thumbs! I can't say anything unless you ask, and then I'll tell you everything.* Though she never responded, his texts always made her laugh.

Andrew seemed to get an idea. "Do you still have all that stuff? If we drove back to Golden Grove, could we pick it up?"

She was so surprised by the suggestion that for a moment she didn't answer.

"Wow, Mom, are you afraid Andrew might win if you share your secrets with him?"

"No, of course not. It's just—" She hesitated. It had been over a month since she'd left Golden Grove, but it felt like much longer. She'd let administration know that she was away for a time, but she'd done a terrible job of answering Walter's texts for reasons she didn't understand entirely or like to think about. Yes, texting was hard for her these days, but she could have managed it. Part of the problem, no doubt, was Andrew's response when he read Walter's texts. Initially it had seemed preposterous to her. Then more messages came—funny ones that made her laugh out loud—and she had to wonder: *Was* Walter flirting?

The more she thought about the two months they'd spent meeting daily for Scrabble practice, the more she had to admit, she had *liked* being the sole focus of Walter's attention, and she loved having him behind her between every game, leaning into her ear, whispering the exact information she needed to beat her next opponent. *This* was how she'd made it to the finals so miraculously, winning her afternoon games against stronger opponents than she'd ever played before: Walter was with her—physically and mentally. For four hours, they joined forces, two against one, and then, when he left her side in the game against Toby because he couldn't bear to watch, the magic evaporated. Now that she'd thought of this, she wondered if this was the reason they'd said so little on the bus ride home and hadn't spoken once since that day—that neither of them could understand or name what had happened between them and were frightened to try.

Rachel didn't read through Walter's texts when Sally asked for her help, but she saw how many there were and how long each one was. "Wait, Mom, he's been texting you this whole time and you've been ghosting him?"

"I don't know what that means."

"Ignoring people when they call or text."

Sally felt a sharp pain in her stomach. Oh, this was awful. She certainly hadn't meant to *ignore* him. "He knows I have a hard time texting. I can manage short ones but I can't do this—" She waved her hand at the phone. "Witty banter. How does *anyone* type all that?"

That's when Rachel showed her the microphone button and demonstrated the voice recorder. "Welcome to the twenty-first century, Mom." She held up the phone for Sally to read. "See? It just typed all that."

It had.

"Technology is here to make your life easier. Especially when your body—" Rachel hesitated. "Gets older."

Rachel was right. Learning this technology and practicing it would help her manage. But this had all been days earlier, so why had she still not reached out to Walter? She'd dictated the start of a few texts:

I want to apologize. I should have answered sooner.

My son hasn't been well and it's taken all my focus.

She deleted both because she didn't want to use Andrew's struggles as an excuse, and besides, it wasn't true. Yes, she was worried about him—about both her children, unfortunately—but worrying didn't occupy fourteen hours a day. She could have written Walter. Or called him. She hadn't because the prospect of it made her too nervous. Now Andrew was suggesting a visit to Golden Grove, where she might run into Walter, which made her even more anxious. Her hands, as if trying to communicate what she couldn't say, started to shake. "I have no problem sharing my study materials. It's a good idea. I'm just not sure about driving right now." She held out her hand. "Look at this."

When to stop driving was a debatable issue for all Parkinson's patients. One doctor assured her that she should be fine for a few years, so she hadn't considered giving it up—until now, apparently, when her heart was beating so hard, she needed an excuse.

"I'll drive if you want," Rachel offered. "But if I'm going, you have to come too, Andrew. We'll get out of the house! It'll be good for us."

Soon Rachel had talked them all into making a day of it, stopping at a farmers market and also the Apple store because Rachel's phone needed a new battery. A day-long adventure and somewhere in the middle of it, Sally might see Walter.

She probably wouldn't, she reminded herself, sitting on a bench at the farmers' market, as she watched Rachel lean over the displays, picking up squashes and bouquets of fall mums. Walter didn't leave his apartment much, especially during the day. Then she thought of this new incarnation described in his texts—Walter, the upbeat club joiner, the lobby raconteur. She checked her phone: In the last week, he hadn't texted her at all, but before that every message was a dining room anecdote or about a new club he'd joined in her absence.

He was obviously moving on from Scrabble and having a fine time without her. Undoubtedly, others were seeing that Walter was a charming man with a good heart. If they hadn't recognized it before because he was too shy or self-conscious, those days were over. She could easily imagine Walter spending his after-dinner evenings in the library playing Bananagrams with any number of Golden Grove women, most of whom had been alone long enough to recognize an opportunity and not run from it as she had.

"You okay, Mom?" Andrew asked, sitting down beside her with a sigh.

"Of course. Just saving my energy. This might be a long day."

"I don't think I'm as interested in farmers' markets as Rachel."

"Few of us are." She watched Rachel move between stalls, one arm laden with purchases. *She'll make a wonderful mother someday,*

Sally thought, and then, as if reading her mind, Andrew sighed again. "Sometimes I feel like I have two mothers. No offense."

She smiled. "No, I know what you mean. I hope she gets to be a real mother, too."

"Yeah." Andrew nodded. "Course that would probably make Barry a dad, right? That's a little harder to imagine."

Sally smiled. She appreciated that Andrew was making jokes again, but sadly, there might be too much truth in this one.

The Apple store was located at the center of a busy mall Sally hadn't visited in years. A few minutes after walking inside, she remembered why: the neon lighting, the vacant-eyed shoppers. She and Andrew made their way to another bench outside the Apple store and Andrew looked around. "Maybe I should apply for a job at Spencer's," he said, looking at the store that specialized in "novelty gifts" ranging from tasteless to breath-catchingly obscene. When they were younger, Sally didn't allow her children to go in. "Then I could sell fart cushions and plastic dog poop for a living."

Sally shook her head. Though about a quarter of the storefronts looked empty now, Spencer's had mysteriously survived. "How do they even make money? Who shops in there?" Just as she said this, a tired-looking mother pushing a baby in a stroller emerged with a large Spencer's shopping bag dangling from the handle.

"Lots of people, I guess," Andrew said.

"Do you need to buy anything? I can sit here by myself if you want to look around."

"No," he sighed. "Malls aren't great if you hate shoes, clothes, and computers. I'm bad at all those things."

"That's not true, Andrew. You shouldn't make such sweeping generalizations. You're fine with computers. It's only that—" She couldn't bring herself to finish the sentence: *It's only that you got replaced by one*.

Instead of letting her finish, Andrew held up a hand. "That's why Scrabble feels important to me right now."

"I can certainly understand that." She smiled. Suddenly she wondered if they were all outcasts looking for a purpose—the old, the infirm, the mentally ill. Still here, but unsteady and moving through a world that averted its eyes.

"I know I'm not an accomplished player yet, but I think I could be." He turned and looked at her with an expression she hadn't seen in a long time. "If I really work at this, I think I could get good. I'm excited. It's a nice feeling."

She felt cheered. He'd been going to therapy once a week, but she'd been careful not to ask him what they discussed or mention Karen. Since her mold-inspecting visit, Karen had been thorough in her follow-up, sending Sally links to "interesting articles about mold" and strategies to remediate the problem. It was so kind that Sally almost invited Karen back over to thank her, but she held back, unsure of where things stood with Andrew. Sally hoped they could be friends. He needed to succeed at being a friend before he could hope for more. Even as she thought this, though, she understood: She did too.

She needed to call Walter and explain what had happened and why she disappeared a month ago. The problem was, she didn't know what she'd say. *The prospect of seeing you again makes me nervous, and I'm not sure why*?

Walking into the sunny lobby at Golden Grove lifted Sally's spirits. Nothing had changed: The same movie-night notices sat on the grand piano; the same lobby-watching denizens sat along the wall; the same cheerful faces worked busily behind the front desk. She had no idea how much she'd missed it all until a few people looked up and smiled.

"Sally! What a nice surprise! Welcome home!" Ralph, the friendly activities director, beamed. "And you've got both your children with you. Does this mean you're back to stay?"

"Not today," Sally said cheerfully. "We're picking up a few things from my apartment, but hopefully I'll be back soon!"

"Wonderful," Ralph said and then added with a mysterious smile, "You should pop into the library and see what Walter is up to. He's found a way to fill his time in your absence. I think you'll be tickled."

The smile that had been real a moment earlier froze on Sally's face. She wasn't ready to see Walter; she hadn't planned what to say, and now Ralph would tell him she'd visited. She straightened and turned to the library, drawing a deep breath to ready herself for what she might see: Walter playing Scrabble with another woman; Walter playing some other game with *several* women, all laughing at his jokes. Her mind spun in a million directions at once. Then she got to the library and saw he wasn't playing another woman.

He was playing *Toby Weir*.

# CHAPTER 37

# Walter

DID HIS HEART STOP, SEEING SALLY AGAIN AFTER ALL THIS TIME? FOR A moment he thought it had. He felt dizzy standing up, which happened more these days, even without a million emotions flooding his brain at once. "Sally, it's so good to see you," he whispered. He couldn't stop smiling. "What are you doing here?"

*She's back*, he thought, but then why were these people here with her? They must be her children, which felt ominous.

"We came to pick up some things from my apartment."

He panicked. Were they moving her out? If these were her children, they'd know that he'd pushed her too hard at the last tournament, and they'd want to get her away from him.

She leaned closer. "What's *he* doing here, Walter?" She pointed to Toby.

He hadn't told her about coaching Toby, hadn't told her anything, really. "I can explain," he whispered as she moved away from him.

"No need to explain," she said, stepping back toward the door.

Oh, this was terrible! For weeks, he'd imagined seeing her again, and now here she was, seeing only betrayal in this scene: him playing the boy who'd ended her Scrabble career.

He followed her to the elevator. "He asked me to coach him because he was so impressed with your playing, and you'd told him what a good teacher I was."

As the elevator opened she turned around. "Really, Walter, you don't need to explain."

## CHAPTER 38

# Sally

"ARE YOU *OKAY*, MOM?" RACHEL SAID WHEN THEY WERE SAFE IN SALLY'S apartment, setting a glass of water in front of her.

Both of Sally's hands were in full-blown tremor, forcing her to use two hands like a toddler to drink. "Yes. I'm fine. Let me just collect myself."

"So *that* was Walter," Andrew said, sitting down across from her. "That was weird, right? It's not just my imagination?"

"That was definitely weird," Rachel said. "But Mom doesn't need to hear our judgment. She needs to sit and catch her breath while we look around for your Scrabble stuff."

Sally set the glass on the table. "It's all in the bedroom, next to the desk."

They disappeared and she sat back, wishing she could forget the scene she just ran away from. Why had she let Andrew plant foolish ideas about Walter being enamored with her? Just before the elevator doors closed, Walter had said, "Please, Sal, don't be angry—"

Once she'd started walking toward the elevator, she couldn't stop. Sometimes her legs froze and sometimes they kept moving of their own accord. "I'm *not* angry," she'd snapped.

Now she sat on the sofa and tried to decide. She *was* angry, of course, but was she angry at him or at herself? It was just overwhelming to see him sitting across from Toby, of all people. She'd wanted to tell him about her children, about the challenges they were both facing, to speak honestly the way they had weeks earlier when they were practicing daily, and suddenly the room felt too crowded to say *anything at all.*

She'd seen the joy and relief on his face when he first saw her, but did he understand that she felt the same way? She knew that soon enough Parkinson's would rob her of facial expressions, but were they already gone? Andrew emerged from her bedroom, holding the stack of books Walter had lent her. "So we found ten Scrabble books, two tote bags full of laminated word lists with six-letter stems, and a bunch of flash cards attached to metal rings."

*Oh, Walter*, she thought. She could hardly bear to think about all the effort he'd put into her studies. She'd known this and hadn't let herself *see* it. The time it represented. The generosity. Andrew left the books on the sofa next to her and got the tote bags. "It's great stuff, Mom. I can't believe how much work you did."

"It was all Walter." She shook her head. "I don't know if I ever thanked him enough for all the work he did for me…" Her voice sounded whispery, like a volume button somewhere had been turned down.

Rachel, back in the room now, could see what Andrew was missing. She sat down and took Sally's hand. "He seems like a nice man, Mom. Yeah, that was strange back there, but you'll see him again, and you'll say, 'Sorry I was so weird in the library that day.'"

"He's a good man," she said, feeling tears gather behind her eyes.

"Of course he is," Rachel said and patted her mother's hand.

Sally stayed quiet for most of the ride home while Andrew sat in the back seat, sifting through her tote bags and whistling every few minutes. "This is pretty genius stuff, I have to say…"

At home, Rachel divided her farmers market haul. "I should go. I promised Barry I'd be home for dinner." Did this mean she and Barry were okay? Were they moving ahead toward adoption? Sally had the urge to ask these questions so Rachel would stick around and Sally wouldn't have to think about Walter. Instead Rachel checked her phone and gasped at the time. "Shoot. I'm already late. You should try roasting these brussels sprouts, Mom. They're a thousand times better that way. Bye, you guys! Fun day!"

How did Rachel, in the span of a week, go from sobbing on the sofa to cheerfully passing along brussels sprout tips? Next to her, Sally felt like a slow-moving ocean liner, unable to make a turn in any direction that didn't require a day's preparation. That evening, over a quiet dinner (of roasted sprouts—delicious!), Andrew said, "It's smart the way Walter organized the word stems. He must be a pretty good player himself. Did he do well at tournaments?"

"No—that was his problem. He got nervous and sabotaged his own games, or that's what he always said. I never saw it myself. At our last tournament he dropped out to help me." Just saying this made her breath catch.

After dinner, she went into John's office and sat with her phone in her hand. She needed to call Walter and apologize. The problem was determining what she was most sorry about: Disappearing in the first place? Not answering his texts? Saying so little when she saw him just now? As she mulled this over, her phone vibrated. It was him. "Oh, Walter," she said in this new whispery voice that appeared whenever she felt emotional.

"I'm sorry about today, Sally. I wasn't expecting to see you. It was very awkward."

"No, I'm sorry. I'm the one who needs to apologize to you."

"Fine, but why don't you let me start by explaining why I was playing with Toby." He told her about Toby's sudden appearance at

Golden Grove two weeks ago, along with his request. "The important thing is: He wanted me to coach him because he was so impressed with *you*. He couldn't believe you'd been playing for less than six months. Of course, I hesitated at first, but the more I talked to him, the more he seemed like a decent kid. Which I think he is. At least based on our time together so far, which admittedly has only been a few weeks.

"I have to tell you, Sally, after that last tournament, I wanted to quit Scrabble completely. I tried. I joined your groups and I threw myself into them and it worked to some extent, but I missed Scrabble. I missed you, too, of course, but I also missed Scrabble. So when he appeared out of the blue, asking for a coach, I suppose I was embarrassingly receptive to the idea. I thought of you—of how I would explain such a decision that has more than a whiff of desperate, old-man loneliness to it—but here's the truth: I never figured out what excuse I'd use or how I'd explain it, and I still haven't. Except to say that I missed you and he was the last person you played and maybe playing with him has reminded me of our own lovely times." He paused. "At any rate, I hope your visit means you might be coming back for good soon."

What a relief it was to hear him say all this. To talk again in the same way they used to, playing their games. "I have something to tell you, too." She waited, gathering her breath. "I've been playing Scrabble with my son, Andrew. He likes the game and he wants to enter a tournament. We came back to Golden Grove to pick up the study materials you made for me." After saying this, she wasn't sure why she'd been so reluctant to tell him.

"This is wonderful news! If he's your son, he must be good. I can't wait to play him."

Now she remembered. "This was why I didn't want to tell you. Not that it isn't a nice idea, but Andrew—" She stopped speaking again. Finally she said, "Andrew's illness is depression. He lost a job he really enjoyed over a year ago and he's had a hard time ever since. I did a terrible job of seeing what was going on. I should never have left him to live in our old house alone without making sure he had some supports in place.

"I've spent the last month seeing some important ways that I failed as a mother. My children grew up with a clinically depressed father, but I never talked about it. I thought the best strategy was pretending things were fine and hoping they'd believe it." Even she was surprised at how emotional she sounded, as if she was close to tears and then suddenly she *was* in tears. Good heavens. If Walter had liked her at some point, he was surely changing his mind now. "I'm sorry," she said. "I shouldn't go on like this. It's hard for me to be here and feel so powerless."

"I've been thinking about this subject a lot," Walter said. "I've decided the hardest thing about being a parent is realizing that when your children are adults, there isn't much we can do to ensure their happiness. They have their own lives."

Sally took a deep breath. "I don't know about that. If I could go back in time, I'd do some things differently."

"Like what?"

It wasn't hard to list her regrets. "I wish I'd let Andrew fail more often and practice coming back from disappointment. I wish I'd encouraged him to make more friends when he was younger. He was an odd kid and I always worried about what other children might say. I knew how mean they *could* be, so I always assumed they *would* be. It turns out being overly protective doesn't protect them the way you think it will."

"I tried to stop Gavin every time he threw himself into some new hobby. I complained about the expense, but really I was scared that I'd have to watch him fail again," Walter said. They sat in silence as Sally felt her chest loosen. Walter kept going: "Lately, I've been thinking they should only let people in their seventies be parents. Before that, you're too young. You have no idea what you're doing."

She laughed even as she wiped tears with her sleeve. They talked for another half hour. She told him more about Andrew—how academically competitive he'd once been, racking up awards and scholarships that didn't amount to much after he graduated from college. She told him about asking the doctor about Asperger's.

"Have you talked to Andrew about it?"

"I'm trying to work up the courage. I don't know if it would be helpful or infuriating."

"It might be both. All I can say is, he might surprise you. Being with Gavin again surprised me. I could see how he'd changed. Maybe I have, too."

"Yes," Sally said. "I'm seeing that in little things, but it's hard to tell. Antidepressants take a long time to work. He has good days and bad. Scrabble has been good for him, though. It's definitely improved his focus and concentration."

"He should sign up for a tournament, then."

This was what she feared: Walter embracing Andrew's entrance into this world without understanding how fragile he was. "He wants to but I'm not sure he's ready."

"Doing poorly at a tournament won't kill anyone. I should know."

She lowered her voice. "He might spend a day losing to high school students. It's hard not to worry how that would affect his self-esteem." In the privacy of the bubble they'd established since she moved home, Andrew *was* doing better, but how long would that hold up if he tested the waters of his new passion and lost to people who were either much older than him or—worse—much younger?

"Didn't you just say you regretted being overprotective?"

"I suppose I did."

"I've got another idea. Why don't you bring him to the VFW

club? It'll give him practice playing other people. I haven't been back there since the tournament, but I assume no high schoolers will be there unless something has changed."

This was the problem, she feared. There were so many unknowns.

# CHAPTER 39

# Walter

WALTER WAS RELIEVED BY THE TIME HE HUNG UP THE PHONE. SALLY didn't hate him! She was focused on her child, which he could certainly appreciate. Only later, as he lay in bed, did he wonder if he'd made some tactical mistakes on their call. Had he really said he missed her *two* times or was it *three*? Did she say anything even remotely similar back to him? She wanted to be friends—he felt that now; he believed it. But what if she wanted nothing more? What if she considered her husband, depressed as he might have been, the sole love of her life?

The fear festered in his mind for the rest of the week as he went about his days, filled with what now felt like meaningless activities and empty conversations. Instead of making new friends as he'd been trying to do over the past month, he lived for the short texts he got from Sally as they planned their outing. I'm taking an Uber. Would you like me to pick you both up? he offered in a text.

No thank you, she wrote back. I'm still driving, remember? We'll meet you there.

Don't be overly solicitous, he reminded himself when Wednesday evening finally arrived. Don't rush in too quickly to help. Still, he couldn't help himself. He arrived fifteen minutes early and paced in the parking lot until her car pulled in. "You're here!" he said too loudly, holding up a hand as if she might not see the only other person in the parking lot.

"Of course we are, Walter. We told you we'd come."

In the short walk to the door it was easy for Walter to see how Sally had changed. She still looked beautiful, of course, but she was moving slower than she did a month ago, walking with a stoop, bending forward, as if she needed to keep an eye on her feet. He wondered if the tournament had done this to her—if she still hadn't recovered from the toll that day had taken.

Thankfully, everyone in the club crowded around when they walked in. They all knew about Sally making the finals, but some of the questions were silly. "Is Winston Pryor as handsome as they say?" Some were specific enough to stymie Sally. "How did you counter his three-prong offense?" Walter could see the confusion on her face. She'd played Scrabble more than she'd analyzed it, unlike the rest of them.

"Why don't we give Sally a break and start our meeting," Peter announced over his microphone, which seemed especially unnecessary, as the crowd was small—only ten people, including the three of them.

"Fine, Peter," Dorothy said. "But I'm putting in a request to play Sally."

"Oh, me too!" Ione chirped, before Sally could hold up her hand.

"Thank you, ladies, but I'm not playing tonight. I'm here with my son, Andrew." She turned her hand to the corner where Andrew stood, waving sheepishly. "He's new to the game but he's eager to learn."

Walter didn't understand. He tried to catch her eye. *Just because Andrew wants to play doesn't mean you can't.* She looked at him and quickly turned away, as if she could see what he was thinking and didn't want to discuss it.

Did she regret not playing when Dorothy started her game against Andrew by telling him what a wonderful player his mother was? "What was she particularly good at?" Andrew asked, forgetting, perhaps, that Sally was sitting behind him, listening.

"Boldness!" Dorothy said without thinking about it. "She never held back! If she saw a long, risky move that opened up a triple-word lane, she'd put it down anyway! She taught us all something about playing with courage."

Was Dorothy trying to tell her the same thing Walter wanted to say—*You're a fearless player! Don't be afraid now!* After two games, Walter sat down on the bench where Sally had spent most of the evening. "I have to say, Sal, I don't understand why you aren't playing."

She shook her head. "Don't make too much of it, Walter. I'm just not in the mood tonight. Don't worry; I'm still playing at home with Andrew."

He *was* worried. How could he not be? "I'm concerned that you don't want to play in public because of what happened at the tournament. That business with the dropped tiles."

She leaned closer and whispered, "Maybe you're right. I don't love the idea of my shaking hands ruining games. Is that so crazy?"

"That happened *once*. At the end of a tournament when you were exhausted."

"It'll happen again. It turns out my body isn't something I can control well these days."

"So maybe that limits how many tournaments you enter, but this is different. These are friends. They love you. They won't mind if a tile or two go on the floor."

"I'll mind."

Oh, it broke his heart to think that pushing her as hard as he did two months ago had left her too tentative now to take any risks at all. For a while they sat in silence. Finally, he said, "You know, Andrew might be a decent player. He's making beginner's mistakes, sure, but I do see some of your talent. It'll be interesting to see how he progresses in a few years—"

"Walter—"

"What?"

"Andrew wants to go to Baltimore. He wants to enter the Nationals in a month."

"Oh my." Walter wasn't sure what to say. Technically, the Nationals had an open division for novice players, but it was a long way to travel, expensive to enter, and an ordeal for someone with his level of experience. Walter had made that mistake. The first time he went, he'd only been playing for about eight months. At first, he loved being there, surrounded by people wearing Scrabble paraphernalia and carrying their "lucky racks" from one game to the next. He'd started strong, winning his first two games and narrowly losing a third.

Then he overheard an older man say he had his eye on him, that "next year you'll be playing in a higher division," a kind and relatively innocuous remark that shifted some delicate balance in Walter's brain. Aware that others might be watching him, he became self-conscious. He started missing plays and then, furious with himself, desperately playing phonies that were challenged off the board in seconds. After four days, he ended the tournament with six wins and twenty-five losses, a humiliating final tally after such a promising start. The next year he returned, still playing in the lowest D division, hoping to erase the memory of last year's annihilation, only to repeat a nearly identical record with seven wins and twenty-four losses, one victory thanks to a forfeit by a player who got a nosebleed at the start of their game.

"It can be quite a pressure cooker. I've had mixed experiences myself." Silly to say "mixed" when he had virtually no good memories of playing at Nationals.

Instead of asking about those, Sally surprised him. "Are you going this year?"

He was actually, but how did she guess this? "Yes, but I won't play. I'm going because Toby's parents can't make it, and he needs a chaperone."

He studied her face. Did she think he was a fool for agreeing to spend a weekend helping Toby after all his lies? Probably. Recently, he'd developed a new theory, though. Toby had very few friends at his school and none from his elementary days. "I get to know them better and they decide they don't like me," he said once. Walter hadn't been sure how to respond. "Well, the more I get to know you, the more I like you," he offered. "Plus I'm learning things, too, from watching you play."

Toby sat up straighter. "Really?" He smiled in a way Walter hadn't seen before. On his very next play, he triple-lettered a Z twice and got 88 points. "See?" Walter said. "You're pretty amazing." The whole episode made him wonder about the toll insecurity had taken on Toby. On all of them perhaps. He'd been a distant, critical father to Gavin because he'd had no role model and had been so unsure of his parenting ability. Mothering had come so naturally to Elyse, and he'd been so clumsy.

Years spent in fear of dropping the baby morphed into other fears—ways he might unwittingly harm or disappoint Gavin. Eventually that all became a simmering mix of anger and resentment. He saw the truth now: Confidence made people kinder and more generous. But how could you help people build their confidence? He said yes to the Nationals weekend because he wanted Toby to know that he meant it when he said he liked him.

"Why aren't Toby's parents taking him?" Sally asked. Stillness was hard for her now. Her head bobbed around. There was a new tic in her chin he hadn't seen before. He studied her face and wondered if she even realized these things were happening.

"They're both scientists. I'm told they have an important conference that weekend."

She nodded and sat back against the wall so their shoulders touched again. After a minute or so, she said, "Is it hard being old enough to watch other parents make the same mistakes you did without saying anything?"

"Very." He smiled.

"I don't think Andrew should go down there alone," Sally said. "I realize he's an adult, but the whole thing makes me nervous. He doesn't know what he's getting into."

Was this a reference to her own hard experience at the last tournament? "We could all go down together. Take the train and make a trip of it." She turned and stared at him. Could she see through his ruse—that he was proposing this in order to spend time with her again?

"Do you really mean it, or are you just being nice because you think this might be a disaster for Andrew?"

"I can't predict what will happen. It might be a disaster for either one of them. But Baltimore is very nice this time of the year. We can visit the National Aquarium."

She kept looking at him.

"What? It's an excellent aquarium."

## CHAPTER 40

# Sally

WALTER WAS RIGHT OF COURSE: SALLY *WAS* AFRAID FOR ANDREW. A week ago, he'd asked her what she thought of him entering, and then he admitted he already had. "I knew you'd probably tell me not to do it," he said. "Or else you'd tell me to wait a year and see if I was still interested. But I don't want to do that. I want to test myself now."

The competition was six weeks away, which meant Andrew had time to throw himself into Scrabble study with an intensity she hadn't seen since his school days. He made a schedule that included four to five hours studying Walter's word lists, leaving three to four hours a day to play games with her or online. Even when Karen came over to work on the mold issue, he didn't stop. Instead, he called out from his bedroom. "Thank you for thinking about our mold problems more than we want to, Flea!"

"You're welcome, Glub! You don't know the fun you're missing!"

Strangely, Karen did seem to be having fun, mixing her biodegradable, nontoxic mold solutions to pour down the drain, then afterward dancing to music in her earbuds as she pointed a hair dryer at the problematic pipes. Sally wondered if this was part of a new strategy on Andrew's part—pretending not to care when Karen was in the house—or if he was really so compelled by his Scrabble study. "Maybe a little of both," he said when she asked him.

Without saying too much about it, Rachel started coming over more and sleeping in her old bedroom on nights when she made them dinner after work. "It's just easier," she said. Her work was ten minutes from the house; the condo she'd bought with Barry was a thirty-minute drive. Once, Sally asked if Barry minded her being away from home so much and she shrugged. "I don't think he notices. If he does, he hasn't said anything."

Sally wondered if her children had become adults who erected emotional barricades because they'd grown up with parents who lived at a distance from each other. Was she still making that choice given how many topics she couldn't find a way to ask her children about? The state of Rachel's marriage. Andrew's job prospects. After a few deflections about where he was looking for work, she'd stopped asking. Yes, she was happy that he'd found a sense of purpose in Scrabble study, but surely he knew he couldn't make a living at it. So what did he want to do? Maybe she didn't ask because she was afraid he'd be honest: *I can't think of any job I want to do.* And what if Rachel was honest about her husband? *Yeah, I'm not sure I want to be married anymore.*

Though she couldn't discuss these things with her children, she found it easy to talk about them with Walter when he called, which he did most evenings after dinner now. At first, Sally was surprised. Without a Scrabble board between them, she might have assumed they'd run out of conversation, but they hadn't. He told her stories about his childhood. His difficult father who openly had affairs. His mother who never left him but probably should have. "She didn't think she had any choice. She told me that once, toward the end."

Sally thought about Walter's wife, Elyse, taking the option his mother hadn't. About Walter understanding, subconsciously perhaps, *sometimes women need to figure out who they are without a man.* In return, she told him stories about her children. How Rachel had once been a "mother duck" for Halloween, which meant tying a bonnet on her head and carrying a basket of little rubber ducks they'd found at a dollar store. "Everyone thought she was either Mother Goose or the Easter Bunny." Walter always laughed and then usually said something sentimental: "She sounds wonderful. Just like you."

Often, Walter's stories were about his awkwardness as a father. "Gavin liked ball games and I was terrible at all of them. To practice his pitching, he had to teach me how to hit a ball."

Sally laughed. "Did you really not know how?"

"I had two older sisters. I could cut out dresses for paper dolls better than I could play sports. I was a whiz with scissors, but as you'd guess, that didn't get me very far with the ladies."

"Didn't having sisters help?"

"The closest one was eight years older, so no. By the time I got to high school, they were married with children and living in different states."

"Why didn't they want to live near your parents?"

"Our father wasn't easy to be around." Walter hesitated. "He had a lot of anger and could be unpredictable. My sisters didn't want their children exposed to that, so yes, they moved far away, and I was the only one around to care for him at the end."

"How old were you?"

"Still in college. It wasn't quite as bad as it sounds. He was nicer at the end of his life. My sisters didn't see that, but I did. His dementia didn't make him cruel the way it can; it made him more childlike, I suppose. The great irony was that I wasn't scared of childish behavior until I had my own child and then it terrified me. Four-year-old Gavin would have a meltdown, and I could hardly breathe. My hands would start shaking—"

He paused as they both registered the mention of shaking hands. Then he went on: "Sometimes I worry that I was a bad father out of fear of becoming my own bad father."

They both sat for a bit, their phones held up to their ears in silence.

"I should probably go," Sally finally said. "I hear Andrew downstairs rattling around. Thank you for telling me all this. It helps more than you know."

They didn't speak quite so openly when they saw each other in person, which they now did once a week at the VFW, where she continued to decline all invitations to play. Walter would usually play one game and then come over to sit with her. In person, they were more tentative with each other. More aware of their bodies, their eye contact, what they might smell like. Thanks to Parkinson's, Sally had lost her sense of smell, which didn't bother her much until Walter sat close to her on a bench and then she wondered, *What if I smell terrible and don't realize it?* On these evenings, they talked mostly about Scrabble and avoided the personal topics they spoke of on the phone. Toby had started coming to club meetings, so they could each watch their protégé play and analyze their mistakes.

"Andrew needs to play more aggressively," she'd say, shaking her head.

Walter would sigh. "Toby needed to stop playing phonies. He's beginning to remind me of me, unfortunately."

As the Baltimore trip drew closer, their phone conversations got shorter. They covered the logistics of the train they would take, the hotel rooms they'd booked, and then they'd say, "Well, I guess that's it." Were they both getting nervous?

Sally knew she was. For a host of reasons, starting with the fact that she still hadn't told Walter her biggest news: She and Andrew had a good talk and decided it would be fine for her to move back to Golden Grove after the tournament. For a month now, Walter had been lamenting her absence on the phone. If he wasn't telling her how much he missed her, he was exaggerating how much everyone else did, too. "I don't know if the Wednesday Walkers even meet anymore without you. They tried a few times, and it just wasn't fun." She knew this wasn't true. She read *Golden Grove News and Notes*; she saw their meetings listed every week.

It was like he'd adopted a new persona in the two months she'd been away—adoring fan, willing to say any sentimental thing at all. It was sweet, of course, but that didn't make it *real*. She wondered what he would do if she said the same things to him. More importantly, what would he do when the reality of her presence shattered the fantasy he'd build up around her? Which would happen soon enough. She could feel the changes in her body taking place faster than she ever expected. In the morning her legs were heavy and stiff, making it harder to get out of bed. Her gait was also changing, which she realized thanks to Andrew's inability to censor his observations. "Is that really how you're walking now, Mom? Like an old man shuffling?"

Yes, this was how she was walking now, thank you very much, because walking had gotten *hard*. It required concentration to execute each component: lift foot, move it, place foot down again. Turning was another challenge, one she sometimes couldn't manage without swaying precariously. In the last month, she'd fallen twice, both times on the soft carpeting of her bedroom with no witnesses so she didn't have to worry about Rachel insisting she start using a walker. She hadn't mentioned any of this to Walter.

"Are you sure you're going to be okay with all this traveling?"

Rachel asked. They were sitting in the car at seven in the morning, waiting for Andrew so she could drive them to the train station. "I've told Andrew three times that he can't get so caught up in his games that he forgets to check on you."

"I'll bet he took the repetition of those reminders well."

"The third time he said he would have to kill me if I mentioned it again."

"Very nice."

Rachel smiled. "In a way it was. He's better, Mom. I can tell. I mean, let's see what happens if he bombs out at the tournament, but I think he'll be okay. When you go back to Golden Grove, we'll keep an eye on him. Karen and I."

"Have you talked to her?" Sally asked, surprised.

"Once. She said it was nice to see Andrew and she was happy to be friends again. It's good that you had her come over and gave him a chance to apologize."

Sally felt grateful for this reassurance. "I feel like I've made so many mistakes. There's so much I never talked about when you were kids." She let this hang for a moment. "Did you know the reason Karen broke up with Andrew in college was that he never said he loved her?"

"He *didn't*?" Rachel's eyes widened with surprise and then she thought about it. "But wasn't it obvious?"

"I thought so but maybe if you're young, you need to hear it." Again, she went quiet. "Not only if you're young, I suppose. I worry that your father and I left too much unsaid. We never talked about the reason we did so many things without him. That his depression made him withdraw. Would it have helped if we'd been more open?" She wanted to have this conversation with Andrew. Saying it to Rachel was a kind of rehearsal. Still, her heart hammered in her chest.

"God, Mom. I don't know. I guess."

"Do you think it's left you both afraid of—" She hesitated. "Having those conversations with the people you're closest to?"

"Well, we both know Andrew isn't great on that front, so I guess you're asking about me now, right?"

"I just wish I'd been less afraid. Those talks are necessary." Yes, she was asking about her marriage to Barry.

At that moment, Andrew opened the back door of the car and threw in the two tote bags of study materials. "I've got a lot of studying I want to do. Hopefully no one is expecting me to talk on this car ride," he announced.

"We'd love it if you didn't," Rachel said.

And that was that.

"This is working out just as I hoped," Walter said, grinning, as he claimed the train seat beside her. Across the aisle, Toby and Andrew had started a game on a magnetic travel Scrabble set. They'd played each other a few times at the VFW club and, though Andrew had never won, Sally had been pleasantly surprised. He'd been a gracious loser, and ever since, they seemed to have established a quiet companionship. With a twenty-five-year-age difference between them, there was no need to pretend they had more in common than they did; Scrabble was enough. Sally looked over and saw them both bent over Toby's tiny board, pinching little magnetized letters.

"How is this 'just as you hoped,' Walter?"

"I get you all to myself for the next six hours." He beamed. "Does that scare you?"

She felt herself squirm. *A little*, she thought. And then she thought, *Just say it: Guess what? I'm moving back to Golden Grove next week.* Maybe she still didn't believe it herself, still wasn't sure if Andrew was ready. "Of course it doesn't scare me," Sally said now.

Though of course, it did.

"And five whole days in a hotel together. I can't wait! We'll explore the city!" Walter's face was red. She wondered if the prospect of being together made him as nervous as it made her.

She was already worried about walking any distance. She had her cane folded up in her suitcase, but what was he imagining for nighttime activities if they had no car? Oh, it was silly, all this anxious uncertainty. They didn't need to feel so self-conscious. She should just say: *I have some good news; I'm moving back home.* Maybe she didn't because they were sitting so close. Their elbows touched, then didn't touch, then touched again on the armrest between them.

He'd filled their phone conversations with talk about missing her. What would they say if he didn't have their separation to lament? This was her fear: Living far away, she'd grown a magical patina. When she returned and they were only an elevator ride apart, would they pass in the hallway or meet at the mailboxes and both feel embarrassed? Him for getting so sentimental and her for loving it so much?

"I'd like to say one thing before we arrive," Walter announced after about an hour of small talk and magazine reading.

*Now*, she thought. *I can tell him I'm moving back now.* "Okay."

"I want to say that I've been watching Andrew play for a while, and I think he has a lot of potential. I also admire the amount of studying he's done. He's the only person I've seen learn the game as quickly as you did."

She certainly hadn't expected this. "Thank you, Walter. That means a lot."

"After this tournament, I'm happy to offer my services as a coach if he's interested."

This *was* a surprise. "What about Toby?"

"There's a limit to what I can offer Toby. He needed life lessons more than Scrabble coaching, and I feel like I've given him all I have to offer. We've agreed to scale back on our coaching sessions after this tournament."

She relaxed a little more after this speech. Maybe he wasn't nervous the way she was. Maybe he really was focused mostly on Scrabble.

# CHAPTER 41

# Walter

HE MEANT WHAT HE'D SAID ABOUT ANDREW—HE WAS EVERY BIT AS promising a player as his mother, with slightly different strengths. Sally's spatial ability was unmatched by any player he knew. She could utilize two tiles on the board and weave a nine-letter bingo like a golden thread through other words. Andrew's gifts were more mathematical. As far as Walter could tell, he was a stellar tile-counter, with an internal odds calculator that made him able to predict what letter he might draw so he could make effective use of the word stem lists that he'd already memorized. He did want to work with Andrew, but that wasn't the main issue pressing on his mind.

Ever since Walter saw how slowly Sally was moving at the VFW club a month ago, how her voice had changed, how quickly her Parkinson's was progressing, he'd been thinking about a proposition: *What if you and I moved in together after you come back to Golden Grove? As friends, like Patricia and Pam, perhaps, but (also like Patricia and Pam) as more than friends?* He knew she'd say no, of course. It was a ridiculous idea. They'd known each other six months. He had olives in his refrigerator older than that. But he also knew this: Golden

Grove was a retirement community for "active seniors." It didn't specialize in assisted care. Yes, some people stayed on in their apartments after their health began to decline, but they had either a spouse to help or hired outsiders to come in.

Ever since the Hartford tournament, this thought had haunted him: If she's having trouble handling Scrabble tiles, how is she making her coffee or pouring herself a bowl of cereal? She would need help sooner or later, and the money to afford that help, judging by her urgent talk of selling her house, would be an issue. People with chronic, degenerative conditions regularly left Golden Grove, though it was sometimes unclear where they went. "Her needs changed" was a euphemism used by administration, with the tacit acceptance by residents who asked no questions because they all feared one day becoming the person no one was discussing. He dreaded such a fate for Sally and, judging by the time it took her to board the train and find her ticket, feared it might be coming sooner than either one of them would want. *You're getting worse. We can all see it.* Of course, he wasn't going to say this directly.

He'd need to time this proposal carefully, after a weekend of demonstrating the help he could offer. To this end, he'd called the hotel ahead of time to ask about reserving an electric scooter. Unfortunately none were available, so he reserved a wheelchair. He knew she'd prefer the independence of moving on her own, but this had other advantages: A wheelchair would mean he could push her and, from behind, lean over and whisper funny things in her ear. He'd been looking forward to this—even planning a few jokes—until he saw her face when the clerk brought the chair out at check-in.

"You ordered this ahead of time?" Sally said, staring at it, aghast. "Without asking me?"

Had he already made a terrible mistake? Did she not realize it had taken them almost an hour to get from the train to the taxi stand?

Whatever happened, he'd never point this out, never intentionally make her feel self-conscious.

"You don't have to use it, Sal," he said, blushing at the nickname he'd only called her in his mind before this. "I wanted it on hand in case it might be helpful. Look, we can pile our luggage on it for now." He dropped his duffel bag on the seat.

She stared down at the thing and seemed to consider. She'd already brought out her cane and, even with it, had lurched precariously a few times until Walter had finally whispered, "I'd be so grateful if you'd take my arm." She'd taken his arm and they'd said no more. This was the problem, he realized: Using a wheelchair said something neither one of them had put into words yet. Toby and Andrew were oblivious to this drama, standing across the lobby.

"It's not that I think you *need* it. It's just in case we're late—"

"Okay, fine," she finally said with a sigh. "But move the duffel. We're not going to waste a wheelchair on luggage."

He waited until he was behind her and pushing to smile.

They went to sleep early that night after a dinner in the hotel restaurant. The tournament hadn't started, but still the conversation filled up with Scrabble talk and the surprise of the day: Andrew's first victory over Toby in a game on the train. The two of them discussed it for most of the meal: missed plays, risky moves, one phony played by Andrew, unchallenged by Toby. As their talk went on, Walter caught Sally's eye: *Am I this boring?* She smiled and shook her head and mouthed the word *no*, as if she understood what he hadn't said aloud.

The next morning, Walter was grateful for the wheelchair when he knocked on the door to the room she was sharing with Andrew and realized she wasn't finished dressing yet. "She's a little slow in the morning," Andrew said, too loudly for Walter's taste. Didn't he care if his mother could hear him? "I'm going to go check in at the tournament now. She might need another twenty minutes."

When Walter returned, Sally answered the door. Her hair was uncombed; her cardigan sweater misbuttoned. "Thank you for the extra time, Walter. I'm fine now. Let's go."

She stepped out of her room and sat down immediately in the wheelchair. "We'll be later than we already are if I try to walk."

They spent the morning watching games. From the start, Walter worried about Toby's erratic play, laying down one word, then changing his mind and picking it back up. He started his second game by taking four minutes off his clock before finally playing OBA for ten points. After that, he started making silly scoring mistakes—one turn he took too many points, another he didn't give himself enough. The corrections ate up more time on his clock.

By contrast, Andrew, playing in the lowest D division filled with beginners and older women, was on fire. In the third play of his first game he made LIONIZED out of ZED. Five turns later, he smacked down BOWLINE for a triple-word bingo. Even more surprising, he seemed to be enjoying himself. Except for one moment when he played JIRD and announced at the same time, "This word is good," he seemed as if he'd been playing for years.

To Walter's surprise, he liked being at a tournament without competing. It meant he could talk to old opponents without sounding agitated or wearing a shirt drenched in sweat. Better yet, he could use Sally as a pleasant excuse to end conversations. "We should get going," he'd say, pushing her chair. "Sally's son is competing—doing well so far!" It all felt very jolly except for a phenomenon he noticed during the lunch break, when Jack Trotter walked by them and waved to Walter but not Sally.

"I didn't know you'd played him," Sally said, eating an orange slice.

"I haven't. You have. He must be mistaking me for someone else."

Then it happened again. Winston Pryor, of all people, failed to recognize Sally but nodded and offered Walter a "hello." Sally turned and smiled at Walter. "Why is he saying hello to you and not to me?"

"I have no idea," Walter said. Surely Pryor recognized her. She'd been *sitting in a wheelchair* when they played.

Late in the day, they ran into Esther, who wanted to complain to Walter about the organizers of this tournament and also let him know how badly Toby was doing. "You'll be glad to hear that boy from Hartford is having a terrible tournament. I don't think we'll have to worry about him after this."

Sally gave Walter a sympathetic look. Esther obviously didn't know that Walter was coaching Toby now, but apparently Walter wasn't thinking about this. "Esther, you remember Sally Reynolds, right?"

Esther looked surprised, as if she hadn't seen her, even though Sally was *sitting right there*. "Yes of course, Sally. It's nice to see you again. I hope—" Suddenly she seemed at a loss for words. "You feel better soon."

Sally tried to laugh it off after Walter pushed her away, but he was furious. "These people are being unspeakably rude to you. Jack Trotter doesn't want to remember that he lost to a woman, much less to a woman who might have a reason to need a wheelchair at the moment."

"It's not that bad, Walter. You've played in these tournaments for years. I didn't. I was a blip on their radar."

"You were much more than that, Sally. You were a threat to them, and you still are."

"Please, Walter. I'm hardly a threat to anyone here."

He moved closer so he could sit directly across from her chair, close enough that if he wasn't careful, their knees would touch. "Listen to me, Sally. There's something important I need to say to you."

All morning he'd been listening to Sally quietly point out plays that Andrew or Toby hadn't seen. "Andrew could play KOUMISS off the open O," she'd whispered at one point, studying a tight board with very few letters to play off. A second earlier Walter had been stumped. He saw that she was not only right, but the K would triple and one S would pick up 12 points by tacking on to JAR. Even more surprising, she'd done the same with Toby's games. "What about PINNULAE," she whispered as they watched. "It fits but I'm not sure it's the best play." Of course it was the best play. It would have been a late-game bingo, always hard to find, usually impossible to place. Toby didn't see it and lost the game by 30 points. "I need to stop playing these games in my head," Sally said, laughing afterward. "It's not helping them and it's making me more nervous."

"Here's what I think," Walter said now. "These people have written you off because you didn't enter this tournament, and without asking any questions, they assume this wheelchair means you've stopped competing forever. They don't have to worry about you anymore, which means, in their minds, they don't have to say hello to you either. It's terrible."

To his surprise, she reached over and took his hand in hers. It was the first time she'd touched him since the start of the trip, and he felt so grateful he had to resist the impulse to lift her hand up and kiss it.

"I *have* stopped competing, Walter. It's fine for them to think that." She squeezed his hand, then quickly took hers back.

"But you mustn't say that! All morning you've been playing better from the sidelines than anyone competing. If I'd forced you to enter—which, believe me, I considered—you'd be leaving all these people in the dust."

"That's not true. We both remember what happened last time."

"Yes. You got tired and dropped two tiles. That's all."

"It was more than that. My tremors nearly upended an important game. My mind might be fine, but I can't control my body well enough to play at this level. Period. I don't really want to have any big discussions about it."

For the rest of the day, he stewed over the problem. This wasn't an issue limited to Sally. The competitive Scrabble world had plenty of young men in the top echelons, but by far their largest group of most loyal fans were the rapidly aging retirees. As far as he knew, these tournaments offered no accommodations for people with physical limitations, even though many would develop them soon enough. He thought of Byron Zorick and his macular degeneration—how he could see his own tiles but not the board, so he memorized the grid and asked the others to place his tiles. For years Walter had failed to see what an extraordinary feat of brain power and memory this was, or the possibility that as his sight dimmed, Byron's play might have actually *improved.*

"What you said before is wrong, Sally. You've never played Byron Zorick." They were eating lunch together. He told her the story of Byron's career.

"When was the last time he competed?"

Walter didn't know.

"That's my point. Fine for him to drop by the club, but those games don't matter. These do. These are the rules, Walter. You of all people should know that. You love rules."

He felt his stomach churn. All day he'd battled a nervous case of indigestion watching Toby play, and now he feared he might get emotional again. "You're the best player I know, Sally. Against the stiffest competition, in high-pressure games, with unlucky tiles. You watch these games and see plays no one else does!" Was he about to cry? *Please God, no*, he thought. *Let me express this one sentiment without the waterworks.* He took a deep breath to calm himself down. "They need to make accommodations for people with disabilities. Someone should be able to sit beside you and place your tiles if necessary."

She took a deep breath. “No. First of all, that will never happen. Second of all, I wouldn’t want to play that way. Where I’m obviously different and being accommodated.”

He would have said more but feared his indigestion might produce an unseemly belch if he opened his mouth.

# CHAPTER 42

# Sally

BY DINNERTIME IT WAS CLEAR: ANDREW HAD HAD A GREAT DAY AND TOBY had not. Andrew won all seven of his games with a 230-point spread, putting him in third place in his division. By contrast, Toby had lost all but one of his games, albeit with close scores. In his division, only two people were rated below him.

If Sally was surprised by Andrew's performance, she was even more surprised by the kindness he'd shown when he turned to Toby, sitting beside him in the booth. "I heard you had unbelievably stiff competition, especially in the morning."

"Who told you that?"

"People playing in D division like to talk about you guys." Andrew smiled sheepishly. "You're our role models, I guess."

"Yeah, not anymore."

"You're the youngest player in your division. A lot of people seem really impressed by you. I played one woman who's been going to tournaments for twenty years. She said you remind her of Bobby Carhardt."

"Who's that?" Toby said. Even Sally, who didn't track Scrabble celebrities, knew that Bobby Carhardt, at seventeen, had been the youngest player to ever win the Nationals, a title he held for five of the next eight years, at which point he retired completely and never played in another tournament. He also never gave an interview or explained his retreat from the world he'd so decisively dominated for eight years. People thought he worked with computers now, but according to Walter, that had never been confirmed. "It's an interesting mystery, but I wonder if maybe it's also a lesson," Walter had mused when he told her the story.

"What would the lesson be?" Sally had asked.

"That maybe conquering the Scrabble world doesn't make you completely happy? It's a working theory. I still need time to fine-tune it."

Sally wondered if just hearing Bobby Carhardt's name made Walter uncomfortable or if it was something else. Walter waved his hand and touched his stomach. "No more Scrabble talk for this meal, guys. You need to clear your minds. It's good to take a break."

Sally agreed with Walter except that all around them in the restaurant were other players from the tournament. After their food came, two large tables nearby filled up and the din of Scrabble talk was so loud, Andrew and Toby went back to their conversation and Sally turned to Walter without any danger of being heard. "I had a great day. Watching Andrew—" She hesitated. "Just watching him be with people again. It's enormously reassuring to me. It's the first time I've thought he might be okay."

"He's doing a lot better than okay. He's showing a formidable talent."

She beamed. She couldn't help it. "I mean apart from Scrabble. Watching him talk to people, interact graciously, all that. I wasn't sure I'd ever see this side of him again. It makes me happy. That's all." It *had* been wonderful to watch Andrew move through a group of similar-minded peers, and it showed her that eventually he'd return to the world he'd stepped away from a year ago. It was a mixed blessing, though. If she was seeing—in glimmers—that he'd be okay, she was also seeing, with sobering clarity, that she would not. The wheelchair was a temporary accommodation for now, but soon enough it would be permanent. She'd become a person moving waist-high in a world that assumed it was more polite to ignore her than to acknowledge the wheelchair she was sitting in.

Getting ready for dinner, she'd thought about Walter's suggested solution. He was right to say this wasn't only about her; this issue impacted many people. She thought about Byron Zorick, the polite, soft-spoken man who—with her at least—had bent very close to the board and moved his head slowly over the played tiles to "see" what was there. A few times, he got so close his lips or his chin accidentally moved some tiles.

Walter was right about something else—she didn't mind straightening the tiles Byron had accidentally moved. Sometimes accommodations weren't hard to make. She was glad she'd stood up to Walter and made it clear—this was *her* choice, not his—but the more she thought about Byron, the more she wondered if Walter had a point. A former top-rated player with a brain still sharp enough to memorize a grid of words was extraordinary. He shouldn't be consigned to club play alone.

Of course, needing someone else on hand to occasionally place her tiles wasn't the only reason she'd stopped playing in public. It also had to do with being around Walter, which made her happy but also nervous. When he said flirtatious things, should she flirt back? None of this came naturally to her. The boldest thing she'd done all day was to squeeze his hand. Then, the way he'd squeezed it back, grabbing her fingers and rubbing them with his thumb, scared her enough to pull her hand back.

It was all too much, she feared. She didn't know her body anymore or what it would do when pressed to new limits of stress or excitement. Playing in the Hartford tournament had taught her that her new Parkinson's brain could surprise her in good ways (she believed at least some of her success was owing to a strange new word-accessing clarity) and in terrible ways (the tics, the dyskinesia, the frozen leg). Overexcitement was the problem. She mustn't indulge herself about anything this weekend—not Andrew's success or Walter's kindness. If he was flirting with her and she flirted back, her body might punish her with overreaction. If he leaned in for a kiss, one of her flailing hands might punch him.

# CHAPTER 43

# Walter

AFTER DINNER, BOTH ANDREW AND TOBY SEEMED EAGER TO GET BACK to their studies. Andrew leaned across the table and whispered to Sally, "Will you be okay if I leave you here? Can Walter help you get back to our room?"

Walter wondered if this was a little like parents tiptoeing up to bed when a daughter and her date were sitting on a front porch swing. In all likelihood, not much would happen, but if they remained, nothing would.

They were alone now, sitting side by side in their booth, waiting to pay the bill. After the tumultuous day they'd had, it was wonderful to sit so close to Sally. Walter closed his eyes and leaned his head against the back of the booth. "I worry that I somehow managed to infect Toby with my self-sabotaging tournament anxiety."

"Oh no. You mustn't blame yourself."

"He went 2–6 today, with a point spread that widened to 370. It's given me indigestion all afternoon."

"Whatever's happening with Toby isn't your fault."

"Tell that to my stomach."

They sat and listened to a table full of Scrabblers next to them debate whether CRESIVE was an acceptable play if it was a misprint of CRESCIVE in the latest *OSPD*. Walter had a heated argument over a dictionary error at his second tournament. Now he had to admit that it sounded silly. "I'm trying to think of something besides Scrabble to talk about. and I've just remembered there's a question I want to ask you." He peeked over to see her reaction. "I'm not sure I should."

"Oh, go ahead. Now you've got me curious." Her expression softened into a smile. "Let me guess—you want me to join a new club with you at Golden Grove, don't you? You've decided that mah-jongg is more interesting than you thought. Or no, I know: You've become a quilter and you want me to help you put your squares together?"

"Now you're making fun. I'm not going to ask my question."

"You can ask, but not if it's heavy. Let's keep this weekend light."

"Fine." He closed his eyes and winced through another stomach upheaval. He wasn't kidding. It had been going on all day, ever since he watched Toby collapse in his first game.

Sally touched the back of his hand. "Are you feeling all right, Walter? You hardly ate."

"I'm feeling very happy to be alone with you and also worried that a brutal attack of diarrhea lies ahead of me this evening. There. I've said too much." He took as deep a breath as he could manage. "If I move, I might shake things up in there. If I don't, I'm okay." He opened one eye. "Would you like to take a nap here in this booth with me?"

# CHAPTER 44

# Sally

WHY DID HE SAY THESE THINGS? SURELY, HE DIDN'T MEAN IT AS A terrifying, veiled invitation to sleep together. So what *did* he mean? She felt her heart begin to race. She'd managed to joke him out of asking his question, but how much longer could she keep this up? She wasn't scared of Walter anymore; she was scared of the way he triggered unpredictable responses in her body when he did things like lean over and whisper in her ear as he pushed her wheelchair. Or what he was doing now: tilting his head to rest it on her shoulder.

This was the real reason she'd avoided his question: She imagined him asking something awkward and sweet (*Would you like to be my girlfriend?*) and the embarrassment of what would happen when he saw—really *saw*—the effect he could have on her. For now—for this weekend, certainly—she had to keep this friendship as light and casual as possible.

Outside her hotel room door, her heart began to race. She looked down at her shaking hands. She couldn't keep anything still around him. "I should go to bed," she said, standing up from the chair he'd pushed all the way up the hall—not an easy task, judging by his red face and his heavy breathing. Unless standing here saying good night was affecting them both more than they wanted to admit. "We've both had quite a day," she said.

"Sally, I—" His voice sounded strained. Almost emotional.

She managed to hold out one of her shaky hands. "Let's say good night, Walter. We both need some rest."

Instead of shaking her hand, he took it and kissed it. *Oh, Walter*, she thought, getting herself inside her room and leaning against the back of the closed door. *What am I going to do when I can't hide myself from you anymore?*

## CHAPTER 45

# *Walter*

EVEN AT THE RESTAURANT, WALTER FEARED HE WAS SUFFERING FROM more than simple indigestion. The pain that had roiled his stomach all day had radiated up to his chest and shoulder. Had he strained himself pushing her chair? That didn't explain his breathlessness at dinner. Or the odd places he could feel sweat breaking out, like on his hands and the small of his back. By the time dinner was over, his shirt was soaked.

He blamed himself. He wasn't good at handling big emotions these days, and here he was compressing all of them—pity for Toby, anxiety for Andrew, his crush on Sally—into a single weekend away from home where he also had to worry about sleeping in a strange bed, hiding his diapers from Toby, and not falling in the ridiculous bathtub/shower. It was only after dinner, when he stood up from the booth they had sat in for so long, that he thought: *Something's really wrong*. In the elevator he stayed behind Sally's wheelchair so she couldn't see how hard it was for him to stand. "You aren't the only person who needs this chair," he said, and she turned around with a questioning look. He said no more. He had no idea what was happening. Only that something was.

When they got to her hotel door, he swallowed the bilious taste in his mouth so he wouldn't end this lovely day by throwing up on her shoes. He couldn't remember what he said or if the hand kiss he gave her was meant to be a real kiss and missed, because suddenly his vision was blurring. All night, he'd thought these were the physical manifestations of an old man falling under the spell of a woman again, fifty years after his first life-changing crush. Goodness, he kept thinking as he felt his breath go shallow. *What will happen if I kiss her?* he thought, not daring to let his mind wander any further.

No question, it had been both terrifying and wonderful to have all these feelings over the course of the day. But now he was more frightened than anything else. He couldn't see clearly. His mouth was dry. His chest felt like a vise was squeezing air out of his lungs, and he couldn't get enough air. Panting helped a bit, enough to get him inside his hotel room. He planned to ask Toby to call 911 when he got inside, but Toby wasn't there.

Suddenly he had the thought: *I might die before I get to the end of my story with Sally.* He sat down on the bed and dialed 911, just before he slid to the floor and everything went black.

## CHAPTER 46

# Sally

WHY HADN'T SALLY RECOGNIZED WHAT WAS HAPPENING WITH WALTER? How could she have spent four years tending to John's congestive heart failure and not recognize a heart attack the first time he complained of indigestion, even though he hadn't eaten for hours? Why hadn't she remembered the host of mystifying symptoms—jaw pain, backache, unexplained sweat—that she'd learned over all the years she'd spent worrying about John's heart?

She didn't find out what had happened to Walter until the next morning when Toby called her from the hospital and relayed what he knew so far: Walter had blockages in three major arteries, 100 percent in one and 80 percent in the other two. He needed surgery as soon as possible, which meant doing it here in Baltimore. Thankfully, Toby had gotten back to their hotel room just as the ambulance was carrying Walter away. They'd assumed Toby was his grandson and let him ride with them to the hospital. Along the way, he called his parents, who had connections to good Baltimore-based cardiologists, he said, which both surprised and reassured her.

Toby couldn't answer most of Sally's questions, so she had no way of knowing how much damage Walter's heart had sustained, but she knew other organs could be significantly impacted by a heart attack: the lungs, the brain. She also knew that emergency surgery in the aftermath of a heart attack was riskier.

"I need to get there before he goes into surgery. I have to see him," she said.

"Okay," Toby said. "I mean, I'm not really in charge of anything, but okay."

"Can you tell him I'm on my way—that I'll be there as fast as I can get a taxi?"

"I think they're called Ubers now. But I'll tell him. They just took him for surgery prep to shave his chest. He asked if they'd mind shaving his back too while they were at it."

Her heart soared. He was making jokes! "I need to see him before they put him under."

"Okay." He hesitated. "Do you want me to say anything in case you don't make it?"

What did she want to say? *I'm coming back to Golden Grove!* would sound ridiculous in light of what he was facing. Ditto: *I feel all the same things you say so easily but I can't!* "Just tell him I'll be there as soon as I can."

When she arrived, she made it to the pre-op area, where a nurse asked if she was his wife.

"Yes," Sally said. "I'm sorry I didn't get here earlier. We're not from Baltimore."

"Yes, that's what your grandson said. Something about a Scrabble tournament?" The nurse was walking too fast for Sally to keep up. She stopped at the door outside his room. "We only allow one visitor at a time, but I'm guessing your grandson won't mind taking a break."

Sally had to put on full protective gear before she could go in: a face mask, coveralls, and booties. When she finally got inside, Toby popped up and moved toward the door. Walter had been sedated enough that his eyes were closed. "He's not asleep," the nurse said. "You can talk to him, even if he seems groggy. I'll be back in ten minutes to take him in."

Sally pulled a chair over to his side and took one of his hands. "I told them I was your *wife*," she whispered. "They wouldn't have let me in otherwise. I'm so sorry about all this. I should have recognized your symptoms. I should have seen what was happening."

He held her hand and mumbled something she couldn't understand. In the car ride over, she'd made a mental list of the things she wanted to say to him:

*I'm so glad you're alive.*

*You're my best friend at Golden Grove.*

*You might be my best friend, period.*

*I'm sorry I have such trouble talking about my feelings, but the important thing I want to say is that if you need to stay in Baltimore while you recover, I'd like to stay with you. I don't want you to be alone. Please let me help you the way you've helped me.*

Why was it so hard for her to say all of this? She couldn't be sure, except that she'd spent the last five years of her marriage caring for a man who rarely acknowledged her feelings or expressed his own. She'd trained herself to say as little as possible, and she knew speaking her heart would mean opening it up again. "Walter, there are things I want to say," she whispered.

He squeezed her hand, which encouraged her to keep going. "You've been a good friend to me, but you've also been more than that... You've helped me believe that my life isn't over yet. That I might still surprise myself. With Scrabble but in other ways, too—"

At that moment, the nurse opened the door. "Just letting you know that your son is getting masked up and will be in shortly."

"My *son*?" Sally said. This morning they'd agreed that Andrew would keep playing in the tournament and she would update him with texts on Walter's status.

The nurse nodded and left. Sally took her hand from Walter's and put it back in her lap.

A moment later, the door opened and a man she'd never met walked in. The nurse stepped in behind him, rolling a cart full of equipment.

"Dad," the man said. "My God, I couldn't believe it. Some kid called me and said you'd had a heart attack in Baltimore. What are you doing in Baltimore?"

This must be Gavin, of course. She kept her gaze on the floor and didn't dare say her name. "We were here for a Scrabble tournament," she mumbled, moving toward the door. She couldn't look at him. She had to leave as quickly as possible or the nurse would wonder why Walter's so-called wife needed to introduce herself to his son.

In the hallway, her body went into a full tremor as she sank down on a bench. It was good that Gavin had come down so quickly, but it also meant she couldn't finish the speech she'd started. From what she knew of open-heart surgeries, recovery would be a long, slow process involving an extended hospital stay and rehab afterward. She wouldn't see him again for weeks, maybe a month or more. If he made it back to Golden Grove at all.

When John was first diagnosed, she'd read too many books. She knew what happened when people had heart attacks. The slowing down, the withdrawal from the world, the change in personality. John had never experienced anything as dramatic as what Walter had been through, but still, the diagnosis of congestive heart failure altered him profoundly. Having scaled back at work, he quit completely and cut off what little social life he had. Convinced he had six months to live, he'd soldiered on for another five joyless years. If she dared to suggest an activity, he always pushed back: "I'm dying, Sally. That means I finally get to do exactly what I want, and what I want to do is nothing."

She couldn't imagine Walter returning with this outlook, but she knew he'd be different. She'd seen it at Golden Grove: The people who returned from major surgeries and rehab stays were never the same. Quieter, less apt to show up for meals and activities. Usually you only saw them getting their mail or being pushed in a wheelchair by an attendant. If they recognized old friends in the lobby, they waved absently as their aide pushed them outside to sit in the afternoon sun. Sometimes they closed their eyes when they got there as if it was all too much. The people, the sun, all of it.

She waited until after she got home to call Walter's phone. She knew he'd made it through surgery but she didn't know any more. She assumed he wouldn't be able to answer, but she hoped Gavin would pick it up, which he did. She tried to make her interest sound as neutral as possible. "I'm the friend who was at the hospital when you came," she offered. "Now I'm back at Golden Grove, where we're all worried about him. I volunteered to call for updates so you won't get overwhelmed." She was glad she had planned what to say ahead of time. She was a concerned friend, that was all.

Gavin told her what the doctors reported after surgery: They'd addressed the artery blockages, one with a stent and two with replacements grafted from veins taken from his leg. The operation went well, but both the heart and the lungs had sustained damage from the attack.

"How much damage?" she asked. Her voice sounded like a child's.

"Hard for them to say, I guess."

Over the next week, she called daily and talked to Gavin. Twice, he put Walter on the phone, but he was raspy and breathless and difficult to understand. He seemed to say her name over and over but not much else. Both times, Gavin pulled the phone away before she could say much of anything. Nine days after his surgery, Walter was transferred to a rehab center and Gavin went home, which meant she could speak directly to Walter again, though she still had trouble understanding him. Sometimes he was too tired to say much, so she told him to stay strong, to concentrate on healing, and to have faith that he'd feel like his old self soon. Other times, she heard a glimmer of his old self. He was exercising, he said. He missed salt and Scrabble, he told her. No one in rehab was a Scrabble player. "The only game they play in here is balloon volleyball," he rasped at one point. She had to get him to repeat it before she understood him and then she laughed. "I can't picture that, Walter," she said.

"Don't try," he muttered.

Around Golden Grove, people asked how he was doing, and she kept her answers cheerful and vague. "He's in rehab now! Still complaining about the food but looking for people to play Scrabble with, so I think he's doing okay."

One night Connie cornered her after dinner: "I just want to warn you, heart attacks can alter the brain, the same way a stroke can. My husband spent years in therapy—speech, OT, PT. He never came back. His last ten years, it was like taking care of a child. Does Walter sound the same when you talk to him on the phone?"

Sally didn't want to tell Connie the truth, that he sometimes asked the same questions over and over. He had the most trouble remembering the days just before his attack and asked her repeatedly what he was doing in Baltimore. "We were at the Scrabble tournament, remember?"

"Was I playing?"

"No. We were watching Andrew and Toby play."

"Toby Weir, the cheater from Hartford?"

She had to explain all over again that Walter had changed his mind after he'd gotten to know him. "You decided he was a good kid and you were right, Walter. In fact, we have him to thank for saving your life. You'd called 911, but he was there when the ambulance came. He gave them your medications and what he knew of your medical history. He also got his parents to arrange for your doctors."

Even as she said this, she feared it might be too late. Walter wasn't remembering the best parts of his old self.

## CHAPTER 47

# Walter

IMPOSSIBLE TO KEEP TRACK OF TIME IN THE HOSPITAL. OR TO REMEMBER, from one doctor visit to the next, what was going on. When he first woke up after his surgery, he knew something terrible had happened, judging by the number of machines he was attached to and tubes coming out of him. The worst was the tube down his throat, which was initially more painful than anything they'd done to his chest. For hours it stayed there, making it impossible to ask any questions. Nurses held up whiteboards for him to write on, but he never had the strength to wrap his hand around a pen and ask the questions he most wanted answers to: *What happened to me? Where's Sally?* Eventually the tube came out, and he was moved to a room where nurses weren't always two feet away but came in every hour to take his vitals and tell him to cough, even though it hurt so much he had to hold a pillow to his chest to keep his organs from flying out. He remembered that. He also remembered Gavin floating in and out, sitting in his room but far away, as if he'd been told not to get too close.

He was happy to see Gavin but still confused. *Where's Sally?* he'd say, but his throat was still raw, and for a long time, no one understood him. "I'm not sure what you're saying, Dad. You're sorry? You don't have to be sorry."

For days, possibly weeks, this was how it went. He exhausted himself opening his eyes and sitting up in bed. At some point, two physical therapists came to his room and told him it was time to practice walking. He tried to say no, they must be mistaken, he was still attached to too many machines, but they insisted. "It's not a choice," one of them said. "Doctor's orders. We've got something nice for you if you can walk to the door."

He looked hopefully at the closed door. Was Sally on the other side? He understood that didn't make sense, but what other reward could there be? He swung his legs to the floor and groaned at the dizzying agony of straightening his body. Trying to stand and breathe at the same time made him swoon. Humiliating to have two grown men holding him up while Gavin looked on, wincing with some mix of pain and embarrassment. Moving each leg took a concentrated effort. He wondered if this was how Sally felt in the morning. He remembered her once saying, "I have to talk to my legs, tell them what to do just to get out of bed." Walking six steps took him about twenty minutes, and by the end he'd broken out in a sweat. Afterward, he collapsed back into bed. His reward was a strawberry Jell-O cup.

He did get better. Enough that Gavin could leave after he'd transferred to rehab. When they hugged, Walter told him he was sorry. This time, he meant it and Gavin understood. He *was* sorry—to be so weak and need so much help. He'd never wanted to be in this position and now here he was. His body fragile, his thoughts scrambled, so tired some evenings that Gavin had to hold the remote and switch TV channels.

Eventually his brain fog started to clear. He knew he'd had surgery; he'd seen the zippered scar, both repellent and fascinating, down the front of his chest. He'd talked to Sally and understood that she was back at Golden Grove, but in the hospital those conversations had always involved Gavin holding out the phone to him and taking it back before their talk was over. He'd never been able to say what he wanted to: *Can you come here and be with me? Can we live together after this?* Naturally he couldn't say these things in front of his son, but the terrible surprise was finding himself unable to say them even after Gavin left.

Breathing was hard for him now, but talking was harder. He'd planned what he wanted to say to Sally, but when she finally called, the words slipped away. Instead, he asked her endless, incessant questions, like a child. What happened again? What am I doing here? He wanted to tell her *I'm sorry, I'm not myself. I will be again when I get better.*

To this end, he began to formulate a plan. Instead of dreading the arrival of PTs and OTs who stopped by and asked him to breathe into tubes and walk down the hallway, he readied himself for their arrival. He asked the respiratory therapist if he could keep her plastic gizmo and practice blowing the needle to the green zone on his own. He sat up in bed and put one slipper and then another on by himself before his scheduled "walks." He took ten steps, then twelve and then, on a big day, took thirty and made it to the black tile square in the hallway that a few days earlier had looked impossibly far away. The PTs at his side applauded.

After four days away, Gavin returned and brought a suitcase full of clothes he'd found in Walter's apartment, along with other things he might need in rehab. "I brought a Scrabble set and a dictionary, but I don't know. Do you think you'll find someone to play with in here?"

He wanted to say, "Yes, of course. I'll play with Sally," but this was where the confusion still troubled him. He had to be reminded that he was still in Baltimore, that he had to complete his rehab near his doctors. The fuzziness was worst in the morning, when he woke up disoriented and needed reminders of where he was and what had happened. He tried keeping a notebook beside his bed where he wrote it all out to make these early morning hours less frightening. He started with bullet points:

- *You're still alive.*
- *You had a heart attack and surgery, and you've got three new arteries.*
- *Your chest still hurts and it's hard to breathe but you're NOT having another heart attack. Do NOT press the call button or tell any nurses that you might be having one because you're not and this annoys them.*
- *Sally isn't here. She calls once a day to check up on you. Do NOT call her when you are sad or upset. Wait until you feel better. You don't want to be a burden to her.*
- *You don't want to be a burden to Gavin. You're working to get better as quickly as possible. Please read the schedule at the end of this notebook.*

It was a good schedule that included as much PT as he was allowed, along with exercises he could do on his own, sitting in his room. His first week in rehab, he wasn't allowed to get out of bed by himself or transfer from the wheelchair he still needed. But when he was working out, he *worked*. He took longer walks, now with only one aide at his side. His PT sessions were the hardest, though they involved activities like swatting Styrofoam noodles at a pyramid of plastic cups in a room full of sad sacks doing the same. At first, it was defeating to watch other people struggle with the things that, once he tried them, were almost impossible for him as well. Still, he never missed a session, and some days, if a nice therapist had an extra opening, he asked for two sessions. "I'm working to get out of here!" he told her. She laughed and signed him up.

When he talked to Sally on the phone, he reminded himself to stay cheerful, but it was hard. He told her about the other patients who spent their days parked in wheelchairs in the hallway or lying, fully dressed, on top of their beds. "I used to hate the superficial conversations at Golden Grove about the weather, but all that sounds like Shakespeare compared to the pablum people talk about in here." Even though this was true, he didn't let himself go on. Didn't tell her about the nurses complaining about their shoes and their shifts. Or other patients railing at unseen family members. In rehab, so many people seemed not only angry at being there but angry at being alive *at all*.

On his twice-a-day walks, he tried smiling and waving. "Hello there!" he'd call out to a woman slumped in a wheelchair. "Terrific morning, eh?" he'd say. Or: "Busy day at the nurse's station?" At Golden Grove, such banalities usually opened up a forgettable exchange that could last twenty minutes or more. He'd never appreciated that until he got here.

One evening on the telephone with Sally, he let himself ponder the sadness he saw around him. "I worry that if I stay here much longer I might get seriously depressed."

She didn't say anything. Maybe she was thinking about Andrew. He was beginning to remember more about their trip to Baltimore and her worries about her son. Mostly he remembered the question he'd wanted to ask her before the weekend was over: Would she ever consider living with him? He remembered the list of arguments he'd thought of: They could save money, and they could help each other manage the countless roadblocks they encountered daily, like the health care portals, remembering passwords, working TV remotes.

Every night on the phone now, he wanted to ask her but didn't because he feared she'd say no and he'd get so depressed he'd never make it out of rehab. He wasn't sure why he sensed this. She'd never said, "I don't want to live with anyone again, especially not you, Walter, with your diaper-filled trash bags and your penchant for watching hours of television that you can't remember moments after you've turned it off." If (and when) she turned him down, it wouldn't be personal; he knew that much. Nor did he worry that she'd find someone else more charming who didn't wear diapers at night.

She simply seemed so content alone. She never talked about feeling lonely or scared or—the worst part about living alone—bored with her own thoughts. Instead she often spoke of her *need* to be alone. She'd tell him about her plans to "skip dinner for a night in," or how she'd been "reading for the whole day and hadn't talked to anyone," in a voice so cheerful it was clear these were not only pleasurable activities but necessary ones.

"That's funny," he once admitted to her on the phone. "I can't stand my own company. If I could manage it, I'd like to host a dinner party where I didn't invite myself."

She laughed, then got serious. "What are you talking about, Walter? Are you all right?"

He wasn't, of course. He was frightened and terrified that he'd never make it out of this place and even more scared of what might happen when he did. Would he go back to Golden Grove so physically ruined that he'd last a month and then—in a cloud of humiliation—be asked to leave because he'd grown demented and incontinent, the way others before him had?

Once he'd overheard a woman at dinner say, without a whisper of pity, "Incontinence is the main thing they worry about here. They have to think about their furniture that needs to last longer than any of us."

What a terrible fate, but even worse would be living in a state of cloudy confusion where you didn't see it coming. This was his greatest fear, so large in his mind he couldn't even speak to Sally about it.

Although he'd thought about it for three weeks, getting released from rehab happened faster than he imagined. He went for one doctor's appointment, had a few tests on his heart, and at the end, the doctor asked, casually, "Would you like to go home? Because you can if you want to." As if this had all been only a matter of speaking up.

"Yes," Walter said. "Very much. Yes, I would."

"I think it should be fine. Can you make arrangements for tomorrow?"

His poor fragile heart sped up. "I don't know. I can try!"

As it turned out, Gavin couldn't come the next day but could the day after. On the drive home, Gavin asked what would happen when they got there. "I just take you back to your apartment and leave you?"

"I won't be alone!" Walter said. "Remember I have friends there!"

"Okay. But what if you fall or have another heart attack? What did they say about you living alone?"

He wasn't going to tell Gavin the truth—that they didn't recommend this. Or technically, that they recommended having "live-in assistance" for at least the first week he was back. "I'll wear my emergency call button! All the time! Even when I'm sleeping!"

He hadn't asked Gavin what was happening in his own life or if he'd moved back in with James. It seemed more polite to wait and see if James's name came up. So far, it hadn't. Now so much time had passed that it felt like asking might only stir up sad feelings. More polite to let it go, he thought, and so he did.

Which left them in a car for four hours, unsure what to talk about. He was happy to return to his old life, but had Gavin returned to his? Was he happy these days? Instead of asking directly, Walter thanked him repetitiously for the help he'd been over the last month. "Truly, Son. I don't know what I would have done without you."

"You don't have to keep saying that, Dad."

"Well, I'm grateful, that's all. I'm trying to get better about expressing my gratitude."

"Okay," he said. "Are you grateful to be seeing your friends again soon?"

"Yes, of course. Nothing quite like a brush with death to make you appreciate your life."

"Are you going to see Sally when you get back?"

This was the first time Gavin had mentioned her name. "I hope so. Why? Would you rather I didn't?" Why was he even asking this question? If Gavin said yes, he'd have to say, "Well, sorry, I'm going to see her anyway."

"No. I'm just trying to wrap my mind around it, that's all."

"I loved your mother. That doesn't mean I can't love someone else."

"Right. But it might be hard to watch you be nicer to somebody else than you were to her. That's all. Like it'll make me feel bad for Mom all over again."

Walter tried to take a deep breath but a pain in his chest stopped him. "We were hard on each other. I was always scared of the responsibility that loving someone brought. My parents got sick at such a young age… I was scared of going through all of that again." What exactly was he trying to say? He felt emotions clog up his throat.

"Was that why you didn't help Mom more after she got diagnosed?"

"She didn't *want* help. She pushed me away. That's how I remember it." He worked to keep his voice calm. This *was* how he remembered it. "Your mother was independent. She wanted to prove something to herself before she died, and she did."

Walter was surprised. In the past, Gavin would have dismissed such an explanation or made a joke. *Sure, Dad. You keep telling yourself that.* He didn't say anything for a long time. "You might be right," Gavin finally said. "At the very end, her friends and I were taking turns sitting with her. We didn't want her to die alone, but she kept holding on longer than the nurses predicted. I'd hold her hand and say, 'It's okay, Mom. You can go,' but she didn't. She finally died when I wasn't there and Wendy was in the other room, making tea. It's like she was waiting to be alone."

"I used to think I was like that, too. That we had a good marriage because we were both solitary people, but I'm not sure that's true. It turns out I like living near other people. I don't mind superficial conversations. Your mom hated all that; she would have hated Golden Grove."

When they got there, Walter asked Gavin to pull over to the side entrance nearest his apartment. "I don't want to walk through the main lobby right now." He'd only been away for a month, but he knew people would be shocked at his changes: He used a walker now, with an oxygen concentrator attached to the side and a cannula running up to his nose. More than that, he'd lost twenty pounds and walked with a hunch to protect his poor, invaded chest. His skin was the pale-blue color of skim milk, his voice a register higher. Even his hands were unrecognizable to him. He didn't want to shock anyone or be the topic of dining room conversation tonight. Better to ease back in slowly.

Gavin turned to him. "Don't you want to say hi to all your friends?"

"I'm not ready for that just yet. I don't want to scare anyone."

"You don't look *that* bad, Dad."

"I look pretty bad." He also wasn't sure if he'd be able to make the walk to his apartment without stopping to rest. He hadn't practiced walking on carpet; better for falls, one PT had told him, harder for walkers. As it turned out, she was right. He had to stop twice and catch his breath. By the time he made it to his apartment, he was ready for a nap. "I wish I could help you bring things in," he said, sinking into his TV chair and closing his eyes.

"Don't worry about it. There isn't that much. I'll be right back."

He was glad he'd told Sally that he'd need a night's rest before he saw her.

"I have no idea what I'll feel like after a long day in the car with Gavin," he'd said. "It's possible I might die on the way." These were the kind of "jokes" his brain occasionally produced these days. Sad remarks that made no one laugh and everyone uncomfortable.

"*Walter*," Sally had said sternly.

"I apologize," he said.

When he woke the next morning he read over what he'd written in his notebook in preparation for his return:

1. Whatever happens, DON'T ask Sally to live together right away.
2. Let her see that yes, you're not doing too well physically at the moment, but emphasize that this isn't a permanent state.
3. Show her how hard you're working in therapy. Attend every easy exercise class Golden Grove offers. Definitely try tai chi where it seems like you don't have to move at all.
4. Be cheerful and smile in public so you don't look like the people in rehab who were sorry their heart attacks didn't kill them.
5. With Sally, keep conversation light and limited to topics that won't make you cry.

Reading this over was a useful reminder of the conversations they'd had over the phone. Even though he'd had a roommate and every reason not to embarrass himself by getting overly emotional, too often he did just that, triggered by the most unexpected topics. Sally would tell him about her fear that her daughter's marriage might not survive, and he'd think of Elyse and how ineffective he'd been in their last conversations. Soon his face would crumple and his cheeks would be wet. He also understood this new emotional state he lived in wasn't entirely a bad thing. No doubt it had helped in softening Gavin and defusing the tensions they'd lived with for the last twenty years. These days they hugged easily and sometimes—most surprising of all!—held hands when Gavin joined him for his walks. Yes, it was for balance, but it was more than that, too. He never held hands with any PTs.

The important part was to give Sally both space and time without putting any undue pressure on her. He was still adjusting to his body's changes; she'd need to as well.

"I want to see you as soon as possible!" he told Sally on the phone the next morning, defying all his written promises. "I look terrible and I still can't walk across the room without resting, but I don't care! I want to see you!"

"Shall I come to your apartment?" Sally asked.

Was she as nervous as she sounded? Unfortunately she'd have to come here. Her apartment was an elevator ride and a hallway as long as a football field away. He'd never make it to hers without someone helping him or, even better, pushing him in a wheelchair.

"Yes, you should definitely come here! We can finally talk in person!"

That's when he remembered what her hesitation might stem from: She'd never been to his apartment before. He'd invited her a few times but never minded when she declined. At Golden Grove, women tended to put much more effort into their decor than the men who, all too often, placed a comfortable chair in the vicinity of a television and shuffled the rest of their boxes into a closet unpacked. They meant to get to them, of course, but never did.

"It's so wonderful to see you, Sally!" he said after hugging her for so long she had to pull herself away. "I'm sorry that my apartment is such a dump!" Apparently he couldn't stop himself from saying a single thought he had.

She smiled. "It's not a dump, Walter. It's just a little barren. And maybe you should think about opening your blinds and letting in some light."

"I don't need any extra light now that you're here!" *Dear God*, he thought. *Do I need to fetch my notebook and read it over while she's here?*

Thankfully, he didn't. They talked about his drive with Gavin. "We had our first discussion about his mother where neither one of us got angry or upset. That was nice. Baby steps," and about his therapy schedule moving forward. "I'll have two weeks of someone coming here to help me walk. Apparently you have to do something called cardio to get your heart stronger. Did you know that?" She smiled and his heart melted a little. So many Golden Grove folks looked puzzled when he made jokes. Sally understood them.

Eventually it was her turn. "I did want to ask you something, Walter, but you should feel free to just say no if you're not up for it."

His foolish heart sped up for a moment. Was *she* going to suggest living together? "You can ask me anything, Sally. I'll never say no."

She rolled her eyes. "It's about Andrew. You very kindly offered to coach him before the tournament. I don't know if you remember—"

He didn't unfortunately, but everything about the tournament was a blur. When he asked about this, he was told that in the days before his heart attack his brain was probably only getting a fraction of the oxygen it needed and it wasn't surprising if he didn't remember much.

"I'd be happy to coach Andrew. We can all play together!"

Sally made a face. "He'd hate that, I'm afraid. Serious Scrabble players don't do three-person games. He did well enough at the tournament that he's gotten fairly serious. I'm afraid it's become a bit of an obsession for him."

It occurred to Walter this might be the truest measure of the changes he'd undergone since his heart attack: He'd never asked what happened at the tournament. "How did he do?"

"He came in sixth in his division. For someone who had only been playing three months, he felt pretty good about that. Toby dropped out of the tournament to stay with you at the hospital but Andrew stayed in. He didn't do as well the second day because he was worried about you. We all were. But he hung in there! He finished all his games, and his strong first day gave him a sixth-place finish."

"That's terrific, Sal. Better than I ever did."

For the first time, it occurred to him how much his heart attack had affected other people. In the hospital and later, at rehab, he had felt so alone, left behind by a world carrying on without him. Now he realized what had happened to him had happened to them all. "Did Toby really *drop out*?" The news was surprising, but even more surprising was the question: Why hadn't he *asked* until now?

"Yes. I learned a lot about him on the train ride home. It turns out his parents might not be as bad as we thought. They never hated Scrabble; they didn't like the hyper-competitive aspects of high-stakes tournaments. They were worried that Toby attaches too much significance to his Scrabble rating and tournament performance. They told him those aren't reliable measures of success, but if he still wanted to go, he could."

"My God," Walter smiled. "I'd like to meet these people. I think they might be right."

"Yes they are, but I still don't think it's a good excuse for sending him off to Baltimore and letting you be entirely responsible for him."

Suddenly Walter remembered something. "I wanted that, though.

I had a long conversation with his mother, and I asked her to let me take him. Entering Nationals wasn't even his idea; it was *mine*."

He could see the surprise on Sally's face. "Why?"

"I suppose I wanted to prove that I could have been a better father. More involved and less judgmental. But look what happened. It turns out if you get a second chance, you just make different mistakes."

"It wasn't a mistake to take Toby. He learned different lessons. Important ones. Like taking care of someone in an emergency. He handled all of that beautifully and didn't even call me until he knew you were stabilized and out of the woods. He said he didn't want to wake us up in the middle of the night when Andrew had a day of games still to play. I also think he liked talking to the doctors and being treated like an adult."

"That it's better to act like a responsible adult than a fake child prodigy?" Walter smiled.

"Exactly. He's not abandoning Scrabble. He's just putting it into perspective."

"Are you okay with me coaching Andrew?" He remembered her saying that Andrew's priority should be finding a job. "If he needs to focus on other things at this point, I understand."

"I appreciate that. I've decided the best strategy for me is to let my children make their own decisions. He's put his name on a list for substitute teaching at his old high school, where he and his sister have also volunteered to start a board games/role-play games club."

"Do I dare ask what role-play games are?"

"Probably best not to, but yes, it does involve occasional costume-wearing and creating your own story and rules as you go along. Rachel is doing it in the wake of separating from her husband and befriending the boy she apparently always liked in high school but wasn't confident enough to date owing to his love of role-play games. Now she's decided she loves them, too. They meet in two rooms—Dungeons and Dragons in one room, Scrabble and board games in the other. I suspect for them, it's all an elaborate ruse to find dates. Andrew persuaded his old girlfriend to help out, and Rachel got Charlie to stop by for their first meeting."

Walter smiled. "I'll eagerly await updates."

"In the meantime, I'm surprised. He says he likes being a substitute and is thinking about getting a teaching credential."

"People do adapt, don't they?" Saying this made him feel shy. As if they were both thinking the same thing: *Can we adapt too?*

He tried to catch her eye, but when he did, she looked away. Try as he might, he couldn't remember that last dinner with Sally. He'd wanted to kiss her good night, but had he? Was it possible to ask?

"Thank you, Walter. Truly. It will mean a lot to him."

He spent the next few days rethinking his plan. He couldn't ask Sally about living together now. He was still too weak, too early in his recovery. If he couldn't prove to her that his health was okay now, he'd show her that he was working hard and it would be soon. He went with her to the easiest exercise classes Golden Grove had: Music and Movement, where people sat the whole time and waved their arms around to upbeat music. Though he never stood up, he was still perspiring with effort by the end of the class. Sally sat beside him as people he hadn't seen yet came over to welcome him home. He tried to keep up a jolly veneer. "I'm doing great!" he said breathily. "A little open-heart surgery and I'm raring to go!"

Every morning, he set new goals for himself. One day he walked to the elevator and back. The next he walked out to the lobby. Soon he measured his progress in slow laps around the grand piano in the main lobby. Now that he'd adopted this upbeat new persona, it was hard to drop. One afternoon, a small group of onlookers applauded as he completed his lap around the piano. He took a bow and waved before sinking into a soft lobby chair. After he caught his breath, he noticed a woman staring at him from across the lobby. She neither clapped nor smiled.

"Hello!" he called and waved his hand. "You must be new!"

She narrowed her eyes. "Are you the Scrabble guy?"

Her expression was so dour, he almost laughed. "Why yes! Though I'm branching out these days and playing other games." She nodded but said nothing. "Why? Are you interested?"

"I just moved here. I might be good at Scrabble. I'm very good at crosswords. I didn't want to come here, but someone said, 'Try it, Wilma. There's a Scrabble club.' Now I'm here and they say there's no Scrabble club anymore. The man who started it had a heart attack, and the other lady has Parkinson's. That's it, they say. End of club. So I'm living in a place where there's no Scrabble and everyone avoids me."

Walter widened his smile, hoping she might get the hint. *If you look friendlier, maybe people won't avoid you. Plus maybe don't identify everyone by their health issues.* Admittedly, it had taken him a long time to learn this. His first year, he probably looked as sullen and leery as this woman did. Many people wore that expression early on, to convey the message *You're all old; I'm not.* Even when he finally accepted the fact that he belonged here, he steered clear of the residents who sat in the lobby all day and hardly moved.

Sally had taught him something about finding a middle ground. About recognizing limitations and reality and still pushing yourself a little every day. If you needed the polite golf clap of the lobby crowd to do so, then fine, make a little show of your effort. No harm in that. What didn't help was allowing labels to define possibilities. Saying the Scrabble club died because he'd had a heart attack and Sally had Parkinson's wasn't right.

"I'm afraid the Scrabble club died long before any of us had health issues. I was too competitive and rule-oriented. It put people off."

She considered this. “So what—just because you were serious, everyone quit?”

He laughed. “Pretty much. Eventually they forgave me though and started a different game club. Parcheesi, backgammon, that sort of thing.”

“Do people play Scrabble there?”

“Not so far, but we could! No one’s made a rule saying no Scrabble allowed.”

She considered this and finally said, “I’m very good at crosswords but it’s not a social activity. I don’t know if I’m good at social activities. My daughter says I have to try.”

Walter considered trying a joke: *You’re not too great at conversation either!* He didn’t. “I think you should join us on Wednesday night. Some people might boo if I walk in there with a Scrabble board, but I’ll say I’ve had a special request.”

Later, at dinner, he told Sally about the exchange. “She really was quite sour about the whole business. She didn’t want to play Scrabble, but her daughter said she had to. She assumes she’ll be good based on doing crossword puzzles for the last twenty years.”

Sally smiled. “You forget, Walter. I wasn’t sure about joining silly clubs at first either.”

“Everyone feels that way in the beginning. You were never surly and unpleasant. You always wore a friendly expression even if you felt a bit unsure.”

She rolled her eyes. “Well, those days are gone.”

He studied her expression, trying to decide what she meant by this, but he couldn’t.

# CHAPTER 48

# Sally

FOR THE LAST SIX WEEKS SALLY FELT AS IF SHE WAS LIVING IN A heightened state of agitation. About Walter's health, of course, but her own life had produced no shortage of surprises. She was grateful that her children were taking baby steps forward with their lives, but still she found herself frightened by the unknowns that might lie ahead for them. Worse was the uncertainty about her own health. Two weeks ago she had forgotten to put her medication beside her bed before she fell asleep and, in the morning, discovered she couldn't get out of bed without it. For the first time since moving to Golden Grove, she'd had to press her emergency alert button.

Thankfully Belinda, the aide who arrived to help a few minutes later, seemed unfazed. She handed her the pills and brushed off Sally's apologies. "I'm just glad you didn't fall and break something. That's a lot harder to deal with, trust me. Fetching a bottle of pills is nothing."

Did she understand that Sally *couldn't move* without them? That this new paralysis marked her most frightening new Parkinson's development?

A few days later, she told Rachel and Andrew the time might have come for her to hire someone to help her in the mornings. Rachel had seemed more distracted than usual and didn't understand. "Like to clean? Doesn't Golden Grove take care of that?"

"They do, but I might need someone to help *me*. Getting dressed. All of that." It was hard to admit this. A moment after she'd said it, she wanted to take it back: *I mean not right now, but maybe in a few months. I'll let you know.* Even more of a surprise was how little reaction she got from her children. Rachel shrugged and pulled out her phone. "Okay, I guess. I mean, if you need help finding someone, let me know."

Neither one registered how this might affect them. Rachel had officially moved out of the condo she shared with Barry and was living back home with Andrew. Hiring someone would mean Sally would need more money and would have to sell the house sooner than they realized.

This wasn't the only thing on her mind, though. She was happy to have Walter back, even if he looked frailer than she expected and changed in ways that were mystifying. Suddenly, he was waving and saying hello to everyone they passed. At dinners he liked to give his food order and then announce, segue from nothing, "Well, here we are and I'm not dead yet!" The third time she heard this, Sally touched the back of his hand and said with a smile, "If you keep saying that, Walter, someone might get so annoyed they kill you."

He grinned. "Like you for instance?"

"I won't kill you, but I might not stop someone who tried to."

He threw back his head and laughed in a way she'd never seen before. There were other changes. Suddenly, he was suggesting trips he wanted to take, restaurants "we should try," new Golden Grove groups he'd like to join. "What do you suppose they do in the poetry-reading group?" he asked her one afternoon. He'd started coaching Andrew in her apartment on Tuesdays. He was usually gone by four thirty, with a half hour until dinner, so Walter stuck around.

She stared at him. "That doesn't sound self-explanatory to you?"

"But do they write as well? I've always wanted to write poetry."

She made a face. She wanted to say, "Who are you and what have you done with my old friend Walter?" She didn't because she knew that would be unkind, and as her independence slipped away, she was afraid of becoming a moody person who complained about people who were able to do things she and Walter could not. She'd tried returning to the Wednesday Walkers and the Green Thumbs, but both groups proved to be beyond her now, though of course no one wanted to say this directly. Instead, Greta mused aloud about starting a slower-paced walking group, standing near Sally, who didn't need to hear any more to know that she'd choose her activities more carefully from here on.

Strangely, Walter seemed aware of his new fragility but, unlike her, utterly unselfconscious about it. "I can hardly walk anymore! One lap around the piano and that's it for me!" he'd announce in the main lobby before dinner. She wanted to hiss a warning to him: *Everyone is watching. The worse you get, the more they'll steer clear of you.*

She saw Andrew more after he started his coaching sessions with Walter. She didn't watch them play to give them privacy, but after a month, she asked Andrew to stay afterward and play a game with her. She wanted to hear how his job was going and see if he'd tell her any more about their club. "Is Karen still helping you?"

"She only came once. She said she liked it but she felt guilty paying for day care when she wasn't working."

"Could she bring her son? Have you met him?"

"He's three, Mom. A little young for Scrabble."

"You could do other things with him. Give Karen a chance to play. Get to know him, maybe?" Did he know how to be a friend, or was he too focused on being more than friends? Impossible to say. She knew Rachel had already been on two dates with Charlie and had admitted that yes, he was still a little odd, but maybe that was better for her.

"Let's be honest; I was never much of a workout queen. Three months tops," she swore, about living at home. She wouldn't say more than that, just as she wouldn't say what was happening with Andrew and Karen. "I don't ask. I'm finally realizing it's okay to keep some things private, so we don't talk about our love lives."

After a few turns in silence, Andrew surprised her. "Do you mind if I ask what's going to happen to you? With your Parkinson's?"

It was the first time he'd brought up this subject since he went to the support group with her. Did it mean he'd been listening when she said she might need to hire help soon? "No one can say for sure. But you saw the other people at that group. It'll progress. I'll have to keep increasing my medication levels, and after a while, doing that creates other problems."

"Like what?"

"Dyskinesia. More uncontrolled movement. Eventually I'll have a harder time dressing myself, making coffee, things like that."

"Do you have a hard time doing those things now?"

Had he really not noticed? "Yes, but not all the time. Why… Are you worried about me?"

"No, but Walter is. He thinks you two should live together, but he's scared to ask."

For a moment, she said nothing. "What's he scared of?"

"I guess that you'll say no. I don't know, but that's because I've never had a normal relationship so I don't really understand how they're supposed to go. As you know."

Sally gasped. "We're not in a relationship."

"That's not how he sees it."

"We're good friends. That's all."

"Okay. But that's a relationship, right?" Andrew shrugged.

"Maybe he wants to be friends who take care of each other, I don't know."

"He *said* all this?"

"Yeah."

"While you were playing Scrabble?"

"Yeah."

"I just can't believe it."

"I don't know." He shrugged. "Maybe he was lying. Maybe he just wants to have sex."

She felt so overwhelmed that she told Andrew she didn't want to talk about this anymore and they played the rest of the game in silence. After he left, she sat by the window, alone in her apartment, and watched the light drain from the sky. At four thirty, she called the front desk and told them she wouldn't be coming to dinner and didn't need a meal delivery either. "I'm a little under the weather," she told Marjorie. "Nothing serious, but I'm going to bed early."

The next morning when Walter called, as she knew he would, she told him she was fine. She just hadn't felt like eating dinner, that was all.

"May I stop by and visit?" Walter said. "You sound a little down."

If she said yes, was he going to ask his question? Maybe it would be best if he did. Then she could give him the answer she'd settled on last night and they could put the whole matter firmly behind them. Thirty minutes later, he was at her door, red-faced and sweaty from the effort it had taken to get himself there. He had his walker and his oxygen concentrator. Around his waist he wore his pill-filled fanny pack, and around his neck dangled his emergency alert button. "Are you all right, Walter?"

"Yes, I'm fine. I just need to sit down for about forty-five minutes and catch my breath." He collapsed onto the sofa, but mystifyingly, he was still smiling. She sat down across from him in the one hardback chair with arms she could reliably get out of these days.

For a full minute, neither of them spoke. Finally Walter leaned forward, with his elbows on his knees. "I've wanted to ask you a question for some time now. I've been putting it off because I'm afraid I've overbuilt it in my mind. I'm scared that if you say no, I'll have wrecked our wonderful friendship and I'll have to go back to being the eccentric old codger who no one cares for much because I say odd things at dinner."

"You're long past those days, Walter. You have legions of fans now who like this new cheerful personality of yours."

"Do I?"

"Well, no one has said this to me specifically, but yes. As you know, an affable single man is a rarity here. People take note."

"Have you? Because I've done this all for you Sally. This upbeat, friendly stuff. It's all a bit of an act because I didn't want to come back and seem like a man who'd had a brush with death and now he was doing nothing except waiting for the real thing."

She smiled in spite of herself. "You mean all this talk of loving tai chi isn't *real*?"

"I hate tai chi. Don't tell Connie. I'll keep going because it's the only exercise I can do at the moment standing up, but honestly, watching paint dry might be more interesting."

Sally laughed. She felt the same way.

He leaned back. "I want to ask you about living together. I thought about waiting until I was stronger, so you wouldn't have to worry about what you were taking on, but I wanted this before I had any issue with my heart, so this isn't about being scared or worried about dying alone. I want us to help *each other*. I can fetch your pills in the morning if you've left them in the bathroom. I can help you get dressed. I know you don't need much help, but maybe a little? Doing up buttons and things like that?"

"Did Andrew tell you all this? About my morning episode with the pills?"

"He said something, yes. It doesn't need to be a secret."

"He shouldn't have. That was a mistake. It won't happen again."

"But other things will. You know that."

She couldn't look at him as he spoke. She stared out the window instead.

"We could choose which apartment we want to live in, though of course we'd choose yours because mine is depressing. We wouldn't have to sleep together, though I must admit I'd like to. Or I'd like to try anyway and see how it goes. But you have two bedrooms, and I'd be happy to sleep in the other one if you prefer. I'd still be nearby if you had a fall at night. I've been reading a little bit, and people say night falls are the biggest danger to people with Parkinson's. They wake up groggy and forget their balance is off—"

"Stop." She held up a hand. "Don't say any more. This is a very kind offer but I have to say no." She stopped when she saw how badly her raised hand was shaking. She brought it down to her lap and covered it with her other hand.

"I was afraid this might be your first response, so I have other arguments. The money we could save. The passwords we could help each other remember. You could help me sort out all this new medication I'm taking. I need to figure out a system for it."

"No." She shook her head and kept her tremoring hands in her lap. "I spent the last five years of my life taking care of a man, and I don't want to do it again."

"But I'd be helping you, too."

"I don't want to keep talking about this. I like being alone. One of the most surprising things I realized after my husband died was how much I liked planning my own day and making my own schedule. I couldn't do that if I lived with someone else, especially not someone with as big a personality as you have. I don't mean this as a criticism, but you fill up a room, Walter. It would be impossible for me to sit quietly and think my own thoughts if you were around all the time."

She couldn't look at him as she delivered the speech she'd planned last night, rehearsing it so many times, she was no longer sure what she was saying. After she finished, a calm swept over her. She looked down at her hands, perfectly still in her lap. Here was her body telling her this was the right thing to do. "We can still be friends. I do care about you. Introducing me to Scrabble made me realize that I can still surprise myself. When you get a diagnosis like Parkinson's, it's easy to believe this isn't true, so I will always be grateful to you. More than I can say."

He looked up at her. His eyes were shiny but he wasn't crying. "Was that it? It was all about Scrabble? Because I have to tell you Sally, I don't care about Scrabble that much. I care about you more."

"And I care about you. Very much."

He stood up. "But not enough I guess."

# CHAPTER 49
# Walter

FOR THE NEXT TWO DAYS, WALTER FELT TOO EMBARRASSED TO LEAVE HIS apartment. *Fine*, he thought. *I'll sit here alone and keep my big personality to myself.* On the third day, he woke up furious. He called Sally before he'd eaten anything for breakfast. "I'm sorry if I was ham-handed in how I framed my offer, but I was more honest about my feelings with you than I've ever been with anyone, including my wife, who I loved enormously but apparently never told her effectively. You like being alone. Fine. I understand that. You don't want to share your apartment with a slob, that's reasonable. But I was trying to tell you how much I care about you, with heartfelt sincerity, and your response was, 'I'm sorry, Walter, but you talk too much.'"

"You're right."

This stopped him. "I am?"

"I've been thinking about our conversation. I wasn't telling you the whole truth and you deserve that. I apologize."

He waited and steeled himself. Was he about to hear some new surprising recrimination, worse than what she'd already said? An indictment of his personality that would explain why Elyse had left him and Gavin had kept his distance for twenty years?

"Have you ever known anyone with advanced Parkinson's?" she said softly. "It's not a pretty picture, and the truth is I can't bear the idea of anyone seeing what's going to happen to me, especially not you, Walter. I care about you too much."

He could hear in her voice how difficult this was. "Oh, Sally—" he said. "Sometimes challenges bring out the best in people. I've seen that."

She sighed. "I don't like thinking about myself as someone else's burden."

"None of us do. And all of us will be, sooner or later."

"I'm still saying no to living together, but I'm glad you called. These last two days have made me realize I don't like not being friends. Everywhere I've gone, people ask about you. I ate dinner last night with a woman who assumed we were married."

"Really?" Walter chuckled.

"She said we put off a 'married vibe.'"

"Did she see us be short-tempered and unpleasant with each other?"

"She must have."

To his relief, they both laughed.

"Can I ask if your resistance has to do with the prospect of being intimate?"

For another long stretch, she didn't say anything. He was grateful this conversation was happening on the telephone. Finally she said: "Are you asking if I'm attracted to you, or do I find the whole idea of sex at our age repugnant?"

"I suppose the latter. Awkward as it is, I've wondered if maybe women—or you, specifically, never mind other women, I'm not interested in their answer—reach a point where that whole business seems less appealing."

More silence.

"If I'm honest, I don't know how much Elyse enjoyed that aspect of our marriage. I tried to discuss it and find ways to make it more pleasurable for her, but those conversations only embarrassed us both, I'm afraid, so I stopped. I'll also say this: I'm reasonably sure it's not a great idea for me at this juncture. I can't guarantee that would change."

"That's okay," Sally said. "It isn't sex I'd worry about; it's sleeping together. I'm afraid Parkinson's produces overactive sleeping episodes, where you have nightmares and thrash around and scream obscenities out loud. I know it happens because I've woken myself up."

Walter smiled, though of course she couldn't see him. "*Really?*"

He hadn't laughed, but she must have known he wanted to. "It's not funny, Walter."

"I'm sorry; it's just so hard to picture. Which obscenities?"

"I'm not going to tell you."

"Is it fuck? Do you say fuck? Now you've planted the seed and I want to get an image."

"Stop it."

He took a deep breath. "I know it's not funny. Sally. It's also not funny that I had some prostrate trouble a few years ago and now I wear a diaper to bed every night. I've spent an embarrassing amount of time trying to figure out how I might keep that fact a secret from you if we lived together, and finally I've decided that I can't. I have to make it a joke and pretend to be easygoing, but privately, I'm dying inside as I tell you this."

"Don't most men our age wear those? The worse alternative is *not* wearing them, right?"

"Exactly." He let the thought settle for a moment. "These are the facts of our lives now. We both have our younger selves sitting inside of us, horrified by these developments, but I'm hoping we also have the wisdom of age. We are not defined by the limitations our bodies have imposed on us."

Sally sighed. "When did you become a philosopher, Walter?"

"Last week. Golden Grove was offering a club and I joined."

She laughed and then sighed. "It's sad, this business of turning into a different person."

"It's happening to all of us. No one was born old. It takes adjustment."

"What if I'm becoming someone I don't like?"

He didn't answer right away because it was a legitimate question, one he often wondered about with so many people around them losing their mental acuity. "I don't know the answer to that, Sally. Except it seems less likely if you have someone close who remembers the real you."

He didn't press the issue or ask if this nice conversation erased their last one. "Let's just give ourselves a little time and breathing room," she offered.

"Fine," Walter said.

# CHAPTER 50

# Sally

A FEW WEEKS LATER, AN AFTERNOON SNOWFALL GATHERED IN INTENSITY until dinnertime, when they all sat in the windowed dining room, mesmerized by the snowflakes as big as the lima beans sitting on their plates. "Apparently the weatherman has changed his mind," a man at the next table announced loud enough for other tables to hear. "Now we're getting fourteen inches."

Sally was pretty sure she'd never eaten with the man. Maybe he was new or maybe he was one of the residents who only came to the dining room on special occasions—holidays, speakers, weather events.

"Fourteen inches!" a woman at Sally's table gasped. "That's almost two feet!"

No it wasn't, of course, but no one corrected her.

Nothing drew this group together quite like the weather. So much so that sometimes Sally wanted to point out the obvious fact: They weren't particularly impacted by it. No one needed to shovel a walk. Those with cars never drove if there was any danger of ice on the road. Regardless, they collectively watched the weather like it was a scary movie playing on their windowpanes. That night, an ice storm knocked out the power, setting off an alarm at midnight. Sally had heard of this possibility. She'd always been assured that backup generators would kick in and service would remain uninterrupted, but apparently this wasn't happening. She clicked her bedside light on and off several times. Nothing.

New fears blossomed in her mind. If she pressed her emergency button, would it even work? After twenty minutes, she felt more alone—and frightened—than she had in years. *Think about other people who have it worse*, she told herself. The people more fragile than herself, who depended on electricity for their oxygen concentrators, like Walter. Thinking this sent a new wave of panic through her. *Walter!* She grappled for her phone, only to discover it was out of battery. She had no way to tell the time. No idea how long it would be before the sun rose.

She heard voices in the hallway, and then a knock. Thankfully, it was still close enough to her last dose of Sinemet that she could open the door to Sharon, from across the hall. "I've found Sally!" she called over her shoulder, as if a search had been going on for some time. They were all confused, unsure what to be most frightened of. "Our wing has decided to sit together in the alcove. You're welcome to join us if you'd like."

"Thank you," Sally said gratefully. She wasn't especially close to these neighbors, though they had a "wing meeting" once a month, which usually involved one person taking notes on everyone else's complaints about the food. She followed Sharon to the alcove where she found about ten others, all the folks who lived alone. Newly widowed Florence. Jeffrey, who still spoke of his wife, Peggy, in the present tense though she'd died eight years earlier.

"Here she is! Hello, Sarah!" Gwen called out. Gwen never got anyone's name right.

The two men on the floor had taken time to put on clothes, but the rest—all women—wore nightgowns and robes. Sally sat down on a small, uncomfortable settee that had an antique feel, as if salvaged from a former resident's apartment. She'd never sat on it before and now knew it would be hard to get out of. The whole scene had the feel of campers roused at night, awaiting instructions from a counselor. Beside Sally sat Carol, a cheery, forgetful woman with a habit of singing to fill in any awkward pauses in conversation. She suggested a sing-along now and a voice in the dark said, "Oh please, Carol, no. We're nervous enough as it is."

Another silence stretched out.

"What about a poem," Julia, once an English professor, suggested. "I can still recite 'Barbara Fritchie'!"

"Not that one, Julia," Jeffrey snapped. "We'll be here 'til New Year's if you start 'Barbara Fritchie.'" He sounded harsher than he probably meant to. It left them all quiet.

After about ten minutes, Sally wondered if it would be rude to stand up and walk back to her apartment. As if hearing her thoughts, Jeffrey announced, "At this point I don't think it's safe for us to be alone. We were sold a bill of goods about backup generators when we moved in, and now we have no assurance anything is working."

Everyone shifted in their seats. Sally hoped the others wouldn't start in with more complaints, but of course they did: If the power stayed off, how would they know what time it was? How would anyone make coffee? What if this lasted more than a day? A free-floating anxiety filled the darkness. Sally remembered her mother once saying, *Sometimes you can feel lonelier in a crowd than alone.* This was certainly true now. Just as Sally decided that yes, she would definitely be more comfortable back in her apartment than out here struggling to find conversation with her neighbors, she noticed the bounce of a moving light up the hallway. They all turned to watch as it came closer.

"Hello there," the familiar voice behind the flashlight called.

She almost laughed. It was Walter, inching closer until she saw a maroon box resting on the tray of his walker. He held it up with a smile. "Scrabble, anyone?"

They all laughed and the nervous tension they'd been feeling dissipated. Sally thought about the distance he'd just traveled. His apartment was one floor above hers. He must have started this trek the moment he woke up and realized the lights were out. Then it occurred to her: If the electricity was out, the elevator was too, meaning—almost unimaginably—he'd also made his way down a flight of stairs.

She stood up and said, loud enough for everyone to hear, "Walter, you've just had quite a walk in the dark. Why don't I make you a cup of tea in my apartment? I think the gas stoves should still work."

Who cared what others thought of her issuing this invitation in her nightgown? Really. Who cared?

For a few minutes after they got to her apartment, she was too overwhelmed to say how grateful she was. Then she took a deep breath. "Thank you for coming to rescue me, Walter. I felt like I was sitting on the *Titanic* with passengers I didn't know, realizing we were too old to even consider rearranging the deck furniture. Then you arrived. My gratitude is infinite."

He laughed. "A power outage isn't quite the same as an iceberg."

"Don't tell them. They're all convinced we're going to die and probably won't get any coffee before we do."

He laughed as he set up his flashlight lantern on the table beside the Scrabble board. After a few turns, Walter mused, "I don't think I can remember the names of anyone in that group you were sitting with. Was there a Ginny in there?"

"No."

"There you have it. That's how much those people matter."

She looked up at him in the flickering light of his lantern.

Suddenly it all seemed silly—to insist that she needed her independence more than she needed help or reassurance. Nobody *needed* to be alone more than an hour or two a day. What they needed was connection to others. To look up in the darkness, see a band of light, and be able to say, *Oh thank God. There you are.*

She didn't want him to think she was saying yes because the power outage scared her, so she waited two days and then invited him to her apartment for a glass of wine before dinner. When he got there, she was more nervous than she expected. She still had a hard time imagining them *living* together. Where would he sit when they watched TV? At the moment, she had room for only one easy chair in her small TV/den/office space. Maybe this wasn't such a good idea. "I wanted to tell you that I've been thinking more about your offer." She couldn't look at him as she spoke. She felt too—something. Nervous? Vulnerable? "I've decided that I think you're right. It's not a terrible idea for us to live together."

He let out a whoop of surprise.

"Now don't say yes right away. Think about what this really means."

"Okay," he said and sat back for a moment. "What does it really mean?"

"Well, for starters, people will think of us as a couple. They might treat us differently."

"Better, you mean?"

He had a point. At Golden Grove, couples tended to be more popular, perhaps because there were relatively few of them.

"We'll probably annoy each other. More than you think."

"You could never annoy me."

"But I will. And you'll do things that drive me crazy. I don't think it's helpful to pretend either one of us is perfect. In fact, one of the reasons I hesitated on this is that I'm afraid that you'll be disappointed when you get to know me better."

He considered this, and for a long time neither one of them said anything.

"Have I already disappointed you because this isn't as romantic as you hoped?"

"No," he said and stood up. "But I do think we should try kissing. There's a bit of an unknown factor here, and that might help us."

"I'm not talking about that part, Walter."

He moved toward her. "Maybe not, but even so." He sat down on the sofa beside her. "Maybe this wasn't what you were expecting."

"No. I have to admit, I thought we'd spend most of this visit negotiating all the furniture I'd ask you not to bring when you move in."

"I don't care about my furniture. I'll give it all away."

"Including that recliner chair?"

"Except the recliner. I do need to find a place for that here."

"Do you care about it more than you care about me?"

He tapped his chin in a gesture of consideration.

"Never mind, Walter. Don't answer that. You can bring your chair."

He leaned toward her and closed his eyes. It was, at least initially, a shock. Not unpleasant, but strange. She and John hadn't exchanged more than a peck in years. *Who invented kissing?* she thought. *Who decided two people wishing to convey certain emotions should do so by pressing their lips together instead of, say, their shoulders or their feet?*

Maybe it was a mistake to make this the first thing she said when they stopped.

"We could try those two ideas," Walter said. "But I don't have high hopes."

"I'm sorry. I get nervous and I say silly things."

"Are you nervous now?"

Wasn't it obvious? "Yes!"

"But why?"

"Because you've built me up too much! What will happen when you realize I have many flaws and two children happy to point them out for you?"

"I know that."

"You do?"

"Yes. You're a beautiful, intelligent woman who has done a good job of seeming fine most of your life, but you've always worried what would happen if anyone looked closer and saw the truth. You don't like being superficial, but you also don't like talking about unpleasant subjects like the fact that Andrew only has a temporary job and your health is getting worse. I see that. We can talk about these things, but we don't have to. We can just say, 'I see all that and I still want to kiss you.'"

She sat back on the sofa, for the first time afraid that she might cry in front of him. He bent over to catch her eye. "Do you still want to kiss me?"

She couldn't speak. Her mouth moved but no words came out. She felt overwhelmed. Was this feeling she had for him deeper than anything she'd ever known with John? Instead of saying anything, she nodded and waited for him to kiss her again. Which he did, and this time had felt different. She lost herself in the surprise of touching the back of his head, running her fingers through his lovely, gold-white hair. On an impulse, she grabbed his ears.

"What are you doing?" he said, his mouth still flush with hers. She couldn't see his smile, but she could feel it.

"Holding on," she said.

Walter didn't move in right away. They had to make arrangements and tell their children first. It took some time to work up the courage, and when they finally did, no one seemed upset or particularly surprised.

"I mean it's nice," Andrew said. "But it's also weird, obviously, because it's not like you're going to start having sex, right?"

"We might, Andrew. We're in discussions on that front."

He held up one hand. "Well, don't make me part of those."

"We won't, but thanks for offering."

"I don't like to think about *anyone* having sex, but especially not my mother."

As it turned out, telling their children was less daunting than telling their fellow Golden Grove residents. Over coffee one morning, Sally told Walter, "I think we should make a quick announcement at dinner. We'll be frank and unembarrassed, and we'll refuse to acknowledge any tawdry jokes."

"Can I make some?"

"Absolutely not. We aren't children."

"Oh my. Are we allowed to smile?"

Sally considered this. "I think it will go better if we don't."

The glass of wine they both had before dinner helped. Sally hoped others would see this in a hopeful light: a demonstration of the surprising possibility of love at any age. Still, she didn't want Walter to mention the word *love* in his announcement in deference to their neighbors who struggled with loneliness. Once he started though, he got carried away and abandoned their agreement to keep it low key. "Rest assured that we're not getting married. Or not yet, anyway! I'd like to of course, but I have to wear Sally down. One step at a time!"

Sally darted a look at him: flush with emotion, grinning from ear to ear. She stopped herself from tapping his knee under the table to remind him of their agreement. "We're doing it for practical reasons mostly," she said. "We both have health conditions that will benefit from having someone nearby in case of an emergency."

Even this dose of cold water didn't extinguish Walter's bright smile. "Plus I love her!" he said, grinning at everyone, now too afraid to look over at her.

Afterward Sally was annoyed. "Why would you say that in front of everyone else when you've never said it to me?"

They were back in her apartment. He sat across from her, staring at the birds outside the window so he didn't have to look at her. "Because saying it to you frightens me," he said.

"Why?"

"I don't know."

"Maybe because you're not sure it's true?"

"Not at all. I've known I loved you since the very first Scrabble game we played."

"That's not *true*. You sound silly when you say things like that."

"Maybe so, but for me, it is true."

"Oh, I'm sorry. You were so happy making our announcement, and now you seem sad."

"I am sad and I don't want to talk about it."

"Okay then." She put her hands on her knees and started to stand up but was stopped, unfortunately, by uncooperative legs. She flopped back onto the sofa.

"That's why I don't want to talk about it."

"Because my legs are bad?"

"Because I don't want you to die before me. Please. You can die one day after I do. That would be fine."

"Oh, Walter." She wanted to reassure him but she knew she couldn't. "Listen to me. If we're going ahead, this will be part of it. Sooner or later, we'll both get sicker." She took a deep breath. "And sooner or later, one of us is going to die and it won't be pleasant. Are we still sure we want to do this?"

He turned and looked at her, his eyes rimmed with tears. "I should have killed myself at dinner. I was so happy an hour ago."

"That's not a very reassuring answer. We can't be in denial."

"I wish we could. Denial is easier."

"Not really. Denial makes your worries grow into an amorphous cloud of anxiety." She hesitated. "Which turns into anger." She waited another minute. "I don't want you to move in here if you're going to get mad at me because I might die someday. Is that understood?"

# CHAPTER 51

# Walter

HE NODDED BECAUSE HE COULDN'T SAY WHAT HE WANTED TO. HE stared at his hands in his lap and didn't look at Sally. He couldn't. He wouldn't be able to see her anyway through his tears. By now, Walter had read too much about Parkinson's. He knew about everything that would probably happen (falls, difficulty with dressing and eating) and the scarier things that *might* happen (cognitive decline, hallucinations). He knew that her balance would worsen, and eventually, she'd lose her voice and her ability to swallow. And this: Gradually, her face would begin to freeze. It would happen so slowly she wouldn't even realize it, the books said. But soon she'd start smiling less and eventually her face would have no ability to show her feelings. The next afternoon, as they sat together before dinner, he studied her for any signs of this.

"What are you doing, Walter?" she asked him.

"Nothing," he said.

"You're staring at me."

"Is that a crime now?"

"No, but it's strange. We're sitting here reading, only you're not reading; you're looking at me like I've got something on my face. Do I?"

"No. I like looking at your face. It's a nice face."

"Oh, stop it." Sally waved her hand and went back to her book. But she was smiling, he could tell. She hadn't lost that yet.

It wasn't really a question anymore: Was she getting worse? Yes. Did others notice? Yes. The real question that he couldn't bring himself to ask was: Did she ever cover up the sadness he sometimes felt but tried to cover up himself? He couldn't ask her, of course, afraid that it would only convey how much he thought about it.

As it turned out, they didn't need to ask for their children's help for the move. Residents moved between apartments often enough that for a nominal fee, Golden Grove had a system in place to pack and shift furniture in an afternoon. They attended the Keeping Current club and the Wednesday Tea afterward, and when they returned to her apartment, his boxes and chair and bed were there. They were roommates.

"Here we are!" he chortled. "Living together by magic!"

Of course there was more to it, as they discovered over the following days. First, there was the awkward matter of sex. He wanted to try it. They both did, he was fairly sure, but they were both afraid. "I only wish we'd done it before my heart attack. Now I'm on so many new medications that I don't know what's working and what's not anymore."

"Let's don't give you another heart attack."

"Exactly."

They decided to wait until after he spoke to his doctor before trying anything more than kissing and holding hands, which they did quite a bit. They now slept with separate adjustable single beds in one room with enough space between so they could both get out of bed safely in the dark. "This is better, I suppose," Walter said, gesturing toward the space between the beds. "It makes me sad not to share a bed, but you never know with these bathroom trips."

Their first night in the same room, neither of them could fall asleep. "I feel like I'm at camp again," Sally said.

Walter looked over at her. "Did you go to a terrible camp where everyone took their blood pressure all day and thirty-five pills at night?"

"Just lying here, having someone to talk to. I haven't had that in a long time."

"I haven't either. Elyse and I slept in separate rooms as soon as Gavin moved out."

"Was that her idea or yours?"

"I'm not sure. We were both terrible sleepers and we both accused the other of snoring. By the way, you must tell me if I do."

Sally laughed. "John would sometimes get up in the morning and say he hadn't slept a wink and I'd want to say, 'Then who was that snoring all night?'"

"I had a terrible time sleeping when I still worked. I'd lie awake, dreaming up ways to antagonize my coworkers without getting caught."

"That's terrible. It doesn't sound like you, Walter."

"Oh, it was. I spent most of my working life furious. What a waste of time."

"Hard to control, I suppose."

For a while, they were quiet. When he heard her sigh and roll over, he took that as a sign that she was still awake. "Did you ever waste time resenting someone or something for too long?" he asked. He knew one of her ears was better than the other. She'd already warned him that if she lay on one side with her good ear on the pillow, she probably wouldn't hear him.

Then she said softly, "Yes. My husband and his illness."

He wanted to ask more but hesitated. Did she mean her husband's *illness* or her *husband*? Sometimes he felt like a teenager this way—jealous and looking for proof that he'd won.

"He was self-absorbed. Other people didn't see that, but I did. He wasn't a good listener. To his children. Or me. He formulated one version of us in his mind and that never changed."

"What was his version of you?"

"That I was sweet and a little simpleminded. When I was younger, I worried that braininess might put men off so I acted less intelligent than I was."

Their beds were close enough that Walter could reach for her hand and hold it. "It's hard to imagine anyone not seeing you as the smartest person in the room."

"Oh my," she said. "John never thought of me as that, I can promise you."

"But you are. You're the brightest woman at Golden Grove."

She pulled her hand away. "Don't say that."

She was kidding of course, but still it hurt his feelings. He wanted to say: *Let's try not to hurt each other*, but how could he be sure he could keep such a promise? In learning this about her husband, he'd won the reassurance his foolish heart craved, but he'd opened up new chasms of doubt. There were so many ways for people to inflict damage.

After about three weeks, they agreed to push their beds together with the help of Winona, the housecleaner. Walter had made the suggestion without thinking too much about it ahead of time. "Does this room seem a little too *I Love Lucy* to you?"

Sally laughed. "Do you mean the two single beds with a table in between?"

"Yes. That always confused me when I was a child."

The next day, she surprised him by suggesting they take a shopping trip to buy a mattress space-filler and sheets big enough to cover both.

"Is this a slightly embarrassing errand?" she said as they walked into the department store. "I can't decide."

"I don't think anyone will ask to see a marriage certificate," Walter said.

That night, he helped her into her nightgown as he had been doing for weeks but instead of lifting her legs and swinging her into bed, he said, "My turn now," and got undressed down to his underwear. They looked at each other for a long time. Finally he said, "You've seen prettier sights, I'm guessing."

"You have a beautiful body, Walter," she said, reaching out.

"With a train track down the front of my chest."

She—very gently—touched his scar. This wasn't the first time she'd seen it, but it was the first time she'd touched it. Not so red anymore, just pink and knobby and hard in places.

"Does it hurt?" she whispered.

"No. The opposite. I can see you touching it, but I can't feel it."

# CHAPTER 52

# Sally

THERE WAS NO QUESTION, THE LONGER SALLY HAD KNOWN WALTER, the more attractive he'd become. He'd always had his beautiful blue eyes, which she noticed the first time they played Scrabble together, but now she knew the messages they contained: the raised eyebrows across a dining room table, the crinkle of his crow's-feet. Sitting with others, they had whole conversations with their eyes. *Here goes Lucinda again on her vegetable monologue.* Or: *Does Francis ever tire of talking about the weather?*

They'd made each other laugh out loud with their eyes alone and she felt something new in those moments—a tingle in her armpits, a flutter in her stomach. Similar to the way her hands and feet went warm and then cold when he whispered in her ear. She understood *this is desire*, but sometimes he seemed so fragile she wanted to gather him in her shaky arms and sit him in her lap. Other times, she wanted to curl up in his, pull him around like a blanket, and hide from the world.

She was the one who'd suggested buying sheets and turning their single beds into one because she'd been thinking about the way they reached for each other across the space between their beds. The way caring for each other's flawed body had become a kind of foreplay. He would help her undress with a tenderness she'd never seen from a man before. In theory, Walter was the more effusive one, willing to proclaim his feelings openly, but here was the truth: She wanted to have sex as much as he did.

As she traced his scar with her finger, he said, "I've asked my doctor about this and he said yes, I should be okay. Medically, that is. He couldn't make any predictions about my performance."

Sally was surprised. She narrowed her eyes. "Did you really ask him?"

"Yes. He even offered me a prescription for little blue pills that—as he so awkwardly put it—will help me fulfill my job."

"Walter. You went to the doctor a week ago and got pills and you didn't say anything?"

"I was nervous."

Why had he waited so long to tell her? Did she feel this pull of their bodies more urgently than he did?

# CHAPTER 53

# Walter

HE WAS MORE NERVOUS THAN HE'D BEEN ON HIS HONEYMOON, IF THAT was even possible. But why was this when he knew that he loved Sally and wanted to spend whatever time they had left together? Maybe it was the doctor's joke about "not expecting too much from himself" along with this offer of pills. It all felt foreign, like he was pretending to be someone else for Sally, the one person he wanted to be his truest self with.

After an eternity of silence, she reached out her hand and touched his chest again. "Do you want to try one of those pills?"

"I'm scared."

"Of what?"

"That it will change me into someone else at the time I most… want to be myself."

She considered this. "Changing isn't necessarily a terrible thing. We're watching each other change every day and we're learning to adjust."

"But what if I become a virile, oversexed twenty-year-old?"

She smiled. "That would be interesting."

## CHAPTER 54

# Sally

SHE HAD NO EXPERIENCE WITH VIAGRA. THOUGH JOHN'S LIBIDO HAD waxed and waned over the years, it died completely when his heart disease was diagnosed. Once, she suggested he ask the doctor about this, but he never did. She was touched that Walter had, and she wanted to reassure him. "Just lying next to you in bed will be lovely for me. I don't need to do anything more."

He looked down at his penis, which was, without any prompting from her, growing. "Look," he said, audibly relieved. "I've already taken the pill, as you can see. Apparently it works."

She drew him down beside her. "Does your heart feel okay? Does anything hurt?"

"There's really only one way to address what I'm feeling now," he said, smiling for the first time that evening.

Afterward they were so pleased with themselves that they laughed like two children who'd gotten away with something. "Who would've thought two oldsters like us could perform circus tricks like that?"

Sally lifted her head to look at him. "What kind of circus did you go to?"

He laughed. "Don't all circuses have that as their final act?"

The next morning they felt sore in places they hadn't felt sore in years and couldn't stop smiling at each other. "I think we should try that again some time!" he grinned. "For exercise, I'll take that over tai chi any day."

"Easy does it, Don Juan. I'd hate to get carried away and end up pregnant."

It gave them both a much-needed boost of confidence in their physical abilities. Still, it didn't erase what was happening. Sally increasingly felt the many ways Parkinson's was affecting her life: in the morning the struggle to get out of bed, then the challenge of making coffee. Sometimes these tasks were Herculean; sometimes she got through them without incident. In the beginning, Walter helped her too much. Unable to sleep past six o'clock, he'd rise early, lay out her pills, and pour her bowl of cereal with a sliced banana on top. After a month of this, she wondered if his ministrations made her feel more handicapped. She told him it was important, for as long as possible, to do things for herself. "I'll lose skills faster if I don't keep practicing," she said.

Walter looked dismayed. "It's hard to watch you struggle. I hate it. I'm sorry, but I do."

She remembered this feeling when her children were young. How Andrew didn't learn to tie his shoes until fourth grade. At the time, she'd felt sure helping him was right. He was gifted in certain ways and needed coddling in others. Now she understood the mistake: A person who can't take care of themselves feels powerless.

She started occupational therapy when she realized it took her longer to eat meals than everyone else, especially Walter, who could put away three courses in under fifteen minutes. He tried to help her out, making adjustments, moving her glass, but she just did everything slowly now. Getting dressed could take an hour, with half that time devoted to socks and shoes. "You could wear slippers to get the paper in the lobby, you know," Walter would say. "People do."

"It's a slippery slope. One day you're wearing slippers in public; the next thing you know, you're going to the dining room in your nightgown."

"No one would arrest you for either one."

"Standards are important."

She started speech therapy after Walter commented, twice in one day, that he couldn't hear her if she insisted on whispering.

"I'm not whispering, Walter. Honestly."

"What's that? I can't hear you."

It turned out he was right. This was confirmed by several others at dinner one evening when she felt as if she was talking normally but apparently couldn't be heard. "What I do is read your lips, Sally," Georgina told her. "That makes it easier."

Once she started one therapy, Walter had other ideas for her to try. He wanted her to join a boxing class for people with Parkinson's, which he admitted was an hour's drive away. "Short, explosive movement is the best kind of exercise for you. Pow! Wham!" He stabbed the air a few times with his fist.

She stared at him. "It sounds like you'd like to take a boxing class."

"Believe it or not, you need to have Parkinson's to sign up for this one. But I'd be happy to go with you."

"And watch people with Parkinson's punch each other? No thanks."

He looked down at his notebook. "There's another class called Move and Shout where you sit the whole time, but apparently you scream a lot. That's at the senior center in town, a little closer. I wouldn't mind trying that class either."

"You just want to show off. Your voice is plenty loud."

"Exactly. If people were impressed with me, so be it. The important thing is that exercise protects the dopamine-producing nerve cells. The more varied your exercise, the better."

"Please, Walter, I know all this. I do my walking and my tai chi."

"But do you get enough explosive movement?"

"I'm about to explode right now if you don't stop."

Even the simplest activities required more concentration. Talking as they walked to the dining room grew harder as she focused on lifting her left leg and extending her gait. If she tried to keep up with conversation, her feet sometimes froze to the floor. Whenever she got discouraged, she reminded herself that she wasn't the only one having setbacks. Walter now took a nap every afternoon and sometimes slept for two or three hours. As the dinner hour approached, she'd tiptoe in and sit beside the bed to make sure his chest was still going up and down. Once, he woke up, startled, and she tried to make a joke: "Just making sure you're still alive," she said. Too late, she realized this wasn't funny because it was true.

How simultaneously uneventful and terrifying this life was, walking slowly, side by side, in a terrible state of readiness.

Perhaps the saddest incident was one they never talked about afterward. They were playing Scrabble, as they did a few times a week when her meds were working and her tremors under control. It was a good game, with Walter ahead but only by a little. She still had a chance to overtake him when she spotted a terrific play—FLEX with the X doubled twice. In her excitement, she started to make a joke—*This word is both a game-changer and a description of what I'm doing*—but before she could play the word, a dyskinetic arm spasm upended the board. Tiles scattered across the floor. For a moment, neither one of them spoke.

They both knew the truth: It would take an hour or more to clean this up and count the tiles to ensure none were missing.

"Were you that worried I might win?" Walter asked to soften the bleakness they both felt, along with a new fear: Was this the last game she'd ever play?

They never said this aloud, of course. Instead, Walter moved on quickly, suggesting he attend the other groups she still participated in, including the book club, which meant reading novels he admitted—privately—he neither understood nor liked. "It all seems so made-up," he told her after the second meeting.

She had to smile. "It *is*. That's why it's called fiction."

In the group discussion, Walter's strategy was to smile and nod as if he agreed with every point made. Afterward the group said they loved having him there. No question, the bar of expectation was lower for men than for women at Golden Grove. Still, Sally liked rehashing their thoughts about the discussion afterward. Usually his comments had little to do with the book. "Did you notice Letitia was wearing two different shoes today? They were the same style, but two different colors. I don't suppose women like having things like that pointed out?"

She smiled. "Probably not."

Eventually, they drifted away from some of their earlier activities. Neither of them could be much use to the Green Thumbs; for Sally, Wednesday Walkers was out. Instead they watched movies in the meeting room and attended some of the less demanding clubs. At dinners they were quieter than they used to be. They listened to others, with less to report themselves. Sometimes Sally thought: *This is what it's like to fade from the world.* Because eating was hard, Sally began skipping some dinners, though she always urged Walter to go ahead without her. "No one can hear what I'm saying, but I want you to go. You can tell me all about it later."

After a few dinners, Walter told her he didn't like eating in the dining room without her. "Everyone talks about things I don't know anything about."

She knew this feeling—as if their health troubles had carried them both away from a world that had moved on without them and now it would be almost impossible to catch up.

They watched more TV. One night they went to bingo, where it took them ten minutes to understand how simple the game was. "That's *it*?" Walter said to the woman showing him how to put the plastic disks on the squares called out. "That's all there is to it?" He spun around in his chair. "There must be thirty-five people here," he whispered to Sally. "They all come for *this*?" Afterward, they had a hearty laugh at the silliness of it all. It was an odd feeling, Sally thought going to bed that night: They were happy with each other and a little sad in their life.

Twice, Walter proposed marriage. He didn't do it in any planned way, brandishing a ring or getting on a knee. Instead, he'd brought it up casually: once over morning coffee, once as they readied for bed. "I could call this our nuptial bed if we were married," he said, helping her into it. "To me, that has some appeal."

Both times, Sally said no. "It's sweet of you, Walter, but I think it would throw my children off. Andrew is still getting his bearings."

"You might not want to believe this, but I think Andrew has his bearings. Plus, I don't think he'd want you using him as an excuse."

"It's not an excuse. My children haven't had great luck in their romantic relationships. Why force them to celebrate me finding what they don't have? To me, it seems cruel."

He thought about this. "Or maybe it would be a demonstration of your resilience which they can use as a model for themselves?" His eyebrows went up hopefully.

"I don't think my children see it that way."

His shoulders drooped. He turned away.

"We're already living together and taking care of each other, Walter. It wouldn't change anything, would it?"

"No," he said with some dejection. "I suppose it wouldn't." Then, very softly he added: "I just thought it would be nice."

To her surprise, it was Andrew who suggested shaking things up. "Toby and I were wondering if you and Walter would like to go to the VFW Scrabble club tomorrow night." She almost laughed at the unexpectedness of the invitation. About two months earlier, Andrew had started working toward getting his education certification at the local community college, where some students were as old as he was. He no longer felt so alone, he said, which surprised her. As did this question about the club. It had been a while since they'd talked about Scrabble.

"Have you been back there since the Baltimore tournament?" she asked.

"Oh sure. A few months ago Toby asked me to drive him. He got his driver's license, but as he said—barely. His parents won't let him take the car at night so he needed a ride."

"How often do you go?"

"Usually every week."

"Why didn't you tell me?"

"I thought Scrabble made you sad. Then Toby said maybe we should just ask if you'd like to come back for a visit."

Maybe it would have made her sad a few months ago, but not anymore. Now it reassured her—Andrew *was* moving forward. "You could just watch or…you can try playing. Peter bought some tournament boards where the tiles lock in. He told us to make sure you knew."

She felt a tug in her chest. This club only collected minimal dues; a donation jar sat on Peter's table every week and never had more than a handful of ones. He must have paid for these new boards with his own money, which made her throat tighten as it always did when she encountered quiet, surprising acts of kindness. "Do the boards spin?" she asked softly.

"Yeah, they're great. Everyone loves them. There's only two, but if you come, you'd get priority. Peter said to tell you."

Dear, awkward Peter with his extravagant speeches and his elephant's memory for memorable plays. Those boards probably cost him hundreds of dollars, but if she tried to thank him, he'd probably look confused, as if he had no idea what she was talking about.

"What do you think?" she asked Walter, who sat in his TV chair, his walker forming a fence around his knees. The last time they saw these people was almost six months ago, when she was beating champions and surprising the world. Walter hadn't been back since his surgery. They'd all be shocked by his weight loss at first; then soon enough they'd realize she was the one more physically changed. Her left hand, which had started all this with its tremor, had stiffened and then hardened into a curl. She used to wear pocketed cardigans to hide the shake, but now she wore them to hide the immobilized paw at the end of her arm. Strange how this disorder amounted to a battle between stiffness and excessive movement, a game played by second-guessing her medications and overthinking everything.

Occasionally she still hit the perfect sweet spot and enjoyed two or three hours in a calm body that allowed her to do what she wanted. On those days, she could even make tea and drink it without scalding herself or spilling it on her shirt. A lovely reminder of the small pleasures life afforded when you lived in a controllable body. More often, though, the excessive movement of dyskinesia was the tradeoff for taking more medication. One arm might splay out spastically, or her head might twitch. She watched eyes widen around her when people took in these new tics. She saw what they were thinking: *She's getting worse.*

"I think we should go," she said decisively.

Walter's head snapped up in surprise. "You do?"

For the last four months, she'd limited their activities for obvious reasons—her balance was precarious, his energy unpredictable. They'd stayed away, assuming they were doing the others a favor, but now she was rethinking this. "Andrew says everyone wants to see us."

"Do they know"—he hesitated—"how we're doing?"

Of course they did, at least in theory. They'd sent a group get-well card while Walter was in the hospital. But did they know how her Parkinson's had progressed? Even as she considered this, she thought about Andrew and what she'd asked him to do six months earlier: enter a group of strangers and join them in an activity he'd not yet mastered. She told him, when asked, to say he wasn't working at the moment "for medical reasons." He was the one who told the truth and said, "I'm dealing with mental health issues. I've had some depression but it's getting better." No one looked at him differently or said anything.

When Dotty heard that he was going to community college, she asked if he was working at all, and he told the truth. "Just substitute teaching and odd jobs here and there." She must have assumed (as so many older people did) that he was good with technology and asked if he ever did house calls to look at people's printers. He said he never had, but he could try. "I don't know much about printers, but I own one, if that helps." Afterward, he'd visited Dotty and *had* managed to fix her printer. Was it possible that Andrew, with his quiet courage, was the role model they both needed now?

Walter had wanted Sally to be one kind of inspiration to other members of the club, but maybe they could be a different kind altogether. Neither of them would play at the level they used to. Their brains were foggy; yesterday Walter couldn't remember the word *hamper*. They'd probably lose to people they'd have easily beaten a year ago, but did that matter? Was it better to stay in every night, watching TV shows they had a hard time remembering the next day, than to settle for being worse at something than they used to be?

Sally was surprised at how nervous Walter was, changing his outfit and asking if his walker made him look feeble. "Not at all," she'd said, touched by his sudden, surprising vanity. "Walkers add five pounds because of their thin legs. You look positively robust next to yours."

"Ha-ha. I just don't want anyone to come up and say, 'I thought you died.'"

"Who would say that?"

"I have. Once, when I actually thought the person *had* died. I only realized how terrible that sounded after it was too late. We tried to laugh it off but it was all very awkward."

"Okay, well. You'll do the same if someone says it to you."

"Ha-ha," Walter said, practicing his fake laugh.

# CHAPTER 55

# Walter

*SO IT'S OFFICIAL—I'M THE NEW BYRON ZORICH,* WALTER THOUGHT, inching his way to the VFW community room behind his walker. He didn't have an aide like Byron, but he had two escorts at his side—Toby and Andrew—holding doors, plus Sally, telling him to take his time.

"Attention, everyone! Attention!" Peter called after they'd been there for about ten minutes. It was an even smaller crowd than the last time, which meant that Peter had, mercifully, left his portable microphone at home. "I'd like to start by welcoming Walter and Sally back to our meeting after an absence of—what has it been, Walter?—four months?"

"Six actually."

"Six months! My goodness, time flies when you're playing Scrabble, as we say."

Even Walter could see there was something off with Peter. He'd always been a ham with the microphone but today he seemed subdued. Soon they learned why: "On a more serious note—before we get to tonight's pairings, I have… Well, I have a somber announcement.

As we know, the VFW has been in dire financial straits for a while, and two weeks ago they told me that they're selling the building. We've had some hints this might happen, and I've spent the last three months trying to find an alternative meeting space.

"I hoped to have a menu of options that we might discuss tonight, but unfortunately, I have none. I won't go into all the disappointing conversations I've had with building supervisors, school personnel, and McDonald's managers… Suffice to say the world is suspicious about offering a group of adults a place to play a board game. One suggested we might be a criminal enterprise using Scrabble as a cover. I told him, 'If you watch us play, you won't think that.'" A polite laugh rippled through the crowd and died away.

"It boils down to this: I called the main office of NSPA to tell them of our plight and see if they had any recommendations. The woman said she was very sorry but this is happening all over the country. She said when most clubs lose their space, they all go home and play online. Unless we can find another suitable space, this meeting will be our last."

He paused to let that sink in. Walter looked around, aghast. How had he heard nothing about this? "Are you saying a club that's existed for *over twenty years* is going to end because we can't find a place to meet?"

"We found one McDonald's willing to host us, but it's about an hour's drive away and in a neighborhood with a fairly regular history of muggings in their parking lot. We can discuss that option, but I thought we'd probably pass."

Walter feared he'd planned these lines, looking for a joke to keep this light so no one—most of all Peter himself—broke down and wept.

"Wait… Is this our last meeting?" Dorothy gasped. "But, Peter, we didn't even bring food this week."

Once a month or so, Peter sent out a snack sign-up sheet with a suggested theme usually based around a holiday, or (more often) a word recently used in play. "In honor of UMIAK, we're looking for Alaskan treats or, as a concession, Russian snacks." They'd eaten BLINTZES and PIEROGI, not because anyone had any cultural history with the items but because they all contained useful combinations of high-value letters and hard-to-shed vowels.

"I know," Peter nodded, unable to look Dorothy in the eye. "I thought about putting out a call for snacks, but it was late and I didn't want anyone to feel obligated. I also didn't want to make this last meeting any sadder than it had to be."

Now it was clear—the tears were coming, and Peter wouldn't succeed in holding them back. "I love this group. As many of you know, I don't have too much family left, but I have this family..." He stopped speaking and put a finger to his lips. "I have you people. Some of you I've known for twenty years and we've weathered a lot together. We've had some losses"—he held out a flat hand toward Iona—"and challenges." He extended his other hand toward Walter and Sally. "And still we've found a way to come together every week because we know the restorative power a few games of Scrabble can have on our spirits."

A few people began to cry. Walter looked around the room. To his surprise, instead of feeling weepy, he felt fired up. "This isn't right!" he said, as loudly as his lungs would permit.

"We need to FIGHT BACK!" He held one fist in the air, clenched tight. He might look silly, he knew, but he also knew his new frailty added some gravitas to his message. *We must fight back or we'll die.*

Peter looked sheepish. "We've been trying, Walter. Trust me. If you find a better solution, I'd be happy to hear it."

Afterward, Sally asked Andrew why he hadn't mentioned what was happening with the Scrabble club. He shrugged. "I don't know. It's pretty sad. I didn't want you to have anything more to be depressed about."

Walter spent the whole drive home brainstorming ideas. "All these companies around here have conference rooms that sit empty after five. Why don't businesses donate space for community good?"

He sat in the front seat next to Andrew, who was driving. "Because then they'd have strangers wandering their halls, stealing office supplies," Andrew said gently. "Plus, it's mostly insurance companies around here, and they always say they can't do things for insurance reasons. If someone got hurt, they might be liable."

Walter shook his head because of course he knew this. He'd worked in insurance his whole life. "Town hall! The high school cafeteria! These places won't care about insurance!"

"Actually they do." Andrew shrugged. "Seems like Peter's tried everywhere."

"Have the others helped him? Have you?"

Walter feared Sally might lean forward and tell him not to push the matter, so he dropped it, but the next day, he returned from his morning walk, giddy with a new idea. "I've got it!" he huffed after sitting down to catch his breath. "The Scrabble club can meet here! I've asked the front desk about reserving the multipurpose room and they said it was available."

"Did you tell them what it was for?"

"Yes, the Scrabble club."

"But did they realize it was a Scrabble club full of people who don't live here?"

"Does that matter?"

"I'm afraid it will. Golden Grove has to serve its residents, not random outside groups. They'll probably say no for safety reasons. What if someone came with whooping cough and infected a resident?"

"That doesn't seem very likely, does it?"

"No, but it's a risk."

"What about the risk that this group will die if we don't find a place to meet and save it. Isn't that a risk, too?"

Walter knew that Sally had a point. He requested a meeting with Nicole, the new director of residential life at Golden Grove. She'd only been on the job a few months but was already making a mark. The usual Sunday afternoon soft-jazz trio had been replaced by a rotating lineup of surprising alternatives—a jazz singer one week, a Scottish bagpiper the next. In the past, most residents moved through the lobby politely ignoring the music, but how could anyone walk by a man in a kilt, red-cheeked and dewy-eyed as he talked about his homeland?

Walter started the meeting with some flattery. "I want to compliment you on your Sunday musical lineup, Nicole. It's good for us to have new faces come in. Everyone worries so much about the isolation facing seniors, so you come up with field trips, which is very nice, but there's another solution that you've found and should get credit for."

Her eyebrows went up in surprise. "What's that?"

"You've invited *outsiders in* to visit us! It's been wonderful! You've convinced musicians to come into a retirement community and we've loved meeting them!"

One hand fluttered to her chest. "Yes it has been nice, hasn't it? I'm a part-time musician myself. Some of these folks are my old friends. I wasn't sure how it would go."

"It's been a triumph and an eye-opener! We like them and they like us!"

Was he laying it on too thick? Apparently not, because now her head bobbed in agreement. "They did enjoy it. I've invited performers who say they don't play nursing homes. I tell them we aren't a nursing home, we're independent living, but it's all a blur in their minds."

"There's a lot of bias out there."

"I suppose so."

He shifted in his seat. "So I do have an idea about inviting a group that wouldn't have a problem with that. They'd be delighted to come and bring a weekly evening of games and merriment. At no cost to Golden Grove, I should add."

Though it took a full week to get approval from upper administration, Walter got the final decision on Monday morning: They'd allow one meeting, with a caveat. They questioned how many residents would rejoin a Scrabble club they'd already tried and decided against. "We know you and Sally love Scrabble, Walter, but we can't indulge a handful of residents who like one activity at the expense of one hundred forty residents who aren't interested. We have to find a balance. I'm sure you understand."

He did, unfortunately. Which was why it surprised him when Sally came up with her own suggestion: "How about proposing a tournament as a one-time-only event? Use what's left over from club funds as prize money. Register with NSPA. Ask Esther to help us advertise. It would make more interesting viewing for spectators. People would see what Scrabble is really about at that level and how thrilling it can be!"

It was a wonderful idea. Clubs were encouraged to host smaller tournaments, but this one never had. Walter grinned from ear to ear. "But how will we get good players to come?" Usually money was the biggest draw, but some lower-stakes contests had a history and big names came because they knew other, important players would be there, too. They cared less about the money than the chance to improve their rating and practice against each other. "If we could get one or two top players, others would come. Meaning someone should reach out to Jack Trotter and Winston Pryor and make a personal appeal."

"Why do I have a feeling you want me to do that?"

"Because they'll never come if I ask them, but they might if you ask."

"That's ridiculous, Walter. They didn't even say hello to me in Baltimore."

"They were distracted in Baltimore, but trust me—everyone loves you." Saying this made him realize something: Golden Grove residents wouldn't care about seeing big-name players they'd never heard of. "If we want to get a crowd from here, there's only one person who can do that." He stared at her. "It's you, Sal. They'd come to see you."

"But I'm not going to play, Walter. You know that."

"But if we're in charge, we can do something radical that no one has tried before: We can create a truly accessible tournament. If you need help placing your tiles, we'll allow for a neutral third party to assist you. They'll sign a waiver promising you no help beyond the physical assist of placing tiles where you ask them to." The more Walter thought about it, the more he liked this idea. "By advertising ourselves as accessible, we'll get others who are in the same situation you are—competitive players who have dropped out of tournament play because of the ludicrous physical demands."

"What if everyone who signs up needs some kind of accommodation?"

"We'll ask for more volunteers. Don't you think Golden Grove residents would be delighted to help out?"

Though it made her nervous, she had to agree. If there was a universal trait most Golden Grove residents shared, it was a desire "to be useful." Sally had even pointed this out once—how her symptoms ebbed in the face of Andrew's crisis and how they returned when he improved. Walter kept going, spinning out his scenario: "We'll intentionally keep it small. We'll invite the club members and do a terrible job advertising. That way we can control the situation better. Less stress all around."

Was he doing this for her? Creating a tournament that she'd feel comfortable competing in? "What about Andrew and Toby?"

"Of course they'll enter."

"What about you, Walter? Will you enter too?"

"As the tournament host, I don't think I can." He smiled, not because he wanted to enter but because her asking meant she'd already agreed to play.

Walter had never hosted a tournament, of course. When Peter admitted that he hadn't either, Walter got nervous. "You've been president of a club that's been going for twenty years and you've never hosted a tournament? Aren't all clubs meant to host one?"

"It's a goal, not a requirement. I talked about doing it in the past, but then, faced with all the logistics, I got overwhelmed."

A silence descended. Walter could already hear the chorus of anxious questions from club members. Who will serve as judge? Who will officiate final scores? Where will we get enough game boards, timers, chairs, tables, etc.? For a group of senior citizens, even managing check-in on laptops felt daunting. Peter still ran club matchups on paper spreadsheets and recorded all results in a spiral-bound notebook. He shook his head as he went over the handwritten task-list they'd come up with in a single meeting: It was fourteen items long. Advertising, prizes, judges, officials. For some reason, they couldn't get past the issue of check-in. "What if we ask people to bring in cash or checks for the entry fee, and we just have a shoebox we put it in? No credit-card readers needed."

In the end, they decided to take the simplest route possible on every choice. They posted a listing on the NSPA website, capped the prize money at $200. Enough to bring locals but (hopefully) not draw too many outsiders. He cleared the idea of making this an "accessible tournament" with Peter but didn't want to make too much of it in their advertising, again at the risk of getting overwhelmed. "We'll be happy if we get—what? Thirty players? The room holds fifty-five. We want a good showing but nothing too crowded."

"I'd be delighted with twenty-five."

"Twenty-six would be easier!" Peter added. Odd numbers were a tournament's bane.

"Quite right."

Then, having worried about too many entrants, they checked their online registration a week before the event and discovered only eight people had signed up, three of whom were themselves, plus Andrew and Toby. And Toby was already talking about making this his "retirement party."

"You're sixteen years old and you're retiring?" Andrew said, dumbfounded.

"I think my best Scrabble days are behind me. I'm ready to move on."

"Well, then maybe you'll consider moving on before this tournament and leaving the rest of us with a cleaner shot at the prize money," Andrew grumbled.

"No way," Walter snapped. "We're desperate enough as it is for players. I'm not letting anyone who filled out an entry form quit."

For three days in a row, they had no new sign-ups. Everyone wanted their club to go on, but no one wanted to do what they must to ensure it would happen. "It's infuriating," Walter moaned. "I don't care if people don't like competitive tournaments. They should enter anyway."

"You sound a little dictatorial right now, Walter," Sally said.

"I can't help it. People should listen to me more."

"They do. Or I do," Sally offered. "I talked to a woman at NSPA who said some new tournaments get half their entrants on the same day. People wait until the last minute to sign up."

"Jesus," Walter muttered. "It's like throwing a dinner party and saying, 'Please don't RSVP. Just leave us in suspense. We *prefer* the excitement of not knowing.'"

By the morning of the tournament, they had thirteen entrants, six from the VFW club and three who were unfamiliar names. "I don't mind saying this makes me nervous," Walter said.

"To be playing with strangers? Isn't that the whole idea?" Sally pointed out. "We're building a community. Creating opportunities for isolated people to come together, remember?"

"Well, in theory, yes, but you hate to throw out the welcome mat for any loon."

Walter had a point, especially when so many eyes of Golden Grove residents and staff would be watching. The night before, the dining room was abuzz with confused questions. "Is it true we're hosting the National Scrabble Championships?" Ivy had asked Sally.

Walter rolled his eyes. "No, Ivy. About five hundred people go to that. We're hosting a modest local tournament. We'll expect about sixteen to twenty people at most."

"Do I have to play?"

"Only if you enter and pay the fee."

"No, I don't want to do that. I'm not good at Scrabble."

"Then you don't have to play, but feel free to come and watch us if you're interested."

Preparing for this tournament had had one surprising effect: Walter wasn't trying to *sell* people on Scrabble; he was only trying to *soften* them to the idea. *Come! Have a look! We'll be in the main meeting room!* He found himself smiling more in the hallway, waving at people he'd long ago decided were grumpy, and to his surprise, a few waved back. One man even stopped his slow forward progress and said, "What's this I hear about a tournament?"

"This Saturday!" Walter said. "Spectators welcome! You'll be surprised how compelling it is to watch serious Scrabble players compete."

"I'm going to come," the man pronounced. As far as Walter knew, he'd never seen this man at a single club meeting or activity. In fact, he'd never seen him do anything except eat his one meal a day, often by himself, reminding Walter a bit of his own early days at Golden Grove.

In brainstorming more ideas to involve spectators in the events, Sally came up with some fun ideas. A few xeroxed Scrabble-related games—anagrams, word searches—for audience members to do as they watched, with prizes awarded at the end of the day. She'd also purchased the prizes, mindful that the last thing most Golden Grove residents wanted was more "stuff" they had no use for. Instead, she offered restaurant gift cards and two Boggle sets. "I think of Boggle as a gateway to Scrabble, don't you?" she told Walter.

Walter left "audience cultivation" up to Sally while he fretted over the last-minute sign-ups, some of whom entered under suspicious-sounding names: Samuel Salami being the most obvious example, but wasn't there also something suspect about Patrick Parsons and Charlotte Windfall? He checked with the NSPA database and found none of these players with active memberships or ratings, raising his suspicions higher. He called Peter that morning. "I don't want to sound any alarms yet, but we've got three recent entrants who aren't members with any rating, and I have to tell you, they also have suspicious-sounding names."

"Suspicious how?"

"Heavy alliteration. Like kids who signed up as a joke." Did kids do this kind of thing anymore? He wasn't sure what the joke would be here, but he had his guard up.

# CHAPTER 56

# Sally

SALLY FELT GOOD ABOUT EVERY ASPECT OF THE TOURNAMENT EXCEPT one. Walter had spoken with the president of the National Scrabble Players Association to ask about their official policy on accommodations for people with disabilities. Astonishingly, they only had a few, mostly involving easy bathroom access for people in wheelchairs. Intriguingly, they'd also allowed a man who kept Sabbath to play on Saturdays (when he wasn't allowed to write down his scores) by placing a bookmark in a book on the numbered page that correlated with his score. Hearing this made Sally realize she'd probably need help not only with tile placement but scoring, too. Though she'd played a bit online, she hadn't handled tiles or played a game in person in months.

The night before the tournament, she lay beside Walter and tried to imagine how it might go. "You should be fine for the first two games," Walter said. "Your best hours are usually between nine and eleven so I've lined up 'game assistants,' but I've told them you might not need to call on them." He'd met with the four volunteers once to discuss how she would make her requests using the Scrabble shorthand to identify grid squares on a board (letters going down, numbers across.) They had practiced this system, but not with Sally, so she had no way of knowing how she would play with someone seated beside her. Just thinking about it made her feel self-conscious and wonder if everyone would feel obligated to cheer if she managed to make a single play.

On Saturday morning, Walter and Sally got off the elevator to find Peter standing in the lobby with the entire Scrabble club around him and a box of a dozen doughnuts in his hands. "We want to thank you both!"

They were a good half an hour early. Bob, the janitor, was still setting up tables and chairs. "I feel nervous," Iona said, and Dorothy reminded her that she'd decided not to play and there was no need for nerves. "What if no one else shows up?" she bellowed. "That will be so terrible for Walter and Sally. They have enough problems as it is."

"No," Peter said equitably. "It will be sad for us all because it will mean we've got no place to meet."

Players arrived in a slow trickle. Andrew and Toby first, arguing over a game they'd played a week earlier. Just as Sally started to quiet them, she saw Jack Trotter walk into the room. She looked around for Walter. No doubt this surprise arrival would elevate his anxiety tenfold. Winners and champions still reduced him to a sputtering awkwardness. *Maybe I should get Jack checked in*, she thought. *He probably won't even recognize me.* It had been more than eight months since her surprise victory over him, and she couldn't deny she looked different now. She started to make her way across the room and then looked up to see Walter not only greet Jack Trotter with a handshake and a shoulder palm but lean in to whisper in his ear, as if his appearance wasn't a surprise to Walter at all.

## CHAPTER 57

# Walter

WALTER SHOOK HIS HEAD. OF ALL THE SETBACKS HE'D TRIED TO anticipate, Sally fuming about Jack Trotter's presence wasn't one of them. "You want to start the tournament with a rematch between Trotter and me? That's a terrible idea."

"Why? You're better in the morning. Your meds are more predictable. Wouldn't you rather play him first thing?"

"I haven't played competitively in months! I'll lose in a spectacularly embarrassing way."

"So what if you do?" Even Walter was surprised to hear himself say this. For so long, he'd worked himself into panic attacks thinking his tournament performances and Scrabble rating were an accurate measure of his success in life. What else did he have—with an unremarkable career and a family who only begrudgingly spoke to him? Now he took Sally's hand in his. "Your victory has already happened. You're here and you're bravely agreeing to play again. How you perform doesn't matter a whit to anyone. If it's any comfort, I invited him here because I want him to play Andrew."

Sally shook her head. "You want to put *Andrew* up against the best player in New England? He isn't ready."

"I disagree. In the last month or so, Andrew has been playing like you in your heyday. Beating Trotter awakened you to your own potential. I'm trying this as a strategy. I don't know if it'll work, but I'd like to see if playing Trotter has the same effect on Andrew."

For a long time, Sally said nothing.

"This isn't about Scrabble really," Walter offered.

"No, I know."

"For Andrew, this is about doing something that scares him. I think just making it through a game with Trotter might be a nice victory."

"Did you ask him to take it easy on Andrew?"

"Absolutely not. Andrew would see through that right away."

"What were you whispering with him about?"

"It's Dorothy's birthday and I said she'd be thrilled if he said happy birthday."

Sally seemed sanguine after this conversation, more so than he felt. They were still waiting on two mysterious entrants—Sam Salami and Patrick Parsons. As it turned out, Charlotte Windfall was the name of a real person, new to the area but a ten-year Scrabble veteran. "I was excited when I saw this listing. No one can keep a Scrabble club going anymore, but apparently you have," she said to Peter, who blushed a far deeper red than the compliment warranted.

*Goodness*, Walter had thought, staring at Peter. *Did I look like that when I first met Sally?* He remembered the surprising heat he often felt in his face and his ears, the flutter in his stomach, the adolescent nerves. How funny to see the hallmarks of a crush on another old codger and, at the same time, how heartening. In the end, this day wouldn't be about who won the tournament or even his goals of convincing Nicole to allow the club to meet here on a regular basis. It would be about these unpredictable surprises: that Peter had a bit of life left in him, that Jack Trotter was more generous than he expected.

So who were these last two unknowns they were waiting on? He hated the idea of this group being mocked. That's what happened, he feared. When you advertised for entrants, you made yourself vulnerable.

That's when a familiar voice whispered above him. "Sam Salami here. Checking in."

It was Gavin. And behind him James, who had aged a bit in the eight months since Walter had last seen him. "Oh my goodness!" Walter bellowed. "What are you two doing here?"

"Sally called us. We cooked up this idea as a surprise. We've even played a little Scrabble to practice. What did we get through—three games… Right, James? Or four? Did we play four?"

Walter could hardly contain his delight. He looked over at Sally who was smiling—still able to say with her face, *See? You've helped me with my son. I can help you with yours!* It was wonderful to see Gavin and impossible—in this hectic moment—to tell him why: James was with him! They were laughing together and looked happy. After a lifetime of being afraid to commit, Gavin had shown he could commit to the only thing that really mattered.

He leaned across the table and whispered, "Based on our games, Dad, I'd say I'm a better Scrabble player than you might think, and James is much worse. Seriously, he's terrible. If you have any weak players in this tournament, please pair them with him. I don't want him to know how bad he is. He thinks he's okay, and he's really not."

It was, in its way, the kindest thing he'd ever heard Gavin say. *I want to protect him. I don't want his feelings hurt.*

"Duly noted," Walter said as he made last-minute assignments. "Does this mean you've moved back home?" he asked, trying to keep his voice casual.

"Yes," Gavin said and smiled in a way Walter hadn't seen in a long time.

"Proceeding ahead…?" he said, letting his words trail off so they might mean anything—*with life? With adopting a child? With professional worm composting?*

"Yes, Dad," Gavin said. "We're proceeding ahead."

Gavin rolled his eyes at his father's predictable awkwardness. He didn't know yet how much Walter had changed. How, with the exception of the bleak week they'd spent together, he was an entirely different person than the father Gavin had grown up with. He talked about his feelings (too much for Sally's taste), cried easily (too often in Sally's mind), empathized with characters in commercials and other people he hardly knew. How do you tell someone you've changed when you were never with them long enough for them to see it themselves?

The first game of the day produced some surprising results, starting with Gavin, who played a strong game against Andrew, who ultimately won, 410–395.

"I was nervous to play your son, Walter," Andrew confided afterward. "And then he told me the last time he played Scrabble with you, he was eight years old. I relaxed a bit after that, but not completely. He doesn't have your word knowledge, but he's very good."

When he told him what Andrew had said, Gavin smiled, "Okay, I'll admit, I've been practicing a little online. You're right—it's pretty addictive once you get started."

The next games were starting, and Walter had no time to ask any more; he gathered the score sheets and made assignments. Two games later, Gavin was still holding his own. No one—including Peter, who lost a close match against him—seemed particularly surprised. "He's your son, Walter," Peter said.

Walter didn't want to embarrass himself by saying, *But I haven't played with him once in thirty years and he was terrible back then.*

## CHAPTER 58

# Sally

MUCH TO HER SURPRISE, THE FIRST TWO GAMES WENT FINE FOR SALLY. Walter paired her with Charlotte, the new arrival. Though helpers were on hand, she only needed assistance placing tiles on two seven-letter bingos, which so impressed the Golden Grove crowd that she didn't feel too self-conscious.

She'd been pleasantly surprised by how many spectators they got—sometimes thirty at a time—which accomplished Walter's goal of showing people how exciting higher-level Scrabble was to watch but also had a downside. Too many distracting conversations; too many people interrupting Sally's games to thank her for the puzzles and prizes they were taking home.

"We'll ask the audience to limit conversation as much as possible," Walter announced early on and again, about two hours into the tournament. It worked briefly, but telling this group to keep their voices down was always going to be a losing battle. It also did no good to ask them to refrain from any comments on the games they were watching. "Just saying, 'Nice play!' can be a distraction," Walter cautioned them, and even after this warning, Sally heard Ruth across the room say, "This man has had an X for a while now and he can't find anywhere to play it!"

This excessive chatter wasn't limited to the spectators, unfortunately. After Sally's surprising refusal to play Jack Trotter in the first round, Walter paired Dorothy with him for the first game. Already inclined toward too much table talk, Dorothy seemed unable to stop herself from telling Jack Trotter her whole life story, up to and including her divorce thirty years earlier. "Oh, why am I going on?" she said, pulling out a Kleenex and blowing her nose. "You don't want to hear all this."

Sally, seated next to her, was pleasantly surprised: He didn't disagree but he also didn't seem to mind. Sally watched him intermittently nod, raise his eyebrows, and purse his lips in response to things she was saying. He won the game 417–236.

After the first round, Walter followed the NSPA rubric for tiering tournament games by ability, rating, and the day's performance. It wasn't easy, but perhaps his old skills as an insurance actuarial adjuster came in handy. After each round, people brought their score sheets up to him—covered in notes and random crossed-out letters—and he punched the number totals into his calculator. Sally didn't want to make him any more nervous than he already was, so between games she visited with the Golden Grove folks who'd come to watch. "I don't know how you do it, Sally," Connie marveled. "I've never heard of most of the words you're playing!"

Sally smiled and waved her hand dismissively. "It's like learning to speak a foreign language except the definitions don't matter and you don't have to worry about pronunciation."

Apparently Connie had no memory of the warning she'd once given Sally to steer clear of Walter and his Scrabble club because she leaned toward her. "I think I might give Scrabble a try again. I've always been very good at languages."

"You should!" Sally laughed. If they'd won over Connie, maybe Walter's ploy was working. "Once you get into the rhythm of looking for words and not settling on the first one you see, it gets much easier."

Connie nodded. "'Rhythm' is an interesting word, isn't it? With Y as the only vowel. Probably good to remember."

"It's a wonderful word, Connie! You're right!"

Though Sally deflected the compliments, the Golden Grove spectators were right. She *was* playing surprisingly well. As Walter pointed out, a smaller tournament like this one played to all her strengths: her surprising focus and her ability to access obscure but legitimate words. On her fourth game, she played Jack Trotter, who hadn't undergone a personality transplant but certainly seemed softened by the conviviality in the room. "We meet again, Ms. Reynolds," he said, pulling out the chair across from her. "This rematch might be the reason I came."

Was that the hint of a smile on his face? She didn't dare test it by pointing out that they'd passed each other (twice!) at the Baltimore tournament and he hadn't recognized her. "I'm pretty rusty, Mr. Trotter, so I don't think you have too much to worry about."

As it turned out, he didn't. Though she had a few impressive plays, he pulled ahead halfway through the game, and she never caught up. "That makes us one and two," he said, which confused her for a moment and then she realized it was his win-loss record against her.

"I told you I was rusty. You played a very good game," she said.

He surprised her by leaning across the board. "If you want to know the truth, you're even better than you were six months ago," he whispered. "Your biggest problem is the clock."

Sally was surprised. He was being generous, of course—unusually so for a champion—but the morning was going so well that she'd played the whole game without any assistance. She'd almost forgotten that yes, she had Parkinson's and yes, it affected her play. She wasn't tremoring perhaps, but she was moving slower than she should.

She was grateful her next opponent was Andrew. "I might be coming to the end of my tether," she confessed.

"I don't know what that means, Mom, but I'm having a great day. So far I'm in third place. The only people ahead of me are Jack Trotter and you. I feel pretty good about that."

She smiled. "You should. Okay then. Game on."

"Don't hold back, Mom. I mean it."

She wanted to play her best game, but whatever started slowing her down in her game against Trotter was moving through her, tying her nerve endings in knots. After her first turn, she signaled to Walter. "I need some help," she whispered when he bent down beside her. "Who do you have on the schedule for this time slot?"

He looked at his list. "It's Sharon, and unfortunately I don't see her anywhere." He swiveled, looking around the room for so long that Andrew had hit the clock and it was her turn again. She had a great play—TRYST, with an S hook landing on a double word score so she'd get ZESTS doubled as well, a risky opening Andrew had left behind in order to triple his Z—but at the moment, her hands were shaking so badly she couldn't lift them off her lap. The clock ticked away as she waited for Walter. This was the last game before a break and the finals round. Most of their morning audience had left saying they'd come back before dinner. There were five or six people but no one she could call on for help.

"Do you want me to stop the clock, Mom?"

"Absolutely not," she said. "I'm doing some deep breathing. I'll be fine in a minute."

"Do you want Walter to help you?"

"As the tournament director, getting any help from him would disqualify this game and your result. I don't want that."

"Okay."

Even she could see Andrew didn't want to win this way. She pulled her shaky hands out and made a grab at the tiles she needed.

Eventually she got them, but her hands were moving in ways she couldn't control. Instead of going toward the spot she needed, they rose up in the air as if her intention were to sprinkle the tiles randomly from two feet above. If Andrew registered this ghastly move, he stared at this rack and pretended not to. What could she do? Press her emergency alert button? Scream for Walter at the top of her lungs?

And then: a miracle. Without taking his eyes off his rack, Andrew lifted one hand and brought both of hers—wrists pressed together—to the board. "Drop the tiles," he whispered, "and tell me where you want them to go."

She did.

"I was afraid of that," he said, commenting on her word placement, not her frozen Statue of Liberty pose she couldn't break out of a moment earlier. She was grateful the crowd had dwindled. The fewer witnesses, the better.

They played for a few more turns; Andrew bingoed with EXALTER, which she challenged and lost, giving him the lead. Then, as Sally studied her tiles, preparing for another play, a commotion erupted in the crowd of onlookers. Everyone turned to see Connie with her hand in the air and a strange, frozen expression on her face. Was she trying to signal Sally? Or Walter? Was she going to report the assistance Sally had just gotten from Andrew?

Then she saw Irene put her hand on Connie's shoulder, heard a gasp, and watched Connie slide, as if in slow motion, from her chair to the floor.

"Call an ambulance!" Irene cried, standing up.

After that, Sally's memory blurred. It wasn't uncommon to see ambulances pull up to Golden Grove and take a resident away, but she'd never witnessed a crisis like this. Everyone hovered in a panicky state, uncertain what to do. Walter walked over and crouched beside Connie. Sally heard someone behind him call out, "An ambulance is on its way." He nodded, took Connie's hand, and bent to whisper something in her ear. Sally couldn't see Connie's face. Was she responding?

Walter looked up at the room and continued to hold Connie's hand. "We're going to suspend game play for the moment. For now, let's have all players wait in the lobby."

Sally felt her stomach twist. Whatever Walter saw, up close, must have frightened him enough to make this call. A few minutes later, the EMTs arrived.

A gloomy silence hung in the air of the lobby, Scrabble players now interspersed with the usual lobby denizens. Sally saw Nicole, Golden Grove's activities director, standing in the doorway of her office on her phone. Though it hadn't been his primary goal, she knew Walter had pitched this event as an opportunity for outsiders to see "what a 'vibrant and active community' Golden Grove is." Maybe this was true most of the time, but certainly not in this moment where a collective uncertainty hung over the group. A few people looked at their phones, but even Jack Trotter didn't pull out the pocket-sized notebook of word stems he was famous for keeping on him at all times. Like the others, he sat, wide-eyed, studying the faces around him, wondering, perhaps, who was going to drop next.

"Did you know her well?" Andrew asked, sitting beside Sally. "That woman?"

Already he was using the past tense.

"Connie? Yes, she's my neighbor and the one who first showed me around Golden Grove. She's lived here for ten years and had lots of tips for me. At first I thought she was a little intense, but now I think maybe she's just very good at living at Golden Grove."

"Did she have heart issues?"

"Not that I knew about."

"Wow," Andrew said.

Sally could hardly bear to think about their exchange a few minutes earlier—Connie saying she wanted to try playing Scrabble again.

"Does that happen a lot? Someone collapsing like that?"

"Not that I've seen, no."

"It was a little scary. I'm glad it's not an everyday thing."

"No, it isn't." She tried to say it emphatically, but how could she when one had only to look around the lobby to see the truth: They had lovely decor, an overfull activities board, and an unspoken proximity to death all around them.

You could try to look away, but still it was here.

Though it was rarely discussed, Sally was sure most Golden Grove residents would agree that it wasn't death they were scared of as much as the uncertain period that preceded it—the ambulance ride, the hospital stay, the Herculean efforts doctors might make to shore up the failing organs of people who'd lost interest in putting their bodies through this effort. This was everyone's greatest fear, right after the fear of losing their minds completely. Final days spent hooked up to ventilators or feeding tubes, traveling back and forth to hospitals for dialysis. Everyone agreed they didn't want that.

"You can either have a good life or a long life," Wilma, another neighbor, always said, unaware—no doubt—of how often she repeated herself. "You can't have both." If Connie survived whatever episode she'd just had, this was what lay ahead for her. Choices between a longer life or a better one.

After Walter first moved into Sally's apartment, he had spent a few days being as repetitious as Wilma, arguing against the Do Not Resuscitate orders so many people had taped up in their apartments. "Boy am I glad I never signed one of those! I've got a whole second life! A new apartment! A new love! Life is great!" Walter didn't see the way such proclamations made other people uncomfortable. Finally Sally explained to him: "It sounds braggy. Also, it's disrespectful to people who've signed those."

"I'm not saying that at all! I'm saying, 'Look, folks, it's never too late to be surprised. A year ago I was a social pariah no one would play Scrabble with. Now things are different.'"

"They still don't want to play Scrabble with you."

"True enough. But they all like you and they're happy to put up with me if it means spending time with you."

Now it had been a month or more since she'd heard him make that argument. Hopefully, he understood that the question of signing a DNR was more nuanced and the answers were frustratingly limited. At any moment, they could all be reduced to a shadow of their former selves and consigned to carry on with little say in the matter.

"Do you think Walter is going to start the games back up?" Andrew asked.

"Are you asking because you're currently beating me?" She offered a limp smile.

"Partly. But also, Karen is coming at five to pick me up for dinner."

"Really?" Sally tried to keep the surprise out of her voice. " Do you want to invite her in to watch you play?"

"I would but she'll have her son with her."

"Oh." As happy as she was to hear this, she understood: This might be a scary situation for a young child to walk in on.

A few minutes later, Walter made his way into the lobby, pushing his walker. He looked pale and didn't make eye contact with her, which seemed like a bad sign. "I can't say anything definitive. The EMTs were very professional and she's getting the best care possible. That said, we're going to have to cancel the rest of our tournament. Many of you need to get home, I know, and the room has been reserved for another group this evening."

No one was angry at Walter, of course. Peter shook his hand and said, "Well, we tried, didn't we? Not your fault."

Dorothy said she'd had better birthdays but she'd also had worse ones. "This was in the middle. I hope that woman is all right." She paused after saying this, as if there were something more she wanted to say. For ostensible wordsmiths, the Scrabble crowd could be surprisingly tongue-tied.

# CHAPTER 59

# Walter

THAT NIGHT, WALTER AND SALLY LAY SIDE BY SIDE IN BED HOLDING hands. "Do you want to hear another terrible thing about today?" he said. They still didn't have a final word on Connie except that she'd "been stabilized" and her family was flying in "to make some decisions."

Sally turned and looked at him. "What?"

"I looked at their board, and I'm almost sure Toby would have beaten Trotter."

"Why is that terrible?"

"Because he didn't get to finish and feel the satisfaction. What good is knowing you've outplayed a Scrabble champion for *half* a game?"

"Do you think Toby's biggest problem is not having enough to brag about?"

"No, I think his biggest problem is loneliness. He likes his Scrabble friends but feels like he shouldn't spend all his time with them if he doesn't have something to show for it."

"Would winning a game against Jack Trotter have done that?"

"Maybe. It changed your life, right?"

"No, Walter. Meeting you changed my life. I'm starting to think Scrabble might not have had all that much to do with it."

He turned on his side to face her. "Really? You like me more than Scrabble?"

"Yes, I do. And while you're gloating, I'd like to say something else. It was terrible seeing what happened to Connie today. Even though I know that if the worst happens, we'll say it was a blessing for her to go so quickly, surrounded by friends, doing something enjoyable. But it was also very sad. It reminded me that we need to appreciate the time we have left and celebrate the important things we still have."

After this long, exhausting day, he couldn't believe it: She was smiling with her whole face. Even her eyes. "What are you saying, Sal?"

"I'd like to get married. If you still want to."

He was so surprised he didn't say anything for a moment.

"I was under the impression there was an offer on the table."

"Yes! There was! There is!" He gave her a long, delicious kiss and asked if it was really the Connie thing that made her change her mind.

## CHAPTER 60

# Sally

IN TRUTH, IT WASN'T. IT WAS THE MOMENT A FEW MINUTES EARLIER WITH Andrew, when he reached out and stilled her hands without saying anything or even—really—looking up from his tiles. It reminded her of Walter and all the unspoken kindnesses he offered to her as he went about his day. Maybe Andrew had been watching them together and had absorbed a lesson he never learned from his own father—that caring for others brings its own reward. Later, watching him walk out and get into the car with Karen and her son without fanfare or even an explanation conveyed the most important message she needed to hear: This was private and real. To find this at any age was a blessing; to eschew it was madness.

As they were falling asleep, she said, "I want to get married because I love you and I know you love me. That's all." She couldn't look at him.

For a long time, he didn't say anything. She wondered if he'd already fallen asleep. Then, in the darkness, he said, "Should we start thinking about guest lists and venues? I'd be happy to do the legwork in seeing if the Scottish bagpiper is available. I think we'd both agree he's our first choice for wedding music."

"Who is the Scottish bagpiper?"

"He played in the lobby a few Sundays back. I was touched by his tam-o'-shanter hat and the way he paired a kilt with knee socks. I wish I had a fraction of his personal courage."

"Do you want to wear a kilt at our wedding?"

"I'm afraid I don't have the knees for it but it's sweet of you to ask."

"We should go to sleep now, Walter. It's been quite a day."

"Yes it has. I didn't have Sally agreeing to marry me on my bingo card for today."

Ever since attending the one session, they'd been making bingo jokes like this. Or he had, at any rate. "Did you secretly enjoy bingo and that's why you're always bringing it up?"

"No, I hated bingo and I want to go to the next meeting with twelve Scrabble boxes and tell everyone to put their bingo cards away."

"That's a terrible idea, Walter."

"That's why I need you to marry me. I'm not always spot-on in my judgment."

"I don't know about that. It turns out you've been right about a lot of things." She laid her head on his chest, with her good ear up.

"Like what?"

"Like I think quite a few people who watched our games would like to try playing Scrabble again. Connie said she did."

They were both quiet for a moment. Finally Walter said softly: "We must play while we can. For as long as possible."

She waited for a second, then tapped his chest. "Would you like me to stitch that onto a throw cushion as a wedding gift?"

"Please," he said.

# READING GROUP GUIDE

1. How do Sally and Walter learn from each other throughout the novel? What do they bring from their relationship with each other to their relationships with their children?

2. How is finding love during your youth different from finding love as an older person?

3. At what age do you start to "feel old"? Is that number different between men and women? How much do societal expectations and norms influence what that number may be?

4. Do you play Scrabble or other board games? What do/don't you like about them?

5. Are you competitive? Would you allow someone less accustomed to a game win to let them gain confidence (or to be "sportsmanlike")?

6. Is there something you loved as a child but haven't done in a long time? Why is that? Is there something you do now that you've loved since you were a child?

7. Were you praised for your talents when you were younger? Were they encouraged, or did you feel you had to hide them? What talents are more often praised for boys versus girls, and vice versa?

8. How much should you indulge your children? Is it better to reprimand them for their mistakes? Where is the middle ground between coddling and bullying?

9. Do you think Gavin treats his father fairly? How did their relationship become so strained, and what is helping it become less so?

10. Are there any new technologies that baffle you? How good are you at adapting to new technology?

11. How do some sports and gaming leagues try to accommodate those with disabilities? In what ways could they be more accommodating?

# A CONVERSATION WITH THE AUTHOR

**Where did the inspiration for this novel come from?**

About five years ago, my mother moved from LA to an independent living community near us in Amherst, Massachusetts. From the beginning, I was surprised by how much I enjoyed meeting her new friends, and I even offered to start a writing group, where I've so enjoyed reading and listening to the wisdom they've shared. I've discovered that at a certain age, there seems to be a tendency to speak with a candor that I just adore! As if the main message often is: Life is too short to waste a lot of effort censoring oneself. Speak honestly and from the heart, as Walter does when he realizes his growing feelings for Sally. It's a lesson we can all use, whatever age we are, I suspect. I'm also amazed at how I think I know someone and find out, after months, that they were once a judge or designed early computer systems. I'm most struck by the way these folks don't define themselves by the same yardsticks the rest of us wave around: our careers, our children, our houses, gardens, etc. If anything, they seem less interested in impressing others and more eager to connect with them.

**What is your writing process like?**

I've had the same process for the last twenty-five years, back to the days when I wrote in the mornings, the moment my children got onto the school bus. I write by hand in spiral notebooks, and I don't plot ahead, though I sometimes wish I could shorten the process. Alas, I need to write lots and lots of scenes to find the characters and plot I'm looking for and usually I'm always trying to be as funny as possible, and then I can't help throwing hard challenges at my characters. I don't know why this is, except that I do know life can get hard at times, and finding the funny story in those times makes it easier.

**What kind of research did you do while writing?**

Well, anyone with even a glancing interest in serious Scrabble playing simply must read *Word Freak* by Stefan Fatsis, but anyone serious about playing Scrabble already has read this classic, which is informative, fascinating, and so, so funny. (Also a little heartbreaking at points, my favorite kind of book!) After I read the book, I nervously tiptoed into the Monday Night Scrabble Club of Florence, Massachusetts, that has been meeting under the benevolent stewardship of Brett Constantine for almost twenty years. I told people I was a writer, just there to observe, far too intimidated to sit down at a board, and by my second visit, there I was, shaking a bag and reaching in. The main takeaways I gleaned were these: 1) Scrabble attracts a huge variety of people—from the very young to the very old. 2) Some Scrabble demons don't speak English as a first (or even primary) language! 3) In a time when all of us spend far too much of our day alone, in front of a computer screen, it's remarkable how restorative it is to meet strangers face-to-face over a board game.

**What is it like to write older characters (as opposed to children or teenagers)?**

One thing I think older characters have in common with adolescents is a willingness to reexamine a lot of presumptions they've held onto their whole life. I know this goes against the assumption of stubborn old folks who never change their mind, but in my experience, I've seen many more who look back and question those old assumptions.

**Do you have a favorite character from the book?**

Hard to answer this one, but I do love Walter's willingness to put his heart on the line when the time comes. I'm much more like Sally, reticent and cautious on these matters.

**What would you like readers to take away from Sally and Walter's story?**

Many of us don't want to think about getting older or be proactive about planning what our lives might look like after a certain age. I know independent living communities aren't for everyone, but I also know that isolation is increasingly being seen as a serious health threat. I'd be curious about any research on the impact living in a community has on longevity. Sally and Walter both move into such a community to ensure their future care doesn't fall to their children—they never expect to make the discoveries they do. New skills, new friendships, new love. My hope is that readers will come away from their story energized by the possibilities that lie ahead for themselves…

# ACKNOWLEDGMENTS

First, thanks goes to my sister, Elizabeth, who reminded me of how much fun Scrabble can be with her deadly serious/very funny *Words with Friends* obsession. (Also important to note that *Words with Friends* is NOT Scrabble, and those who start their journey back to the board game will be disappointed when they discover that rules, tile values, and even the board layout are all different. But it's still fun and easy to obsess over!)

Thanks to Brett Constantine, who has directed the Monday night Northampton, Massachusetts, Scrabble Club for eighteen years with a remarkable commitment to making all guests feel welcome and all committed players feel challenged. Thank you, Brett, for this group and for gently suggesting I stop watching people play and sit down for a game myself.

An even bigger heartfelt thanks to Ben Greenwood, longtime director of the National School Scrabble Tournament, Scrabble coach extraordinaire, and a multiple national tournament champion himself. Ben gave this book an enthusiastic and careful read with gentle assessments of my own spelling mistakes and grievous

Scrabble strategy errors. Any of the latter that remain are my own fault, not his.

Thanks to dear friends and early readers of this book—my yoga group!—who all happen to be astute, wise readers: Melinda Reid, Abby Dallmann, and Christine Stevens. Thanks also to my brother, Monty, who doesn't do yoga but reads everything under the sun, including whatever I send him.

A lifetime of thanks to Margaret Riley King who has been a remarkable agent for almost twenty years, which seems impossible, given how young we both still are.

Many, many thanks to Shana Drehs for enthusiastically taking on Sally and Walter's story and loving it (and them) as much as she has.

Love and thanks to Mike, Ethan, Charlie, and Henry. You are always my favorite people to go through life with, and thank you for playing board games with me when I badger you for long enough.

And last but not least, thanks to my mother, Katie, and the Applewood community who have opened their hearts and invited me into their world through a small but stalwart writing group who have taught me so much about aging well.

# ABOUT THE AUTHOR

Cammie McGovern is the author of three books for young adults, *Say What You Will*, *A Step Toward Falling*, and *Just Breathe*, and three books for middle-grade readers, *Just My Luck*, *Chester and Gus*, and *Frankie and Amelia*, all featuring characters with disabilities. She is also the author of *Eye Contact*, a mystery, and *Hard Landings*, a memoir about her oldest son, Ethan, who has autism, and his transition into adult services.